THE
CERULEAN'S
SECRET

THE CERULEAN'S SECRET

DENNIS MEREDITH

Glyphus

For information about this title or to order other books and/or electronic media, contact the publisher:

Glyphus LLC
4159 Summit Rd., Purlear, NC 28665
www.glyphus.com
editor@glyphus.com

Library of Congress Control Number: 2014918779

ISBNs: 978-1-939118-14-1
        978-1-939118-15-8 Kindle
        978-1-939118-16-5 ePub

Printed in the United States of America

Cover and Interior design: 1106 Design

ACKNOWLEDGEMENTS

Special thanks to our eagle-eyed first readers of the manuscript: Mike Bratcher, Vicki Duckworth, Chris Evans, Wendy Hunter, Gary Sharp, and Darlene Suber. They helped make the book as perfect as it could be, although any errors are solely the fault of the author. Also, to Jeanne Cavelos and the Odyssey Writing Workshop class of 1997. Their encouragement and insights were invaluable.

ALSO BY DENNIS MEREDITH

Fiction
The Rainbow Virus (RainbowVirus.com)
Wormholes: A Novel (WormholesaNovel.com)
Solomon's Freedom (SolomonsFreedom.com)

Non-fiction
Explaining Research: How to Reach Key Audiences to Advance Your Work (ExplainingResearch.com)

To Joni

CHAPTER 1

I lay there in the dark like a dead man, still paralyzed under the weight of heavy sleep. Then the horrifying realization began to seep into my groggy brain. I couldn't hear the cat *anywhere!* Jesus, he might be gone! The realization struck like a punch in the face, because, if I lost that cat, I really would become a dead man!

I jumped off the couch, whacking the coffee table with my shins, sending empty cans rolling, clinking across the floor. I held my breath. I sifted through the faint night sounds for the low growling in his throat he'd been doing constantly since the dye job. Or, for a meow, a purr, even the delicate crackle of food wrappings being stealthily nosed. But I heard nothing catlike, and no feeling either of the cat rubbing against my leg in the darkness to say he forgave me.

I couldn't really blame him for being ticked, after I'd dunked him hissing and spitting into a bathtub full of gray dye. He'd probably just decided for spite to retreat to a corner and do private cat-things, ignoring me, like cats will do. I rubbed my eyes and tried to shake my head clear of cottony sleep-stuffing. I'd really gone down hard after a week of running and hiding and then wrestling with a big, all-muscle, ticked-off cat. I hadn't meant to fall asleep but just to rest a little before working on some plan of action.

The torn window shade flapped in a puff of wind, making me jump. That sound must've been what woke me in the first place. Outside, the rain still fell steadily, leaden and liquid, as it had when I'd passed out from exhaustion. But now a wind had risen, occasionally gusting through a broken pane, injecting a cool dampness into the musty, still room. Fully awake, heart pumping, I held my breath and listened hard again. The old apartment house produced only a few distant creaks at this hour from my fellow anonymous tenants moving around. No more muffled hollering and explosions from the viddie next door. The guy had finished watching his movie and gone to bed. But also no cat sounds.

Enough listening; I needed to start looking. I bumped around the table, tramping through the fast-food sacks scattered on the floor, flattening a spare hamburger in one. I felt my way around the room, fumbling on lamp switches. I'd need as much light as I could get. He was dyed dull gray now, not being his natural genetically pumped iridescent blue, so he could hide in any shadow. I made a quick, hopeful scan of the living area—torn couch, battered chest of drawers, water-stained walls—and didn't see him.

The hard little knot of fear in my gut grew to a big, rocklike chunk of panic. I realized it was a pretty useless exercise, searching an apartment that was only the one bedroom, a prefab plastic kitchen wall unit and a tiny old bathroom. I found the bathroom empty of cat, too, but still showing the gray spatters marking our struggles; still smelling of pungent hair dye. I even checked in the cracked plastic tub, where I'm sure he thought I'd tried to drown him. It still held six inches of scummy, gray water but no cat.

As if the disappearance hadn't buzz-freaked me enough, another jolt struck when I passed the bathroom mirror and saw the puffy second-skin face and brown-dyed hair of a stranger. My translucent secondskin disguise had sagged a bit off my left cheek, and the right jawline had curled up at the edges. This was my last set from Rudy the makeup guy, so I smeared a little more glue from the tube under the loose flaps and, with careful little fingertip-pokes, smoothed them back into place. I experimentally frowned and smiled and screwed around my mouth and cheeks, to make certain a piece of jaw or a nose wouldn't drop off in public, showing part of my real framed-for-murder face.

2

Repairing my disguise gave me a chance to calm down, to think a little. Cats could curl up in the smallest space, so I needed to search every little hidey-hole. I flopped down onto the scarred wooden floor and scootched around, peering into the shadows behind and under the couch, the chest of drawers, and the cabinet that held the decrepit early '40s plasma TV. No cat—just dust balls and random gobs of grunge that I didn't want to know any more about.

As the very last thing, I looked into the opening in the cat's old cardboard box. Maybe I saved the box for last so I could savor the anticipated relief when I found him curled up there, staring at me with accusing slitted eyes. Or maybe I wanted to put off the disappointment when he wasn't. But the box was empty except for the rumpled piece of old quilt, smelling cat-musky, with a few shiny blue hairs marking where he had slept.

Down low where I crouched, I could see smudgy paw prints and drips on the floor, and even up the wall, where the dye-soaked cat had literally gone ballistic before I caught him and wrapped him in the towel. Boy, had he zanked out, bouncing like a SuperBall from wall to door to window, yowling and cursing me! But still, no cat.

The poor cat. He really was a great cat, an amazing cat, in fact. He had an almost spiritual presence, exuding a powerful animal energy, as if the scientist who made him had condensed all nine of his cat lives into one intense cat. It was like squeezing a bunch of plain old light into an ultrabrilliant laser beam.

He'd saved my life a couple of times, and we'd become friends, even though I was this young, dumb guy who'd kidnapped him, or catnapped him . . . or whatever. In fact, I'd really gotten attached to the big, genetically engineered cat with amazing cerulean fur that made people treat him like a god, calling him the most beautiful cat in history. I felt like some sadist the whole time I was dyeing him, like a guy slopping house paint all over the Mona Lisa. But it was the only thing I could figure to save his life and mine. Basically, I guess I was just too stupid to come up with a better plan.

Also, I must have missed a way he could get out! My multi-stupidity brought me to a boil against myself.

"You syntho-brain!" I cursed myself, sitting up and looking around. "You canky, worthless spit-bubble! Think!" Calling myself names pumped me up, focused my thinking. The broken window, of course! When we'd arrived, the wind hadn't been blowing, and I hadn't thought to check for a broken pane. I dragged a flickering floor lamp over to see better and yanked the grease-stained window shade, letting it clatter up. In the yellow light, the dark mirrored surface of the glass showed smeared paw prints below the hole, which was at the top of the window. He was some really smart cat to figure out how to get up on the chair and wait for the shade to blow out, so he could then launch himself from the chairback and pull himself through. I stared, puzzled, at the chair, the rickety collaborator in his escape. I was almost sure it had sat by the door before. Obviously chairs don't move themselves. Had the cat actually moved it? Was he that smart? Nah, I decided. I must have done it in my stupor; cats don't move furniture.

I took a deep, shaky breath and stared at the battered wooden door to the hallway and the rest of the world. I knew I had to find the guts to open it to search for the cat somewhere in the murky, rainy night in a dangerous Seattle slum. Could I do it, knowing the cops might be out there with their guns and their Cop Network cameras? I'd make good viddie going down in a hail of bullets, leaving a glorious multi-punctured corpse for the virtie-viddie vampires to feast on.

Could I do it knowing that out there might be the killer, Julio Miravelle, sleek and dangerous, aiming his black pistol at the door, waiting?

Or, could I face . . . I fought a wave of fear-nausea . . . a Big Nasty programmed on my scent, ready to rip out my chest in one swipe of his taloned claw? I'd never really known what evil was until I encountered the genetically concocted killing machine I'd dubbed a Big Nasty.

I could open that door. Of *course* I could open that door. I stood up and took a few deep breaths. Sure I could. After all, I'm the Gopher. That's what my dad nicknamed me when I was a scrawny little kid and I'd come home around supper time covered with layers of grime from running wild in the North Carolina woods all day, building earthbases, battling evil aliens. He'd smile tolerantly, shake his head and go back to watching the news, and Mom would make tutting noises, guide me upstairs with a single finger in my back and make me skin my dirt-stained clothes off to soak clean in the bath. She always threatened to burn the clothes but never did. I wouldn't have had any clothes left after a week.

Sure, I could open that door. The Gopher would do just about anything, even go out that door and look for a cat. Especially a cat that was my only guide to getting me out of this mess and to finding two people I loved, Lulu and Callie. Somewhere, Miravelle held them hostage, and the cat was both bargaining chip and clue. I ached over the plight of the beautiful, bright-eyed Lulu, who made me even more goofily infatuated every time I looked at her. And over her mom Callie, my greatest friend, who'd saved my life, even though she'd never even met me before this all began.

I'd survive only if I figured out what the cat knew and what secrets lay in the tangle of its stitched-together genes. And I'd figure out the cat only if I found the cat . . . out that door.

CHAPTER 2

I'd stalled long enough. I unlocked the door and eased it open, eyeball peering through the crack, ears listening for raspy animal-breathing or the cocking of guns. The hall was dirty, dim, and quiet. No cameras, no guns, no six-inch claws; only the stained, peeling wallpaper whose dark blotches had been bright little flowers a hundred years ago. No cat either, so I slipped out, down the hall, out the front door and across the porch into the street.

I took a deep breath of damp night air and tensed, waiting. No bullets, no claws here, either. The chill rain on my head washed away the last tattered remnants of my grogginess. The cold water also shocked me into some realistic thinking. Standing out in the muddy gutter, I realized I knew absolutely nil, nada, nothing about where the cat had gone. And I didn't even know how to call it. If I yelled "Cerulean!" some mindslug holed up behind one of these dark windows would surely figure out the famous cat was here and call the cops or maybe the company that built it, Animata, for the reward.

So, as my shirt wetted down into a soggy, cold, clinging shroud, I experimented with a loud, whispered "kitty-kitty-kitty," and began to circle the old apartment house. I kitty-kitty-kittied up the narrow, gloomy alley, peering into the garbage cans and crouching down to look down the steps of the basement side entrance. No shining cat eyes. I kitty-kitty-kittied over to the next block, where more cars splashed along and an occasional person walked, hunkering down against the rain. I trotted a ways down it, past other paint-challenged apartment houses, still finding no cat.

The exercise didn't much warm me up from the cold, slithery rain dribbling snakelike down my neck. The water loosened the secondskin even more, and I poked it back into place, feeling it squish beneath my fingers. All I needed was for my face to start coming apart. I squeezed a clump of hair and held my fingers up to a street light. I saw a little brown dye, and if mine was coming off in the rain, so would the cat's.

I approached a bent old guy wearing a rain slicker, limping across the street from a hole-in-the-wall bar. He kept his head down and pulled back like a turtle's inside the hood, maybe to keep the rain out of his face, maybe to avoid dealing with me.

"Sir? Sir? You seen a cat?"

"Seen lots of cats." He squinted at me suspiciously as he limped faster, pegging me no doubt for some wimpy cat lover who'd lost his precious puss. Well, okay, maybe I was a cat lover. So what? I'd really started to like that cat.

I kept up with him. "A gray cat. Big."

"Looking for a gray cat at night?" He wheezed a kind of wet gurgly chuckle. "They's all gray at night, boy." He shook his head inside the plastic hood and hurried away.

"Well, if you see him . . ." but the old man was gone. I knew if I'd mentioned the Cerulean, he'd have whipped back like a yo-yo.

I decided the best way to look was to take a quick run around as large an area as possible, so I took off slogging down the sidewalk, my sneakers splatting on the water-skinned concrete. I circled the block trying to look like a regular jogger-guy just out for his routine nightly run on this cold, wet mess of a night. Yeah, right, a routine jog wearing soggy jeans and a t-shirt.

I slowed, wiping the rain out of my eyes to get a better look at the alleys, the building entrances, the porches. I reached a main street of darkened shops and food joints, where whispering electrics and an occasional gas car sped past, splashing through rain-filled potholes with rattling thuds.

In the flash of passing headlights, I caught sight of a crumpled gray form on the street. The panic-rock in my gut seemed to heat up. Panting hard, I jogged closer and peered down. Just a greasy rag! I blew a puff of relief and ran on, circling and circling blocks and blocks, going farther and farther away from the apartment house. I passed a tabby sitting in a house window, and a yellow one slinking away down an alley. But no big gray with that odd searching look it always had on his face.

I hoped his dye hadn't washed out. I hoped I really wouldn't see him dead in the street. I hoped I wouldn't hear a growl from the shadow of a dark alley that told me a Big Nasty had me cold. The thought dredged up the agonizing memory of torn-apart flesh and the staring open eyes of dead men, sending shivers through me that had nothing to do with the cold rain. I ran harder to escape the image, to work it out of me.

After a few miles of running, I finally just lost my steam and bent over gasping with hands on rubbery knees. I waited until I got my breath and my bearings and trudged back to the apartment house. I stumbled up the apartment house steps and back into my rented room. I stripped off the soggy clothes, ran a towel over myself, patted the lifting secondskin back on my face, and pulled on dry jeans and a shirt. The gray towel showed some brown dye from my head, but the mirror reflected a fully brown-haired guy, so I was okay in the hair area. Probably, the cat was, too—a little good news.

Since I only had the one pair of sneakers, I put them in the microwave on low. I unwrapped some of the fish I'd brought him from the Seattle waterfront market and plopped it into his red bowl. I wrapped the musty blanket from the bed around me and went back out in my sock feet onto the front porch. With the bowl as my lure, I'd sit there a while on the rusty metal chair under the light and wait. When I got back my wind and my legs, I'd find a raincoat or something to keep me dry so I didn't get pneumonia, and I'd spend the night running, looking. I convinced myself it was okay to allow myself to rest on the front porch. He was about as likely to come back here as anywhere.

And, I convinced myself I was safe here at the apartment for the time being. I'd taken it as Nick Adams, not Timothy Boatright. And I'd paid with a non-traceable cashcard, which the old lady who ran the place scanned with the little scanner pulled out of her baggy housedress.

She looked at me—standing there fidgeting and holding my cardboard box full of hidden cat—with narrowed, suspicious eyes, but accepted the money and gave me the room.

As I sat hopefully on the porch, the rain drummed steadily on the roof, reminding me of the winters back home when a rolling storm would sweep across the sky from the mountains. I'd sit warm in my room and watch the quicksilver sheets of rain sweep across the bare gray woods around my house. I missed those woods. I missed home. I forced myself back to my predicament.

I knew I needed the cat, and I also absolutely knew that somewhere in the history of this unholy mess lay clues that would get Lulu, Callie, and me out of it. I had to go over everything about how I got here, chasing a genetically engineered cat and being chased . . . by just about everybody.

Chapter 3

It all started on a day I drove my cab like always, and New York stunk the way I liked New York to stink, with the sharp tangy aroma of electrics, the fumes from the gas cars, the aromas of sidewalk food, and the general rich, organic funk of people and the city. As it got hotter, all the great smells just sort of cooked themselves together like a steamy bubbling stew. Everybody immersed in the stew busied themselves acting the way only New Yorkers do. The drivers inched along in bumper-to-bumper Manhattan traffic, cabbies cussing and big traffic-scarred trucks double-parked, with everybody trying to squeeze in on everybody else.

The sidewalks could barely hold all the people: salaries in suits, slickies in their randomweave hemp jackets, funkies in trashwear, shifty peddlers selling junk, sex-joint hustlers passing out wiggly-naked-woman electroholograms, and tough, pretty New York girls, proud and knowing, wearing just about anything.

As usual, the crowd included robot Helpers, striding along with the purpose their owners had given them, on some errand or another. The mechie Helpers looked like the machines they were, with metal heads and arms all clinky and clanky. The humanalogs, however, with their electrogel flesh and secondskin covering, looked more and more like people with every new model. All the people and Helpers flowed and swirled along the city canyons like the rapids boiling over and around rocks in the mountain gorges back home in North Carolina.

Through my cab windshield, I could pick out all kinds of interesting people from the flow. I saw a terrific long-haired funky-guy striding along wearing a long shimmery trashwear coat woven of plastic strands from six-pack holders. He wore shoes made from milk jugs and a vest from stitched-together flattened beer cans.

I saw a salary-guy wearing a conservative blue suit and dark tie stuffing a sexy holo from a hustler into his pocket. Tonight, I'd bet he'd postpone dinner with the wife and kids to sit in a squirt-strip joint trying to spray a naked dancing girl with a water pistol to make her naughty chem-tattoos show up.

I saw a pretty, long-legged girl shimmering along in an electrofilm dress with constantly changing, swirling rainbow colors. She walked arm-in-arm with a slickie in a light gray randomweave suit, his own electrofilm tie showing alternating Picasso images.

When there wasn't much to see on the particular street I drove down, I could watch my fares in the rear-view mirror and talk to them if they were willing. I enjoyed talking to a family of tourists I took from the Waldorf over to the Met. They chattered so much about all the things they planned to do, I could barely hear the central cab computer report the route with the lightest traffic. They were the kinds of folks who were friendly enough that we could swap stories. They said they were the Newcrofts from Pennsylvania and they'd come to the city because Mr. Newcroft had business he couldn't do virtual-reality in the Mirror, so they all came along. Marie, the mother, designed data-sites in the Mirror for small businesses, and the two girls went to grade school, both real and virtie. The parents believed in real school, not just virtie.

I tried not to stare at the two girls, but I was trying to figure whether they were twins or clones. Probably clones, maybe of the mother. They had her straight little nose, and matching mouths with cute little short upper lips. But I didn't say anything, because it wasn't polite. Clones had enough problems as it was.

They said I was one of the few native-born Americans they'd seen driving a cab. I told them how I'm going to be a writer, and how, after

I got my degree in English from the University of North Carolina at Asheville, I decided that coming to New York was the best way to do that. Actually, my degree should have read American Literature, I said, or even more specifically Hemingway. Once I started reading Hemingway, I realized I had to be a writer. He wrote about this guy, Nick Adams, who got into all kinds of adventures, and Nick Adams was really him, but he was me, too. I held up the copy of *For Whom the Bell Tolls* I keep on the front seat.

One daughter asked why I had a dead-tree paper book and didn't just use an e-paper reader or download it and read it on my viddie-googles. E-papers were handy for reading, I admitted. They consisted of a single foldable display page that I could swipe my finger across to read through whole books, or even libraries.

But I told her I preferred printed paper books. They had a kind of literary feel to them you didn't get with an e-paper book. And as for googles, the cops ticket cabbies for even having googles in their cars. And passengers didn't trust pavement pilots who might have just come off their breaks buzzbombed from using the virtual reality glasses to immerse in some virtie role-playing game or done something weird in some Mirror sex-joint.

Anyway, just when we reached the Met, I'd gotten around to telling them I came to New York to learn about an entirely new place and get into the publishing industry. But they had to go before I finished, so we said goodbye, and they cashcarded the fare with a nice twenty-dollar tip.

After taking a salary in a suit to Battery Park, I got a slim older woman in an expensive red pantsuit, who held some kind of furry animal in her arms. I didn't get a good look at it, but I think it was one of those genetic cat-dog combinations. It made a kind of mewy barking sound once, so it probably was a dat or a cog. She wanted to go to Madison Square Garden, which I should have figured. When I'd taken a fare by there the day before, the screen out front showed a big sign advertising a cat show, with animated images of herds of cats running around. As I think back on it, the screen did advertise a special appearance by an amazing cat, which I guess meant the Cerulean.

After the traffic computer reported I'd get there fastest on Hudson to Eighth up to the Garden, I asked the lady about her animal, but she just made a little polite noise like people do when they don't want to talk. She was too busy looking at some booklet.

It surprised me that she didn't want to talk about her pet. Most of the time, people who buy expensive, genetically engineered animals are only too happy to give you the whole story. They take their animals on talk-show programs and rattle on about what it's like to live with a bear-dog or a lion-lamb combination. Or, if it's a really cool animal, they get it a big contract to advertise for a soap or something. My favorite ad animal was the feather boa . . . an honest-to-god snake with feathers. It slithered around in its feathers in some kind of perfume ad.

Or, people take their animals around and exhibit them for fifty bucks a look. I'd seen a hard-shelled, snake-necked snurtle and a furry, winged hamakeet up close at the state fair. The animals had gotten to be a zillion-dollar business. Dad said he thought it was pretty interesting, but Mom and the ladies at the church agreed with all the protesters who picketed the company and tried to get their Congressmen to pass laws against creating the animals.

Anyway, I didn't get to talk to the lady about any of that, because she really concentrated on the booklet, which I think was a cat-show program. Of course, now I know that the Cerulean's premier appearance was probably why she was so intent.

She and her animal and her program made me particularly primed to pay attention to animals in my back seat. I let her off and had just started to pull away from the curb when somebody pounded really hard on the side of the cab. Scared the biscuits out of me! I thought I'd hit somebody! I stopped, and, as I turned around, the back door whipped open, and this guy piled in with some kind of box covered with his raincoat. He was a thin, bald guy, with beads of perspiration popping out all over his expansive forehead. I asked him where he wanted to go, and he just sat there breathing hard and swallowing. I heard a shuffling sound inside the box. He peered out the window like he was expecting somebody to join him and then told me to take him to the Castle Hotel. I repeated "Castle Hotel" into the microphone, and my traffic computer took a second to find out from central control about open routes. It told me how to get there, but added an ominous "level 4" notification. That's cabbie code for a dangerous area, meaning that we can refuse service if things don't feel right. It didn't bother me, though, because I live in one of the most dangerous parts of the city, and it was broad daylight, so I didn't even flick on the cab's external navcams, which I really should have, it turned out.

I swerved into traffic, cutting off a honking truck, and my passenger put on his googles. I couldn't see his eyes, but I could see that he had this little birdbill of a nose that came to a downward point, with a tip that looked like something was dripping off it. I heard more shifting sounds from inside the box. He mumbled something into the googles . . . a number I guess . . . calling somebody up.

"Where the hell were you, you dumb bastard?" the bird-guy shouted into the mike on his googles.

I knew he wasn't talking to me, but I flinched all the same.

He kept hollering at the dumb bastard. "I don't care! I don't care! Shit, I don't care!" He was really ticked off! "You almost screwed the whole thing up. We got maybe ten minutes before . . ." He glanced up, remembering that I was there. ". . . look, I'll be where we said. You damn well be there!"

I got a stop light and tried as casually as I could to adjust the mirror to get a better view of what he was carrying. His raincoat had slipped a bit, and I could see that his box looked like an animal carrying case, which he'd wrapped his arm around tightly like he was afraid it would get away. More muffled thumping sounds of movement came from inside.

He finished his conversation and perched the googles up on his bald head and again twisted around to look out the back window. He moved like a bird, too, with quick darts of his head, as he checked the scene outside the windows. Finally, my curiosity about him got the better of me.

"So, you been at the cat show?"

"No . . . yes. I . . . uh . . . I had a cat in it."

"That the cat?"

He cackled a triumphant laugh, but sarcastic, like a squirt of acid. "Well, not this one. Another one." Then his face clouded up again. "Just drive, okay . . . Boatright?" He'd checked my name on my cabbie picture ID on the back of the seat.

"Sure, fine, sir."

He twisted around again to look out the side and back windows, and, while he was concentrating elsewhere, I adjusted the mirror again to get a better look at him. He had little ears and a fringe of stubble around his bald head. He had on a dark green shirt with a small anteater logo.

Traffic was light, so we got into upper Manhattan pretty fast. The buildings were old and canky, the newest being mid-twentieth century. Tired, tattered people slumped on the worn stoops and watched the cab go by with blank, bored expressions. A skinny, squirrelly looking guy on the corner stopped in the middle of selling a small white box to a fat guy. He waited until I passed in case I had my cameras on. The cops could use the images as evidence.

"Hereherehere!" The bird-guy said as I neared the hotel, to my surprise stuffing an actual hundred-dollar bill in my money tray. He quickly shoved the door open, and I twisted around really quick, like I was only grabbing the bill, but really so I could look straight-on at him as he got out. That's when I saw it!

The raincoat had slipped even more as he dragged the case out, and a furry, puffy tip of a tail poked itself out of one of the case's little side windows and wiggled back and forth. The tip was colored this shining, glowing blue, like the blue poof-ball from a Roman candle arcing into the night sky. It shimmered when it caught a little sliver of sunlight, mesmerizing me even though I didn't know what it was then.

In an instant, the tail withdrew, and the bird-guy saw the coat had slipped and yanked it back in place. He glared at me for a moment to see if I'd noticed anything. I remember those nasty little brown eyes looking at me and a whole collection of perspiration drops glistening on his forehead. Even though I was sure he hadn't caught me seeing the blue tail, I made it a point to grin innocently back at him and say "Have a great day, sir!"

He slammed the door, and I stayed put, pretending like I was talking to the trip computer, so I could see where he went. Hefting the box at his side, he hurried right past the hotel entrance, to the end of the block, and disappeared around the corner.

And that was how it all started.

CHAPTER 4

I had a crazy zooming-around shift that day, so I didn't think much more about the bird-guy and his case with the blue tail sticking out. I took fares to LaGuardia and to midtown hotels and to buy groceries. One lady dragged a big stuffed Panda into the cab for her granddaughter who was sick. And a young couple did juicy-feelies on each other going down Fifth Avenue. They made me remember that after my shift I was going to see Elizabeth, who is sort of my girlfriend.

I rolled back into the taxi barn about nine p.m., after the rush hour and the early dinner-crowd. The barn is a big hulking warehouse way uptown that's held taxis for what looks like a century. It's black with greasy dirt and has a layered smell with old oil underneath, and the tang of electricity on top. The electrics with their egg-shaped plastic bodies are lined up on one side hitched to their humming power lines, and the few boxy scarred gas cars that have survived sit on the other side of a wall across the garage, with the mechanics changing oil and banging around beneath their hoods.

Tucked in the back, behind another wall whose top half is yellowed scratched Plexiglas, is the cabbies' trash-strewn lounge, usually filled with cabbies sitting around on old plastic chairs, drinking coffee and soft drinks and hollering at each other for one thing or another. They holler because they all speak different versions of English. I think each cabbie believes if he hollers loud enough, his version will become the version of choice. And they holler because they've been out their whole shift fighting traffic and catching hell from fares. It's a great place for somebody like me who wants to be a writer.

The cabbies always include me in their hollering at each other, because I'm best at English. I can translate from one foreign accent to an American accent so the other guy will understand. I think that's probably why I was hired, besides the help from Mushie. When I first landed at LaGuardia, I'd gotten into this cab driven by Mushie, a rail-thin little guy with perfect dusky black skin and beautiful white teeth that flashed when he grinned. I liked him immediately and began telling him all about coming to New York to become a writer. I asked him about what being a cabbie was like and whether it was a good way to meet people. He giggled.

"Oh, sure. We see the best people. Every damn day we see very best damn people in whole damn world."

"You think I could be a cabbie?"

"You are not stupid enough. You look like a bright boy."

I convinced him I was really stupid, and he laughed and said he'd do what he could. And he did. We kind of clicked together, like we'd been friends a long time. His real Bangladeshi name was much longer than just Mushie, with lots of k's and n's and r's in it, but Mushie was all we could manage. The last name was easier—Biswas—but we never used last names. Mushie really pushed Louis the dispatcher to hire me, even though he didn't want some kid like me working for him. Since I was new, he made me drive one of the old gas cars instead of an electric, but I didn't mind.

Mushie also helped me get to know the other cabbies, which was easy, because I started helping them with English for their citizenship exams. They especially like my English, because I've got this North Carolina twang they liked to imitate. Big Petrov said that, for some reason, the examiner went easy on him because he told the guy "Hahdy!" and answered the questions in a southern-fried Russian accent.

So, when I walked into the cabbies' lounge after my shift, Rasheed, Big Petrov, Nuzhat, Bonabo, Jorge, Chin, and Mushie were sitting around the table on the plastic chairs, hollering. A couple of other guys sat off in a corner using their googles—watching a viddie or making phone calls. I'd brought an after-work snack from the old GoodEats diner down the street. A half-pound cultured meat burger with a thick slab of onion, mustard, pickle slices and a great slather of melted cheese.

"So, you have survived another day." Mushie grinned. "Now you will go and see your girlfriend and stay up all night 'talking'. Oh yes, talk, talk, *talk!*"

"Yeah, we talk. We do!" I protested, but they didn't believe me because they'd seen Elizabeth.

They all laughed, both at Mushie and at me, because that always got me to blush. Mushie apologized, and clapped me on the back with his small, bony hand. I accepted, and he bought me a Kava Squeeze from the machine in the lounge to go with the burger. Between bites and swigs, I spent some time translating for the guys: "Ahvdue" into "overdue" for Nuzhat trying to explain a bill to Rasheed. "Kleekul" into "clinical," for Bonabo trying to ask Big Petrov about doctors. We had a generally good time.

We started talking about fares and I mentioned the bird-guy with the carrying case with the tail sticking out. Chin suddenly jumped up, waving his hands as if trying to coax the right words out of his mouth.

"Shooleen Kot!" he finally said, nodding his head vigorously. "Shooleen take away. Burra big, big thing to happen! Kot! Kot!"

Even I was stumped at Chin's rattling on, so Big Petrov, who knew some Chinese, talked to him for a bit. Finally, Big Petrov clapped his ham-hands together and told me.

"Ah! He says this cat was taken. The . . . *Cerulean* cat. Very famous, expensive genetic cat who was made in laboratory."

The room echoed with shouted questions in all accents, until I told in detail what had happened. This was a big deal, they hollered. I let them go on while I finished the burger.

"So, should I go to the police?" I asked when the hollering died down.

Everybody hollered together, this time "NO!"

"You will get only grief," said Mushie.

"They will interrogate you," said Big Petrov.

"You might be taken away," said Jorge.

"Son, you really wanna get your butt in trouble over a little piece of tail?" hollered Rasheed, making everybody roar with laughter.

While they kept on, I thought about whether I should just let it drop. But I decided that as a future writer, I really needed to know what had happened to that cat.

I needed to send out my angel.

I've got a really good angel, a Microsoft 6.2 CyberAngel, really the best piece of software I ever had. My mom and dad bought it for me as a graduation present after college, because they insisted that when I went out in the world, a good angel would make the difference between success and failure. Sure, I knew "Angel" was an acronym for "Agent for Neural Guidance to Electronic Libraries." But like most folks, I really liked the idea of the agents as angels watching over us in cyberspace.

From my locker, I retrieved my processor and googles in their black plastic belt pouch. I put on the googles, sticking the earphones in. My googles looked almost like regular wraparound glasses, with the microphone built into the earpiece. Of course, the processor just looked like a little black box with a red on-off switch, an indicator light and a row of plug-in jacks. But it was a magic box to me.

My folks bought them both for me, too. They wanted to make sure I didn't have the excuse of broken old equipment not to stay in touch. Maybe they also wanted me to remember them and feel a little homesick and guilty about going off to New York. It worked. I always felt a twinge when I put on the googles.

I ignored the twinge this time because I was hot on a trail. I didn't need to go to a linkbooth to get high bandwidth; I wasn't going into the Mirror. I could just download the few three-D virtie-viddies I'd need—where you can move around inside a viddie as it played, seeing it from all angles. So, I dragged a chair over to a corner and asked the guys to leave me alone for a little bit while I downloaded stuff on this stolen blue cat.

But Mushie came over twiddling a pair of borrowed googles in his hand.

"Mind if I plug in?" he asked hopefully in his tongue-rolling accent. "I would like to know about this cat also." With his big family, Mushie couldn't afford the glasses or angels, so I let him tap in with me whenever he wanted.

"Yeah, actually I want you to see these. You tell me whether I should go to the cops."

"You know my answer. No bloody way." Mushie plopped his skinny frame down on the old couch and folded his legs, and I plugged him into a spare processor jack.

I flipped the switch on my processor, the world faded into black and my angel materialized in three-D, with her snow-white feathery wings, shining halo and all. She floated in front of wispy digital clouds, smiling her pretty, dimpled angelic smile, wafting her wings up and down. Her filmy gown and golden hair billowed softly about her. She didn't have to worry about gravity. She was only software and she was in cyberspace. Some people like their angels to be just efficient geometric icons that flash signal colors at them, but I liked my smiling angel icon. The sight of her gave me a little tickle in my libido. Except for one problem.

"Hi, Timmy. Warning. Your battery's low," said the angel in my mom's voice. Mom had asked a hacker friend of Uncle Ned's to program that little feature in, as one of her little practical jokes. It still worked okay, but made me feel self-conscious sometimes. Like when the guys back home got me to go to that synthosex room in the Mirror. There I was with all these incredible luscious syntho women offering to do anything my heart desired, to morph into anybody my heart desired! In virtual reality anyway. And there I was with an angel mouthing my mom's voice.

"I'm sorry . . ." I caught myself. I never could get out of the habit of apologizing to software. "How long do I have?"

"Two hours."

"Okay, I'll charge it later. Look, I need you to get me information on the Cerulean cat."

We went through a few questions and answers while I specified what I wanted. After a few seconds, my angel shrank to a small fluttering Tinkerbell-like figure in the corner of my vision, with the parting admonition:

"Wash your dirty socks." Mom also had programmed in reminders about my bad habits. Like the voice, the hacker had hidden them so well in the software, I hadn't managed to delete them.

Mushie and I started immersing ourselves in new viddies showing how the cat was stolen from the Madison Square Garden Cat Show. We wafted along rows of wire cages spread out across the arena in perfect rows, with cat-people milling around them—including a fair number of plumpish older women in big print blouses and pants, and men in baggy sport shirts and hang-dog expressions at being hauled to a cat show. We peeked into some cages, where fancy cats peered out with blank cat eyes—cats with long fur or short, colored white, black, brown, tan, orange, yellow, gray—cats in solid, stripes, spots and swirls. The cats looked pretty calm, considering cops were bulling their way from cage to cage pulling back fancy lace curtains and shoving their cop hands in to pull up plush carpeting and big plump cat beds and generally tossing the cages the way they might toss a room looking for drugs.

Another scene we immersed ourselves in showed a shaky long shot of white-coated people loading what looked like a blue cat into a carrier. But the scene wasn't very high resolution, so the people were fuzzy and not really three-D. So we couldn't zoom in much and circle all around them. You could always tell when a virtie came from one of the freelance vampires who hung out with their virtie-viddie cameras and sold whatever stuff they could shoot that involved blood, explosions, or major mayhem.

Still another virtie scene showed a shot of a big stone building with a sign that said Animata and a logo that was strands of DNA shaped like an ark. The TV reporter in voiceover called the cat "the pride of the high-flying genetic engineering company, Animata, Incorporated." Then there were scenes in which we could float around scientists working in laboratories with fancy machines, bottles, and tiny tubes. We zoomed in for a close-up look at the bottles, but they didn't look like much special. We heard the reporter say "Today was to have been its public debut, the beginning of perhaps a billion-dollar career as a celebrity animal."

Virtie-viddie from the Cop Network was the best, as usual, because it was from the cops' badge cameras. It started with a gray-haired cop in a dark suit with an Exxon patch and a big gold badge. "We have a full investigation underway," said the cop in his best Cop Network voice. "And we expect to find the perpetrators and the animal and return it to its rightful owners," I recognized him as the famous Lieutenant Rocky.

"There's not many places that anybody could hide such a distinctive animal." Other Cop Network virties showed the armored car that had transported the cat and the guarded dressing room where it was being kept when it was stolen. A cop held up a dyed blue cat that hung limp, like it had been handled a lot. We zoomed up close to the cat. It was a pretty sorry-looking puss.

"The perpetrators switched animals to give themselves time to escape," said the cop holding the bored, floppy cat. "Until the case was opened, nobody knew the cats had been switched."

Then I remembered the bird-guy's funny cackle when I asked him if he had a cat in the show. He'd said, "Not this one," or something like that. He'd brought in the decoy cat!

I zipped through the rest of the viddies to get more details about how the catnappers had switched the cases when the guard stepped out of the room to take a pee. But nowhere did anybody even give a sketchy description of the kidnappers.

"Mushie, y'know, I might be the only witness!" I whispered as we watched the viddies. "With a zillion people carrying a zillion cat cages around that arena, one more likely wouldn't have been noticed."

But Mushie didn't say anything. In fact the room was dead silent.

I flipped the googles up and gave myself a chance to refocus on reality. Everybody stood like statues staring at the door, where Louis the dispatcher, a little guy who combed about twelve long hairs across his bald pate, stood with two big guys in suits. Even from across the room, I could see the little red lights glowing from their badge cameras, which were little black squares on their chests. The dispatcher pointed at me, and the cops came over.

"Timothy Boatright?" asked the bigger of the two. I recognized him immediately as Lieutenant Rocky, which was both cool and scary. I was on the Cop Network!

"Yes."

He spun me around and ratcheted handcuffs down tight on my wrists.

"We're taking you in for questioning in connection with the theft of the Cerulean cat."

CHAPTER 5

My wrists still hurt a little from the handcuffs, but I was too freaked to care. The other cop, Al-Somebody, watched over me while Lieutenant Rocky went off to get a cup of coffee. A jowly guy in a gray pompadour and a tailored suit, he just stared at me, I'm sure trying to freak me even more, so I avoided his gaze by looking around the main room of Manhattan Center, probably the most famous station on the Cop Network.

The place was crammed with old desks with the big beefy precinct cops barely squeezing into squeaky old chairs. They pecked away on old dirt-smudged computer keyboards or talked in growly voices to shifty-eyed snitches and sullen hookers. The walls were grubby and stained and the ceiling fixtures cracked. I noticed, though, that the grubby walls were painted to look that way, and the old desks were actually new ones with battered-looking wood glued over them, all for the benefit of the Cop Network viewers, I realized. The room smelled like a combination of decaying old building, fresh coffee and cologne.

For about fifteen minutes, I sat in a hard wooden chair staring at a desk sign that said "Lt. Rockefeller Lundquist, sponsored by Exxon." Then he showed up with a Cop Network mug in his hand.

For the first time, I got a close look at him. He had thick, bushy eyebrows that each sat above his eyes, like scrub brush on a mountaintop. He also had a big nose that looked like it had been broken a few times and curly brown and gray hair that had retreated back on his forehead, like it was intimidated by the eyebrows. He took off his jacket with the Exxon patch and cop badge, and pulled his matching machine pistols out of their shoulder holsters, making sure I got a good look at them before locking them in his desk drawer.

"Pal, we're going to NCA ya. That okay?"

"Yeah . . . okay." I should have known! I'd seen tons of perps hauled in and stood up in front of the Noninvasive Credibility Assessor before. I didn't have anything to hide, so I'd be fine. I was sure . . . sort of. They stood me up in front of this machine that looked like an old-timey bank cash machine I'd seen in a barn once back home. But instead of all the bank information, this avatar appeared on the screen. He was a pleasant-looking guy, I knew meant to put me at ease.

Meanwhile Rocky rolled his shirt sleeves up on hairy arms and sat down at the readout screen, taking out a pen and his notebook. He didn't really need to write anything. That was all for the Cop Network viewers. The machine would keep a record of my answers.

I concentrated on the avatar-guy on the screen. The NCA would measure my subtle microexpressions, eyeball reactions, fidgeting, stammers and all kinds of cues that I might be lying. I determined to keep a straight face and be steady-eyeballed, fidget-free, and smooth-talking. But the first question got me.

"Full name?" asked the avatar.

"Uh . . ." Dang! I thought. Bad start!

"Full name?" repeated the avatar, smiling.

"Yeah. It's . . . Kayak Timothy Boatright."

The avatar didn't react, but Al snorted and Rocky gave me a scowl. But I knew that the computer had already verified my name. I'd no doubt flashed a screwed-up embarrassed face that the avatar caught. Mom had given me the name Kayak. Her and Uncle Ned. See, Mom was born in 2002, a palindrome year; the same backward as forward. When my Nana told her what palindromes were, she fell in love with them. That's probably why I'm a writer, sort of. While she was still a kid, she started collecting palindromes like "A man, a plan, a canal. Panama!" And when I was born, she wanted a palindrome name for me. Dad tried to persuade her to name me Bob. No such luck. For some reason, she listened to Uncle Ned, who, like his big sister, got all involved in palindromes, too. He thought Kayak would be a hoot, because it fit with Boatright. Thank God my dad also persuaded her to give me the middle name Timothy, after my great grandfather. It wasn't until Kyle was born that Dad thought to argue that the name Bob was related to boats, which is why my brother is Kyle Bob Boatright.

"Address?" asked the avatar, bringing me back from my recollection.

"You want my address?" I was really not doing well, here. I didn't want to give my address because of the canky neighborhood. If I lived there, I *must* be up to no good.

"Address?" repeated the avatar patiently.

I gave my address, face-scrunching and shifting around, aware that the cops' computer system had already pegged it as a high-crime area.

"Are you associated with any criminal activity?"

"Well . . ." I didn't know what to say. See, I'm a writer, and words mean a lot to a writer. I am "associated" with criminal activity. I don't do anything illegal, but I know Miguel Salvo. And boy is he ever associated with crime! I finally answered "No."

Al shook his head. It's illegal for the cops to reveal the results of an NCA exam. But the Cop Network cops know how to make it clear to viewers what they think without saying anything.

"Were you involved in the theft of the Cerulean cat?" Boy, that avatar got right to the point, but he was still smiling like we were just having a nice chat.

Again, I had a word problem. I *was* "involved" in a way. I'd accidentally picked up the bird-guy and the cat. So, that makes me "involved." The avatar repeated the question.

"No," I finally answered.

Rocky kept his scowl cranked up to intense. With one last look at the screen, he dragged me over to a chair and sat me down.

"Well, Kayak, your computer records showed you picked up a fare at the Garden about the time the cat was taken, and dropped it down on 129th. That's a level four area, but you didn't turn on your navcams. Why the hell not?"

"I'm willing to tell you I saw it . . . or a part of it anyway."

"It's in parts?" He got right in my face. "You confessing to something?"

"No, no. I don't mean the cat's in parts. I . . . I mean I saw its tail sticking out of a carrying case . . . in the cab."

"So, you going to give up your partner?" Rocky sat on the edge of his desk, folding his hairy arms. I became acutely aware that my family and friends were out there watching.

"What makes you think I'm involved in this?"

Rocky looked back at the NCA machine. I knew I'd done pretty lousy on it, but all he said was, "The fare wasn't cashcarded."

"He paid real cash."

"Yeah, right. Kayak, nobody pays real cash."

"Look, I'll tell you everything."

"I'm listening, Kayak."

I told him the whole story, including the bird-guy, his phone conversation with the dumb bastard, the blue tip of the tail, and the drop at the Castle Hotel, where the bird-guy didn't stop. Rocky took a lot of notes and asked terse, clear questions for the Cop Network cameras.

After I finished, Rocky hit a couple of keys to bring up a rendering program, asking me to describe the bird-guy for a composite sketch. I stumbled around some, but managed to get the program to sketch the guy's beaky nose, fringe of hair and little ears. From watching a story about the sketch program, I remembered to use words the computer would know. Like, I didn't say "beaky," but rather "thin and drooping."

Finally, there before me on the screen rotated a pretty good three-D image of the bird-guy, hair-fringe, beak-nose and all.

Next, Al took me to a bare little room where they wanted me to look at mug shots. A technician taped electrodes to my head that would register the characteristic blips in my brain waves when I recognized a mug shot. The brain record was good evidence in court, because witnesses' brain waves triggered involuntarily when they recognized somebody. I hoped none of the mug shots would show Miguel Salvo or his gang. I'd be in even deeper trouble if the cops found out I recognized a big local drug boss. But Salvo didn't look like the bird-guy at all, so I was pretty safe.

For an hour, I sat there in the big chair watching three-D images of thin, bald guys flash on the screen. Some looked a lot like my bird-guy, but none rang the brain gadget.

Rocky came back in and sat down beside me.

"Look, kid, we don't know whether you're giving us straight information or not. There's nobody to back you up. Nobody's come forward to say they saw this guy with the case. And the thieves screwed up the cameras in the area, so we've got no viddie."

"So, I'm a suspect?"

"Just don't go anywhere." He got a call and left, so Al finished up with me. He was friendlier, maybe being the good cop.

"Son, you have an agent?" He leaned against the wall of the mug shot room and smiled, showing very nice teeth.

"Well, no. Didn't think I needed one. I just thought I was a witness . . . maybe a suspect."

He chuckled knowingly. "This is a big case. You ought to have an agent." He fumbled around in his pocket. "Tell you what. Here's my agent's card." He passed a shimmering holo card over to me. I'd put it in a card reader later and go over all the stuff embedded in it. Then he reached over and touched a button, and a form appeared on the viddie screen.

"It's the standard short-form contract for witnesses." He waved his hand at the screen. "We have rights to show you on first encounter, but this protects you from now on. Just touch the screen with your index finger."

"So I'm a witness not a suspect?"

He ignored the question. "It says you give us rights to use your image and your information to the Cop Network only. But . . ." He held up one big index finger and waggled it back and forth ". . . . you get to keep ancillary rights . . . . syntho books, movies, games, theme songs, live-action figures, so forth."

"And if I don't sign?" All the trouble they'd given me made me ornery.

"No skin off our nose. They're your rights." He indicated again I should put my fingerprint on the screen.

"Paperbacks, too?" Even in the fix I was in, I knew I had to worry about such things.

He wrinkled his brow. "You mean like printed on paper? Oh, I guess, if they still make them." He showed teeth again. "Oh, and you're automatically entered in the witness lottery." I already knew about how a witness could win trips and stuff. I shrugged, touched the screen, and the computer registered my fingerprint.

Free for the moment, I pushed through the battered bulletproof plastic doors of the Manhattan Center and stopped outside, squinting against the glare of the permanent camera lights shining on the old brick building. Even though I'd gotten rousted around, the battered hulk of a building still impressed me, with its pockmarks from gunfire and its wild colored swirls of graffiti.

Two cops with Dunkin' Donuts sponsor patches on their shirts had just wrestled a canky-looking suspect out of a patrol van and stood his sorry bedraggled self up in front of the station, probably so they'd have a good camera angle. They were reading him his augmented Miranda rights, which I'd heard lots of times before.

". . . You have the right to makeup," continued the younger cop. "You have the right to an attorney and an agent. If you cannot afford these, the court will appoint a makeup artist, attorney, and agent for you . . . ."

I stood wondering if I'd hear those words as a suspect soon, when my processor beeped. I slipped on the googles, but it was a voice link from Mushie.

He asked if I was okay, and I described being hauled in and questioned. Then came the bad news.

"Louis says that you are not needing to come in."

"I'm fired?"

"The boys and I have persuaded him that he should not fire you, but he says until you are cleared, you are not to work."

"Jeez, that's not fair! I just saw the cat is all! I'll call him. I'll talk—"

"We will work on him, Tim. Don't worry, friend, the boys are with you."

He asked if I needed money, which I would soon, unless I wanted to call my folks, which I sure didn't. I thanked him and hung up, facing the prospect of getting a job waiting tables or something. And maybe my girlfriend Elizabeth would offer a sympathetic shoulder and more for an out-of-work suspected thief.

Tonight the publisher she worked for, Gigaday was holding a publishing party for the first commercial synthobook she'd helped edit. She said the party would run late, and I could come by if I wanted to. I wanted to.

CHAPTER 6

The cavernous marble lobby of the Gigaday building billowed with hanging rainbow electrofilm fabrics by the designer who does the fancier parties. Spotlights played over the shimmering cloth and the crowd of people who looked as if they'd designed themselves for such parties, displaying their glasses of champagne like awards for their shiny, swirly clothes and shaved and sculpted hairdos. I decided a long time ago that jeans and sneakers would do for any party I needed to go to. They'd have to; they were all I could afford. But I enjoyed seeing all the fancy capes and dresses the other people wore, filing them away for future reference to clothe my characters with someday.

Crowds of the dazzlers still filled the hall, because the buffet still held heaps of food, and the bartenders still poured freely. And weird-looking humie Helpers circulated holding trays of drinks and nibblies. Their secondskins were designed to look like characters from the synthobook that was premiering—wizards and warlocks and knights, and so forth.

I snagged a beer and wove through the crowd until I found Elizabeth standing beside a young guy with a neatly shaved oval on top of his head, the bald spot tattooed with a yin-yang symbol. Elizabeth wore a long multi-slitted black dress that accented her creamy skin and long auburn hair. She had a dancer's graceful posture, as the dress's low cut, thin straps and snug fit around her waist revealed. She smiled at the young guy, flabby and pale, who rested his arm across his paunchy stomach, his elbow on one hand and his champagne glass held bent-wristed, as if too tired to bear the weight of the glass without bracing it. He slouched as he talked. He must have been very tired.

Elizabeth gave me a measured smile that played prettily around her delicately curved lips and brown eyes, and I smiled back. But she offered no hug or kiss.

"Timothy, you came. You remember Klaus?" I remembered Klaus, but I was more interested in Elizabeth's long legs that peeked out of the multiple slits in that dress. Her ballet classes had made them very expressive legs. She used them creatively when we made love, wrapping and unwrapping them around me, and even flipping them all the way over her head. I snapped myself back to the present.

"Sure, Klaus. How're you doing?"

Klaus didn't abandon the job of supporting his glass to shake my hand.

"Yes, you're the farmer from Kentucky, aren't you?"

"North Carolina, and my dad's also in the furniture business."

"Of course . . . furniture . . . how nice." He sipped his champagne, spied someone he knew, waved, and excused himself.

"I saw you were on viddies. You were arrested?" Elizabeth's voice was as flat and measured as a ruler.

"No, not arrested. I think I saw that cat. The Cerulean that was kidnapped."

"It looked like you were arrested. Look, I've got to go mingle." She waved to a large man in a flowing rust-colored robe and left, showing peekaboos of silky white thigh through the dress slits as she walked. Lots of promise prowled beneath that dress.

She was a little cool tonight, but maybe she was just being Elizabeth. Not Liz, not Beth, but Elizabeth, she insisted. Like Elizabeth Barrett Browning. She said that the full name Elizabeth was more fitting for a big-time publishing executive, like she planned to be. I thought she already had a great job. After she'd graduated from Vassar, this big publisher Gigaday hired her to screen all the synthobooks that people submitted unsolicited. She said the job was the Stygian pits, spending whole days wandering through "syntho-slush" virtual-reality stories created by warped minds whose only distinction was their sick delusions.

I decided to give her the benefit of the doubt and made a strafing run down the buffet, trying out the little meatlike protein balls, the (fake) lobster dip, and the (almost real) cheeses. I skipped the weird-colored genetically engineered vegetables piled around bowls of brown and tan dip. Even though they were the fashion, I couldn't get my taste buds up for red carrots, striped blue-and-white tomatoes or purple broccoli.

Once stuffed, I checked on Elizabeth, but she was in the middle of a crowd, so I wandered over to a long table holding googles and chest-woofers. A couple of other people had linked into the synthobook, and they were waving their hands around like lunatic mimes on drugs, manipulating virtie stuff. They also wore the chest-woofers, paddles on their chest that vibrated their whole bodies, tweaking their emotional brainwaves and immersing them in the action. One guy ducked and let out a whoop. An actor came over, dressed in a ridiculous medieval outfit with a puffy white blouse, purple tights and pointy shoes, and offered to help me get hooked up, but I declined, waiting for an opening with Elizabeth.

Instead, I watched the viddie screens that showed scenes from the synthobook. One screen showed the title in swirly three-D letters: *Castle of Destiny,* by Brendan Oatley. Another screen showed a user in a great stone hall with a long, battered oak table and huge fireplace. Hunched over the head of the table sat a wizened old man wearing a black suit that loosely shrouded his frail body. He was a very good syntho. I could clearly see the wrinkles in his haggard face, and the wild, wispy hair that gleamed in silvery strands backlit by the fire. Virtual people were getting better all the time.

Still other screens showed a user skewering a bad knight with a sword, making realistically gooey virtual blood squirt out. Another screen showed a player waving a wizard's wand over a gnarled, ugly warlock, making him melt into what looked like a puddle of blue oatmeal.

Standard stuff. At least Elizabeth hadn't had to work on one of those freaky synthos where people turn into chairs and get sat on, or fall down holes into simulated stomachs and get digested. Or, one of the bloody ones where you blow up monsters and destroy planets.

Since Elizabeth didn't seem inclined to come to me, I'd go to her. I found my way through the crowd to where she stood talking to a tall balding man in a dark suit with a carnation in his lapel. They stood beside the table showing *Castle of Destiny* toys, music, jewelry, watches, t-shirts, theme vacations, frozen dinners, candy, tattoos, and condoms.

I finally got my chance and drew her aside to talk privately, but her eyes roamed the room, as if avoiding my gaze.

I asked, "You want to get together? My place?"

"Uh . . . sorry . . . I've got obligations." She started to go, then seemed to decide that her answer wasn't definitive enough. "Look, Tim, you've got into trouble, and I'm sorry about that. But my editor asked me about it. He said it's not a good idea to get involved with people who got arrested. The corporation and everything. I've got a career to think of, and . . . well . . ." She trailed off, blushing slightly, the rose color conspicuous on her milky-white skin.

"So, it doesn't matter that I wasn't arrested?"

"You were on the Cop Network. Handcuffs and everything. C'mon, Tim, see it my way."

"I do see it your way Elizabeth. And it's not a good way. It's not how I treat my friends."

"Well, you just better learn about life in the big city, Tim. I'm sorry, okay?" She cocked her head and made a rueful face, squeezed my arm and moved off through the crowd, not looking back. I really regretted watching her walk away. I liked Elizabeth. She was a snot sometimes, like now, but she was clever and smart, and when she was in a less-snotty mood, she was fun to be with, like when we were rolling around in bed, with her laughing and shouting, "Oh, farmer Tim, plow me, sow me, reap me!"

I'm sure one reason she didn't stick by me was that she really didn't believe that I'd be a writer. But I knew I would, eventually. I remembered what Hemingway said about how it's hard to write if you were enjoying people and places and having a good time. He said when it came time to write, it would be like peristalsis. I guess my creative peristalsis hadn't started up yet.

But for now, though, maybe I just needed some quiet time in my apartment to digest all that had happened.

CHAPTER 7

Riding the subway home, all kinds of different feelings came and went just like the subway stops. The cops had really ticked me off for hauling me in and making me into some kind of minor public enemy. Louis for laying me off. Elizabeth for being such a snot about one little sort-of arrest.

Not having a job worried me. What would my family think about me being unemployed? They kind of accepted criminals. We had criminals in the family. Like Uncle Ned, who'd seen some cells in his time. But everybody had a job.

After sorting through it all, though, I finally decided I felt more excited than anything else. This is what I'd come to New York for—to get into adventures I could write about, and this seemed like a pretty cool one. So, what the hell. None of this stuff made problems I couldn't handle.

I could tell when the train got closer to my neighborhood. As people got on and off at the stations, the regular people with legitimate purposes in life thinned out. They were replaced by scruffies and gang-bangers, whose eyes either dead-stared into space or darted around looking for trouble. They all pretty much left me alone. I didn't look like I had any money, and I did look ready for any stuff they might want to try. Besides, I think the word was out even beyond my neighborhood that I was under special protection.

My stop came up, and I got off behind a trembling, raggedy little man who stopped and informed me he was looking for Jesus, and could he have money to support his search. In front of him walked a bulky, hairy guy with a gold fang and steel bracelets who, if I hadn't been on the platform, would've probably helped Raggedy get to heaven and see Jesus for free.

Raggedy flopped down in a corner of the station, his smell rising around him, and I climbed the subway steps behind the big guy, and right into a dope deal. Just outside the entrance, one of Salvo's ratty-looking humie Helpers was passing cartons of nickies to a customer in a Volvo electric at the curb. The customer had the driver's window down just enough to pass money and nickies through. Salvo's Helper paid me no attention, even though his customer stopped in mid-sale, put the window up and shifted the Volvo into gear as a precaution. But I knew I hadn't really stopped the sale. The customer wouldn't go anywhere until he got his nickies. Ever since nicotine got banned in cigarettes, people would do anything for a carton of nicotine smokes, even hang out in my neighborhood.

Then I ran into a *big* problem I hadn't even thought of—Granite-head. The huge, muscular man loomed in front of me, his shiny bald head looking like it was carved from a single block of rich brown granite. He had onyx eyes and ivory white teeth that gleamed with a predatory smile. He reached out and gripped my shoulder; the bulging cylinders of his arms jutting out of the sleeves looked like they'd been carved from the same granite. I called him Granite-head; I never wanted to get to know him enough to learn his real name.

"We takin' a little trip, you and me." Behind him stood his backup, Fancy-hair, my name for a lanky guy known for his shaved and sculpted hairdo. Tonight's fashion-do was a sort of corkscrew of ebony hair that looped around and down past his ear. He giggled.

"What do you mean? Trip where?"

36

"Mr. Salvo, he want to see you."

Miguel Salvo, the biggest drug boss in this part of the city. Torturer, killer. An all-around interesting guy. I figured the meeting had to do with our past mutual interest.

Granite-head, who was Salvo's resident tough-guy in my neighborhood, spun me around and walked me to the corner where Salvo's big, black electric limo waited. He herded me inside and followed, slamming the door and waving the driver on. The limo glided ice-smooth through the streets for just eight or ten blocks, and we pulled up in front of a brownstone sheathed in construction scaffolding. Granite-head walked me through the iron piping, past two large, ugly guys standing on the front steps looking very wary. They knew Miguel Salvo treated any slipup in guarding him as a capital offense, I was sure. Inside, the brownstone smelled of new wood and paint. Its swaths of plastic sheeting, piles of boards and buckets of paint told of the final stages of a renovation. Granite-head motioned me into a new elevator, and I felt like a dwarf standing next to the huge thug. On the third floor, the door opened, and Granite-head pushed me out into a hallway with a single door leading into a spacious apartment still sheathed in raw wallboard, with some exposed studs and fresh plywood, and partly covered with new oak flooring. Over in the corner sat two tall crates with the Helpers, Inc. logo, undoubtedly Helpers that Salvo wanted to give his mama, along with the apartment.

I turned back to Granite-head, but the door had closed, the mean, brown mountain vanishing without a trace. He was only an errand boy. Now I had to deal with Salvo's major line of defense, and offense—Max. The mountainous black-suited Max lumbered toward me from the next room wearing a stainless steel cap screwed to his bald skull, pocked with rows of threaded bolt holes for mounting hardware. He'd screwed lethal-looking spikes into four holes—on the front, back, left, right—obviously for goring opponents. The helmeted face had no eyebrows and a forehead like a rock ledge, shielding little beady eyes set way back underneath the outcropping. His large nose was flattened and gnarled from countless battles. A scar that looked like the Mississippi River slashed down one cheek.

Max greeted me as usual, with one hand in his coat gripping his machine pistol. He surveyed me with predatory eyes, like a cougar that got into our barn one time and went after our dogs.

"Hi, Max. It's been a while."

He said nothing. Max never said anything. I could probably whang Max over his metal-covered head with a crowbar and just barely get his attention. He reached out and patted me down, his left hand showing the row of tattooed hash marks that Freddie Dunk, my landlord, said was Max's body count. The right hand showed a similar row, and Freddie said he thought the difference might be people shot-versus-stabbed. I thought I could detect a fresh hash mark on the left hand. I wondered whether there was a new body stuffed in a dumpster somewhere.

Satisfied that I didn't pose a threat to his employer, Max stepped back and waved me into the next room.

The first face I saw there was a beautiful antidote to the ugliness of Max's—an exotic female face of rich, caramel brown, with long-lashed almond eyes, a little turned-up nose and a wide, expressive mouth that held sensuous promise, all framed in a fancy feathered helmet-hat with silver beads hanging down either side.

Salvo's girlfriend, Yani, wandered about what would be the apartment's spacious living room, her long brown legs shown off by a very short, tight, look-at-my-fine-butt gold beaded dress.

"Hi, there," she said with that honey-smooth voice. I'd sometimes fantasized how that voice would purr in my ear during lovemaking, but knew of course that I would quickly become a hash mark on Max's hand after that.

"Hi, where's—"

Miguel Salvo strode in, compact, like a coiled steel spring. He had an oval face, electric in its intensity, from which shone snake-cold eyes, pitch dark. His small, nose, cocked slightly to one side told of old fights. A slightly protruding jaw gave the face a pugnacious look, the thin lips a cold authority. His shiny ebony hair was immaculately cut, brushed back flat against the skull.

"How is she?" he asked in a surprisingly soft voice. His jaw tightened almost imperceptibly in frustration. Here he was, such a big guy and he couldn't find out for himself how his own mother was. "She need anything?"

"She's fine." I said. "It's too late to see her tonight, but I'll see her tomorrow." I stammered a little bit.

"I wanted you to see this." He waved his hand around at the unfinished apartment. "It's for Mama, to get her out of that little place. You tell her it's nice. You tell her she should move here when it's done."

"Sure, I will." Yani sat down on a folding chair, looking bored, and stretched her long legs out, looking like a tawny animal resting before a hunt. I looked around, trying to avoid looking at Yani's legs. "Yeah, it is nice." Salvo counted on my influence with his mother, especially after what I'd done that night two months ago, when I'd practically saved the life of the mother of the biggest drug dealer in this part of New York.

The first weeks in my apartment hadn't really been that promising. I'd promptly been ripped off, losing my furniture, money, clothes, viddie screen. But I decided I'd just have to live without stuff, because I'd determined to live somewhere interesting, besides the usual places with people like me.

The only other tenant on the floor was a nice old lady, Mrs. Salvo. She had tired eyes and sparse, frizzy white hair, wore old print dresses and reminded me of my Nana. I'd helped her unstick a window and carried her groceries up the stairs, and she showed me pictures of her late husband, and of her three kids. I could only see two. One of the faces was covered with a piece of masking tape.

Then one night, I had come out of my apartment and heard a groan at the bottom of the stairs. Mrs. Salvo had tripped carrying the garbage down and lay there crumpled at the bottom of the steps crying in pain. I felt around gently on her old body and she winced when I touched her shoulder. I banged on Freddie's door, but he wasn't home. I got my googles and called an ambulance, switching on my locator, so they could home in on us.

And I waited. I kept calling, but the ambulance never came. I found out later, ambulances took their time coming to this neighborhood, if they showed up at all. Finally, I called Mushie, and he whipped over in his cab. We helped Mrs. Salvo in and took off for the hospital with her slumped over, breathing in gasps. I thought she was going into shock, so I did my best to comfort her and keep her talking. Even after we got her to the hospital, they left her out in the waiting room in pain, so I went a little nuts, hollering at the doctors and jumping around like a loony. I guess I did that because she was like my old Nana. The doctors were really ticked off at me, but they treated her.

After that, I visited her in the hospital every day, and when she got home, I carried her groceries and ran errands and made sure she ate and took her pain pills.

Then one day, I came in from my shift to find all my stuff returned, including my viddie screen, which had even been hung back on the wall. That night, I found out why my luck had changed, when I first met Miguel Salvo and his friends. Salvo showed up outside my apartment door with a scared-witless Freddie, who warned me I'd better let Salvo in, even though he was a bad guy. Turns out Salvo had just gotten back into town, to find out that this new hick kid . . . me . . . who lived in his mother's apartment building had just about saved her life. Since she wouldn't talk to him, I became his link with her. And, he'd put me under his protection, as signified by the initials M.S. that Max had gouged into my door.

Now, he stood in front of me, his lips pursing slightly, the passing flicker of the look of a hurt son, before his face crystallized back into a gangster's again. The black eyes bored into me now. Tonight, he had more business with me than asking about his mom. He glanced over at Yani, who immediately left the apartment, taking the elevator down.

"You talked to the cops. You said you saw something."

"Well . . . uh . . ." I stammered, suddenly realizing that Salvo really wouldn't have liked the idea of me going anywhere near Lieutenant Rocky. Maybe I should've just left town.

"The cat, man. You said you saw the . . . Cerulean." He motioned for Max to signal into the next room, and this tall guy I'd never seen before came in. He had a big, coarse face, with a big nose, big lips, big ears, big head, big brow. And, he had big hands, with bulbous knuckles and fingers with tips like paddles.

And, he had this zombie-blank look on his face, like a syntho with a deleted personality algorithm. He stood there, slack-jawed, staring with eyes that gleamed metal-shiny behind wire rimmed glasses. The eyes seemed to glow with a light of their own.

He had implants! I'd heard of fanatic onliners having microscopic laser scanners implanted into their corneas, but this was the first I'd ever seen. This guy, obviously Salvo's personal 'liner, could have viddie images scanned directly onto his retina, cruising the Mirror without glasses. I should have known that anybody as smart as Salvo would have a 'liner to act as his early warning system, his spy in the Mirror.

"Lamb, say what you found out." Salvo didn't look at his 'liner, but spoke to him while looking at me. He was reading my face.

"He got taken in," Lamb, the big-faced 'liner, said in a deep throaty voice that matched his looks. "Cops thought he had something to do with the cat. He said he saw the man who took the cat. He did a computer sketch and looked at mug shots. He spent three hours in the police station."

"What else did he tell them?" Salvo still looked dead-straight into my face, watching for any little twitch that would tell him I'd said something about him.

So, I held my breath. In fact, I almost forgot to let it out when it hit me that Salvo's 'liner must have a daemon! None of that procedural detail ever went on the Cop Network; only in their computers. I'd never seen a guy with a software daemon. Everybody had heard rumors about daemons, but nobody ever confirmed they even existed. It was against the law for even the government to have one. The legend was that a daemon could tap in anywhere, access any computer, find anything that was online. "Daemons go where angels fear to tread," was the saying about them.

"He told them nothing." Lamb wrinkled his big brow and continued to stare into cyberspace, still searching for a hint that I'd betrayed his employer.

"You didn't talk about me?" The inflection in Salvo's voice activated Max to move his black-clothed mass between me and the door.

I suddenly became very aware of Max and his tattooed hash marks and the machine pistol in his holster and the various other pieces of killing equipment hinted at by assorted bulges in his black suit.

Nervous jitters flipped around in my stomach. They'd brought me here to this deserted place just in case I needed to neatly disappear, without causing any commotion in Mama's apartment. A bullet to the head, wrapped in plastic, left in a landfill. I'd felt intrigued by Salvo's use of me before; now I knew I felt like only an expendable tool.

"No, you never came up." I tried to sound as confident as I could.

"You know who the last person who talked about me was?"

"No."

"He lived in your place." Suddenly, I realized why the usually slovenly Freddie had carefully repainted before I moved in.

"You be straight with me, man, you be okay." Salvo moved off, walking around the room, inspecting the carpentry work. The air in the apartment seemed to lighten a little. I was still on his good side.

"I am. I will be."

"I tell you something, Tim. I am a businessman," he said, running his hand across the marble mantle of the fireplace. "I see why this cat was taken. It was good business. Man, I don't interfere in other people's business, so they don't interfere in mine. That's all I say."

I thought I understood him. He would still protect me from his people, but if I'd gotten myself into any problems because of the cat, I was on my own.

He came back to me, staring me in the face as he issued a last warning.

"And you don't bring none of this trouble to my mama's building. Not even on her block."

I nodded in agreement.

"Perez is in trouble," the vacant-eyed Lamb suddenly announced.

Salvo's voice lowered, becoming whispery and cunning. "What you see, man?"

"Cops've pulled up his name in their computers. They've tagged him with the nickie shipment."

Max knew the drill and lumbered out the door, with Lamb behind him.

Salvo turned just before making his own exit. "You see Mama, you tell her I'm okay. You tell her I think about her. You tell her I gonna get out of this business someday. But not now. And you tell her she should move into this nice place I build for her."

"Sure. I will."

I felt my stupid, young-kid confidence overwhelmed by a fear-rush, like I'd just fallen into a swamp full of thick-as-your-arm water moccasins and made it out alive. Before, I'd been just buzzed; now I was buzz-freaked. I needed to settle myself down and think what to do next. I needed to go back to my apartment.

CHAPTER 8

The cab let me off in front of my apartment house, and the driver floored the pedal and sped away to avoid being robbed. There had been no limo ride back. Salvo was finished with me for the time being.

The cabbie needn't have worried. My block sat in the middle of the no-commerce zone Salvo had decreed around his mother's apartment house. It had cost him business. That's why I suspected his campaign to move his mom to a new apartment was as much a business decision as a sign of devotion. He needed more retail space for his drugs, professional ladies, and other products to service every orifice.

Normally, I felt safe in the zone, but as I walked up the steps to my apartment, I had the uneasy sense of something weird, something out of place. It wasn't Salvo's threat. I'd managed to calm myself down from that. But something was strange that my conscious mind couldn't perceive; maybe a scent, a vibration, like when I hunted the woods back home as a kid and I would suddenly feel on edge. Once a cougar appeared, and another time I almost stepped on a copperhead, so I always listened to my intuitions.

I paused at the top of the steps and looked around for the source. A gray car rounded the corner and passed by. A guy sat on a stoop across the street with his legs stretched out, making something with his fingers. A kid a few doors down, wearing a blue t-shirt, idly bounced a ball against the steps. I could see the bodega's lights down the street, the little store still open even this late.

I finally shrugged—maybe this time all my troubles had just buzzed my imagination—and let myself in the rattly wooden door. I climbed the concrete stairs to my apartment on the second floor and stood in the hall deciding whether I should look in on Mrs. Salvo this late.

"Hey, boy."

I jumped at the high crackly voice at my feet. Freddie Dunk had heard the front door and come up the stairs to poke his saggy, whiskery face between the railings of the second-floor bannister.

"Hi, Freddie. You scared me, there."

"So sorry, son. So very sorry." He smiled, showing crooked, nickie-stained teeth. "Thought I saw you on my camera. Just wanted to make sure it was you. Just say hello. Make sure you was okay. All that." Freddie was always ultra-polite to me, even though it was hard for the normally nasty-tempered little guy. He worried that I would move out. If he chased off either of Salvo's favorite tenants—me or Mrs. Salvo—parts of him might turn up in various New York landfills.

"I'm fine, Freddie." I decided to see Mrs. Salvo tomorrow and turned to unlock my door.

"That's fine, then. Real fine. Just wanted to check. Make sure you was okay. You . . . uh . . . saw him then?"

"Yes. He's not mad at me for going to the cops about the cat. And he's not mad at you for anything, Freddie." I decided not to mention the new apartment Salvo was renovating. It would've set Freddie off on another round of freaking out.

"Oh, good. That's fine . . . well . . . okay." He pulled his relieved face out from between the bannister railings, waved and disappeared down the stairs and into his apartment by the front door.

I let myself into my apartment, with its faint odor of new paint and old hamburgers and shut the thick steel door with a satisfying clunk. I fastened all the locks and as a final punctuation clanked the steel bar into place to brace the door. I was home.

My place consisted of a big, high-ceilinged living room-dining area with a little bedroom and bathroom to the left, and a closet-sized kitchen off the little dining area. In the four months I'd been here, I'd lugged up a tattered overstuffed sofa, a wing chair with only a couple of rips and a wooden table with unmatched dining chairs that creaked in individualistic ways. Dad would've hated the furniture and made me take new stuff from his warehouse, but I liked it. I'd hung posters in the living room, two portraits of Hemingway and one of a misty Blue Ridge Mountain morning. The wall opposite the sofa held my viddie screen with the dent in the edge, gotten either when it had been swiped or returned.

I stopped and looked around the room. That uneasy sense had followed me into my apartment. Had somebody been here? I noticed the message light blinking on my base processor so I flipped it on.

"Hello Timothy," said my angel in my mom's voice.

"Hi. Do I have any calls?"

"Your dear mother said to call immediately, anytime. Your mobile processor battery's almost dead. You should call your mother more often." My mom had programmed those little digs very cleverly.

I obediently unclipped my processor from my belt and plugged it into the base unit for recharging, and told my angel to call home.

The viddie screen flashed "Call Attempting to Connect" for a long time before she appeared on the screen, her puffy face lined from worry and sleep, fumbling on her glasses. She saw me and perked up, launching a rapid-fire burst of mom-isms.

"Tim, are you all right? We saw the police pictures of you being arrested. Are you mixed up in something? You should come home. You look pale. Are you eating?"

"It's okay, Mom. I just got called in to talk about seeing that cat. How's rat-boy?" That's what I always called my brother Kyle, to get him riled up and into a wrestling match. Mom didn't like the name, so she made a disapproving face.

"He's fine. He's asleep. You should come home, son." She waved her hand off-camera. "Daddy, you come here and talk to this boy of yours." Dad appeared, his thinning hair sticking up, yawning, in the frayed bathrobe with his initials on it that we'd given him years ago. He rubbed his unshaven face and focused, waving to me.

"Talk to him, Stuart." Mother was not to be denied.

"Son?"

"Yes, Dad."

"You got a bedroom suite? Bed, dresser, chest-of-drawers?"

"No, Dad."

"You want one? We've got a really nice floor-sample suite. It's—"

"Stuart, that's not what I meant!"

But Dad was not to be side-tracked. "—oak."

"My bed's okay, Dad."

"This is one of those electrogel beds. Big. Adjusts . . . and everything." I wondered whether my sly old dad was hinting something about my social life.

"I'll think about it."

Mother looked thoroughly exasperated at her husband.

"Stuart, tell him to come home. That's what you should tell him."

Dad took a deep breath and put his arm around Mom. "Okay, okay . . . Tim, you all right?"

"Yeah, Dad."

He gave my mother an eyebrows-up, resigned look that said "He's going to do whatever he's going to do."

"Okay, then, son, you promise to call if you need us?"

"I will, Dad."

"And if you want that bedroom suite, I can bring it up in a truck. Ned will come along to help. And maybe a couple of the boys. We can be there in a day."

"Yes, Dad. I'll call if I need the furniture." I knew this was Dad's way of offering to help without seeming to interfere and make me lose face. He'd managed to get Uncle Ned out of lots of scrapes with that low-key way of his.

"Fine then, let's all get some sleep."

I could see Mom getting her steam up to scold him. Then she thought better of it and simply turned to me, smiling resignedly.

"Pa's a sap." It was her favorite palindrome.

"Ma is as selfless as I am," responded Dad, yawning. It was his favorite palindrome. He'd given in to Mom's palindromania.

"A motto, Ma." I answered with my standard reply. They waved goodbye and left me alone in the room with the guilty memory of their worry.

I needed to relax bad, which usually meant I needed to eat something and drink a few beers. I found a chicken pot pie I bought last week and nuked it and set it on my eating board with a beer. I sat down on the couch with the board in my lap, telling my angel I wanted a new movie, something dramatic.

She knew I liked Hemingway and came up with a musical version of *The Old Man and the Sea* starring Elvis Presley. I was pretty sure he had been a real person at one time, but he was probably dead now, so he couldn't have just made the movie new. They must have used him as a model for a computer-generated syntho-actor. Syntho-Elvis was pretty good in the role, although he didn't look much like the fisherman I'd envisioned in the book.

Just as I'd finished most of my pot pie and beer and gotten to the part of the movie where Elvis was singing to the big fish, the door thunked three times.

I left the remains of the pie and beer and ogled around through the seehole, catching sight of this old lady standing there with a big canvas bag on her arm. She wasn't as old as Mrs. Salvo, but she was old, maybe in her fifties. I ogled around some more, because, like any good writer-to-be, I observe people to try to figure out their character before I actually meet them.

Her wrinkled little face looked like it had spent a lot of time in the sun, and set in the leathery skin were two of the brightest blue-gray eyes I'd ever seen. Some of her wild mop of gray hair hung down the sides of her face, and the rest was pulled back in a loose, floppy bun that sagged down the back of her neck. She'd poked a big, red chopstick-looking thing through the bun, like she'd stabbed it when it tried to escape.

She wore this big peasant blouse with pictures of cats jumping around all over it, baggy black pants and tennis shoes. Around her neck dangled a big gold necklace with an ivory cat face, and she wore several gold rings on her fingers.

She shifted the canvas bag to her other hand and knocked again, looking behind her. "Say . . . you in there?"

She must've heard me leaning against the door while I was ogling her. "What do you mean am I in here?" I asked. "Who are you looking for?"

"Well, who are you?"

We went back and forth like that, and she got more and more ticked off. I thought it was kind of fun.

"Listen, son, quit messing around. If you're the kid who saw the cat, we got important talking to do."

I decided to open the door. She was less distorted without the goggle-eye perspective of the seehole, but she was still a pretty outrageous old lady. She definitely didn't remind me of Nana.

"You Kayak Boatright?"

"Jeez. Tim! It's *Tim!*"

"Okay, whatever you want. You saw the cat?"

"I think so, yeah."

"Well, in that case . . . ." she opened the canvas bag and rummaged around. I tried to see what was in it and was not happy with the result. She came up with an ugly nine-millimeter pistol. I jumped like I'd grabbed an electric fence, hollered a cuss word, and slammed the door, whipping around and wedging my body against it. Who would've thought an old cat lady would come to kill me!

"Hey, kid!" she hollered back. "What's all this?"

For an instant, I thought I was safe, but something wasn't right about my door. When I shifted around to lock it, I realized she'd poked the pistol barrel in the door, wedging it open.

"Take the gun out!"

"Can't. You got to open the door!"

"No way. You could shoot me."

"I'm not going to shoot you, sonny."

"Could've fooled me, lady."

"It's Callie. I was trying to give it to you."

"I *bet* you were . . . Callie."

"The gun. I was trying to give you the gun so you'd trust me."

I looked through the seehole. She had a bag strap in her teeth, rummaging around in the bag some more. She came up with a holocard and poked it through the door, above the pistol. I kept my weight full against the door and grabbed the card, reading "Callie Lawrence, National Cat Fanciers League, Manhattan Chapter."

"You're going to shoot me because you think I took the cat."

"No, I'm going to save your life, dummy!"

CHAPTER 9

We were stuck in a standoff. I wasn't about to open my door so some nutty old lady could shoot me, and I could tell she wasn't about to give up and go away until she'd talked to me face to face. Looking through the seehole, I didn't see another gun. And since she couldn't have shot through the steel door, I was reasonably safe in the standoff.

"I'll give you money," she said.

"Why? To do what?"

"So you'll open the door a crack and let me get the gun out. And listen to me."

I heard rustling and clinking while she dug around in her big bag. A cashcard sailed through the crack and fell to the floor. Luckily, it landed with the display side up, so I could see it had $3,500 credit on it.

Given my current unemployment, that card looked pretty good, so after figuring I was younger and faster than an old lady, I decided to risk it.

"Okay, on three, I'll open the door just enough so you can get the gun out. Then maybe we'll talk."

"Yeah, okay, sport."

I braced myself, in case she shoved against the door, even though her little old body couldn't have pushed hard. I counted and opened the door a crack, letting the pistol loose.

She pitched the gun into the room! It clunked onto the floor, lying there looking dangerous, and challenging me to come up with some logical theory of what this lady was possibly up to.

"Now, you see?" Scolded her muffled voice from the other side of the door. "Now, you see that I'm trying to help you?"

"You just dropped it."

"Do I look like I'd drop a gun?"

"Well, you're old and all."

"Pick up the gun, smart ass. Let me in."

"Can I keep the card?"

"If you let me in and listen to me."

"Just don't try any fast moves."

"I'm old, remember?"

I picked up the pistol and managed to pop the clip out and see that it was loaded, pulled the gun's slide and snapped a round into the chamber. It worked like an automatic Uncle Ned had taught me to use. He kept the gun to shoot rats he said, and one time an International Harvester robotic tractor, which he plugged right in the processor. He claimed the machine had sassed him.

I picked up the cashcard and stuffed it into my pocket, secure in the certainty that possession and a loaded pistol were probably more than nine tenths of the law.

I clicked off the safety, opened the door and stood back. She walked in, looked around, wrinkled her nose and dropped the bag with a thump by the door. The bag had cat faces on it, all kinds of cat faces with big cat-eyes.

"Kind of dumpy, but I guess it's okay for the neighborhood." She scanned my posters on the walls. "You like Hemingway?"

"He's my favorite."

"I met a woman once who had him."

"Really? Had? Like in . . . *had?*" I reminded myself to keep the gun up.

"Yeah, she picked him up in a bar in Key West, I think. She was really old when I met her, and her memory was kinda fuzzy. She said they got drunk together. He wasn't very good, but I think he put her in a story later."

"*For Whom the Bell Tolls?* Wow! Was she Maria?" I tried to remember the lines from the book. "*She had high cheekbones and a straight mouth with full lips. Her hair was the—*"

"Look, we got more important business. You're in deep shit, son." She walked into the kitchen and I followed, gun at the ready. She looked in the refrigerator, made a phooey sound at the contents and after a moment chose a can of beer and opened it.

"You don't mind, do you?" She held up the beer.

"Well, it's only a few hours until breakfast time."

"I've had beer for breakfast before." She went back into the living room, sat on the couch, took a healthy swallow of beer and began. "I've been hanging around outside there in an alley for hours. I found out where you lived, and I suspect the next thing that happens will happen here."

"What do you mean 'next thing that happens?'"

"About the cat. See, I'm really smack ass in the middle of the thing. I'm in the Manhattan Cat Fanciers, like it says on the card. They put me in charge of security for the Garden Cat Show."

"You?" I smiled at the idea of this kind of goofy old lady with cats on her shirt and a big bag in charge of security for anything. She saw my smile and shot me a frown that said I should keep my opinions to myself.

"Yeah, *me*. And since the Cerulean was taken, I've been the one who's catching hell over it."

She took another swallow of beer and burped politely. "Besides, when it comes to cats, I'm a little obsessive. I don't like to see any cat stolen. And this cat . . . this cat . . . ." Her blue-gray eyes seemed to stare far away, dreamily. "I actually saw that cat before they took it. It was the most beautiful animal I'd ever seen. Just amazing. A cat like that needs to be kept safe. People need to see that cat."

I thought for a minute she was going to get religious or something. "So what are you doing here?" The question brought her back to our business.

"Like I figured, something's going on out there. On your street. There's a car out there that comes by about every half hour."

The gray car I'd seen! I knew something felt funny out there. "So?"

"I figure whoever's in that car is waiting for your lights to go off up here. I just get that feeling. Let's just call it middle-aged intuition."

"Fine, thanks for your intuition, but I can take care of myself pretty good. Or I can call the cops."

She made another phooey sound. "You think they're going to make it in time to this neighborhood? And even if they do show up once, you think they're going to come screaming back every time you call?"

"Well . . ." I thought about it. She was probably right. I'd seen special viddie programs memorializing brave, dead witnesses. I wasn't brave, and I didn't want to become dead.

"Look, kid, I'm here already. Just in case I might know a little something about these things, why don't you let me stick around? We'll turn the lights off and see what happens."

"I can take care of myself. You keep your money." I dug the cash-card out of my pocket and dropped it in her big bag. "I'll keep the gun. Why are you so interested in my welfare, anyway? The cops must have all kinds of leads besides me."

"Maybe, but I've just got a hunch you're the key. You saw the guy. There's probably other things you didn't tell the police you didn't even know were important. Besides, you seem like a nice kid who's gotten into something that's too much for him."

"But this is just a cat. Why would anybody come after a witness to a catnapping?"

"It's a *billion-dollar cat*. The company that created it will pay big bucks to get it back. Or, a collector would hand over big money, no questions asked. People do things for a billion dollars they wouldn't do for just a million." She finished her beer and attempted to stuff the can into my overflowing garbage pail.

"But I've already given the cops a description. I've already done the sketch and all. Why would they still be after me?"

"You're still critical for a lineup. And your testimony in court. You wouldn't make a very good witness if you were dead. In fact, the cops might think you were just an expendable accomplice and go off in the wrong direction."

Again, I thought about it. She did seem to know more than I did about this stuff. Besides, she was sort of an interesting lady. "Okay, what's your plan?"

"You make a big lump in your bed like you're sleeping there. With old clothes and pillows. We turn off the lights, we wait in the kitchen. You can even hold the gun. I've got another."

I considered whether to get schizo over the fact that she still had a gun. I decided she seemed to know what she was doing.

"Y'know, that door's steel. Nothing can get through it."

"We'll see." She headed for the bedroom, stopping by her bag to extract a chrome-plated revolver, which she held pointed up like she'd used guns before.

I gathered dirty clothes from around the floor, threw them on the bed and poked and whacked them into a long, person-shaped-lump. I looked around for my pillow to add to the lump. I couldn't find it. Strange. The uneasy dread came back. I shrugged and covered the lump with my dingy tan blanket. After smoothing it around some, I stood back and looked at her for approval.

"Yeah, okay," she allowed, giving the lump a critical scan. "It ain't Michelangelo, but it'll do."

I turned off all the lights, and we went back to the kitchen and sat on the floor, so we could peek out into the living room. That sense of dread helped my heart start thumping some, like when I'd crouched in a hunting blind as a kid. The pistol warmed in my hand until it seemed a heavy extension of my arm. As my eyes got used to the dim light from the front window, I could see that Callie's face had hardened into a determined geography of wrinkles.

She had settled in with her bag beside her, with her legs crossed in the lotus position. She was pretty limber for her age. After nothing had happened for about half an hour, we started to talk.

"How'd you learn about guns and sneaking around?" I whispered.

"My husband had a store here. He kept guns for protection."

"Does he still have a store?"

She harrumphed. "Well, not here. He left years ago. He's running an ice cream parlor in Dallas. Has some forty-year old chickie."

"Oh, I'm sorry. Do you have kids?"

"Do I ever!" She rummaged around in her bag and came up with a wallet and opened it to two holograms. I strained, trying to see them in the darkness.

"Oh, yeah. You need a light." She rummaged around and came up with a penlight, which she clicked on and aimed so I could see the three-D images. One was of a smiling guy, older than me with short brown hair sitting at the tiller of a big sailboat.

"That's Russ. He's got a business in China. Fine boy. He'll give me grandchildren soon."

The other picture grabbed my gaze like glue. The slim girl was about my age, wearing a t-shirt and cutoff jeans, barefoot, leaning sort of cockily against a tree with her arms crossed. Her tanned oval face had an impatient grin that said she wanted to get on with it, and be somewhere else. She had a cute, dimpled smile and Callie's impish blue-gray eyes. Her hair was medium length, silky brown and tousled by the breeze.

She reminded me of sweet, saucy Cindy Jasper and the summer nights at Uncle Ned's farm. I still felt Cindy's arms holding tight around my waist as we rode that old mare bareback through the warm night to the cool river. And the two of us swimming naked, and making dripping-wet love for my first time in the river, then again in the breeze on the soft blanket.

"That's Lulu," said Callie, her voice dropping a half-step.

"Your daughter?" My voice cracked a little.

"She was named Lulu because from the minute she was born, she's been a Lulu."

I finally made myself stop staring at Lulu, and she clicked off the light. We talked about Russ and Lulu in the dark, and I politely asked questions about Russ, trying not to make it obvious that it was Lulu who interested me.

A noise tickled the quiet, a faint grinding, crunching noise. We froze and listened.

"Somebody's trying to get in," whispered Callie, unfolding her legs and peering around the kitchen doorway into the living room.

"Not through that steel door. That's a tough steel door."

There came more grinding, crunching, like something digging. Or gnawing. I stood up and looked out over her head. Callie pushed me back.

"No, not your tough, steel door," she whispered. "Your cheap, thin walls!"

I poked my head back out, peering into the shadows. It was true! Somebody was coming through the wall!

The noise grew louder, blossoming to the sound of a hole breaking through, the faint spattering of plaster on the floor. A low, angry animal grunting added itself to the mix. An animal was squeezing itself through the wall, apparently right beside the front door.

"Should we turn on the light?" My palm sweated on the gun's grip, and I wiped it off. I clicked off the safety, my heart accelerating.

"No, then they'd either start shooting or take off. We've got the element of surprise." We peeked around again. The spattering, grinding, crunching continued, and Callie motioned for me to stay put. She crouched low and duck-walked out of the kitchen and between the dining table and the sofa.

A soft thump of the animal hitting the floor, the scratching and clicking of claws on wood. A scrabbling noise, more low, steady grumbly growling. It was like the animal was talking to itself. I saw the dark shape that was Callie move up against the sofa, and I moved out behind the table.

From the bedroom erupted snarling and tearing noises. The animal had gone straight in, almost like it was trained, and started ripping away at the person-lump. And it was really mad!

Callie stood up and crept toward the bedroom, her sneakers crunching on pieces of plaster. The snarling, tearing sounds suddenly stopped, replaced by more low growling, this time of an animal alerted, wary. I followed close behind, gun up. Callie paused at the bedroom door and crouched down, peeking around the door jamb. Gripping the pistol so hard the nubbing on the grip bit into my hand, I stepped into the doorway of the darkened bedroom. I began to make out a shadowy form scuttling around on my bed.

Callie had just grabbed my arm to yank me back, when the form lunged screaming through the blackness straight at me, slamming into my stomach, back claws braced against the waistband of my jeans, razor-sharp front claws slicing flesh, drawing blood. With searing pain came the smell of animal stench, the heat of animal breath. I grabbed madly with one hand at thick, short fur, underlying hard muscle, the other hand using the pistol as a lever. I couldn't fire for fear of shooting myself or Callie. I staggered sideways, slamming against the bedroom wall, feeling the animal's thick muscles straining to pull itself upward toward my throat. I could barely hold it back, pushed it sideways, felt it still straining upward, heard snarling, the teeth snapping. Powerful jaws clamped down on my shoulder, tearing into muscle, and a vicious pain erupted, making me almost faint. Trying to pry the jaws loose from my shoulder with one hand, I hacked at the body with the gun. I felt Callie tear the creature away, fling it onto the bed.

The deafening explosion of her gun brought a strobe of light that illuminated bared teeth, hateful shining eyes, a body crouched for another attack. My shoulder flamed, but I leveled my pistol and pulled the trigger. The room strobed over and over with our gunfire, the rapid-fire blasts sledgehammering my ears, the acrid stench of burned gunpowder filling my gasping lungs. Each flash revealed the animal's writhing body, fangs snapping, fur becoming raw bleeding meat from the bullets ripping into it. And between the explosions came the animal's dying screams. They ended in a liquid gurgle as blood filled its throat, and it lay still.

Its sound stopped. We stopped. I stood panting with pain and shock, my ears ringing from the pounding gunshots, my skin feeling stickiness soaking my shirt, my nose smelling the stench of the animal's death permeating the smoky smell.

"The light," commanded Callie. I fumbled for the switch and turned it on. Pain ripped through my shoulder deep into muscle.

Through the gauzy shroud of gray gunpowder smoke, the dead animal sprawled on the shredded lump that would have been me, its blood soaking the blanket. The side of its long-snouted head blown away, what remained of its mouth gaped open, showing fangs stained with my blood. It once had a large, muscular body, now torn apart, and forelimbs with curving talons. A deformed dog or wolf? A huge, fanged rat?

Callie poked it once, then turned to me. "Son, you've been torn up a little there." I continued to stare dumbly at the animal, still trying to figure it out, as she guided me around the bed and into the bathroom.

"What was it? I've never—"

"We'll figure it out later. Let's just see to you first." She helped me strip off my soaked shirt and used it to wipe away the blood. I watched in the mirror, seeing my face dead pale with shock. I determined to pull myself together. I'd been torn up before. I could handle it. I was the Gopher. I took stock. I had a big, oozing gash in my left shoulder that burned like hellfire, and deep clotting cuts all over my chest. Feeling woozy, I sat myself down on the toilet. Luckily, I'm a good clotter, so I wouldn't bleed to death. If I hadn't been, I'd never have survived all the cuts and gashes I suffered as a kid.

While I pressed my bloody shirt on the wound, Callie found my extra sheet under the sink and tore it up to make temporary bandages. She seemed pretty practiced at bandaging. I wondered dully if she'd been a nurse at one time.

Once she had me all bandaged up and my head cleared, we went back out into the bedroom. The thing still laid there, its body blown apart into a bloody, furry mess. I found a stick I'd used to prop my window open and turned the carcass over to get a better look. The blood had begun to dry, sticking it to the shreds of my blanket and clothes. It did look like a giant rat, only with bigger teeth and claws than any rat I'd ever seen. Its canine teeth were pointed like a wolf's, and the claws more like a bird's talons. It also had big gnarled fleshy ears, and its remaining small eye was dull black.

"It's a mutant," said Callie. "I've heard of them. Looks like maybe based on a wolverine. Meanest little bastard around. But maybe with some other genes thrown in . . . rat, hyena maybe. The genetic companies make them. Nasty things."

"Yeah, nasties." Then it dawned on me. "Oh, Jeez, these are those things that—"

She finished my sentence, "—that they genetically engineered as the ultimate guard animals. You're not going to believe this, but that thing's good news!"

"Yeah, right." I was getting woozy again.

"Really. It means you've got somebody scared."

"You mean besides me?"

She smiled, examined my bandages and patted me gently on the arm. "We've got to get you to a doctor, killer." She went back through the apartment turning on lights, found her bag and reloaded her revolver. For the first time, we got a look at the small, jagged hole that the animal had gnawed through the wall. That thing was quite a digger all right. I realized my pistol was still clutched in my hand. I motioned for her to give me bullets, too, and she handed me a full clip. I managed to eject the old one, slip the new one in and click the safety on. I unplugged my portable processor unit and got my googles and asked her to stuff them into her bag. When I got a look in the bag, I saw that even she carried a mobile processor, but it was an old one, like a phone with a little screen. You were just naked without a processor these days. Speaking of naked, I realized I'd need to get out of my bloody clothes, so I asked to stuff a fresh t-shirt and jeans into the bag, and dug them out of the box where I kept my cleanish clothes.

I took one last look at the dead Nasty, and unlocked my door just as we heard distant sirens. Callie slipped through the open door, pointing the gun expertly left, then right, ready to put a hole in any other surprises that might be waiting in the hall.

"Freddie must've called the cops." I looked over the railing to see if he was at the bottom with the old sawed-off shotgun he kept next to the door, but he was notably absent. After Salvo left, he'd probably drunk himself into a stupor as usual, aroused only by the shots. And now he was hiding in his room. "Wait till I tell the cops what happened. Rocky'll bring an army down."

"Kid, I don't think it's a very good idea for you to get involved with the cops right now," said Callie. "You're in deep enough with them as it is."

"But they're the law."

"Yeah, well, look how well they protected you so far." She took my hand and smiled like my mom did when she was trying to get me to do something for my own good. "Let's just get in my car and go to a doctor I know. She's a friend of mine, and she can fix you up right. You can always show up later and tell the cops what happened. We need to lay low and think about this."

True, my shoulder was really hurting. I needed a shot of anesthetic and a spray bandage. And besides, this business had me both curious and mad. When I get either way, I tend to take matters into my own hands, and both together really get me zapped up. Finally, there was the fact that Callie had saved my life, not the cops. I'd be a bloody corpse on the Cop Network without her.

The memory of Miguel Salvo's warning finally launched me to follow Callie out the back hall window and down the fire escape. I needed to disappear until I could find out whether he'd be mad at me or mad at whoever sent the animal for causing a commotion in his mama's apartment house. And if I went to the cops again, Salvo might also vent his displeasure in dangerous ways.

Callie drove her car, an old rusty gas Toyota, rattling across town to a quiet street with a really nice townhouse, where Callie rang the bell until a round lady about her age answered the door in her bathrobe, yawning. They had a short conversation I didn't follow because my shoulder hurt so much. The lady doctor, named Dr. Annie, took me into the small, neat treatment room of what must have been her private practice. She gave me a couple of shots, the last of which made me feel really *fine*. I laid there happily on the treatment table watching the ceiling light wander round and round, while she glued the big wound shut and sprayed on an aerogel bandage that toughened into a clear covering that would last until the wound healed.

She helped me put on my fresh clothes, and by the time I stumbled slowly out to the hall where Callie waited, daylight was streaming through the front window and traffic noises had started up outside. I had my wits back and asked Callie to wait while I called the cab company to leave a message for Mushie to look in on Mrs. Salvo. She'd be scared, with all the gunfire and the cops showing up and everything.

When I finished calling, Callie almost ran to the car with that clunky bag and got in. Gripping the wheel with her little wrinkled hands with the big, gold rings, she launched the car away from the curb and down to the main street. Without hesitation, she plunged it like a big, rusty knife into the honking, cussing, bumper-to-bumper mess of whining electrics, buses, gas cars, and trucks that was rush-hour traffic.

"We're not going back to your place," she shouted over the noise. "There'll be vampires all over." I flinched as Callie zoomed through a yellow light, barely missing a cab. "We shouldn't stay at my place either," she shouted. "Vampires there, too. But we have to stop there first. I've got to get some things." She wove through traffic lanes like a pro. People who she cut off suggested that she perform physically impossible acts, but she ignored them. She would have made a good cabbie. I noticed that she had blood stains all over the prancing cats on her blouse, but she didn't seem to bother about them.

"So where do you suggest we go, then?"

"Lulu's."

I liked that idea a lot. I remembered the fine, fascinating girl in the picture with the dimples, the pretty eyes. Meeting her would make a bad day end well, so I could start out tomorrow fresh, figuring things out. But I knew one thing for sure already. I'd come to New York to get involved in interesting stuff, and I sure wasn't going to retreat back home just because a bunch of cops, criminals, and a killer animal had got after me. Besides, that cat must be really something to stir up all this trouble. Maybe it was stupid, but I decided I was determined to see that cat somehow.

I was still so woozy that the next thing I knew we were leaving Callie's apartment building, walking down the sidewalk to her car, Callie hauling a big square trunk with holes punched in it. It kept bumping her around, like something inside was bouncing around. I tried to help her by grabbing the handle, but she yanked it away. She made it clear this trunk was not leaving her hands. I remembered only vaguely that she'd come out of her apartment with the trunk after our stop to pick up some "important cargo." She'd left her bag in the car, parked a couple of blocks away and told me if she didn't come back in half an hour I should just drive off and not come back. I thought her plan was flea-market crummy.

"I owe you my life," I'd told her. "You're not going in there alone. Another Nasty could be in there."

"Piffle! I can handle a little Nasty. You're too important to risk."

"I'm going!"

"You're not!"

62

"I am!"

"Stubborn young twit!"

"Stubborn old lady!"

We'd glared at each other, our jaws set. Then we both broke into embarrassed smiles and agreed to compromise. I would wait on guard in the lobby with the pistol, my googles on. Callie promised to call me the instant she got into her apartment.

Before she'd left, though, she pressed the cashcard with the $3,500 credit back into my hand.

"Just in case," she'd said. "It's even fixed, so nobody can trace the money to you. A member of my bridge club knows how to jigger them like that."

So, I leaned against the wall of her lobby worrying about her, wondering what kind of bridge club she played in. The doorman watched my every move, eyeing the obviously pistol-shaped bulge under my t-shirt. But before he'd gotten suspicious enough to take action, she'd called to reassure me that the apartment was safe, and she was getting what she went for.

So now we were back on the street, with the salaries and funkies all staring suspiciously at the trunk bumping and shifting.

"What've you got in there?"

"You'll see," she smiled and winked. We reached the car and she slid the trunk ever-so-gently onto the back seat.

"It's my box of pure love!" She opened the top and a cat head popped up, wide-eyed, long-whiskered and furry. Glimpses of spare ears and tails told me that there were more inside. The head was attached to a big slinky Siamese cat, which slithered out, complaining loudly with a high baby-cry. It paced the back seat until it said what it had to say. Then it jumped onto the rear window shelf and stretched itself out, lazily eyeing the cars and people outside.

"That's Shank," said Callie, holding the lid up for the next appearance. A white head emerged with brilliant blue eyes and a snub-nosed face that looked like it had collided flat with a wall. Callie held the lid so the white Persian could step out and assume her place in the center of the back seat, carefully licking down her mussed fur, and raising her head to observe.

"This is Priss. Gorgeous, fairly bright, but deaf as a post."

Once Priss established herself, Callie reached in and drew out a massive round clump of tiger-striped cat, which immediately launched a rattly purr that sounded like an old rumbling refrigerator we once had on the back porch.

"This is Albert." She nuzzled the huge cat. "Hims don't move unless there's a bomb under hims."

Callie then proceeded to pet each cat with great ceremony, explaining to them precisely what was happening, where we were going, and why they were being inconvenienced. Finally, she turned back to me.

"My babies understand now. Would you mind sitting down?"

I took the front passenger seat, wisecracking "Stack cats." Never thought I'd find a use for that palindrome. Mom would be proud. Callie ignored my cleverness and got behind the wheel. Albert managed to squeeze between the seats, and hefted himself onto my lap, peering into my eyes as if searching for the answer to some eternal question. The question was probably whether I'd make an adequate bed, because he rubbed tentatively against my shirt, then with a plump, laid down, taking up my whole lap, and curled up to sleep. It was like having a furry hot water bottle on my legs. In fact, it felt comforting to have an animal that wasn't trying to tear my throat out.

"Hope you don't mind. Albert thinks any lap rightfully belongs to him."

"No problem." Actually, I identified with Albert. We both liked laps, although for Albert either sex would do. All three cats had settled into what were apparently customary places, as Callie slammed the old car into gear and roared back out into the morning traffic.

"You really think they understood all that talk you gave them?" I stroked Albert's acreage of furry cat fat. He shifted himself on my lap, making clear with his difficulty that mine was not the ideal lap. Not big enough or soft enough.

"Well, they seem to. Except maybe Priss. But I think she reads lips."

I pondered the worrisome facts that this woman talked to cats, believed that one cat could read lips, and also carried deadly weapons. Callie drove on, enraging two cabbies, a delivery van driver and a fat guy crossing the street. Within half an hour we were driving down into the narrow streets of a grungy retro neighborhood housing all manner of weird and interesting artists, funkies, retros, 'liners, syntho-builders, and neural-zappers.

She squeezed the car into a parking place and re-stacked her cats back into the carrying trunk. I carried her other canvas bag which was heavy with two pistols and other stuff I couldn't imagine.

"They don't mind being carried like that?" I asked when Shank muttered the feline version of a curse.

"Nah. Each one of them spent a lot of time as kittens inside my trunk. It's like home."

"Are they show cats?"

She hmphed. "They'd be strays or dead if it wasn't for me. They were all abandoned for one reason or another."

Our mutual sideways glances at each other showed we were both thinking the same thing; that I was another of her strays.

Lulu's loft was a godawful mess, even for somebody like me who wasn't too particular. Draped over the couch in the big main room were a couple of party dresses, pantyhose, jeans, and a towel. The paint-splattered wooden floor was a minefield of boots, a shoe, socks and stockings of various colors, a knit shawl, piles of colored plastic scrap, and a rubber snake. Callie nudged the shawl with her toe.

"So *that's* where that went to."

The walls held posters of Van Gogh, Kandinsky, Warhol and the holograms of Latislaw. One animated hologram showed a pair of intertwined dancers. They seemed to float gracefully out into the room, whirling around, as we picked our way along the scattered islands of clear floor. A big metal mobile hung in one corner, daring anybody to disturb its exquisitely balanced curvy pieces and cubes balanced on extended wires. Another sculpture, a big upright multicolored glob of gel, perched on a black square pedestal between the main room and a door that I took to be the bedroom.

"Guess she's gone to work," said Callie, as she poked her head into the bedroom. The sculpture responded to her presence, shifting toward her, changing to solid blue and sprouting bulbous appendages. She walked away, and it settled back into its blob shape, remaining blue.

"She an artist?"

Callie didn't answer, but the fleeting scowl of a mother's annoyance at an unruly daughter crossed her face. It was quickly replaced by concentration, as she looked for a landing place for the thumping trunk. She spoke to the trunk. "Coming in for a landing, babies. Get ready. Shank whined as she set the trunk on the couch amidst a pile of clothes and opened it. The cats emerged all bright eyes, cocked ears, and quivering whiskers. They all began to explore the room in their own way, sniffing the scattered clothes, rubbing against the furniture. Shank prowled about, lithe and sinuous. Priss stepped with great care and haughtiness. Albert seemed to drag himself through the loft, no doubt looking for a new lap, or a reasonable facsimile.

Now that I'd come within range of a safe bedroom, all the energy suddenly drained out of me. My head felt like a lead weight balanced on my neck. I'd worked a full shift, done a fancy party, dealt with a drug boss, met a woman with three cats and two guns, and been mauled by a mutant Nasty.

I'd had a busy day.

"Think she'd mind if I crashed?" I mumbled to Callie.

"Jeez, you're starting to look like something not even my cats would drag in. Sure." She guided me to Lulu's bedroom. We passed the animated blob, which greeted me by turning green and white and sending out a curvy extension that looked like a big smile.

The bedroom was just as messy and held some indefinably delicious aroma that must have had something to do with Lulu. I cleared enough junk off the bed to lie down. I instantly plummeted into the soft darkness of a fathomless sleep.

CHAPTER 10

I felt smothered in murky dreams of tattooed heads, guns going off, a cat's glowing eyes, our barn at home filled with scurrying rats that flowed around my feet like a single, furry creature.

A dream of hanging on a window ledge, fingers bleeding, waiting for Death to pry the fingers loose to send me into the void.

Dreams rising like fish in murky water only to sink away into invisibility again.

I emerged slowly from blackness into the gray stuff of half-awake. I moved my hand and felt something furry . . . a Nasty!

I yelped and sat up, my chest thudding. I looked down at my hand expecting to see open jaws, poised claws, and black-evil eyes. Albert only lifted his great cat head slightly and twitched his tail in mild annoyance. He stretched his bulk and went back to sleep.

I laid back down and closed my eyes to recover. I heard rustling in the room. I opened them again and found myself looking up at two sets of blue-gray eyes, one old, one young.

"Well, *Mother,* he is pretty. Has he got nice buns?" She said "Mother" with a kind of sarcastic snap.

"Lulu!" Callie hadn't sounded like a mother before, but she did now. A scolding mother.

"Probably brainless," snarked Lulu. "You're always bringing me brainless ones."

I smiled and put one hand behind my head and tried to focus on her. "You must be Lulu." She stood with her arms folded, like in the hologram, making the short t-shirt she wore ride up a bit, showing a flat, smooth stomach and belly button above her jeans. She had an inny.

I looked up from the inny and into eyes that stared at me with a twinkly, impish honesty. No shyness, no pretense. I also felt like she could see into my lusting soul. Those eyes shook me up some.

She stuck out her small hand. "Hello, Meat."

I shook her hand and felt a firm grip. I must have given Callie a puzzled glance.

Callie frowned at her daughter. "Lulu, I told you he's not—"

"Meat? Sure looks like prime sirloin to me. But, *Mother,* you know I'm a vegetarian."

I moved to get up and winced, as a slashing pain reminded me of my shoulder's damage.

"Well, I tell you, I feel like meat that's been hanging on a hook for a while."

"Ooh . . . . Meat's got a right nice southern drawl," teased Lulu, mimicking my North Carolina accent pretty well. "You want coffee?"

"Sure. Black. No tenderizer, no ketchup."

She tossed her head to flip unruly strands of fine hair out of her face and flashed a quick wry grin. Like I remembered from the picture, she made cute dimpled cheeks, showed nice teeth, a delicate jawline and a slim, smooth throat. She left me looking dopily awestruck, striding away with long-legged steps into her living room, picking across the debris past a happily undulating blob sculpture. "Sorry about the clutter," she said over her shoulder. "It's my way of organizing."

Callie stayed back to watch me rise slowly to my feet. She made a concerned "Hmm" when I winced.

"Let's take a look at that wound." She gestured that I should pull off my shirt, so she could check on the slash on my shoulder. It was visible through the bandage gel, and she began to examine it, touching it gently.

Albert watched until he decided the bed would no longer be occupied. Seeing no prospect of a replacement sleeping partner, he thumped to the floor and waddled off to the other room.

"It's healing just fine. I should explain about Lulu calling you Meat . . ." she said as she peered at my other less-than-prime cuts. ". . . although you do look a little butchered, here. Y'see, I sometimes take the trouble to introduce my wayward daughter to young men who I think might be nicer than the hounds she normally associates with. She doesn't appreciate my concern." Callie hmmed a final approval of the healing process, and I said I wanted to take a shower.

Lulu's bathroom was like the rest of the apartment; cluttered with all kinds of stuff . . . hair stuff, bath stuff, smell-pretty stuff. Bottles and tubes and little vials and soaps and lotions. I looked around for male stuff, but didn't see any, which made me happy. In the mirror, I saw a ratty-looking male with a serious morning grunge-face.

I showered and washed my hair, and shaved with a pink girl razor. After a hair-combing with one of Lulu's brushes, and putting my fresh jeans and t-shirt back on, I looked fairly human. As I picked my way across the cluttered main room to the tiny kitchen, the blob sculpture sprouted an arm that seemed to wave good morning, turning red then yellow.

Lulu was clumping around in her small hiking boots getting coffee ready. Callie was arguing with her about her not showing up somewhere she should have shown up. I grew acutely aware of Lulu's cute bottom encased in the faded jeans, as we cleaned the table of dirty cups, two books of poetry, an art book with lots of torn paper bookmarks sticking out, and a glass with a sprouting sweet potato. Paper books! I realized she had paper books!

Lulu sat down and made a serious face with pursed lips as she handed me a steaming cup.

"*Mother* said you're in trouble about that blue cat." She cast a suspicious glance at Callie. "*Mother* lies, though. Convince me you're not just meat." Callie made a disapproving face back at her impertinent daughter and took a sip of coffee.

I started downing serious gulps of coffee, and as it kicked in, I managed to get across pretty dramatically what it felt like to have a mutant Nasty going for your throat. She was impressed. I was seriously cool. I also realized I was dead-empty starving and suggested we find some food. Callie and Lulu started to debate where to eat—Chinese, deli, hamburger, vegetarian, blah blah blah. They seemed to argue about everything, as if they exercised their arguing muscles on each other. I could sure see in Callie what Lulu would become in a few decades. It was actually pretty cool, except maybe for the wrinkles.

While they were narrowing the decision to vegetarian restaurants, I realized I'd better let people know where I was. I grabbed my googles from Callie's big bag, sat down on the couch beside a dozing Albert and checked the news. Sure enough, I was still mentioned in the stories as a suspicious character, with viddies showing me being hauled into the station. But strangely, none of the accounts reported that I'd been attacked, and none showed the dead Nasty. Maybe the cops were wanting to get all their clues together first.

I had my angel send a message to my folks. I told them I was okay and with friends but couldn't talk to them now. I knew if they saw me all banged up, both of them would be on the next plane to New York, maybe with Uncle Ned and his guns.

Callie and Lulu finally agreed on a restaurant, and Callie proceeded to explain the plans to the cats. I thought they took the news that we were leaving very well, probably since she fed them some leftover doggie-bag chicken Kiev that Lulu had saved for them from the refrigerator.

At the little restaurant around the corner from Lulu's, a big lady in a green robe, with a bleached-white top knot sprouting out of her shaved head like a fountain, served us bowls of steaming vegetarian stew and great slabs of fresh bread. The stew had some meat-like chunks in it. It was okay, but I dreamed of a big beef hot dog slathered with chili and onions and two or three cold beers.

"The cops are out of the question," said Callie, taking a bite of the stew and chewing it critically. "Can't trust 'em. I think we've got to somehow get this kidnapper's trail. Figure out who he is."

"Well, how?" I asked.

"There are ways," Callie answered, taking another bite. I thought I caught Lulu giving her mom a suspicious look.

I managed to swallow my own mouthful of meat-substance. "I think we go right to the source."

"What do you mean?" asked Callie.

"Who lost the cat? Who got hurt? Whoever wants the cat back the most, they'll tell us everything they know." I took another bite and got a nice chunk of potato.

"Well, that would be Animata."

"Corporate scum . . ." muttered Lulu. She scowled, her brows shadowing those blue-gray eyes; and the cute cheeks went away as she set her jaw. ". . . out there in their big labs putting together animals out of pieces of DNA like some low-rent Frankensteins! Felicity is right about them!"

Here was a new name I hadn't heard before. "Okay, so I know Animata is the company. I remember from the viddies. But who's Felicity?"

Callie sat back and finished a bite of bread, chewing and thinking. It was like she kind of went off into talking to herself. "Yeah. Losing the animal hurt Animata bad. They've made a ton of money designing and making all those animals, but this cat was their biggest success. This cat was the ultimate."

I tried again. "Hello, ladies? Who's Felicity?"

Callie was still talking to herself. "Felicity might've taken the cat. They hate all this genetic engineering business. The announcement of the cat really set 'em off. Protests, marches, so forth,"

I kept trying. "Felicity is a they? So they could have taken the cat? Now, who are they?"

"People with a conscience," said Lulu. "Biowarriors. Religious—"

"Agitators," interrupted Callie. "They're sure suspects." She held up a hand and extended her multiringed fingers. "Hell, we've got no want of suspects." She ticked off her fingers with the tip of a fork. "There's Felicity, there's that other company, GeniPet. They'd dearly love to take the Cerulean off the market. There's organized crime, for ransom. There's rich collectors. There's religious nuts . . . the Hindus worship cats. This cat would be a big-time god."

"So let's start finding stuff out," I said, my belly full of meatlike substance and ready to go. "Let's start with a little trip in the Mirror!"

CHAPTER 11

"Are we not drawn onward, we few, drawn onward to new era?" That was one of Mom's palindromes I always recited when I went into the Mirror. It just seemed the right thing to say before the hot-damn rush I always got when plunging into virtual-reality cyberspace.

The Mirror always buzzed me bigtime, just thinking about its hundred million computers all linked together into an immense worldwide virtie network. My dad had told me about how excited people were at the old World Wide Web. But 'liners really changed the world when they invented this incredible mind-trippy cyberspace mirror world.

"What'd you just say, kid?" asked Lulu. "We're going to be drawn onward?" She brought me back to the business of getting into the Mirror. We sat scrunched together in a little linkbooth in a virtie shop near Lulu's apartment. They sat on either side of me, plugged into my processor, wearing rented googles.

"It's a palindrome. Same backward and forward."

"Cute, Meat," said Lulu wryly, but I think she was impressed. My glorious angel materialized on our googles, floating pure and white and smiling.

"Who's that?" Callie sounded a little schizzy. She'd only been in the Mirror a few times and made it clear she didn't much like zipping around in three-dimensional cyberspace.

"That's his angel, *Mother*." I could just imagine Lulu pursing her cute lips in annoyance. "She . . . it's . . . like a guide in the Mirror. Like a protector."

"She's beautiful," said Callie.

"She's software," hmphed Lulu, probably not approving much of angels.

"Hi, Timmy," said the angel. "Did you shower today, stinky? What can I do for you?"

A little embarrassed at the motherly advice, I ignored the first question, holding my hands in front of me, so the system could synch. It recognized my fingerprints and synched with my hands, and I saw two three-D virtie hands materialize in cyberspace in front of me. "I want to go into the Mirror," I told my angel.

"Certainly, Timmy." She smiled again her angelic smile.

My angel shrunk to Tinkerbell-size in the corner of my view. There was a grand trumpety electronic fanfare, and a "Welcome to Mirror World" logo materialized in three-D shimmering letters that oscillated from red to blue to green and all colors in between. The logo faded, and we found ourselves in my personal Mirror Room, my virtual control panel floating within reach of my virtie hands.

"What's this place? This your place?" Callie fidgeted beside me.

"My Mirror Room. It's where I keep my Mirror stuff."

"It's messy," said Lulu. I started to apologize, but realized she was complimenting me.

"Yeah, well . . ." It was true. My Mirror Room was cluttered with virtual filing cabinets and a wall of virtual books on one side, and a wall full of labeled shortcut buttons on the other that linked me to other Mirror-sites. A third wall held a whole bunch of software icons that looked like shiny, colored Christmas tree ornaments of all kinds. I could just press one with a virtual finger and bring up software to send videomail or whatever I wanted to do.

I touched the control panel joystick with one virtie hand and floated around my room. As far as I could tell, it was precisely the same mess I'd left last time I was here. That was reassuring. Sometimes rogue 'liners broke in and screwed up your room or hid logic bombs. But my angel was a good watchdog, even deleting the sneakiest invading viruses.

"You guys got your brains in gear?"

"Yeah, sure," said Lulu. "I've spent time in a lot of the galleries here." I sensed that Callie had nodded. She didn't realize I couldn't see her.

"Angel. Give me any news on the Cerulean cat."

A pause, while my angel analyzed the request. She replied "The latest bulletin says . . ." My mom's voice became a news-announcer's voice, the angel's face became the announcer's. "Police are following a great many leads to the theft, including those supplied by their witness, Kayak Timothy Boatright. They expect to make an arrest soon in this theft of the billion-dollar cat." I winced when I realized that Lulu had found out my first name. But then hers was Lulu, after all, so she probably understood.

Callie exclaimed a triumphant "Hah . . . see? They're still not even admitting they found a dead whatchamacallit in your room and that you're missing!"

"Wonder why not?"

"Hell, they think they screwed up and let the catnappers get you! I told you they couldn't be trusted to be straight."

She was right, I guessed; we had to do our own data-gathering. "Angel, take me wherever I need to go to find out more about the Cerulean cat's background."

There was a pause as the angel processed. "I will take you to the Animata complex."

My "okay" triggered the wall of my room to dematerialize, and the angel to vault us out to soar high above Mirror World.

"Whoof! Damn!" gasped Callie, grabbing my arm. "This is just exactly what I didn't want to do."

But she managed to calm herself, and we sailed through virtual reality space like in the dream where you can fly just by willing yourself into the air.

The absolute darkness of no-data enveloped us, making even more brilliant the shimmering virtual landscape below, sprinkled with teeny data-buildings in a spectrum of colors. At this distance they seemed but masses of colored, twinkling lights along luminous streets, like somebody had scattered glowing stars and ribbons on a dark earth.

Other avatars sailed past us—animated icons that represented users in the Mirror. A white Star of David floated by, linked to a red floppy hat, with an angel leading the way to some Mirror business. A writhing, neon-glowing yellow snake with big shiny green eyes slithered through the dark cyberspace just below us, stopping to look up at me with fathomless black eyes. I was always buzzed seeing the weird avatars people come up with to represent themselves in the Mirror.

One time my dad showed me an old Monopoly game, where players could be shoes, top hats, or cars. It was like that in Mirror World, except people could be anything—animal, vegetable, mineral or imaginary. Of course, I'd chosen Papa Hemingway as my avatar. So, most people thought I was really an old guy with a beard.

My angel grew to her usual size and flew ahead, her wings gracefully beating the digital atmosphere, her software hair billowing out behind her. I always felt like Peter Pan flying to Neverland when we traveled through the Mirror this way. Third star on the right, and so forth. I could almost imagine a cool wind in my face.

A lot of Mirror-users just materialized wherever they wanted to be in the Mirror, but flying to a site always helped me get my bearings and discover neat stuff I didn't know about.

"God, this is nerve-wracking!" grumped Callie, bringing me back to business. "I never could get used to it."

"It's okay, *Mother*. It's not real." Lulu was trying to be cool, but I could tell she liked the exhilaration of flying over the virtie cities of lights.

"Animata lies in the city just ahead," said my angel, banking into a dive. I touched the controls to follow her, plunging like a virtual skydiver, showing off a little.

"I'm getting sick! Cut that out!" Callie cuffed my arm.

"Sorry. It's what they call 'virtiego' . . . dizziness from flying in the Mirror. Just close your eyes."

"*Mother,* maybe you should take off the glasses."

Callie took a deep breath and made a grunt of determination. "Nah, I'll survive. I've taken worse."

I reluctantly slowed my descent, as the mass of lights resolved into Mirror World cities of colored geometric shapes spread out to the horizon. It looked like somebody had dumped a huge load of shiny kids' toys on a world-sized carpet.

We homed in on one city, passing a floating sign that marked it as Mirror-Philadelphia. The geometric shapes now resolved into individual buildings with facades as detailed as real ones, but in luminous computer-glow colors. We passed a fire-engine red skyscraper and a humongous orange sphere studded with glittering lights.

Mirror-Philadelphia City Hall rose in the distance, a virtual copy of the real thing, a big stone wedding cake with all its statues and fancy decorations. Surrounding it were boxy-looking bank and government buildings that looked like ones I'd seen in real Philadelphia.

"It looks so real, yet so fake," said Callie.

"Yeah, they shape the virtie buildings just about like the real things. Everybody can find their way around easier. You should see the Eiffel Tower and the Kremlin. I dive-bombed them on trips to Mirror-Paris and Moscow."

Once we reached street level the sounds of the Mirror enveloped us. Not the usual horn honks, engine rattles and airplane roars of the real world, but a rich symphony of voices, music, electronic dings and warbles, and all the other signals the Mirror World used to communicate its business.

I jerked the controls to avoid an Abe Lincoln zipping past us and pulled up short to let a buffalo float down in front of me and clump into the entrance of a company's Mirror building.

"You hit another avatar, sometimes your data files get mixed," I explained to Callie, who vice-gripped my arm in protest at my sudden stop. "Even with an angel, you have to be careful."

Mirror-Philly was a lot more crowded with avatars, so I moved more carefully, following my angel through purple toads, sexy women, Tweedle Dee's, devils, robots, and burning bushes. I told my angel to pause, so we could watch the virtual crowd.

"I can't believe how busy it is," said Callie in my right ear.

"I can't believe some people spend their lives here," said Lulu in my left ear. "God, they sit in their little dark rooms in their virtie chairs flying their little avatars around here all day. It's not real. It's so . . . syntho."

"Yeah, well, this is where the stuff we want is," I said. Lots of people made good money in the Mirror. Some made big money organizing data, analyzing data, even sometimes ripping it off. I just wanted to find out about a stolen cat.

I was about to tell my angel to take us to Animata, when a knight in elaborately embossed armor floated toward me, heavy-metal rock music blasting out of its head. The song sounded like one from a syntho group, maybe like Bowel Sounds or Digital Insertion. The knight's faceplate flapped as he spoke.

"Say, old man, I see you got an angel. You mind asking her where the fun is around here?"

"What kind of fun? Synthos? Games? Adventures?" Even on a mission, I didn't mind helping him. Asking advice from somebody else's angel was considered okay manners in the Mirror.

"Well, a good rock bar, man, with fine-looking syntho women." The knight made a kind of funny, eager dance suspended in space, clanking his heels together. The user-guy had really done a great job of animating his avatar.

"Warning! Viruses detected!" My angel announced, inserting herself between me and the knight, frowning.

I immediately pulled away. "We may be in trouble. This guy's infected." People like him who didn't bother with guardian angels usually ended up with viruses. I held up my virtie hand to let him know to keep his distance. Viruses can't transmit through cyberspace, but you never could be too careful. "Look, my angel says you're infected," I told him. "Let's just go our separate ways, okay?"

"HIV detected!" warned the angel. She'd narrowed down the virus, turning herself a danger-red color, a really bad sign.

"What's HIV?" asked Callie. She was finding out how wrapped up you could get in the Mirror.

"Heuristic Internet Virus. Started about six years ago. You get infected, it eats through your defenses and messes up files, until finally you're deleted."

"I knew this one girl, Julie," said Lulu. "She worked in the Mirror. Hung out at bad sites. Got deleted by HIV. There was a Mirror funeral and everything. She was a real 'liner, and she went to pieces and had to get help from a shrink. A real shrink, in person, since she couldn't get into the Mirror."

The knight, who'd heard my angel, floated closer, metal-shiny gloves out, pleading.

"Hey, man, have a heart," his faceplate flapped. "I couldn't help it." Most avatars don't show expressions, but he seemed sad. "Just pass me the data, I'll be on my way."

I pictured this lost user-guy, sitting in some crummy little room somewhere, his googles on and a nickie in his hand, living out his last days in the Mirror. He was a 'liner, no doubt, who didn't have a life except online in the company of other 'liners and synthos. Just passing him data wouldn't hurt, I guessed. I asked my angel to make a list of some good places in Mirror-Philly.

"Look, just stay clear. The angel will pass you a data packet." I was okay as long as we didn't share read-write access to each others' file directories. After a moment, a small blue box materialized in my angel's hand, and she sent it floating over to the knight. It melded into his chest.

"Thanks, man." He saluted me with a glove to his helmet.

"You ought to get an angel," I told him, even though it was really too late. "It's dangerous without one."

"Nah, I'll just keep screaming around the Mirror to see what I can find. Well, until I can't . . ." His voice trailed off and his knight avatar did the same little dance step, but now there was something pitiable about it.

He waved goodbye, as I turned and told my angel to continue on to Animata. As we began to ease away from him, my angel turned snow white again.

"He'll be deleted then? Permanently?" asked Callie.

"Yeah, eventually. He'll never be able to get into the Mirror again. HIV will make sure of that."

"I wonder how close death here is to the real thing."

"Just as final in its way, I guess."

Suddenly, my earphones brought a horrified "NO!" from behind me. It abruptly ended, along with the rock music that the knight had been playing. I whipped into a turnaround to look back in the direction we had come.

Only empty cyberspace remained where the knight had floated. I jerked in surprise, sitting in my chair in the linkbooth.

"Angel, where is the avatar we just talked to?"

My angel swooped away, wings spread wide, searching back and forth in the now-empty region. I know that software can't have emotions, but she seemed puzzled.

"The avatar has been deleted."

"Did the virus do it?"

"No," said my angel. "No remnant data structure is detectable."

"Then how did this happen?"

"I have no information," said my angel. "No remnant data structure is detectable."

That really spooked me, because the Mirror's operating system just doesn't allow an avatar to disappear without a trace. I scanned further for any sign of the knight, but saw nothing. It was like he'd been murdered, but his body had vanished into thin air . . . well, virtie-air.

"What the hell's going on?" asked Lulu. "I know this isn't supposed to happen."

"Well, maybe a serious system error, maybe a wrinkle in the Mirror World. We shouldn't stay here. Angel, let's go!"

My angel sped away, and I hit the controls, launching instantly up to speed, since we were free from inertia in cyberspace.

I followed my angel down to the massive granite-looking Animata building I'd seen on the video. Close up, its large multicolored doorway held images of fantastic animals like unicorns, sea serpents and abominable snowmen. We slowed, easing up to the door, which slid open to reveal a vast entry lobby with marble-patterned floors and walls hung with holographic prints of whole zoos of animals. I'd just moved in to explore, but this handsome, young guy-avatar in a blue uniform with an Animata logo patch floated up and made a welcoming wave.

"Welcome to Animata, the birthplace of wonder. Can I help you?"

"Eat my shorts." I guessed he was a syntho and not an avatar representing a real human.

He continued to smile. "I didn't understand. Can I help you?"

"He's a syntho," I told Callie and Lulu. "That's my favorite test. My dad uses that expression sometimes. You say something that's outside

a syntho's programming, and he doesn't react like a human." I circled
the syntho guide and scanned the room. "We'd like a tour, and we'd
like to find out about the Cerulean cat."

"Certainly, may I have your name?"

"No."

"Rude little snot, aren't you?" said Callie.

"Not really. Mirror sites like to get your name so they can send
you advertising or trace your movements for all kinds of commercial
purposes. I don't like giving mine."

"He's got rights, *Mother*. He can have his privacy." Lulu and I were
in synch here, which was cool.

I asked my angel to put out a NOYBIE, so nobody else would ask, and
the synthoguide took my "None of Your Business" sign with the calm
acceptance of good software. He led us away on a tour that started with a
general corporate overview. Canned recitation: "Pioneering company . . .
founded to serve customers with the finest in genetically engineered pets
and farm animals . . . highest standards of quality."

"Blah blah blah," mocked Lulu in my left ear. "Guys, this is just
the official corporate line. You can't trust it."

"We'll see. Angel, turn on the bullshit detector." It's a neat feature
of a really good angel. She would record all the statements and correlate
them with downloaded information from independent sources, so I
could check whether we were being lied to. She shrank down to be out
of the way and rode along with us.

We floated along, following the guide through the virtie marble
halls, passing other avatars following other guides, stopping at video
walls showing the company's products.

A viddie showed the company's very first product, a Christmas
mouse with antlers, including a team hitched to a miniature sleigh.

Other viddies showed later products, including various weird animal crosses—dats and cogs, snurtles and takes, churkeys and tickens,
and cigs and pows. The viddies were just getting into some really exotic
animals when I felt Lulu fidgeting around next to me, all agitated. She'd
taken off her googles.

"God, I just can't stand this! This is sick! This is unnatural!" She
whapped my arm in frustration.

"Yeah, well, some people like them, I guess."

When, I told the guide to lead us on to the next viddie, she put her googles back on. The scene showed a pudgy little guy working in a lab. He had a sparse frizzy beard and a round chipmunk face with chipmunk teeth. He kept eyeballing the camera nervously while he worked, like he was afraid it was going to do him bodily harm.

The smiling syntho guide told us that Animata was founded in 2042 by the guy in the viddie, Vasily Rozoff, a Russian émigré who'd come over to work for American drug companies. Rozoff was a rare chipmunk, a genius in both computers and genetics. On the screen, Rozoff turned stiffly to the camera, like he'd no doubt been directed to. The high-res, three-D screen showed he was wearing carefully applied makeup.

"I realized that powerful ultracomputers and genomic engineering technology represented an opportunity to do genetic alteration of animals as never before," he recited in a thickly accented, quavering high-pitched voice. His eyes darted back and forth as he talked, probably only partly because he was reading from a prompter. He really didn't like what he was doing at that particular moment.

He licked his lips, darted his eyes and continued reading. "More and more complete DNA sequences of animals were being produced and stored in computers."

The scene cut to a white-coated Rozoff standing inside a large room, wearing googles and surrounded by floating three-D molecules, anatomical structures of animals I couldn't even guess, and the hieroglyphics of computer code. Also in the same room stood the ghostly images of three other people watching as Rozoff grabbed a virtual molecule and poked at it to adjust its structure.

"His playroom?" asked Callie.

"VROOM," I said. "Virtual Room. People who want to collaborate virtually from anywhere can put on their googles and meet and be surrounded by data or whatever."

"Yeah, like porn," snorted Lulu.

Rozoff continued to fiddle with the molecule, a glimmer of gold reflecting off his right wrist, from some kind of identification bracelet. His Russian accented voice declared "We found we could use ultracomputers to predict how genes mixed together from different animals would interact in a new construct. We could then generate—"

"Pause," I instructed, and the image froze, leaving Rozoff with his mouth open, the molecule halted in mid-fiddle. I turned to the guide. "Where's this guy now? Can we go see him?"

The guide smiled a perfect synthosmile. "I am sorry, but Doctor Rozoff is no longer with the company."

"Where is he?"

"I am sorry, but Doctor Rozoff is no longer with the company."

"Is he retired?"

"I am sorry, but—"

"Is he dead?"

"I am sorry—"

"Angel, where is Vasily Rozoff?"

"Searching for information requested," said my angel.

"What is this bullshit?" demanded Callie.

"Corporate bullshit," said Lulu.

"My angel goes way beyond bullshit," I said.

"Search complete," said my angel. "Vasily Rozoff. Missing since May 14, 2049. Last seen in Qualton, Washington."

"Angel, what is the significance of Qualton, Washington?"

"Listed as place of residence."

"Angel, store the complete file on him in my Mirror Room."

"Okay, Timmy. Brush your teeth twice a day."

Callie poked my arm in emphasis. "So, not only is the cat missing, but the guy who started the company!"

Suddenly somebody grabbed both my shoulders hard and yanked off my glasses. I yelped as vicious pain knifed through my damaged shoulder. The abrupt google-ectomy disoriented me, like people always get temporarily when they suddenly leave the Mirror. I struggled to focus, to return my senses to reality. There were rough, commanding voices, Callie and Lulu yelling and cursing. Somebody hauled me out of the linkbooth, sending more waves of pain shuddering through my body.

Lieutenant Rocky thrust his face into mine, and I managed to focus on him. His teeth were clenched, the veins on his forehead standing out. He looked as if he could crack walnuts between those muscled eyebrows.

I could tell he was being tough for the cameras, because the little red light on his badge camera was on. We were live on the Cop Network.

"Where've you been?" He growled. "Who're these people?"

"Friends," I answered.

"Accomplices!" he spat.

"Actually, the lady saved my life, which is more than you did."

"We found blood in your apartment, and you were gone. You were instructed to remain available. It's not a good idea to ignore police instructions." I wondered what was going on. He never said anything about the Nasty. I'd thought they were just keeping the fact under wraps, but something else was going on. I decided not to mention it in public.

"And the blood and this thing on my shoulder don't tell you that I'm a witness, not a suspect?" I scanned the vertie shop. Several customers stood glowering at two cops shoving Callie and Lulu against the wall pat-searching them. The cops grabbed their wrists and slapped on handcuffs.

"You know who you're dealing with?" shouted Callie. "By God, I'm the security chief of the National Cat Fanciers League . . . *Manhattan Chapter,* by God!"

"Goddamned fascist syntho-brains!" bellowed Lulu, face flushed, jaw jutting out, eyes narrowed, hair flying. Boy, was she cute when she got really ticked off!

CHAPTER 12

Now I'm sitting on a bench in the grungy hallway of the Manhattan Center station, watching cops haul sullen guys wearing handcuffs and electronic tracker-chokers into the interrogation rooms. Lieutenant Rocky put me out here. Actually, he almost *threw* me out here. When we got back to the police station, I made him even more ticked at me. I couldn't help it; he really got my dandruff up after rousting us like that.

"Dammit, I'm mad!" I declared to myself palindromically.

It was the cops' fault. For one thing, they'd dragged us like criminals out of the linkbooth and past a big crowd and into squad cars back to the station. Rocky said he wanted to take me into custody for disappearing like that. He took Callie and Lulu along as possible accomplices, although he wasn't sure what they helped me do. Even after he realized he couldn't hold us on anything, he'd refused to let us go.

At first Rocky started out real cool, even the clenched teeth going away.

"Look, kid, the blood told us you got attacked, that you might be just a pawn in this. But we still have suspicions. We hear that you're protected by Miguel Salvo."

"Well, then, you know that it's because I helped his mother, and that's it." My shoulder hurt, making me ornery. I told him all about the Nasty and how it was a big mutant monster-thing, but he rolled his eyes and made a disgusted sound at this kid who was trying to lie to him.

"Despite this bullshit, maybe you're straight. So, show us. Help us out and wear a badge camera. It'll show whatever you see."

"Nope," I said. On the Cop Network, I'd seen enough camera views from witnesses looking down a gun barrel just before the screen went blank. Bang! No more witness, but good viddie for the Cop Network. And when a witness got blasted, they showed his last seconds over and over, slo-mo, close-up, enhanced and everything. I didn't want my folks seeing what happened to me, if something did.

So then, Rocky's teeth clenched a little and, he asked if I'd activate the locator on my mobile processor and give them permission to track me.

"Nope," I said. He ground his teeth a little now. I knew my rights, I said. They had to have my permission or a judge's order before they could keep tabs on me. But they had to convince a judge I was in trouble or a fugitive. The blood in my apartment gave them cause to track me to the virtie shop. But now that they'd confirmed I was okay, and couldn't link me to the kidnapping with certainty, they couldn't continue.

Rocky wanted to give me a guard.

"Nope," I said.

Rocky wanted me to report in every hour.

"Nope," I said.

First, Rocky had switched off all the cameras. Then, he yelled "You goddamned stubborn little dink!" Boy, did he clench now; his dentist would've really been mad at me. "Here we're trying to help your cracker ass, and you give us this 'nope' shit! Get the hell out of my office and think about how your life won't be worth a chewed-over cigar butt if you don't cooperate!"

That's when he threw me out in the hallway.

By then, I probably had "that look" on my face; the one I get with the scrunched up lips when I get really stubborn and mad, like when Mom would say "Don't you give me *that look*, young man!" I decided I needed to be obstinate here. That's what Nick Adams would do. He wouldn't let the cops push him around.

So now, I'd been sitting here for about half an hour watching the cops drag people in and out. Callie and Lulu still hadn't been let go. I couldn't decide whether to start hollering. It might get them out, but it also might make Rocky madder, and he'd keep them there longer, even the maximum twenty-four hours.

I was just about to finally ask for a lawyer when this slickie walked in—a guy so slickie-sleek, he looked streamlined. He wore his dark, shiny hair combed back tight against a small skull. His narrow hawk face had a straight nose, small thin-lipped mouth and smooth jaw. Really smooth jaw. He could have been a male model, except he looked too dangerous. I couldn't see his eyes, which hid anonymously behind wraparound black sunglasses.

He wore an expensive black randomweave hemp suit, custom-fitted by laser-scan, no doubt. Beneath the jacket, he wore a white silk collarless shirt buttoned at the throat. I'd seen his expensive, pointed-toed black boots in the windows of fancy shoe stores. Except for his light olive skin, he was a crisp picture in black-and-white in the dirty-brown world of the police station.

He turned his head in my direction and flashed a faint ghost of a smile that disappeared without leaving a trace. The desk sergeant greeted him like he knew him, and he acknowledged the sergeant with a nod, but headed for me. He slid into the seat next to mine with a kind of animal grace, like he was used to making precise moves. This guy would make a good character in a book, whenever I started writing.

"Timothy Boatright?" He stuck out his hand, the sleeve pulling back a bit to flash part of a really expensive gold watch. Firm handshake, quickly released. "Julio Miravelle. I'm director of security for Animata." He had a fluid Spanish accent and a soft, quiet voice like a velvet-covered bullet. "Mr. Talbot, our president, would like to meet you. To discuss how Animata might help you."

Just exactly what I wanted; to get into Animata to find out what they were up to.

"I can't go anywhere. They've still got my friends."

He flipped his hand in a little gesture of dismissal, and gave me his radar-blip of a smile. He strode over to the desk sergeant and leaned close to him, talking low, the elegant slickie to the chunky, big-jowled cop.

The desk sergeant looked over at me, his expression suddenly really serious. He sat up straighter behind the tall counter, like he'd just received official information that he had to deal with officially. As Miravelle slid back into the chair next to me, the sergeant glared at his back, making an urgent phone call.

"I simply pointed out that Animata employs many lawyers," Miravelle explained in that soft-over-steel voice. "And many publicity men." He glanced down at his watch, then threaded a wire out of his inside jacket pocket, plugging it into the side of his sunglasses. I realized with a 'liner's delight that his glasses were viddie-googles, the zillion-dollar Italian designer kind. I could just make out the other hair-thin wire leading from the glasses to the tiniest earphone in his ear. He spoke Animata's Mirror address and waited a moment for contact.

"Miravelle here. Please tell Mr. Talbot that we will be there in an hour," he said into the air. "There are no . . ." A quick smile at me. ". . . difficulties."

Within a minute, Lulu and Callie stormed out of the interrogation rooms, their faces showing major matching mother-daughter mads. Rocky followed them, also scowling, transferring his scowl to Miravelle, like he recognized him, too.

Lulu and Callie spewed a volcano of insults, each tumbling onto the other's.

Callie: "—damned cops, think they—"

Lulu: "—bunch of fascist overlords! We didn't—"

Callie: "—couldn't investigate their way out of a paper bag. Why they—"

Lulu: "—more interested in their damned viddie ratings—"

Callie: "—let this poor boy almost get—"

"LOOK!" Rocky bellowed at me to stop the bombardment. "We picked you up for your own safety. And we're proceeding with the theft investigation that we—"

"Squat!" spat Callie. "I bet you got diddly squat or we'd have seen it on the viddie already!"

"That's confidential," Rocky glared at Callie. "You just stay out of it. Yeah, sure, we know *who you are!* But you still stay the hell out of it!"

It seemed odd, the way Rocky said "who you are" to Callie. It seemed maybe he meant Callie was more than "the security chief of the National Cat Fanciers League, Manhattan Chapter." But I didn't think much about it, because I was busy watching Lulu scan Miravelle up and down. I recognized it as a "Who-the-hell-is-this-character?" scan, but I felt a little itch of jealousy anyway.

"Lieutenant, we will take good care of him," said Miravelle.

"Yeah. Right. I just hope there's enough left to put a toe tag on," muttered Rocky, spinning on his heel and leaving.

Miravelle smiled again, this time more broadly, and introduced himself to Callie and Lulu, asking "May I take you to Animata?" like he was inviting them to tea.

Callie shrugged and allowed that was a good idea. We followed Miravelle out the bulletproof doors, spurring to action a small clot of viddie vampires across the street behind the police chain. They thrust their cameras up to get a good shot, whistling and shouting for our attention. We ignored them, standing on the sidewalk letting their cameras roll on.

Lulu took me by the arm and whispered. "I'm not going there. Animata. I hate that place. It's built on making poor mutant creatures. It's a sick place!"

"Well, we've got to, if we want to figure this out," I said, hoping Lulu would come along.

"I'm late for work, anyway."

"Doing what?"

She ignored me. "*Mother*, we'll talk. You watch yourself. And don't . . . y'know . . . start up again." She turned and strode away from us without a backward glance, whistling down a cab before the vampires could reach her.

"What's she mean?" I asked Callie. "Start up what? Do you start things?" Now it was her turn to ignore me. By this time, an electric limousine had eased silently up to the curb, and a big-chested guy in a dark suit pulled himself out of the front seat to help us in.

Once we settled into the limo, I tried my Lulu-question on Callie. "What does Lulu do?" I remembered how Callie had done a slow, silent burn last time I raised the subject. Now she hmphed. "Won't tell me.

Probably something she knows I wouldn't approve of. Like the time she was an artists' model."

I tried my best to picture Lulu posing naked in a studio with golden sunlight playing over her body, her cute inny navel in shadow.

Miravelle said little during the ride, but busied himself studying the traffic out the windows. He'd taken his glasses off and I could see he had dark eyes that constantly flicked around suspiciously, seeming to accuse everything he looked at. He was probably a very good security man.

"So you're Animata's security guy? You were guarding the cat when they took it?"

He flicked me an annoyed glance, his smoothness ruffled a bit. "My people were." He switched on the limo's navcameras and watched the rear view on a viddie monitor set in a rich walnut console.

"What happened? How'd they get the cat?"

"Information leaked." He targeted Callie with an accusing gaze.

"Hey, don't blame us," said Callie. "You were supposed to guard the cat."

They were about to start an argument, and I didn't want that, because I needed more information. "Exactly how did they do the job?"

"Yeah, how?" asked Callie. "The cops wouldn't give out details. I think they're still screwing around trying to figure out the whole story themselves."

Miravelle put his googles back on and mumbled something to them. The little viddie screen changed to a scene of a large room with green cinderblock walls. Battered lockers and benches lined one wall, and a big massage table stood in the middle. The other wall held mirrored makeup tables and an entrance to what looked like a bathroom.

"This is the dressing room in the Garden. No windows, one door. It's built for security, to protect whoever's playing there from intrusions. Like rock stars."

"Yeah, no way in or out. I remember." Callie leaned forward, peering intently at the image of the room.

"No way," said Miravelle. The viddie cut to a close-up shot of the table in the middle of the room. "They set the cat here in its case. We did this reenactment." The same big dark-suited man who was now driving the limo appeared in the viddie frame and set a carrying case on the table. The case looked just like the one the bird-guy carried.

"Yeah, and . . . ?"

"And this is what happened." Suddenly, the center of the table sank smoothly out of sight, carrying the case with it. The case immediately reappeared, but something seemed different now.

It took a bit, but I got it. "That's not the same case! It's got different scratches on it."

"Perceptive," said Miravelle. "The table had a mechanism for switching cases. We also figured out the remote signal that triggered it. Somebody knew the plan was to bring the cat in, set it on this table. Somebody knew early enough in advance to build a trick table that could switch cases. And switch cats, too, substituting one that had blue-dyed fur. Somebody knew all the details pretty damned early on."

"Didn't you have cameras?"

"All over the room. But they were tapped. That's extremely difficult with digital fiber optics, but they did it. And they figured out the security coding on the signal. And when the guard left for a second, the bastards knew. They switched the security camera image to show the room with nothing happening, so, my people couldn't see the switch."

"And then we came in and took the fake cat out to the staging area," Callie said. "It was maybe fifteen minutes before we opened the case and found the fake. We were watching the crowd, not the cat."

"And after you left the room with the fake cat, nobody cared what was going on in that room," I said.

"Everybody followed what they thought was the Cerulean. Hell, they could have taken a lion out of there."

"How about the guard? It was pretty convenient for him to go pee."

"Yes, it was. He's ours, but we're checking him. Nothing so far. No big car, no women, no big spending in the Mirror. I think it was you cat people who screwed up . . . maybe on purpose."

Callie glared at Miravelle. "That's bullshit. Tons of people knew the cat would be parked in that room. For a month they knew. And the Garden is a public place. Anybody could have come in a week before and put in the table mechanism. That's why I'm going to figure this thing out, to show we didn't screw up."

We both kept badgering Miravelle for details, as we traveled in style to Animata. The limo dropped us at LaGuardia, where we met this big Animata helicopter, all gleaming white with the company logo on the side. It lifted off for the Philly headquarters, and Callie and I leaned back in the big leather seats and toasted with cold beers at being in such luxury. I had some little meatlike sandwiches, which were okay, but I would've preferred roast beef. We eased down for a landing on a big grassy hill, right next to the real version of the Animata building. Same huge granite building, like some Egyptian tomb with the same swirly DNA ark logo in shiny steel.

We ducked through the helicopter's wind blast up to the same big multicolored doorway with images of the strange animals we'd seen in the Mirror. But it was real now, not with that kind of digital-smooth computer graphic look. And the plants and bushes around the entrance weren't in the Mirror version—exotic plants with strange flowers that looked like they must have been genetically engineered.

Miravelle led us inside to the real lobby, with real marble and real video screens and real visitors watching them. Also, there were real guards, not even Helpers, with real blazer uniforms, and with real bulges in their jackets. Pistols. But I noticed differences between real and virtie.

"See, there's more doors here in the real-life building," I whispered to Callie.

"Oh, yeah," she whispered back. "I guess a company doesn't show you everything in the Mirror."

"Sure, like places they don't want visitors. Maybe just broom closets. But maybe also high-security areas."

We reached an elevator with big, shiny brass doors that you could see yourself in. I realized I looked kind of sloppy next to Miravelle, but who wouldn't? At the elevator, Miravelle looked directly into the camera, so the computer could scan his iris pattern. The computer confirmed that he was, indeed, Julio Miravelle, and I'm sure it scanned Callie and me, too, for future reference.

We rode the carved-wood-paneled elevator up to the top floor, and when the doors opened, stepped into the richest, coolest office I've ever been in, with big, thick carpets and antique chairs, tables and armoires that my dad would have really admired.

Another guy, dressed in the same blue blazer as the guards, led us down a long hallway to an office with big double doors richly carved with all kinds of mythical animals—gryphons, dragons, three-headed dogs, abominable snowmen. The doors were old, I'd bet from some castle. Dad would've known.

In the office, a man sat in a high-backed leather chair behind a massive marble desk.

"Hello, I'm Kenneth Talbot." He said, rising to reveal a fine suit that matched Miravelle's in quality. He had thinning blond hair, neatly trimmed and combed to perfection and skin that had seen too many tans, making it like fine, brown parchment. He smiled, creasing wrinkles around his eyes, and waved his hand toward the other side of the room. "Sit down, won't you? Refreshments?" He asked in an upper-crust British accent, no doubt carefully shaped by family and education.

In a corner beside floor-to-ceiling bookcases, sat massive wine-colored leather couches and a huge, ornate chair, like a carved-wood throne with thick cushions. The guy in the blazer hurried around the desk and pulled Talbot's chair out of the way.

Talbot stepped back and turned, leaning forward slightly and moving out from behind the desk. He took studied, precise steps as he walked across the room, heading for the chair, his shoes making a faint thunk when they landed.

I realized with a start that he was wearing an exosuit—one of those artificially intelligent computer-controlled electroplastic pants-things—surrounding his legs and torso. I'd seen them on viddie news, but never in reality. The suit attached to hundreds of hair-thin electrodes inserted into his back that sent little tickles of electricity into the spine, stimulating his leg muscles to contract, so he could walk. And the pants brace gave him support when the stimulating didn't work right.

The pants brace fit closely around his body, adding only a little bulk underneath his suit. I caught a glimpse of a battery and computer pack wrapped around his waist under his jacket, and his hand held a small wireless remote control, whose buttons and joystick he manipulated with practiced expertise.

I watched fascinated, but trying not to stare, as Talbot sent programmed waves of electricity into his spine to walk him across the room with this strange, automated smoothness. He was like a computer-controlled puppet, except he held the strings. He reached the chair, turned, and directed his muscles to lower him onto its big seat. The guy in the blazer pulled up another chair for Miravelle, who sat in it without saying anything.

I couldn't believe it! Kenneth Talbot, multibillionaire, old-time aristocrat, big-time corporate chief . . . was a paraplegic!

Chapter 13

I politely said I didn't want refreshments. Even though the little meat-like sandwiches and beer hadn't filled me up, I decided it wouldn't look good for me to chew and gulp while I talked to a multibillionaire. Seated in his big chair, Talbot extended his hand, with an apologetic wave. "Sorry about not getting up. Damnable legs, y'know." I jumped up and shook his hand, receiving a measured refined handshake, like a British aristocrat might give. Callie plunked her big bag beside the couch and did the same.

Throughout the whole greeting business, Miravelle never looked at Talbot, but steadily at us, like he expected us to go for guns. That's what security people did, I guess.

"Y'know, you're a brave fellow," said Talbot, settling back in the chair, his dead legs not moving unless they were stimulated to.

"Me? Why?"

"Well, telling the police as you did. Sticking with the problem, even after that attack. Bad news. Terrible attack. We saw video of the bedroom."

Callie propped her ankle on her knee and frowned at her sneaker for a moment, then looked up at Talbot. "What do you think about that? About the animal that went after Tim?"

"Rotten business. Sorry we ever created them."

"I bet you are." Callie glared at Talbot and drummed her fingers on the arm of the big leather couch.

"*You* created them?" I hadn't known that little fact.

"Oh, well, yes. Improved guard animals for the military. More intimidating than dogs. Smarter. Called them 'GenESents,' for Genetically Engineered Sentries. But we decided in the end it was a bad sort of thing we didn't want to be into. Sold off the patents."

"Who to?" asked Callie.

"Genipet."

"You think Genipet's behind all this?"

Talbot set his leg-control box on the table and folded his hands on his lap. "Can't really say. Surely don't want to slander anyone, but it's a possibility we're considering." He glanced over at Miravelle, who gave him a cool, deadpan look back, like he was assuring his boss that he had the whole thing covered. Talbot continued. "Or maybe it was Felicity. Or maybe somebody after money. We're just interested in recovering the Cerulean, the poor animal."

"But Genipet's your main suspect?" I asked distractedly. I was puzzled by that box. I wondered why Talbot hadn't decided to get his brain neural-dusted. That's where surgeons infuse your brain with nano-sized receiver/transmitters that the brain incorporates into its circuitry. That way, Talbot could just control his legs directly with his brain. Then it hit me. He was probably getting his spinal cord regenerated. Somewhere there was a jar with pieces of his spinal cord growing, and which surgeons would implant to restore his legs. In the meantime, he used the exosuit and control box. Talbot's answer about Genipet brought me back to the matter at hand.

"Well, to be honest, we're not terribly confident of their ethics. They're still developing the GenESents. They've got a military contract. Perhaps one of the animals came into the hands of a bad sort. That's what attacked you."

"Bootleg beastie, eh?" said Callie.

"Well, that sort of unpleasantness was why we wanted to stick with making pets and farm animals and such. And the endangered animals. Especially the tigers. Remember the last tiger in the wild?

Sad thing. We were glad to start making them. Really less liability in all that, y'know."

"Liability," Callie muttered under her breath. Then, to Talbot: "That's all you're worried about? Liability?"

Talbot smiled tolerantly at the question. He nodded to his assistant, who knew what the nod meant and fetched him some kind of bubbly water in a really nice blue crystal stemmed goblet. Talbot didn't use Helpers. He liked real people serving him.

"Mrs. Lawrence, we know there are those who disapprove of our industry. Even some in my own family." He picked up the glass and took a sip of the water. "But we make a product. Genetically engineered animals. No different, really, than the selective breeding humans have done for thousands of years. Our farm animals give people better nutrition. Our pets give them pleasure. The exotic animals are like living sculptures, tributes to the ingenuity and the aesthetics of the human race."

I thought I'd heard that speech somewhere before, like on a viddie news show one time when the building was surrounded by really mad people with signs.

"Yeah, well, one of your damned sculptures almost killed this boy."

I had to get Callie off that horse, so I changed the subject. "So, what are you doing to get the cat back?"

"Well, there's the five-million-dollar reward for information leading to an arrest and recovery. Our own people, supervised by Mr. Miravelle, are working with the police. We'll do whatever we can to help."

"So why'd you want to see me?"

"Well, to thank you for coming forward. And to make sure you know you're in for some of that reward if there's a capture."

I must've perked up visibly, because Talbot gave a little smile as he took another slow sip of his water, probably to let that fact sink in, and continued.

"But the main reason was really to find out what you saw. Maybe we can assist the police better if we knew more. Might be a bit of information, y'know, that we'd recognize as important that you wouldn't; that the police wouldn't. We'll even show you our facility. Maybe something will jog your memory. Something you didn't tell the police. Maybe you'll even see somebody you saw on the street and didn't remember. Any clue at all would help. You willing, Timothy?"

"Heck, yeah!" I settled back in the big chair, seeing visions of a cashcard with a big, fat balance. I decided to ask for a drink, one of those new invented-flavor Crokes, which also came immediately in another blue goblet. I took a couple of big drinks out of that fancy glass and felt the cold tingly liquid cool my tongue, making it kind of thick. But I kept that tongue warm by blathering away, rattling off the whole story, including every little detail I could possibly remember.

Like when I heard the first thump on my cab that scared me; how the bird-guy got in; exactly what he looked like; what the carrying case looked like; what he said to the dumb bastard over his googles—

Miravelle interrupted here and asked how I knew the bird-guy was talking to another guy and not a woman. I took a sip and explained that I didn't think even the bird-guy would cuss at a woman like that. At least, people didn't where I come from.

"Clever fellow," said Miravelle in appreciation. I did feel really clever, because I hadn't really thought of that until Miravelle asked. So, I kept on, and when I finished, the aide refilled my Croke, and Miravelle and Talbot asked bunches of questions. Like exactly what the bird-guy did when I let him off at the Castle Hotel. Like which way he went. And like did I think he was looking for another cab or walking.

I thought about the last question for a bit, then said, "Well, he kind of walked away fast lugging that case. And he was kind of a skinny little guy with a big case. So he probably expected not to have to carry it that far. I'd bet he either had a car waiting nearby or a place to hide." I was really being smart, I thought.

Talbot nodded and sat for a long time then without saying anything, looking at us without really seeing us. Callie interrupted his staring. "Look, he's told you everything he knows. When's your man here going to reciprocate? What've you figured out about this? What do you think the cops know?"

Talbot nodded and made a face that said "fair question," and gestured to Miravelle to tell us what they knew. So, Miravelle told us in that smoothly accented voice that they didn't know diddly. Only he said "the information is sketchy." He said the cat had disappeared, the cops were still looking, and that was *that*. I could tell Callie was getting a little steamed up. Talbot probably could, too, because he took up his control box, pushed a few buttons, fiddled with the joystick and stimulated his leg muscles to make his body rise like a garage door going up. The aide stepped forward, all attentive.

"Well, we should show you how we make our animals," said Talbot. "I think you'll be quite amazed."

He strode stiffly toward the double doors, which swung open just as he reached them. An aide held each door. Rich guys must have people watching their every move. The elevator doors had opened, too, and we stepped in. Miravelle followed, staying just behind Talbot, so he could watch us, no doubt.

We descended to the basement, where a big electric cart with leather upholstery waited for us. I moved toward it, but Miravelle stopped me.

"Which hand do you prefer?" he asked.

"What?" I looked at my hands. "Well, I guess they're both pretty useful."

A big guard stepped up and handed Miravelle two metal bracelets.

Miravelle took a bracelet and held it up. "Which hand? You have to wear a PID on one wrist."

"Personal identity device," said Callie. "It sends out a locator signal so the security can track you." She held out her wrist and the guard snapped a bracelet on.

"What if I didn't wear one? I'm not going to run off anywhere."

Miravelle stood staring at me impatiently, but I really wanted to know. "The security computer would register your body heat, your motion. Unless it detects a bracelet, it would assume you were an intruder and take . . . action."

"What action?"

"That is a security matter." Miravelle took the bracelet and held it up, like he was giving me a last chance.

"Standard procedure, Timothy," Talbot said from the cart, beckoning. He had walked himself over to the cart and fiddled with his control box, managing to get his legs to climb into it. The aides stood back, not looking too comfortable, but pointedly not helping him. I'd bet he got pretty touchy about people helping him. One of the aides got in the driver's seat and adjusted the mirror so he could see Talbot.

"Sure, okay, cool." I shrugged and held out my right hand, and Miravelle clicked the bracelet on. A little green light glowed on it.

"You'd better tell him the whole story, though," said Callie, looking at her bracelet like it was some disgusting thing that had wrapped itself around her wrist.

"Certainly," Miravelle nodded. "Since you're a visitor, you have to stay within ten feet of Mr. Talbot or myself. The security system tracks you very precisely. It knows who's near you."

"And if I don't?"

"You hear a little warning beep. Just a little beep."

"Tell him all of it," said Callie. "If the system detects that you've taken off on your own, it sends a warning signal that zaps you with an electric charge. It'll feel like your arm's been set on fire with a blowtorch. And if you still don't comply, it blows you to bits."

I looked at the little bracelet. It sure looked harmless enough. I shrugged. "Well, if I took it off?"

"It's locked on. And anyway, after a minute it knows your heartbeat like a fingerprint, so you can't put it on anybody else." Callie looked over at Miravelle, who smiled that instant smile and nodded.

"I'll just have to keep up, I guess." I got in beside Talbot.

The cart eased silently forward and carried us through a long tunnel decorated with fancy tile mosaics of all kinds of animals. We passed pictures of elephants and swans and snakes and alligators and lions and monkeys. But no pictures of Animata's genetic combo animals. We passed smaller carts going in the other direction, carrying people in white lab coats or in regular jeans and sneakers, like me. The silent aide drove, and since Talbot was sitting beside me, leaning forward and talking to us, I looked him over. He was perfect, the way people were when other people did everything for them. Everything was smooth surfaces, like a living sculpture. His clothes fit just so, with creases and folds and buttons just where they were supposed to be. His face looked tended by a barber, not a bit of stubble showing, as was his razor-perfect-cut hair. Everything worked perfect except his legs, and I'd bet that really ate into him, but he didn't show it.

Callie must have been thinking the same thing, because she interrupted his recitation to ask "How'd you do that?" pointing to his legs.

He stopped abruptly and a strange look crossed his face, kind of calculating, or maybe angry. "Sailing accident. Up the mast in a race, trying to fix a fouled sheet. Boat heeled, safety line came loose and I fell. Hit a stanchion." He stopped. That was all he was going to say. He pointedly resumed reciting company history.

Callie nodded and leaned back, also with a peculiar look on her face. There was tension going on here . . . maybe. It was almost like they were having some kind of contest.

CHAPTER 14

The cart finally reached what was probably the basement of a huge, gray brick building that I'd seen looming behind the headquarters. We emerged from the tunnel into a hangar-sized hall, about the size of a dozen barns; solid brick all around; no windows, two-story ceilings. The air felt cool and dry and perfect; only a faint hiss of ventilation tickled the vast stillness. One side of the room held a glass-walled chamber, in which sat rows and rows of room-sized steel globes. A stocky guy wearing a big tool belt squatted on the floor in front of an open globe with a hole in the floor beside it. He bent over a thick sheaf of fiber optic cables jutting out of the floor. When he jiggled the cables, little gleaming pinpoints of light twinkled out of their tips.

Across the cavernous hall sat a line of seven doors, their spacing hinting that behind them lay rooms as big as my whole apartment.

"This is where we do our designs," said Talbot, pointing at the domes. "Besides the usual wall screens, we've got this series of vrooms connected to a network of parallel cryogenic quantum zettaflop ultracomputers.

"Whoa . . . try to say that three times fast!" cracked Callie, standing there holding her big bag. Talbot ignored her.

"Our designers work in there. Let's go in one." He swiveled himself out of the seat and fiddled his control box to trundle himself over to the door. The aide opened the door and we entered to find ourselves in a darkened room with three people wearing googles, sitting in chairs and waving their hands in the air. There were two young fuzz-faced guys in jeans and a little old oriental lady in black pants and a white blouse.

The aide handed each of us googles, and when I put mine on, the room was suddenly crowded by a bunch of shimmery *virtual* people. Like the real people, they were either watching or fiddling with floating mathematical equations with Greek letters and exponents, charts with zillions of numbers, graphs with squiggly lines, strings of genetic sequences, and three-D rotating molecules. It was a brainbanging incredible sight!

The three real people realized we were there and straightened self-consciously when they saw our group included Talbot.

"Carry on," he said brightly. "Just a bit of a tour here."

The oriental lady smiled and nodded, did a little bow, and reached for a sequence of a gene. I could tell it was a gene, because it was all letters ATGTACGTGCGTA, like the genetic code I'd learned in biology class. Next to it was a three-D molecule that looked like a bunch of colored pool balls. I think it was a protein that the gene was the blueprint for. She poked at a virtual control panel hanging in mid-air and changed one G to an A. The bunch of colored pool balls folded itself around into a different shape.

"These are the genes for a new animal we're trying to build, I suppose," said Talbot in a surprisingly reverent whisper. "We've decoded the genes for most animals now. So, when we get an idea for a mix, like our chicken with sable fur, we plan it here. We actually feed mathematical models for two or more animals into the ultracomputers. It's like having a virtual zoo living in the computer. Then we run simulations of how they can be viably combined."

"And Rozoff? What did he do?" I asked.

"Vasily developed Genesis, the simulation program. Quite an incredible achievement, y'know. Genesis can input specified changes in different combinations of animals' genetic blueprint . . . their genes . . . then predict how those changes would interact to produce a new kind of animal."

"What happened to him?" Callie didn't look at Talbot, but stood there with her bag, watching the molecule rotate above our heads

Talbot ignored the question, still in his explanation mode. "It's something like putting together a building. You change the blueprint, which changes the bricks and girders, which changes the shape of the building. Don't really understand all of it. But it's enough they do," he waved his hand at the real and virtual people crowding the room.

"What happened to Rozoff?" Callie repeated louder.

"Sorry. Got carried away. Dearly wish we knew. Just disappeared after he gave us the cat. To be honest, he was a strange little fellow, but we all liked him. Shall we move on?"

The cushy electric cart carried us past the rooms, into a big freight elevator and up to a floor of laboratories filled with more machines, this time with little pumps sluicing colored liquids through tubes, and viddie screens with bunches of numbers scrolling down them.

Talbot waved for the cart to stop, but didn't get out. "Here's where they assemble the genes . . . molecular engineering and all that. Synthesizing and insertion into fertilized eggs . . . oocytes. Standard stuff. The difficult part is next."

"DNA-land," I said, smiling at my palindrome, but since Talbot wasn't into palindromes, he didn't get it.

We went up another floor. This time Talbot got out of the cart immediately and propelled himself into a sprawling, muggy culture room with long rows of shelves holding gallon-sized tanks with little pinkish globules floating in hazy yellowish liquid. Mechie Helpers fitted with long arms and clamps rolled up and down the rows. One stopped at a tank, reached up and unhooked hoses that circulated liquid through the tank. The Helper clamped onto the tank, slid it onto a cart, and rolled it away, leaving the gap in the row.

"Embryos," said Talbot, walking himself along the rows, steering clear of the trundling Helper. "We insert the genes into eggs and create embryos. Grow them up a bit. Then insert the mammals into host mothers, and they grow into the animals." He stopped at one tank and peered in. "Or, like this one here, if it's an egg-laying animal, they don't need a host mother. We just grow them up until they're ripe."

I peered into a bottle that had a little pinkish Something-Alive floating in it. I tried to make it out. I could see a little round head, maybe with a beak, and a body with a long tail. Maybe like a chicken-snake. The Something-Alive jiggled a little bit in the liquid, like it was trying to get itself comfortable. I'd seen chicken-snakes on viddies, but not in real life.

"Was that one dead?" asked Callie, making a pickle face and motioning at the retreating Helper. "What's your failure rate?" asked Callie.

"We prefer to talk in terms of a *success* rate," answered Talbot smoothly.

"Okay, how small is your success rate?" she asked sarcastically.

"It's highly satisfactory," said Talbot spinning on his mechanical heel and marching off.

"And even after they're born, you don't know what you'll get," said Callie, following him.

"That's why our animals are so difficult to create. God has a much better record than us."

"But you're like little gods, right?" asked Callie. "Lesser gods."

Talbot remained unflustered at Callie's needling. "Like drug companies, we start out with a lot of candidates, but only a few make it to market."

"And the mistakes?"

This time Talbot's jaw clenched. "The nonviable constructs are disposed of humanely. We learn from our mistakes."

I followed them down the row. "And the good ones? You can't just breed them over and over?" I didn't have to worry about my security bracelet zapping me for wandering away, because Miravelle followed closely, maybe watching to see that I didn't swipe an embryo. I peered into other bottles with things that looked like little turtles or lizards or birds . . . but not exactly.

"Wish it were that easy," said Talbot, swiveling himself back toward the electric cart. "They're all sterile. Like mules. You understand how that is, Timothy. You're from farming country, I hear." We followed, making our way down the rows of bottles, past all those pinkish embryonic globs.

"Damn good thing they're sterile," said Callie. "Government would shut you down, you let some of these things loose and they bred."

"*Government,*" Talbot said, like it was a fungus. "Went through quite a bother with the government. USDA . . . EPA . . . tons of reports. Proved our animals posed no threat. Couldn't reproduce. Mules. Like mules, y'know."

"That's why you don't just clone 'em?" asked Callie. "Run copies out like a Xerox machine?"

"Of course, we could clone these animals ad infinitum," but Talbot's wrinkled-brow frown said he dismissed such a distasteful idea. "But we do see ourselves as something of a boutique for collectors, especially the ones who like the really exotic mixes . . . our Beautipet or Artanimal or Mythic Creatures series. Those really are exhibit-quality animals. It would be like photocopying a great work of art. So, for their sake, we enforce a strict cloning policy. We do offer our customers a single-copy cloning service for their purchases, once the animals live a natural lifespan." Talbot pointedly ended that subject by climbing back into the cart. We barely managed to get ourselves in before the cart sped away, out of the tank room, and past another large room with no windows.

"What's in there?" I asked.

"Birthing room, pathology, so forth," said Talbot. "Not terribly . . . aesthetic. So, we don't take folks in there."

Callie made a "hmph." I could imagine how yucky that place might be, with living and dead embryos and all the stuff that went with them. "So, where do you keep the young animals?" I remembered seeing viddies of herds of weird animals in a field, with the place being picketed by people with big signs.

"Our farms and ranches around the country. We do a lot of field-testing. Make sure the animals can forage for themselves. Make sure the big ones can get along in herds. We give our customers quality-tested animals."

"Did the cat grow on a farm?"

"The Cerulean was different. Just after I came in, Vasily isolated himself at his place out in Washington. Had a whole computer design setup out there in the woods. He was a special sort . . . a bit eccentric . . . and he needed a bit of rest, so we left him alone. That's where he designed the animal."

"And how'd the cat get . . . uh . . . built?" The cart turned back toward the elevator.

"Well, about a year after he left, he came back in and started working with the technicians to build genes for a new animal. Said he was onto something big, so I told our people to go along. Then he put the egg together and implanted it in a host mother cat. Then he took the pregnant mother away. And then a couple of months ago, he just presented us with this incredible animal and disappeared. We were flabbergasted. We figured he wanted to get out of the business and this was his pièce de résistance."

"Just like that. Here's the cat and good luck?"

"And with none of the data. We never found his data. We wouldn't know how to duplicate the cat. Amazing achievement. The cat isn't really blue, in fact. The color's prismatic. Vasily somehow figured out the genetic program to create the prismatic structure of a bird feather in its fur shaft. Like a peacock feather, or maybe an indigo bunting. That's why the animal has this stunning iridescent quality. We saw it when we examined a fur snippet. But we couldn't even dream of sampling the skin follicles to figure out how those structures formed. Didn't know how delicate the cat was, y'know. We've had animals die just from having a blood sample taken."

Callie piped in: "You didn't think this whole secrecy thing was weird? Him just showing up with this cat?"

"That was Vasily's way . . . working alone, y'know. And, it's our policy to grow up a new animal before we make it public . . . to make sure there are no—"

"Monsters," Callie muttered.

"—non-viable constructs."

Callie said something under her breath I couldn't hear. It had some b's and s's and t's in it.

I tried to head off an argument again. "I only saw a little of the cat on viddies. Got any viddie of your own? Got any pictures?"

Talbot didn't say anything right away, but waved the driver on and we entered the big freight elevator again. Miravelle in the front seat turned around to see what he would say.

"Certainly. Made a video to introduce the cat." Then to the driver: "Showroom."

"That's it? Just one viddie?" asked Callie.

Talbot smiled like a cat who'd eaten a canary, or maybe one of his genetically engineered versions.

"It was a clever little trick the marketing department dreamed up, actually. If we'd allowed too much footage, invariably some would leak out. Lots of vampires out there, y'know. And marketing told us if people didn't see the animal on video before the unveiling they'd come see it in person. But mainly, if we licensed it to a company . . . cat food or such . . . we wanted to give them utmost exclusivity. Enhance the novelty value, and all that."

We stopped at a floor and left the cart to enter one of the showrooms, where Talbot showed us the viddie, as we sat in big armchairs. The viddie began with a fancy three-D Animata logo, with a syntho orchestra playing an overture in Immersound, which made it seem like the musicians were all around us. A clarinet player sat behind me.

Then the screen showed the cat in three-D, all blue-furry and pretty, sitting in a white room. The scene cut to dramatic close-ups of the cat's blue tail, back, and head, and then to swooping long shots of the cat walking and sitting. A narrator with a deep voice told how incredibly cool the cat was.

But I thought it was just an okay cat. Just a blue cat. Not that special somehow. Maybe the viddie wasn't very good, because even that little real-life tail tip I saw seemed more special than this whole cat on the viddie. The viddie showed the cat from one side and the other, but they were quick shots.

"That's a crummy viddie," Callie whispered to me in the darkness. She'd noticed, too. "I saw the real cat. It was incredible. Its fur! Its eyes! They don't show the eyes!"

The viddie ended, the lights came up, and I dutifully said the cat was incredible, but it wasn't really. It just looked like a blue cat. Callie didn't say anything else. She seemed immersed in some kind of dark mood. We rode the cart back through the tunnel to the main building and up the elevator to Talbot's office. As we were leaving, he laid his hand on my arm. He had shiny nails.

"Timothy." He patted my arm and smiled. "You're our only lead. You're in danger. Let Mr. Miravelle give you one of our best men to watch over you."

"We're doing fine, thanks," answered Callie.

"Frankly I'm worried, Mrs. Lawrence," Talbot leaned toward her, smiling. "This isn't something you two should get involved in. It's dangerous. You should let the professionals take care—"

"We can handle ourselves," interrupted Callie. "But there is one thing you can do."

Talbot shook his head sadly. "Whoever stole the Cerulean is desperate, Callie." He said her name with a faint condescension, and I could tell it riled her.

"How about getting us into the next animal auction?"

Miravelle shook his head again. "How can that possibly help? Not much chance the thief will show himself there."

"Yeah, well, it might stir something up when they see Tim. And I know people in the business who might be there who I can talk to. It's a chance."

Talbot looked at us with furrowed brow, pursed lips, deciding. Then he nodded to one of his assistants, who handed us a card. "Oh, very well. At least you'll be where we can help if you get yourselves in trouble. Give my card to the guard at the auction tomorrow. It'll get you in the door and any cooperation you need."

Callie thanked him, we said goodbye, and the guard took our bracelets off. Good! I wouldn't blow up! Miravelle escorted us back outside and to the limousine. The silent, dark-suited driver held the door for us to get in. Miravelle didn't follow, but nodded goodbye and closed the door behind us.

I twisted around and watched out the back, as the Animata complex receded into the distance. "Why did you turn down the bodyguard? I thought it was a good idea to have one of those guys with us."

"They had motives that wouldn't have helped you." Callie stabbed the button to close the partition between us and the driver.

"Like?

"Greed, Tim," she whispered in my ear, digging through her bag and bringing up a package of mints, offering me one. She waved her hand around and touched her finger to her lips, telling me she figured the limo was bugged. "These guys are only after their damned precious animal."

I took a mint, picked off the lint and put it in my mouth. I whispered back. "Talbot seemed like a pretty nice guy."

"Yeah, they all seem *nice*." She hissed the word "nice" with a sarcastic emphasis. "But let's say you get attacked again. Say they had a choice whether to stop the killer or let him succeed, so they can follow him back to the cat."

It dawned on me. "I'd be dead."

Callie slapped me on the knee and rolled the mint around in her mouth. Now she talked out loud. "You're learning about big city ways pretty fast, sport."

CHAPTER 15

The next day found me very happily sitting beside Lulu in a cab. She was grinning at me, making dimples, and had an amused twinkle in her eye. "The cop was right. You are a stubborn little dink, aren't you?" I could tell she meant it as a compliment, so I sat back in the cab seat and took it that way.

We'd kind of given Callie the slip, and we were on the way back to my place. "Well, I promised Mrs. Salvo . . . and her son . . . that I'd take care of her."

Lulu shifted sideways on the seat, leaned back against the other cab door and cocked one jeaned knee up on the seat, wiggling her boot. Behind her, the scabby stores and brownstones of my neighborhood slid by. The cabbie shook his head again, clearly unhappy about being here. His computer had told him level 4, and he switched on his navcams, including the one aimed at us. As if a couple of young and dimpled people like us would rob him.

"*Mother's* sure going to be pissed when she finds out you went back to your place," she said.

"She's going to be even madder when she finds out you decided to come along."

"I go where I want." She sure did, I thought, as she paused to look out the window at all the hinky goings-on we passed. The nickies being sold on street corners. A couple of hairless nearly nude smoothie-baldies doing their sinuous dances and trying to get people to join their cult that celebrated their e-tatts. The suspicious-looking guys lounging up against the buildings behind dark googles, probably plugged in and committing link crimes.

The night before, I'd gotten to sleep in Lulu's bed . . . good news. But the bad news was she wasn't there. When Callie and I had returned from Animata to her loft, we found a note saying she was at "work," and wouldn't be back until morning. Callie had made a sour face and grouched about her daughter being up to no good and out all night.

So we went to bed, Callie insisting that I sleep in Lulu's room for protection, because it was farther from the front door. She and her cats had piled together on the couch with a pillow, a comforter, and the nine-millimeter on the floor beside her. It was just as well Lulu hadn't been there last night. I probably wouldn't have tried any kind of romantic move anyway. I'd have tended to lose my concentration on Daughter when Mama had a loaded pistol.

Anyway, Lulu had shown up the next morning, her hair wild and blowy from the night. And dressed in feathers! Yes, feathers! She had all kinds of shimmery colored feathers attached to her body in a way I couldn't figure out at first. Then I got it. Secondskin. She wore a sec-ondskin body suit that fitted her just like real skin, and it was covered with feathers. While the feathers were strategically arranged to show off her slim body, unfortunately they covered the good parts. After I spent some time wishing for molting season, I noticed that her secondskin suit appeared to include no pockets, meaning that she carried no googles or any other communicator. That was really strange these days, I thought.

She'd stood over me, given a flip of her hand and a "Heeyaahhh, boy," like a cowgirl herding cattle, and rousted me out of her bed so she could sleep. I sure wanted to ask where she'd been and why she didn't carry googles. But I kept my mouth shut, obeying my eviction. She curled herself up looking like a nesting bird, fluffing a feather here and there, and closed her eyes. I showered, shaved and sneaked out past the happily undulating blob sculpture, and a sleeping Callie and her cats, to a coffee shop for breakfast. Great breakfast! Three-egg cheese omelet, double real bacon, double home fries, toast, big coffee. Cheap, too. Forty bucks.

When I got back, Callie was up and mad at me for going out alone, but I argued that nobody would notice me with all the schizzy artists and brain-warped funkies on the street in the neighborhood. But I finally agreed to 'frigerate, to stay cool, so I spent the rest of the morning hanging in the apartment with Callie and her cats and plugged into my processor, peering through my googles.

I watched all the news viddies about the Cerulean, seeing myself over and over. They said I'd disappeared and showed my bloody bed, but still no Nasty! But all the blood still made great Cop Network viddie. They said the investigation was proceeding rapidly, and they expected an arrest in the catnapping soon.

I also spent the morning checking my messages on my googles. I had forty-three! I'd never been that popular before. Twelve from my folks wanting to know if I was okay. Two from Elizabeth wanting to get together, saying she knew this agent. Bunches from cops, viddie news people, a girl who wanted to meet me, and a guy who screamed the cat was a demon from hell, and I should kill it with a stake.

Callie decided to go visit some people who might have useful information. But first, she got right in my face and said "Kid, you stay here, okay? And don't send any messages; they can trace the calls. Don't even breathe loud."

After she left, I spent an hour going over all the viddies, articles, news releases, government reports, and other stuff about Animata that my angel had dredged up, using her bullshit detector to check facts. Allowing for the corporate hype, all the statements we'd heard on the Animata tours, real and Mirror, just about matched up with public information. The company was a skyrocket that had started making zillions of dollars, but had to deal with all kinds of protests and government regulation. And Talbot had come in when the company started getting too big for Rozoff—who was a great scientist, lousy businessman—to handle.

But as I sat on the couch with the cats studying all this, I remembered that Mrs. Salvo was alone, and that she needed me. She was just too important for me to stay stuck in Lulu's apartment. Then Lulu came dragging out of the bedroom, yawning and, having peeled off her secondskin, wearing a saggy old nightshirt that gave me a nice look at her legs. I told her I was going out. She'd insisted on my waiting for her to wake up and come along.

So, now here we sat in the cab five blocks away from my apartment house. Lulu's attention returned from the scene outside, and she continued as if she'd not even stopped. "... anyway, when you said the old lady was like your Nana ...." The tone of her voice softened, her expression wistful. "... reminded me of my grandma. She raised me mostly. I miss her so much."

"*She* raised you?"

"*Mother* was off saving the world, but you know about that." Lulu searched my face for comprehension, but found none. Her eyes widened and she laughed in wonder. "Hell, she never told you, did she?"

The cab jerked to a stop behind a double-parked truck. The cabbie tweedled his electronic horn and rattled off a bunch of curses in Indian out the window. He stomped the accelerator, and swerved around it.

"Told me what?"

"Timmy, who ... what ... do you think *Mother* is?"

"She's a nice cat lady, I guess."

"My mother was a spook."

"Spook? What's a spook?"

"She was a spy, Tim-boy. Guns and secret codes and stuff."

I must've looked really dumb, because she laughed again and slapped me on the knee. The cab zoomed through a changing red light, triggering horn honks and tweedles from the side streets.

"Y'know, I thought she knew too much about guns and sneaking around for a cat lady. Who'd she spy for?"

"Us, dummy. You remember when you were a kid ... well, you're *still* a kid ... when you were a *little* kid? And there was all this drug mess in South America? Cocaine, crack ... stuff like that?"

"Barely."

"You remember a big drug war? Remember, they shot the vice president, and we sent the army down and rounded 'em all up?"

"Yeah, I think I saw viddies about it in school."

"That was *Mother*."

"What was Mother?"

"She'd got in close with the drug lords. Real close. She was a . . ." Lulu either couldn't or wouldn't say the word for what her mother did.

". . . spy."

"Yeah . . . spy. She made the whole thing possible." Lulu raised an eyebrow. "What did she tell you about my father?"

"Well . . . something about him being in Dallas. Running an ice cream place. With some young—"

"Hah! My *Mother!*" Lulu threw back her head and laughed again, but it was cackly, sarcastic. "The ice cream parlor story!"

"Where is your dad?"

Her face grew stony. "Never knew him."

"Did your brother?"

She looked out the window. The subject was closed.

"Do you love your mother?" The question just popped out.

Lulu looked back, startled. "Of course! What kind of question is that?"

"Well, you guys always fight."

"We just have a history, *Mother* and me. We're both strong personalities."

"No kidding."

I told the cab to pull over a block away from my apartment house, so we'd see if any vampires were still hanging around. Fortunately, Salvo's thugs had swept the area clean. I gave the cabbie a good tip, and he sped away, propelled by the sight of Granite-head hanging out on the corner. As we passed Granite-head, he glared at me and took out his googles. Salvo would find out pretty fast that we were here.

We reached my apartment house, and I let us in. As we passed Freddie's door, he didn't come out, but the little red light on his hallway camera told me he'd know I'd been there. My door looked like it always had, except for the hole ripped in the wall beside it. Freddie had left a bucket of plaster beside the hole, as if he thought the hole would suck the plaster up and fix itself. I showed the hole to Lulu and she whistled and said "Mean little bastard, eh?"

We knocked on Mrs. Salvo's door, and after lots of clanking of locks being undone, she opened it. She saw me and threw one wrinkled old arm around my neck, the other one still in a cast. She wore little pink house slippers and a cotton print dress, always so neat. She was bent over, and her thinning gray hair was done up in a little bun held with bobby pins.

"*Dios Mio! Ay, Dios Mio! No sabia que te habia pasado!*" she cried.

I don't know Spanish, but I thought she was saying she didn't know what had happened to me. She kept on, holding me tight, using words like "*sirenas*" and "*policia,*" and one I really recognized: she kept saying "*animal diablo*" over and over.

I had to calm her down, so I stood there for a while, enjoying her soft Nana-like hug.

"You saw it? You saw *animal diablo*?"

"*Si*. Heard noise. Looked out door," she said, pointing down the hall toward my apartment. "Saw it go into wall. Then you leave . . . man come. Carry . . ." She gestured as if wrapping up a big bundle. "Carry big thing in blanket away. Then *policia* come. I so worry about you!"

So, whoever sent the thing to kill me retrieved its carcass! Somebody really did want me to be in trouble.

"I'm okay, Mrs. Salvo. It didn't hurt me . . ." She patted my shoulder and I winced ". . . much."

She drew in a shocked breath and said "*Dios mio!*" again. Her face wrinkled up even more than it was usually, and she made me bend down so she could look under my shirt at my wound.

"You come in now," she said in her thick accent. "I was so afraid for you. *El animal diablo!*" she muttered as she led us back into her apartment. "*Ay, madre de Dios!*"

She made us sit down and brought us iced tea, refusing to let us help her serve. She finally eased herself into a chair across from us, worry in her old eyes, pain wrinkling her brow. She held her arm cast close to her like it was some kind of treasure, but I knew it was because she hurt.

"Have you been taking your pain medication?"

"I was so worried for you. I heard the guns and the *policia*. They scared me."

"I'm fine. Have you taken your pain pills?"

"I saw you on the television show where the *policia* are."

"The pills, Mrs. Salvo?"

"Oh, pills, pills, who knows about taking pills?"

"Do you have enough food in the apartment?"

"That nice little man. Your amigo who took us to the hospital. He came. He went to the bodega and brought food back. You want *pollo* and *frijoles negro?*"

"Maybe later. But you need pills." I went into her bathroom and rooted through a medicine cabinet full of old-people medicines and found the bottle of prescription pills I'd had filled at the drug store. It was almost full. I got a glass of water from the neat little kitchen with the flower pots on the window sill and came back in. She was lying on the couch, holding her cast to her chest, with Lulu sitting in a rickety wooden chair beside her massaging her temples. Her eyes were closed, and her old face looked much more relaxed. I stopped short, surprised at seeing Lulu do that, after she'd acted like such a toughie.

"This always worked with Grandma," she whispered, smiling like she was remembering a nice memory.

Up until now, I just thought Lulu was a really fluffy-looking girl with a kick-ass personality and a cute smile and those magic eyes. But seeing her like that made her click into place for me, like we were a couple of puzzle pieces fitting together. I stood there just staring at her, until she made a silly cross-eyed face at me and tossed her head impatiently to get me over to help.

We lifted Mrs. Salvo so she could sit up and take a couple of pain pills, and Lulu kept massaging her temples and talking to her softly. I slipped out of the apartment and went back down the hall to my own, partly to get my clothes and partly to shake off the thunderbolt that had just hit me. There weren't any surveillance cameras on the door. The cops couldn't do surveillance without the owner's permission, and Freddie wasn't about to give it. I let myself in and went into the bedroom. The bed was stripped down to the mattress where the Nasty had been bundled away. There wasn't blood on the bed, but there was blood on the wall. Mine. I shuddered at the memory. I rummaged in the cardboard box in the corner where I keep my cleanish clothes. I wash everything every couple of weeks, and in the meantime just sort through for the cleaner ones. The really dirty ones go on the floor.

The box was almost empty! Somebody had taken my dirty clothes, too! No jeans, no t-shirts, no socks. Just a couple of pair of underwear and a towel. All the really dirty clothes on the floor were gone, too. I remembered that my pillow had disappeared earlier. I stood up, trying to figure out who would do such a weird thing. The cops? They wouldn't be interested in my underwear. It began to dawn on me. The Nasty had gone straight for my bed! It was homing on my scent. And now all my well-scented dirty clothes were gone!

A sound in the hall! The big steel door to my apartment creaked open. I froze. I didn't have a gun or anything. Footsteps crunched across my floor, until they reached the squeaky board by the bedroom door. I backed into the bathroom, looking around for a weapon. Soap in a sock? I just had slivers left, and no socks. My toothbrush? Good for close-in, poke-in-the-eye fighting, but not for holding somebody off.

The shower curtain rod! I yanked a couple of times, tearing it off the wall, and sneaked out into the bedroom holding it like a lance, the moldy old yellow-flowered shower curtain still attached, dragging the ground.

"You big damned dummy!" Callie stood with her bag in one hand and nine-millimeter in the other. "What're you, some kind of Lancelot with a shower curtain? Christ!"

I shrugged and pitched the shower curtain onto the bed, but Callie hadn't finished with me.

"Damnit, I told you not to come here. Somebody could pick up your trail. Somebody could be hanging around, just waiting for you to pull some dumbass stunt like this!"

"Well, y'know, Mrs. Salvo—."

"Mrs. Salvo didn't have some damned thing try to rip her throat out!" She glared at me for another few seconds, stuffed the pistol into her bag, and stomped out the door and down the hall. I followed, locking my door, finding her in Mrs. Salvo's apartment glaring daggers at Lulu, who had her finger to her lips in a be-quiet gesture. Mrs. Salvo raised herself off the couch and smiled, the pain and fear largely gone from her face.

"You are *Señora* who is mother of this angel?" She patted Lulu's smooth face with her wrinkly old hand.

"I claim her. And you are Mrs. Salvo?"

"*Juanita Salvo.*"

"*Soy* Callie Lawrence. *Usted Mexicano, Señora?*"

"*Soy Cubano. Vine aqui con mi familia hace muchos años.*"

Callie turned back to us "She says she came here with her family many years ago." Then, to Mrs. Salvo: "*Su esposa?*"

Mrs. Salvo rattled off a long answer. Callie told us what she'd said. "Her husband is dead. She has a daughter in Los Angeles and a son in Cuba working for a big company. She won't leave here because her husband is buried in New Jersey."

Callie sat down in the worn easy chair with her bag at her feet. She asked a long question that had the word "animal" in it several times.

"She said she saw the animal go in, and the man take it away, and then the police came." Callie leaned forward smiling, and asked another question using the words "*la vida a este muchacho.*" I think she told Mrs. Salvo my life was in danger.

Mrs. Salvo put her head back and opened her mouth as if remembering something, and said "*Vi a unos hombres calvos!*" She continued on, excited.

Callie turned to me, frowning. "She said now she remembers. After the police left, she saw bald men head down on the street. She says they hung around looking like they were up to no good. I think they were trying to pick up your track."

"Remember, the guy in my cab with the cat? He was bald."

Callie turned back to Mrs. Salvo, asking something about the bald men and the animal. And Miguel Salvo.

Mrs. Salvo switched back to English for emphasis. "I have no son by that name," her old face wrinkled in sadness. Then she shook off the memory, smiled at Lulu, patted her face and got herself up and hugged me with her good arm. "I am very tired now. The pills make me sleepy. I will go and sleep now." She shuffled toward her bedroom. She stumbled slightly, and I took her arm. I helped her into bed, tucking her in under an old quilt made from flannel work shirts and pieces of cotton fabric like her dress. She smiled at me tiredly, said "*Gracias. You are nice boy.*"

"You ever think of moving? A nicer place away from this neighborhood?" I decided not to tell her the new apartment would be provided by her estranged son.

"I never move," she said sleepily. "I raise my *muchachas* here. My Juan, he die here." She patted my hand. "*Via con Dios.*" She closed her eyes.

By the time I got back to the living room, Callie and Lulu had already worked their way through an argument over Lulu's letting me come here and also coming herself.

Callie let out a final exasperated hmph at us two foolish kids. "Look, we've got places to go. The Animata auction starts in an hour." She sat me down and looked me straight in the eye.

"Tim, I want you to understand something clearly. Sources I've been talking to say your existence as a witness is stirring things up. They say they don't think this is an ordinary theft; that this whole business has complications. We need to show up at this auction so you can check people out, but also to make the thieves nervous, make them do foolish things. Then we can—"

"Bait, *Mother*," interrupted Lulu. "Why don't you admit he's just *bait.*"

"Hey, I don't care! This bait's damned mad at being jerked around," I said. "And this bait's ready to do serious fishing."

Callie slapped me on the knee. "Okay, sport. But I'll be watching you every second. You just make sure you don't do something stupid. I'm kinda getting used to you hanging around."

She got up to go, looking sternly at Lulu. "You coming, Miss Independent?"

"Wouldn't miss it." Lulu marched out, with me following like some puppy dog. Callie closed the door quietly behind us, so as not to wake Mrs. Salvo.

Actually, besides the thrill of the fishing, I was pretty buzzed about going to the auction. I'd get to see some of Animata's latest weird animals in real life. My freak-obsessed brother Kyle would want to know everything.

CHAPTER 16

We hustled out of the cab and past the line of Felicity picketers, who booed, chanted slogans and waved signs that read "Animata Antichrist" and "Genetic Purity for All God's Creatures." They looked angry, like they were ready to swing a sign at somebody. With my pre-existing cuts and slashes, I didn't particularly want any new ones from being bashed with picket signs.

As they surged against the police barricades waving their signs and haranguing the well-dressed people streaming into the auction arena, I could pick out three distinct types of Felicity picketers. The Syntho-Jesus Freaks wore robes and long straight hair and glazed half-smiling saintly expressions. The mostly middle-aged True Christians wore antique traditional twentieth-century polyester pants and dresses and angrier expressions. And the Eco-Rad Funkies wore elaborate trashwear made of old plastic and metal scraps, and determined scowls. Felicity had created some pretty odd partnerships, but they'd sure united to give Animata and Genipet a tough time.

"I'd almost join 'em," said Lulu nodding at the demonstrators. But I just found all the weird animals interesting. I didn't see much harm in them, except maybe for the Nasty that had tried to kill me.

Callie handed Talbot's card to a guard, who became really respectful and ushered us inside. We squeezed through the crowd, down a long corridor lined with booths selling genetically engineered bugs. For a thousand or so dollars, people could buy a purple striped beetle, or a butterfly with their initials on its wings, or an orange spider. I'd heard Animata made good money on the bugs, because they sold so many of them. But the really big money was in the animals they auctioned off.

We entered the big auction arena to see spread out before us what looked like an acre or so of wealthy people taking up every one of the plush seats around the center show ring. The smell in the arena combined the fragrance of expensive cologne, the essence of excitement-sweat, and the faint, musky odor of animals I couldn't even begin to imagine.

We settled into seats near the last row, and Callie poked me in the ribs. "You stay put this time. Keep your eyes open for anybody who looks familiar."

"I drive a cab. Everybody looks familiar."

Callie immediately saw somebody she knew in another section and left to sit with them, talking and pointing up at me, trying to find out what they might have heard about the theft.

I obediently scanned the audience. Many were well-preserved older ladies wearing expensive dresses and swirly hair, and husbands with yacht tans, gold rings, and meticulous laser-razor haircuts, all private collectors, no doubt.

Others clearly weren't collectors. In front of us sat a beefy guy with a shimmery vested suit. Two young slickies next to him took notes and peered through fancy designer googles, probably at the online auction catalog. They were certainly commercial dealers or exhibitors, and would bid heavily on really outrageous new animals to show around the country for a hundred bucks a peek.

And farther down front sat some really conservative-looking types, probably advertising guys looking for a mascot to use in ads. With all their corporate money, when they wanted an animal I'd bet their bids would blow the other people out of the arena. The Cerulean would've brought gigabucks from the corporate guys, I was sure.

Right down on the show ring in a cordoned-off box, I could see slickies stopping and bending down respectfully to talk to somebody there, then quickly moving on. A guy standing in my way moved a little bit, and I recognized the well-groomed back of Talbot's head. He sat there all polished and cool, letting everybody bow down to him to say hello. Miravelle strode across the front, scanning the crowd. He bent down to talk to Talbot, who nodded. Then Miravelle waved to a guy by the door, signaling that the auction should start.

People gripped their numbered identification paddles, ready to bid. The paddles were a peculiar touch, I thought. The auction could've had computers registering electronic bids, like at cattle auctions back home, but here they still used the traditional old hold-up-the-paddle method. I guess the waving got everybody excited and bidding higher.

Lulu wisecracked about the people, but still craned her pretty neck to see as many as she could. "See that guy? Bet he's cheating on his wife." Lulu pointed to a sleek gray-haired guy, sitting two rows down, next to a matching sleek lady.

"How can you tell?" I was more interested in Lulu's slim body, with all its sweet warm promise, sitting so close to me.

"It's clear as New York tap water. He's brought Mrs. Wife here to buy her expensive animals. Keeps the old lady happy while he bounces some Betty in the Bronx."

"I'm impressed. You sure know a lot."

"Yes, I do," she grinned, recognizing teasing when she heard it. "How old are you?"

"Twenty-two."

"A child! Well, see, I'm twenty-three. I know a year's worth more than you."

I worried over the age difference, until the tuxedoed auctioneer marched out into the blue-carpeted auction ring and started his announcements about bidding and payment. He finished and with a flourish, waved the first animal out, and everybody hushed, sat up and got all tense and expectant, ready to be amazed. Some of these animals had never been seen before.

The auction started simply. First came a large cat-dog "cog," a big furry, cat-eyed pointy-eared animal with a doggy-looking body, loping along at the end of a leash. Its fur had a cat-like tortoise shell pattern, but was long and silky like a spaniel's. It stumbled once and nervously strained back against the leash, but despite the strange temperament, the bidders started out fast, lifting paddles discreetly and coolly, keeping the excitement and the price down. A big four-sided display screen visible all around the arena lit up with genetic symbols I didn't understand. But the dealers wrinkled their brows and took in the information like it was from the Bible. The price jiggered its way up, bid by bid, to half a million, and the cog was sold.

Below us, Callie moved across the arena to somebody else she knew, huddling and talking, gathering more intelligence.

The auctioneer kept the animals coming, now only cogs and dats—they called them Beautipets—escorted by girls and boys in tuxedos, and the collectors got more and more excited, waving their paddles high.

The last Beautipet, honest-to-God, was a dog-fish "*dish!*" It flip-flapped out on webbed paws, wagging this floppy finlike dog tail, with shiny scales and black fishy eyes and fish lips over doggy teeth.

"My God, how blecchy!" exclaimed Lulu.

But the collectors and dealers went crazy, bidding up and up and up. The handlers had to spray the animal with water every once in a while to keep its scales wet, and its bark sounded kind of gurgly. It was one ugly, oddball animal, but it would certainly attract crowds, so it went for ten million to one of the exhibitor guys in shiny suits.

They'd just started auctioning the bigger animals—Artanimals, they called them—when Callie came back and asked me if I'd seen anything. I hadn't, because I'd been looking at the animals, with an occasional sneaky side glance at Lulu. She had great little ears, too, with cute little lobes.

"Good job, Sherlock. Remind me to order your junior detective badge."

I shrugged and promised to try to do better. I did pay more attention to the crowd until they brought out the next animal, a long-haired white leopard! Gasps rose all around, but not much applause, because everybody tried to look seriously cool. The leopard padded around at the end of its leash, its fur hanging down all silky and shiny. Like the cog, it stumbled a little bit every so often, and I wondered whether the genetic engineering had left it a little lame. That didn't appear to bother the bidders, and paddles shot up all over, as bidders whispered to one another and talked on the googles. The leopard went for twenty million, causing little sighs of amazement to flutter across the arena.

Lulu grumped some more about the poor creatures, but I kept quiet, still thinking the animal was really something. Callie saw somebody else she knew and left for another huddle.

Then the lights went down, eerie electronic music filled the arena and a spotlight lit the center as the auctioneer announced the beginning of the Mythic Creatures series. The dramatic lighting and music aimed to drum up excitement, but I couldn't see how the crowd could be more excited. They fidgeted in their seats and craned their necks for a better view. Now we'd see animals out of our oldest dreams, our oldest stories, our oldest nightmares.

A guy led this beautiful white stallion into the arena, and people began oohing and aahing. For an instant, I couldn't figure out what the big deal was, until I realized that folded tight against its body were these feathered wings. A Pegasus! The sleek animal pranced around showing off those wings, muscular haunches, and a beautiful mane. Then the handler shouted a loud "HUTHUT," and the animal unfurled those huge, white-as-snow wings, flapping them mightily and rearing up on its hind legs. The crowd went nuts!

Now the sleek, gray-haired guy two rows down grabbed the paddle from Mrs. Wife and started bidding himself. So did the corporate guys, who probably had a car they wanted to name the Pegasus. Again, up, up, up went the bids, so fast the auctioneer was dancing around the ring trying to keep up. The Pegasus went for a hundred million bucks, and the rich guys who lost clenched their jaw muscles in manly disappointment.

I had to pee. The coffee and juice and water I'd drunk that morning suddenly announced to my bladder that it was time.

"I gotta go," I whispered to Lulu.

"*Mother* said to stay put." She sat forward to find Callie, who had moved again.

"I don't think these seats are waterproof."

She looked at me like I was some kind of child. "Kids! Well, then I'll go with you."

"And what? Hold my hand? I need both. C'mon. What could happen to me with all these people around?" I stood up, determined to go.

Sure, well, maybe partly I was trying to impress Lulu a little, but I was also sure nothing could happen in a crowded arena.

She shrugged "It's your funeral, boy."

What really convinced her to stay was what was happening in the arena. Attendants had wheeled out a huge covered cage. As I squeezed down the row and into the aisle, they whipped off the red silk cover to reveal a dragon! Despite my complaining bladder, I stopped in the aisle for a look.

A handler poked the twenty-foot-long beast to get it riled up, and it tossed its big, scaly, frilled head and opened its mouth to show huge, pointy teeth. Then it hissed so loud we could hear it in the stands, like a gas station air hose let loose. It looked like maybe a mix of horned toad, crocodile, maybe a Komodo dragon and all kinds of other genes from slithery things. But it was close enough to a dragon for me.

The rich guys and the exhibitors and the corporate guys all thought so, too, because they forgot all pretense of decorum and started waving their paddles like crazy. I thought a few of them were going to swat their neighbors.

The ringmaster's voice seemed to pump up a notch. "Ladies and gentlemen, behold the dragon! Oriental symbol of royalty and good luck. Legendary guardian of great fortunes! Now let us see what fortune this remarkable creature will bring."

The bidding hiked upward at a million bucks a shot, reaching one hundred twenty million, but I really, really had to pee, and I figured the bidding would go on for quite a while. So, I pushed through the crowd at an entrance and into a hallway that circled the arena, spying a men's room door. The dragon had drawn everybody else into the arena like a magnet, but when I have to pee, even a dragon can't keep my attention.

The men's room was empty, and I stood up against a urinal and started my business, staring at the wall. Somebody else came in, no doubt as bad off as me, but I kept staring at the wall and the nice tiles and let the relieving stream flow on.

I'd just realized that the guy hadn't taken a urinal but had come up right behind me when I felt a sharp jab in my back. I flinched.

"Don't turn around!" said a whiny flat voice. "Don't even move!" I felt another jab and winced.

"What the hell—"

"I've got a hypo-gun needle at your back, kid. It's full of stuff they use to put horses down . . . even elephants. You move, I punch you full of this shit, you're dead."

About that time, I seized up, shut down, lost all interest in peeing.

"What do you want?"

"Put junior away. Just walk out in front of me."

"Can I wash my hands?" The request wasn't as goofy as it sounded. I was buying time to figure something out. Maybe get a look at him in the mirror.

"Hell, no! Just move! Out the damned door!"

I got myself stowed away and zipped up, and stepped back really slowly, so as not to get jabbed again. We passed the mirror on the way out, and I quick-glanced sideways, getting a look at him. He was short and squatty, with a fat round jowly face, a flat nose and little crinkly ears. And he was bald.

CHAPTER 17

Bald Squatty marched me past the ushers and the guards and out the door. We passed the picketers, but they were too busy picketing to see that I was being kidnapped. The hypo-gun wouldn't have shown anyway. I'd seen in the bathroom mirror that Squatty had draped a coat over his hand.

I was so scared my guts churned like I was on a heaving ship, and my knees were wobbly and near to giving out. But at the same time, part of me hung in there, trying to figure a way out. That same brave part also determined that it wouldn't show Squatty that he had me scared.

I couldn't break and run. The little tugs on my t-shirt told me he had hold of it with his other hand. So if I pulled away, he'd hold me long enough to pull the injection trigger, then turn and walk away quiet-like, while I collapsed and died.

We walked out to the curb and he poked me with his hand, like you'd guide an elephant, to go right. I did, and we reached a battered white van sitting at the curb, motor running. Squatty poked me to climb in the seat behind the driver and gave me another jab with the gun to remind me why I should mind him. Squatty got in behind me and slammed the door, but the guy in the driver's seat didn't turn around, showing only the back of a head with long, stringy brown hair.

"Hands behind ya!" barked Squatty, holding the gun against my neck. I turned sideways in the seat and put my hands behind me, and a band tightened hard around my wrists, biting into the flesh.

"Look, I don't know what—"

"Shuddup! Not another damn word." Squatty whacked me on the back of the head. "Awright, gogogo!" he commanded the driver, and the van jerked forward, throwing me back against the gun's needle-point.

Everything went black, and for an instant I thought I'd been injected, but Squatty had dropped some kind of hood over my head. I sucked hard to draw in breaths under the suffocating, hot cloth and trickles of sweat ran down my temples. I worked hard to convince my churning stomach, wobbly knees, sluicing sweat glands, and other panicked body parts that I'd get out of this. Somehow.

To figure out where we were going, I tried to pay attention to how the van swerved as we turned corners, and strained to pick up characteristic street noises. After all, I was a cabbie. I ought to be able to figure those things out. But my concentration was a little distracted by the band cutting into my wrists and the smothering hood over my head and the poison-filled needle against my neck.

We bumped over a bridge and rattled along potholed roads for a while. The van made one last turn, stopped, and I heard the rattly metallic sound of a big steel door opening. We jerked forward, probably into some kind of garage. Squatty opened the door and dragged me out. I smelled old oil. He pushed me forward and I stumbled and started walking, feeling with my feet. My foot hit something metal and I fell over, bashing my face onto a concrete floor.

"Take the damned hood off! He doesn't know where he is."

I knew that voice! It was the bird-faced guy! Sure enough, when Squatty yanked the hood off, there he stood with his beaky nose, holding a wig in his hands. They'd taken me to a big abandoned warehouse littered with rusty car parts and old tires and piles of metal junk. It looked like a place where car thieves might have stripped stolen cars at one time.

Squatty shoved me through an old steel door and up some metal stairs to a big office/locker room. We walked over stained, cheap gold carpet past a couple of side rooms with unmade cots in them. Finally, we entered a big workroom with large frosted windows, an industrial steel sink and a table with a microwave and empty dinner trays piled on it. The room also held a saggy, torn couch and some battered wooden chairs. Squatty sat me onto one and found some rope to tie my hand-cuffed wrists to the chair back and my legs to the chair legs.

"You won't need these for a while, buddy," he said in that nasal voice, yanking my processor pouch from my belt and pitching it onto the littered table. My googles popped out of the pouch and landed in a used instant dinner tray.

I looked around for a way out. The big, grimy, frosted windows filtered daylight through them, so they probably looked out onto a street.

The bird-guy went off to flick on a monitor and stare into it for a while. They must have set up cameras to watch the front door. Squatty sat down, looking into my face, grinning a stupid, fat-faced grin that showed annoying gaps between each of his teeth. He held up the hypo-gun, showing its cartridge filled with a yellow liquid. He touched the plunger with his thumb and a little spurt of the liquid leaped from the tip, which loomed bigger and wickeder all the time.

"Okay, look, we just want to know what they know . . . Animata . . . the cops. You tell us, we'll just take you way out somewhere and leave you. Okay? You won't know where this is, and everything will be just okay. Okay?"

A faint meow came from across the room.

"You feed the cat?" asked Squatty, without taking his eyes off me.

"I thought you fed the cat," said the bird-guy, his words muffled because he had a mouthful of something.

"You're the goddamned cat expert, Lyman!"

So Lyman was the bird guy's name! Lyman turned and pitched an empty beer can at Squatty, who ducked.

"You stupid asshole! I'd just as soon the kid didn't know my name!"

Since Squatty was, no doubt, the "dumb bastard" Lyman had called from my cab, I wondered whether "stupid asshole" represented a promotion.

Another faint meow. I took a chance at moving and twisted my head around. On the floor against a wall of peeling green paint sat an animal carrier, the same one I'd seen in my cab under Lyman's overcoat.

Brilliant golden cat-eyes peered out the wire-mesh window at the front, and around those eyes, blue fur.

Lyman rummaged around among the food wrappers and came up with an open can of cat food. He smeared some onto a plate and filled a plastic bowl with water and took them over to the carrier. He bent down and opened the carrier door.

And out walked an animal more beautiful than any I had ever seen in my life! Or probably ever would.

The Cerulean was a really big armful of a cat, maybe twenty pounds. It walked with the lithe, muscular stride of a small tiger, carrying its body with the easy, sinuous confidence of an animal that knew its power.

And its *fur!* Its amazing, cerulean fur! Long and luxurious and the brilliant blue of the crystal-clear mountain skies that I'd seen when I climbed to the highest peaks with my dad as a kid. And its fur also shone with a mile-deep shimmering that seemed to generate its own light. Like God had ground up the brightest nighttime stars and sprinkled them into the sunlit daytime sky.

The cat wore a gold chain around its neck with perhaps a gold identification tag, as if anybody wouldn't instantly recognize such a stunning animal.

The cat watched me steadily as it approached. Its gleaming golden eyes—with black vertical slits sharp as knife slashes—harbored a depth, a seeming wisdom beyond what I'd thought possible in an animal.

Time had stopped for me only twice before in my life. Once at a swimming pool, when I stood in dumbstruck sixteen-year-old awe, gazing into smiling green eyes belonging to the most beautiful girl I had ever seen. She had smiled so warmly at me, her silky sunlit golden hair wafting in the breeze, and her slim, young body tanned to a perfect coffee-with-cream. She was Cindy Jasper. And time had also stopped when I first read *The Old Man and the Sea,* and I sat in the dark in my room utterly lost in the stunning power of its words, wanting so badly to make such thoughts come alive.

And now time stopped again, as I stared at a cat so fascinating that—here I was kidnapped, tied up, threatened by a poison-filled gun—and I still couldn't take my eyes off it.

And the big cat didn't take its eyes off me. Ignoring the food and water, it strode right past Lyman and walked up to me, holding its tail high like a banner. It twitched that glimmery blue tail back and forth a few times, sat down and curled the tail gracefully around its blue paws. Its ears swiveled forward and it stared at me with those glowing, golden tiger-eyes. All the animals I'd seen at the auction—the cogs and dats and the Pegasus and dragon—paled next to this amazing creature.

"Damned fine-looking animal, ain't it?" asked Lyman. I realized he was talking to me and nodded.

The Cerulean looked me up and down, like it was analyzing my situation, assessing my character. I'd never had a cat do that. Regular cats look at you with vague cat-interest, maybe checking to see if you have food for them, or if you're going to step on them. But this cat was sizing me up, I swear to God. Its look was not a cat look. Something really different was going on in this cat's head.

A stinging wallop across the face took my mind off the cat.

"Now that I got your attention, you ready to talk to us, asshole?" asked Squatty.

"What could I possibly know?"

"You went to Animata. Tell us what they know. They mention us? They say anything about us?"

As the cat still watched, he grabbed a fistful of my hair and held the gun's needle-tip right up close to my eye, squirting out a few drops of yellow liquid to remind me what was in its injection cartridge. I held as still as I could, trying to hold down my trembling. One flinch would bring an eyeful of poison.

"As far as I can tell, they only know what you already saw on viddies. I told them about the bird-guy . . . uh . . . Lyman . . . and what I saw in my cab, but that's it." Squatty put down the gun, and I relaxed a little.

"Yeah, but how are they trying to find the cat? Where are they looking?"

"Look, they aren't going to tell me—" He punched me hard in the mouth, pain slashing through my face.

"And the cops? What do the cops know?" asked Squatty, pulling back his fist for another shot.

"The cops showed everything they know on the network," I lisped through a swelling lip. "Beyond that, they don't confide in me." Squatty punched me a few more times, snapping my head back, raising starry twinkles in my brain. Warm blood trickled out of my nose and down my lips. I felt a loose tooth with my tongue. My head lolled forward as I grew woozy, so Squatty left me alone for a while to clear up, as he went off and huddled with Lyman, arguing about something. My eyes started to focus again, and I looked around for the Cerulean. It had eaten its food and drunk its water, and was gliding around the room, examining things—the windows, the door, the table. I kept getting the feeling that the cat was figuring something out. Dusk darkened the room, and Lyman turned on the lights. Squatty came back to me, apparently with a new bright idea.

His whiny voice took on a tone of mock sympathy. "I remember seeing on the viddie how you got your shoulder hurt. Is it okay now, buddy?"

Before I could answer, he ripped my shirt neck down over my shoulder, saw the healing wound and slapped it hard. It hurt like hellfire, but I kept my mouth shut tight. Tears began to well in my eyes, but I took deep breaths and forced them to stop. By God, I wouldn't give him the satisfaction of seeing me cry!

Satisfied that he'd inflicted the optimum amount of pain, Squatty sat down in front of me again, his fat face in mine.

"Okay, kid, one more time. We'll go over everything you told Talbot and the security guy. And everything you told the cops."

I was about to get stubborn again and not tell him diddly. But I realized there was really no reason to hold anything back. Anyway, I could buy time to figure a way out of this mess. So, I started talking. I talked slowly and carefully through swollen lips for maybe ten minutes, when Lyman suddenly barked "Hey!" He bent down, staring at the viddie monitor. Squatty's attention left me.

"What?"

"Somebody downstairs."

"Who?"

"Shit, I don't know. Can't tell. Get the gun." Lyman leaned forward and stared at the screen even more intently.

Squatty pulled a big, black automatic pistol from a jacket hanging on a hook on the wall. He slid back the bolt with a snap. "Say, Lyman, don't get freaked now. It's probably Geni—" He stopped and looked at me. "It's probably the guy, y'know? Coming early."

"Great! Great! We'll get this over and get our asses out of here. Put him in the closet. I'll get the cat." Lyman scooped up the Cerulean and put it into the cat carrier. Squatty untied me from the chair, checked my plastic wrist cuffs, yanked me up and walked me over to a closet. He shoved me in, and I fell hard onto a pile of boards and rags.

"Look, pal, you make a sound, I put a coupla rounds right through this door. Hear?" I just glared at him, so he slammed the door and locked it. After my eyes adjusted, the sliver of light beneath the door gave me enough light to see that the closet also held a metal clothes rod, but nothing that would help me get loose.

The door was thinner than they realized, because I heard Squatty say real low, "We still going to put him down like you said?"

"He's the only witness they got. And like I said, a little prick for a little prick." Lyman laughed that same acid cackle I'd heard in the cab.

I managed to get up and back myself against the closet wall. My heart pounded so hard it rattled my whole chest. And my knees felt jittery-rubbery, and my stomach knotted into a solid chunk of twitching muscle.

I'd decided on a plan. Whenever the door opened, I'd push off and slam into whoever opened it. I'd knock them down and get up as fast as I could, given that my hands were tied behind my back. I'd run hard at the nearest window and try to crash through it. And take a chance that I'd survive the gun, or the broken glass, or the two-story fall. Pretty lousy plan.

CHAPTER 18

Through the door, I could hear Lyman and Squatty whispering, figuring out what to do. Then, sounds like Squatty going to the outside door, readying himself for whoever was coming up.

The sound of a massive shattering of glass exploded into the room and Lyman hollering "WHAT THE HELL—," then loosing a scream of pain that abruptly cut off, with a wet sound of something ripping, like meat. From his carrier, the Cerulean loosed an unearthly screaming yowl.

Squatty's footsteps pounded past the closet door and the thunder of gunshots shook the room, wild, like a desperate man trying to shoot something that couldn't be hit. A deep, resonant, snarling growl rose from a huge throat, furniture shattered against the wall, and Squatty begged "OH, NO, PLEASE! JESUS!" then made only terrified gibbering sounds in that high flat whiny voice. A loud thud rattled the closet door, like something slamming against the wall next to it. Squatty's gibbering cut off, followed by a liquid sound, like somebody pulling a clenched fist out of a tub of Jell-O.

The cat continued to yowl like a demon. Even through the door, I could sense *Something* hulking moved around the room. It continued to give out a deep, grunting growl, like a big animal hunting.

Something sniffed at the closet door, and the sliver of light at the bottom darkened into shadow. I froze absolutely still, breathing through my mouth, trying to will my thudding heart not to explode out of my chest like I was sure it was about to do. The *Something* scratched at the door and bumped it experimentally, the deep thud telling me that the *Something* lurking on the other side was really big, really vicious.

A splintering crash interrupted the scratching, like somebody had kicked in the front door. "Down! Down!" said an unfamiliar voice. The sniffing and scratching started up again. I kept quiet. The cat still yowled in rage.

"Jesus, shut up, will you?" said the voice. But the cat continued, now adding spitting and hissing, like water on a red hot griddle.

"Okay! Okay, cat!" Then the voice changed to a command, apparently to the *Something*. "Go to the truck! You hear? Truck, now!" The sniffing around my door stopped, the sliver of light brightened and the grunting faded into the distance. Then a tell-tale scraping sound, like the cat's case being moved. A low cat-growl going past the closet door, like the cat was being carried out. Then all grew quiet.

I waited a *really* long time before I did anything. I listened hard for any little sound—a sniff, a growl, a shuffle, a rustle. Anything that would tell me that the *Something* still crouched on the other side of the door waiting for me to come out. What could that thing have been? Certainly not the little Nasty that had attacked me. A *Something* much bigger, A *Something* monstrous. I decided to think about that much later. I struggled to my feet, took a bunch of deep breaths, steadied myself, and listened some more. Finally, I braced myself against the back wall and kicked hard. The door held. I kicked again. Still it held. I got claustrophobic, standing there in the dark with my hands bound behind me.

"Okay door, cooperate," I whispered, prayed.

I gathered all the strength I had left and really walloped the door. The lock tore off and the door swung open, but a soft obstacle stopped it from swinging all the way around against the wall.

The sickening, metallic smell of blood vapor filled the room. Red spatters speckled the walls, even up the windows. One large window was shattered, large chunks of glass scattered beneath it. A dark red pool of congealing blood spread across the dirty wooden floor in front of me, looking like some sick abstract painting. I peered through the crack between the door and the hinged jamb to see what had stopped its swing. An abstract mound of glistening red and pink. I stepped out and nudged the door closed with my foot.

Squatty slumped over behind the door, leaning against a blood-smeared wall, his legs twisted at a grotesque angle. His stomach lay ripped open, glistening pinkish-white intestines hanging limply out, as from a butchered deer. His left hand twitched, his mouth gaped open in the remnants of his last horrified scream. His dead eyes were wide open, his round face showed a puzzled expression. I retched, barely avoiding vomiting and backed away into the room.

I looked across the room only to see the top of Lyman's bald head on the floor wedged against the old couch. But I realized with another wave of shock and nausea that the couch was too low to have a body stuffed under it. It was just Lyman's blood-spattered head.

Head reeling, stomach volcanoing, I leaped for the big sink and threw up everything I'd ever eaten in my life. Every bit of food, from this morning's breakfast to that triple hamburger I had two weeks ago. When I was emptied, I gagged and spit and tried to wipe my watering eyes on my shoulder. I gathered myself. A screaming-crazy panic tried to engulf me, but I was determined not to let it. I spat again and took a couple of gasping breaths, turning back to see Squatty lying there, eyes fixed.

I forced myself to think about what I had to do. First, I had to get my hands free. I found a kitchen knife by the sink and took it down the narrow hall past the bedrooms. I had to get out of that bloody room. As I'd been looking for the knife, I'd glimpsed what I thought were more body parts scattered around. Maybe I saw a piece of Squatty's guts, but I was determined not to look at them straight on.

I stood in the hall and tried to work the tip of the knife between my wrists to push the blade against the plastic band. But my hands were so numb, I dropped it a couple of times and had to lie down on the floor and grapple for it. Finally, I had the blade in place and began to saw.

It seemed to take forever, standing there in the hall sawing . . . sawing . . . sawing. And listening for growling or sniffing or scratching. I tried to distract myself from the pain by remembering what was important back in that room. I tried to remember if my googles were still there. I thought they were.

The band stretched, then snapped, and my hands came free. The thin white plastic strap still clung to one wrist, embedded in the deep red welt there. I peeled it away, pitched it against the wall and rubbed my wrists until the feeling started to come back in my hands. I took a few deep breaths. My face and head ached bone-deep from the beating, and the welts on my wrists felt like they were on fire. Not to mention the slashed shoulder and cut chest. Now what would I do?

My answer came in the form of the distant whine of sirens. The cops had finally gotten around to checking out whatever call had come in about gunshots in a crummy part of town.

I could picture what would happen when they came in and saw this bloodbath. Lots of questions, no answers, no cat, no killer. Just me. Then me in custody as the surviving accomplice, and Callie and Lulu out there with some kind of murderous monster that would rip them apart in a heartbeat if they got too close to the cat. And unfortunately, Callie was smart enough to get really close. Things had changed, I realized. I didn't just need Callie. She needed me. I couldn't be just a kid who'd gotten himself caught up in a mess. I had to help fix it.

The sirens grew louder. I took a last deep breath, steadied myself, then went back into the bloody room. I retrieved my processor and googles from the table, taking care not to walk through the pools of blood. But even without my footprints, I knew the cops would figure out what had happened. Their forensic team would do DNA tests and stuff. Soon enough, they'd figure out that the cat and I had been here, and that something had smashed through a big, thick window and torn apart two people. But that figuring would take some time.

And maybe during that time I could figure out what in God's name was going on.

CHAPTER 19

Just as the cops pulled up at the front of the warehouse, I managed to shove open an old rusty door at the back. The scraping and squeaking must have attracted their attention, because I heard a shout behind me and the sound of feet clattering their way across the junk in the warehouse.

I ran hard down the dark alley, stumbling over a pipe here, a box there, trying to put distance between me and the cops. It didn't work.

"Halt! Police!" sounded behind me, then a clang of garbage cans and a curse. I ran as hard as I could. My legs had quit shaking, glad to have something to do, and I pumped them hard to forget standing in that dark closet and then coming out to see those torn-apart corpses.

I reached out and grabbed air, pumping my arms, running hard, but the cops ran just as hard. I decided I'd better pay attention to what was around me, to figure out some way to lose them. I realized why Lyman and Squatty had chosen this area, dead empty at night, with no people at all; just some old, rusty metal warehouses, a couple collapsed into rubble.

I reached a corner and two shots exploded behind me. A chunk of brick bounced off my head, giving me a hard knock. They must have found the bodies and pegged me as the killer. I zipped around the corner and pounded ahead harder. Now I wouldn't be just captured. I could be killed!

Above the sound of my panting and my running stumbling feet, I heard a low, steady thumping ahead down the alley. I ran out onto a street crowded with motorcycles, battered old gas cars and bicycles. The thumping was louder now, and I recognized it as the bass rhythm to brainbangers-loud rock music.

Another holler behind me spurred me on. Another shot and the thwang of a bullet off a car. I'd apparently had the bad luck to be chased by cops in good shape. I crouched low next to the building, sprinting toward the light of an open door, reaching it and launching myself through it.

The sound, the odor, and the sight all hit me at once like some big engulfing mass. The sound of wailing synthesizers and guitars; the odor of sweaty, oiled bodies, a funky jungle-smell, warm and moist.

And the sight of an undulating sea of near-naked, oiled, shaved bodies, covered with e-tatts. The e-tatts, powered by body heat, glowed and moved across the skins of the bodies as they danced a waving and slithering dance. I'd never seen so many smoothie-baldies in the same place. Their computerized, electroluminescent e-tatts animated in glowing rainbow colors across glistening skin. How they stood the pain of having those millions of nanoparticles shot into their skin I'd never understand. One slim, young woman had an e-tatt snake slithering up her belly and around her neck. A herd of white horses galloped across the shiny chocolate skin of a man. A really fat woman had room for a whole body-canvas of dizzying, swirling colors.

I'd stumbled into an oily-ball, one of those schizzy parties that smoothie-baldies held. Elizabeth and I'd been invited to one with a writer she knew, but we hadn't had the guts to strip down, shave, oil up and go. And we certainly didn't want to get e-tattooed. Too crazy-weird. I waded into the mass of slick, hairless, shiny arms, backs, heads, bellies, legs, breasts, and butts, all wiggling and jiggling and gyrating to the thundering music from a band on a high steel scaffolding.

"Hey, hairy! What the hell you doing here?" I heard behind me, but it wasn't the cops. It was a massive, beer-gutted smoothie-baldy bouncer, dressed only in a small loincloth that was mostly hidden under his belly.

An animated e-tatt tiger leaped at me from his chest over and over. The bouncer had no eyebrows, no hair anywhere, and he didn't like me and my eyebrows at his party.

I shoved away from him through the crowd, but a rising exhaustion dragged me to a dead stop. I'd reached an area of small tables, with e-tatted smoothie-baldies lounging, drinking, and slicking themselves down with oil. I leaned, panting, against a railing beside the dance floor as the bouncer loomed toward me. But a glimpse of blue uniforms at the door, and the glint of drawn guns, jolted me back to life with the energy of fear. I hurdled the railing and plunged back into the mass of shiny skin, keeping my hairy head low. The crowd didn't like me there, with my clothes on and blank skin.

"Damn! It's a hairy!"

"Shave yourself, fuzzy! Be clean! Get bright!"

"Watch it, furball!"

The oily, sweaty smell enveloped me as I kept low and wove quickly through the fleshy, glowing, tattooed forest. At my level, I pushed through lots of bellies, butts, and the occasional glistening globes of female breasts. The private parts were only semi-private behind small loincloths and thin bikini briefs.

A wave of shouted "COPS!" rolled through the crowd over the head-rattling music.

Another wave of "EEKS!" rolled toward me, but it wasn't a reaction to cops coming. The jiggly people were jumping out of the way, avoiding a snakebot slithering toward me! The cops had released it to come find me! I could see its metallic scales glimmering under the lights as its body wove back and forth, its googly camera eyes searching for me. I stumbled forward, knowing that I couldn't outrun it. I turned back, expecting to face the bot just as it sank its hypodermic fangs into me, injecting a knock-out drug. But it wasn't there. Instead it was whirling round and round above the crowd at the end of a long muscled arm. A smoothie-baldie had snatched it up! After half a dozen whirls, the arm released the snakebot to sail high over the crowd and out an open window. Smoothie-baldies hated the cops' bots as much as they hated the cops.

A powerful hand vice-gripped my arm, hauling me up short. The jut-jawed eyebrowless face of the bouncer thrust into mine.

"Cops after you, man?"

"Uh . . . yeah. I didn't do anything! I was just—"

But before I could finish, I felt myself dragged through the crowd like a kid's doll behind the massive chunk of muscled smoothie-baldie.

"Cops!" I heard again behind me, along with deep-throated commands that sounded like they'd come from cops in a hurry. Over the hammering music, the scream of an indignant girl; the hoarse, drunken bellow of an angry guy.

The bouncer-baldie dragged me through a curtain and into a small back room. He peered out of the curtain, then back at me with little close-set eyes above a broken nose.

"Go through the window. We don't need the hassle of cops in here. Anyway, them bastards is always after people. You got hair, but you still don't deserve a bullet or a bot-bite."

He shoved me toward a small window, just big enough for my skinny body. I waved a thanks at the baldie and dove through it, slamming onto dirty pavement in a dark alley. I rolled once, slicing my hand on glass, and leaped up, running again.

No cop-shouts behind me now; only the fading music and the dim light of an occasional street light.

I didn't stop until there was absolute silence. I reached a building with a dark, recessed entryway and gophered—burrowing deep into the doorway and scrunching as far back into the dark shadows as I could get. Sirens ate into the stillness.

I sat there until my breath came back, then flipped on my processor and fumbled on my googles. I worried that the processor might have been damaged in the chase. It had been thrown around a lot, but after all, it was a solid chunk of silicon and diamond. I'd seen demos where they threw one off the Golden Gate Bridge and it still worked.

My angel appeared as usual, all white and smiling and golden-haired, and I breathed a sigh of relief. She was only binary code, but she was beautiful.

"Hi, Timmy. What would you like?"

"Where am I?"

She paused, still smiling, as she consulted the GPS chip in my processor.

"Latitude and longitude, or street address?"

"Street address."

"You're at 14257 Industry Boulevard in Jersey City. Clean out your yucky refrigerator."

I chuckled in spite of my predicament. Even here, Mom's joke angel-commands were still funny. And it felt better to put a name to where I was, even though it didn't move me one inch away from the place.

Now what? I couldn't go near Lulu or Callie, because the cops were after me and that murderous *Something* lurked around. The *Something* was like that Little Nasty that had attacked me, only big. It was a *Big Nasty*. The name suited it.

I needed somebody who wasn't involved, wasn't known. I needed Mushie.

He didn't have googles, so I asked my angel to contact Louis the cab dispatcher. I talked Louis into linking me with Mushie's cab. Anybody could be listening in, so I had a plan. He answered, and I was nanosecond-quick.

"It's Tim."

"Oh, Tim! We were thinking you had died! What do you—"

"Listen, call me back from a land line. You know the number."

I hung up and waited in the darkness. Mushie would let off his fare, then get to a phone or a linkbooth.

I had time to think. Was this how Hemingway got started, getting himself into dangerous stuff like this? Yeah, it was. He fought in a war and all, and bummed around. I wonder if he ever got kidnapped.

My googles buzzed, and I answered quickly. A cop car whizzed past, lights on, siren off, but I'd scooched so far back in the shadows, he couldn't have seen me. I gave Mushie my location and hung up fast. I flipped off my processor and waited.

I knew I should be dead, by all rights. That Big Nasty should have ripped the closet door off and torn me apart. It must not have been programmed to my scent. Sure, whoever ran that creature didn't even know I'd be there, or I'd be a torn-apart corpse, too. I shivered and settled into a dozing stupor, the Gopher hunkering down.

Next thing I knew, lights shone in my eyes. Headlights. Cops? I jumped up and got ready to run.

"Tim? Where are you, Tim?"

It was Mushie's unmistakable accent. He stood beside his cab, peering down the alley. I limped toward him, squinting at the light. He put his skinny arm around me, helping me toward the cab.

"My God, you are all bloody. You are all hurt! And you smell like cooking oil. I will take you to my home."

I climbed in the back seat of the cab and laid down on the floorboard.

"You can't take me to your place," I whispered up to him. "Your family. Something is going on I don't understand, and I can't put your family in danger."

"I will take you home," Mushie said, with a stubborn finality.

We bumped along over potholed roads, onto an expressway and over a bridge back to Manhattan. Inside an hour we pulled up to his little matchbox of a house with its carefully tended postage-stamp yard out in Yonkers. I stayed down while Mushie went inside. After a minute, a bunch of big dark eyes stared down at me through the car window. The big grownup ones were Mushie's wife and mother, and the little ones belonged to his kids. Mushie introduced me to his wife Lina, a sweet, round-faced woman with a red dot on her forehead. They helped me into the house, and he introduced his mother, whose name I couldn't pronounce. She did her part by chattering a constant stream of worried exclamations in Bangladeshi.

They showed me to the bathroom, where I took off the oily, blood-stained shirt and stared in the mirror at my swollen lip, bruised jaw, opened shoulder wound, sliced hand, and all-around rotten-looking miserableness. I'd finished washing up, when Lina knocked gently and came in with bandages, which she expertly applied. She gave me a big floppy cotton shirt that must have been Mushie's. I came out and sat on the couch, and Mushie's Mama Biswas brought me some ice wrapped in a thin towel for my lip. Then she brought a glass of hot tea with a straw to get it past my iced lip. All the while, she fussed in Bangladeshi over my sad state.

When she saw the welts on my wrists, she insisted on bringing some kind of medicine-smelling salve to rub on them. The salve eased the pain and the tea was good once I got it past my lip, and I felt my appetite sneaking back to see if everything was okay. After a while, Lina brought hot rice and a lamb curry, and I ate that very carefully through my fat lip, while they sat and watched me with great sympathy.

Finally, I told my story. They deserved to hear it. Lina translated for Mama, who gasped and rolled her eyes when she heard all the bad parts. There were lots of bad parts, I realized. They started talking among themselves, and finally, Mushie turned to me.

"You will stay here. I have to go back to my shift, but you will sleep. We will figure things out in the morning."

I was too tired to argue, so they settled me in on the couch, Mama Biswas tucked me in, and I began to doze off. I thought about telling my angel to leave a message for Lulu and Callie that I was okay. But I realized that since the cops had no doubt declared me a fugitive, they could legally trace my calls and after getting permission from a judge, even use my processor locator to find me. I would have to cut myself off from all electronic communications. I'd have to go bare, to ditch my processor. I felt really scared at being so isolated. I stopped Mushie before he left and gave him my processor to put in my locker at the cab garage. The cops would find it, but they wouldn't be suspicious. I kept my googles, though. Maybe I'd need them to plug in somewhere else.

I slept like a corpse, which I might have easily have become over the last day. And I dreamed of corpses. I was surrounded by corpses, dark bloated corpses, but I couldn't get away. So I climbed away, clawing and dragging myself through a black sludge, up to the top of a mountain with trees overlooking a gray flat ocean. I dreamed other dreams, but mostly just lay there in a sleep of leaden darkness.

I slept almost until noon and woke to the giggles of Mushie's kids playing in the kitchen, with Lina trying her best to shush them.

I ached all over as I sat up. Mama Biswas brought me more tea with lots of sugar and some soft eggs that I could chew, and I thanked her. She smiled a sweet old-mama smile and patted me on my bandaged hand, saying reassuring things in Bangladeshi. The kids came in and crawled on the couch beside me, all round-faced and cute, and watched me with big, dark eyes. One leaned over, touched my lip gently with small fingers and said gravely

"It'll be all right. Don't worry, Timothy."

But I was worried. Not much about the lip, though. Now I had to figure out what to do next. I sat and thought for a long time, and a plan finally started forming itself, just as Mushie came in looking like he'd had a rough shift. He said the cops had come in and found the processor. He flopped onto the couch and I tried out my plan on him. It was a really screwy, really dangerous plan, but it was the only thing I could think of to do.

"You are bloody well crazy," Mushie concluded after hearing it. "If you try this, the great Vishnu himself will not be able to help you."

"Well, I've got you on my side, Mushie. Will you help? Will you do what I need you to do?"

I could see the whites of his eyes as he rolled them. "Sure, sure, of course. You'll need all the help you can get."

CHAPTER 20

My plan started as Mushie eased his cab down my street. I stayed down out of sight, asking him to stop on the corner where Salvo's guys hung out. They liked that corner because they could see down the side streets and watch who came out of the subway. I'd stayed at Mushie's house until it was dark, playing computer games with his kids and thinking.

I scrunched down farther into the darkness of the back seat. I'd gotten really familiar with the floor in the back of Mushie's cab. I'd found an old coin of some kind, which was weird because nobody had carried coins for years. I touched my swollen lip, which was getting better. My shoulder still hurt, but it was getting better, too. Mushie let the window down, and spoke to somebody, probably one of Salvo's guys that I described to him.

Next thing I know a voice above me said. "Say, lanky-ass fool, what you hiding down in the bottom of that car for?" It was Granite-head. He wrinkled the brow on his shiny bald head.

"I'm in a little trouble. I need to see Salvo."

"Shit, boy, you think I don't know you in trouble? You hiding there all folded up in the bottom of some damn cab all scabby-looking? You think I'm some kind of big-pack nickie-sucker? Shit!" He pulled open the door, jumped in, slapped the back of the front seat and told Mushie to drive on.

He took out his googles, perched them on his nose and ears and spoke a couple of commands. He was immediately connected. He told his contact that he had the "white little mouse who's up at mamacita's" with him. He said I wanted to see the boss. He listened a minute.

"Okay, we goin'." He leaned forward and told Mushie an address, and Mushie took a left and headed there.

We drove a long way across town. Granite-head didn't say much, but kept looking all around the whole time, swiveling that bald, brown head suspiciously to see inside every car that came near us. I wondered whether I should just forget the whole thing. Just take Granite-head back to my corner and give him some money for his trouble and forget it.

Salvo was probably a murderer, drug-runner, God knows what. And he might be so ticked off at me for endangering his mother, he'd just have Max kill me on sight.

But I had to risk it. He was the only one I could ask for help.

Before my better judgment made me jump out of the cab, it was too late. We reached a big silvered-glass tower building and dipped down into an underground garage. Granite-head got out first and looked around some more. Then, he motioned for me to get out.

Mushie just sat there and looked at me with that worried look. I told him I'd be fine and waved him away. Finally, he drove off.

Granite-head and I went up to a blank steel door, and he hauled me up beside him while the security camera recorded our iris patterns. The security system okayed him, the door lock clicked and we went in. Inside the little lobby was an elevator with a fancy "M S" in gold overlay on polished stainless steel. We took the elevator up to the penthouse, and emerged into a paneled, carpeted foyer that was very crowded with one guy . . . Max.

Salvo must have been planning a party, because Max had what looked like a bottle opener and a corkscrew screwed into his shiny steel skull cap.

He didn't acknowledge our deep past friendship, but silently patted me down. All the time, Granite-head twitched and fidgeted, making it pretty clear that Max was The Man, as far as he was concerned. Max turned, still without saying anything, and unlocked another door, leading me down a long hall and into a huge living room I could've played basketball in. Except I wouldn't have wanted to break one of those floor-to-ceiling windows looking out over the East River. And I wouldn't have wanted to get the room dirty. White carpeting, white couch, white walls, white chairs. All that white made any people in the room look like dirt smudges.

The only color was a couple of red and yellow swirly paintings and a slinky, caramel-brown Yani lounging on the couch in black silk pajamas and no shoes. She was fiddling with her short, dark hair and scanning pictures of fashion models on an e-paper. She looked up and smiled and I tried to smile back without being too friendly. Max went and stood in the corner until he was needed.

"You don't look very well, precious." She leaned back, stretching out her legs, pointing her toes, showing off her figure.

"Well, uh, I—"

Before I could finish stammering, the door opened and Salvo walked in, wearing brown slacks, a beige silk shirt and small beige loafers. He looked like a dangerous animal that somebody had tried to dress up nice so it wouldn't look dangerous. Like a wolf with pants.

"I hear you're in some shit." He motioned for me to sit down, but I was too nervous. Besides, for some reason I decided I'd prefer to die standing up. He sat on the couch by Yani, who curled up making nesting movements like she was glad he was there, but went back to her e-paper.

I launched into my apology. "First, I want you know that I never would have endangered your mom. I didn't have anything to do with—"

"Mama called," he interrupted, with maybe the slightest hint of pride in his voice. "First time in a year. She told me to take care of you."

I collapsed onto a chair in relief. What an irony that a sweet little old lady had saved me from one of the biggest drug lords around.

Salvo told me to give him the whole story, so I explained all about the attack by the Little Nasty, how Callie had saved me, the Animata auction, the kidnapping by Lyman and Squatty. And seeing the cat. And being beaten and thrown in the closet. And hearing the Big Nasty smash through the window and rip two guys into little pieces. And escaping the cops.

"Lamb says the cops are looking for you, but just because you're missing. The woman and her daughter went to them. They think maybe you're dead. The cops are trying to figure out how the two guys got spread all over that room, but the lab tests haven't connected you yet. Lamb says the results will be ready tomorrow." He smiled a cold, predatory smile. "That thing that killed those *gringos*. Wonder if I could get me one, y'know? I'd send it to see some people I do business with." Yani shivered, switched off the reader, and shot him a mildly scolding scowl.

I got a chill, too, but I needed to stay on the subject. "Can I get your 'liner to help me?"

"Nothing he can do to help you. That's all he knows. Cops don't have any lab results yet."

"No, I mean help me find the cat. There's got to be some trace of where it went. Some record in the Mirror. In a database, on a camera record . . . *something*. Your 'liner's got a daemon, right?"

"You want the cat?"

"Well, until it's found and returned to the company, Callie, Lulu, me . . . we're all in trouble, I think. The two guys that took it, they're dead. Pretty soon whoever has it now will find out I was there. And I'll get another visit, this time from the Big Nasty."

He smiled slightly. "Yeah . . . the animal . . . that's a good name for it. Big Nasty." He waved at Max, who left the room, returning with Lamb, who was all sparkly-eyed with his usual electro-zombie-from-Mars vacant expression. Without saying anything, Lamb sat in one of the chairs, his big hands covering the chair arms, his big feet in scuffed black lace-up shoes planted in front of him. He plugged his processor into a data port installed in a table beside him. Rich people didn't have to go to linkbooths for high-bandwidth Mirror access. They just ran ultra-high-capacity optical fiber lines right to their apartments.

Salvo waited until Lamb had settled and asked me "Who do you think has the cat?"

I remembered that Squatty had slipped and mentioned Genipet. I suppressed nausea, as I nightmare-flashed on the fact that Squatty's tongue, and most of his other salvageable parts, were now zipped up in a body bag in some morgue. "I think Genipet."

"What's that?"

"A company that makes animals. Like Animata."

Salvo stared at me for a long moment, with those black-marble eyes. He was considering how deeply to get involved. "You go somewhere for a while. Come see me tomorrow. I got to decide if this is some bad shit I don't need to get into. Yeah, you took care of Mama all right, and she said to take care of you. But I got to be careful, you understand? Got to see what's what."

"Sure. But I don't know where I can go."

"That's your problem. Come back tomorrow."

"Look, can you make an untraceable call to Callie Lawrence?"

Salvo chuckled. "Lamb here can do anything."

Lamb took that to mean he should go ahead, because he tipped his head back and assumed an even more vacant expression, if that was possible. Probably communicating with his daemon to find Callie. I suddenly realized that Lamb didn't have to move to communicate with the daemon. And he didn't have to wave his hands around to control movement in the Mirror. Unlike Talbot, he *was* neural dusted—his brain infused with nano-sized receiver/transmitters that his brain had wired into its circuitry. So, he could control his Mirror navigation just by thinking. I stared at this weird wired human, wondering at how that would feel. Then he did move, shaking his head.

"No contact," he said, in his low, guttural voice, like water bubbling up from a weed-choked pond.

"She's probably got her processor off. Maybe even left it somewhere. Can you try Lulu Lawrence?"

Again, Lamb whispered to his daemon. But this time, after a minute, he nodded his head. He'd made contact. "What do you want to tell her?"

"Tell her I'm alive. Ask her where I can go that's safe."

Lamb's lips moved again. He stopped and turned toward Salvo, but with eyes that only dimly registered the real world through an overlay of cyberspace images.

"She said she would pick him up here. I gave her directions."

I said goodbye to Salvo and Yani. I didn't bother with Lamb, who had resumed his head-back vacant stare, probably navigating himself through the Mirror. I followed Max out the door, into the elevator and down to the basement. Granite-head was gone, no doubt back to the street corner to watch over Salvo's ventures.

I stood in the basement garage with Max, waiting. It was like standing next to a boulder. I didn't say anything. He didn't say anything. I tried counting the hash marks. Before I could get a good count, though, Callie's old car rattled into the garage, with Lulu driving, and I jumped in.

"My God, Tim, we thought you were dead! Thank God you're alive!" Lulu hugged me with one arm and aimed a kiss for my lips, but at the last instant, detoured it to my cheek. I couldn't figure whether it was because she saw my puffy lip, or she wasn't ready for lip-kissing.

"I've had a few . . . problems."

"You do look like hell."

Yeah, I do, I thought. *But getting close to you made it almost worth getting the crap beat out of me.* She accelerated out of the garage, leaping into the street and screeching into a turn. She drove like her mother.

"Yeah, well, I'm okay. So you were worried?" That made me happy. She looked really good sitting there in that little shirt and slim, tight jeans with those long legs reaching all the way to the car pedals.

"Well, we were all worried."

"But *you* were worried."

"Yes, okay. I was worried. You're such a child. You happy?"

"Yeah." We left the garage and I slumped down in the seat. No doubt, vampires roamed the night with their cameras, ready to sell virties of me to the nets or the cops.

"Where's Callie?" I asked from the floorboard.

"She made some calls. Said she might know where you were and took off. Left the car for me, in case you showed. Tell me what happened to get you so banged up."

I told her about the kidnapping and the beating and the closet. And the cat; the big, beautiful, incredible cat. And I told her about the Big Nasty. And the bloody chunks of Lyman and Squatty spread all over. I could tell she was schizzed, but she stayed cool, her face deep in thought. She looked really nice when she thought.

"Look, boy, we can't have you wallowing around on the floors of cars and sneaking around. We've got to fix it so you can go out in public, even with cops and guys with animals after you."

"Fix how? Fix what?" I asked from my slumped position.

"We're going to change that face of yours."

CHAPTER 21

The fat guy who opened the door looked ugly as a rotten stump. A big, red-veined nose protruded from his face like a giant wart, his cheeks showed deep purple pustules, and his slash of a mouth dribbled slimy green drool. Lulu jumped and yelped "Jesus Christ, Rudy! You scared the shit out of me!"

The big ugly man shrieked in laughter, grabbing her in a bear hug, and she allowed the familiarity.

"Ah, my little art thief. You like Rudy's creation?" He released her, whirled around, billowing out the gaudy gold silk caftan he wore, and pranced away, waving his hands in the air with glee. "It was such a terrible thing to do, making myself ugly. But that is my art, dear. That is my marvelous art! But come-come-come! I must remove my creation." We followed him through a big living room with huge overstuffed sofas and a skylight. We entered a studio whose walls were covered with face masks. Staring out at us were pretty girls, gangsters, trolls, monsters, old men, children, animals. I stopped and stared around. Standing along the wall was a collection of full-body secondkins meant for covering humies—maids, butlers, sexy women, houseboys, and so forth. It was like standing in a silent crowd. The ugly man whirled around again, fixing his gaze on me.

"And this boy? Who is this pretty boy with these horrid bruises?"

"Rudy, this is Tim."

"Hi," I stuck out my hand and Rudy took my fingertips.

Rudy looked at me, but spoke to Lulu. "And what does the pretty boy want? Pretty boys can have just about anything from Rudy."

"He likes girls, Rudy."

"A *lot*," I added emphatically.

Rudy's eyes widened. "Oh? So, then you are lovers?"

Not yet, I thought.

"No," said Lulu firmly. "He's in trouble."

"That's just like you, little thief," Rudy petted her hair. "Just like you to help out a boy in trouble."

"He needs a new face. He can't go out in public."

I took another look at Rudy's ugly puss. "Look, I don't want some kind of surgery."

Rudy laughed. "Oh, no surgery, boy! Just Rudy's magic." He waved his hands extravagantly and sat down at a dressing table, smoothing his caftan. With great care, he worked his pudgy fingers under the gnarled jaw and picked at it. He lifted off the jaw and cheek to reveal smooth skin beneath.

I stared in fascination. I'd never seen secondskin removed. It looked like he was taking off his face. The skin seemed absolutely real, with blemishes and wrinkles and the translucence of real skin.

He peeled off the protruding brow and finally the big wart of a nose. He wiped his face with a cloth, fluffed back his long thinning hair and opened his hands in giddy triumph. Now he was a round-faced man with mischievous eyes, a pug nose, and a broad grinning mouth.

"Voila! Once more, I am *gorgeous!* That was a test face for a play I'm doing makeup for. The character is a monstrous man who abducts and kills children. I think I captured his *espirit de corpse* perfectly." He giggled at his little pun.

Lulu leaned on his shoulder and gave him a peck on the cheek. "Of course, you were brilliant, as usual, Rudy. Now, what can you do for my friend?"

I said "Look, Rudy, just make me look different. Not, y'know, disgusting."

Rudy studied my face intently. "Rudy knows," he said absentmindedly. He touched my nose, my cheek, turned my chin this way and that. "You certainly have been abused, boy." He touched my lip, still swollen. "Rudy will have to allow for the swelling. And he will have to make you blend in. Rudy can do all that." He glanced slyly at Lulu. "But Rudy requires a consideration."

"*Rudy*," warned Lulu in a cute growly voice.

"Just a teensy favor, dearie. Don't get bitchy on me."

"How teensy?"

Rudy stood up and laid his fingers on his cheek, studying me from a distance.

"Oh, well, considering all the bother, I guess maybe that lovely Friedman you stole the other day. I saw it in his studio when he'd finished it."

Lulu rolled her eyes. "God, Rudy, that sculpture's worth a fortune! And it's not for you, anyway. It's for . . ." She looked at me. She realized I'd been hearing too much about what she did. ". . . no, Rudy."

"Well, then . . ." Rudy made a pouty mouth. ". . . if you're going to be a little bitch about it, just take your pretty boy and go. Rudy was ready to help, even though it's probably illegal, and Rudy will have to deal with the police maybe, but . . ." He made a bye-bye wave with his pudgy fingers.

"Damn. All right. The Friedman, you old—"

"Delicious! I know right where I'll put it. Out there in the foyer. I've got the cutest pedestal that I—"

"Rudy. Do the face first."

"Yeah, and not ugly," I reminded.

Rudy clucked his tongue a few times, made an indignant chin-up expression at my lack of confidence, and led me to a large gray console in the corner with a chair and a large black plastic cylinder suspended over it. Watching me from the wall were faces of a devil, a fat eunuch, and a pirate with a big scar. I got worried. I hadn't seen anybody on that wall who was normal. Would I be walking around looking like a pirate? Or worse, a eunuch!

Rudy motioned for me to sit in the chair and pulled the cylinder down over my head. It was dark and smelled like lots of other heads had been in there.

"We'll put your head in here and do a scanny-wanny. Get your pretty face in the computer. Then you can see how I'm going to make you plain and simple."

"Not too plain," I said.

"He's already simple," said Lulu.

"It's a laser scan. Close your eyes," Rudy instructed. I did, and humming sounds started up all around my head, rising and falling as if little mosquitoes were buzzing about me. They lasted a minute, then Rudy lifted the cylinder off. He sailed his caftan over to a big leather chair facing a wall-sized viddie screen, floated himself down, and waved for us to pull up chairs beside him. He hit a few buttons on a remote control. His viddie screen lit up with my head floating there in three-D. The shape, the texture, the skin were all exactly like my head. It looked like he'd just removed my head and put it on the screen.

"And there's your pretty self," said Rudy, rotating my virtual head around, cocking it up and down, and examining the scan. "Coloring looks good. No data dropouts. Now Rudy's ready to do his wonderful magic."

For the next half hour, he used hand gestures, a keyboard, and voice commands to reshape my face. He joked around a lot, pulling my nose out like Pinocchio; giving me lips the size of airplane tires. But when he finished, he'd done what he promised. The resulting face was older, anonymous, bland. A nose a little broader, cheeks a little fatter, jawline pointier. But somebody who wouldn't stand out in a crowd. He even made fake ears, to thwart the ear-recognition scanners that the cops used.

"Well, you're not pretty anymore, just ordinary. Okay, my boy?"

"Sure, fine."

Rudy hmphed, pulling himself up in mock indignation. "More than fine. A sculpture worthy of a genius. Shall we do the skinsies?" He heaved himself up and waltzed, humming, over to a big clear-walled chamber, flipping on a few switches there.

We watched inside the chamber as a gray glob of translucent gunk formed itself into the new face Rudy had created. "Electrogel?" I asked.

"Yes, little one. We form your old and new faces using it. Then put them together and inject the secondskin between to make your appliance. So very complicated, but Rudy understands it all." After some more button-mashing, the machine had fashioned my secondskin mask.

"And, voila!" He announced grandly, opening the chamber and peeling off the secondskin with exquisite care, laying the pieces on a tray. He took them up one by one, and used a paintbrush to dab pigment onto the skin, making a blemish, adding a little white scar, perfecting the stunning illusion of real skin.

"And now, boy, we make a new you." He sat me in the chair in the corner and precisely applied the secondskin with adhesive. It stuck to my face, feeling like real skin. He carefully fitted the fake ears over mine, giving me new ones that wouldn't be recognized.

Finally, he held up a mirror, and somebody else stared back at me. The fuller-faced older guy from the viddie screen. I touched the skin. It felt real, too.

"Fine, just fine," pronounced Lulu. "And this will fool the recognition scanners?"

"Oh, dear, you have any doubts?" Rudy made a disdainful *of-course* face that told Lulu her question was absurd.

"Okay, now make him a couple more sets. You know how these things wear out after a while. And also some sets of retinal overlays, to get past those scanners."

"Missy, I am an artist, not a factory hand!" Rudy stood, touched my face here and there, and turned to go.

"You don't have that Friedman sitting in your foyer yet, do you, Rudy?"

"Bitch," he pouted, regarding her with narrowed, accusing eyes. "Little bitchy thief." Then, he grinned magnanimously and kissed her on the head. "Okay, for you I do quantity."

"For the Friedman you do quantity."

We walked out of Rudy's with me wearing one secondskin face and ears, and two more sets in little bags. Rudy had also fitted my eyes with retina overlays, which would fool retinal scanners. Now, I could walk the streets. We climbed back into Callie's car and Lulu swung back into traffic. It felt good to sit up.

"Well, now you're pretty safe. But you can't come back to my place. I did lose the cops going to Salvo's, but I'm being watched. I know a place, though, where you can put up for the night."

"Why did Rudy call you a thief?"

Lulu ignored me, calling somebody to ask if I could stay with them. But I didn't give up.

"C'mon, tell me. Why'd he call you a thief?"

"I'm kind of an art dealer."

"An art thief?"

She swung into a narrow street and pulled up to an old movie theater. "Look, I just make good deals. It's late, and I need to get you settled in here and go check on *Mother*."

We got out and pushed through old wooden doors into the lobby. A big, neon cross hung on the wall across from the doors. And on the cross hung a holographic animated Jesus, writhing around in three-D, multicolored agony. People in robes or shirts and baggy pants sat around on the lobby floor talking, and the old candy counter held all kinds of books and little statues.

Above the candy counter hung a realistic painted mural of a guy in a monk's robes, surrounded by animals . . . rabbits, lambs, cows, birds . . . all kinds, with rich colors, like an old Master had painted it. I think it was St. Francis of Assisi, who I heard about when I went to vacation Bible school as a kid.

I'd just noticed another similar mural of Noah's Ark hanging on the wall where stairs led to the theater balcony, when I heard a voice behind me.

"Greetings," said a tall, really skinny guy with a sparse beard in a white burlap robe. He smiled a smile that took up his whole face. His eyes sparkled like he was on some natural high. I could almost imagine a halo floating above his head. He extended his bony hands to clasp Lulu's. "Lulu, how good to see you again."

"What is this place?" I asked.

"Welcome, brother," he said, turning to me and taking my hand. "Welcome to Felicity."

CHAPTER 22

Felicity! The nut-cases who were hollering and singing outside Animata. I must have looked uneasy, because the guy in the robes spread his hands in a friendly "I'm-a-really-holy-guy" gesture.

"Please, don't be worried. My name is Michael. We're here to help you."

"Sure, fine, thanks, well . . . uh . . . I've got to be going."

"Going?" asked Lulu.

I excused myself from Michael, who stood there still smiling. I took Lulu across the room under the Noah's Ark mural. "What is all this? You're putting me here, right in the middle of a bunch of people who might have taken the cat? They've picketed the auctions, and they've protested the animals. Didn't they even try to steal some and let them loose?"

Lulu pursed her lips and wrinkled her brow. "Okay, I'll give you that they're against Animata. But look at them, Tim. Could these gentle people possibly have sent that animal to kill you? Could they ever have kidnapped you?"

Michael had squatted down to talk to some people sitting in a circle with Bibles. They were smiling, ever-smiling. Uncle Ned once said that people like that probably smiled when they took a dump. The smiles seemed fake, like they were really up to no good.

But then I thought about the Little Nasty that went after me, and the Big Nasty that had killed Lyman and Squatty. No, these people certainly couldn't be behind that. I remembered that Squatty had let Genipet's name slip, too.

"Yeah, okay, maybe they didn't send the Nasties," I conceded to Lulu. "But they still could be connected with the guys who took the cat. Like helped them, or hired them." Sure, Felicity was probably harmless, but this business had been so screwy, I had to remain suspicious. I realized sadly that I had to be suspicious of Lulu, too! After all, she'd brought me here.

I warily nodded okay, and we went back over to Michael, who had just finished with the smiley group.

"I appreciate your help," I said.

"Well, we're glad to do it. And we wanted you to see the other side. Lulu told us you'd gone to Abomi-nata." He said the word with a sneer, which made his imaginary halo slip a little bit. "Let me show you our church. We're very proud of it." He led us toward what used to be the movie auditorium, and I lagged back to whisper to Lulu.

"How do you know these guys?"

"I knew the artist who painted these walls. He's a church member. He introduced me."

Inside the theater a big crowd, almost a full theater, of old ladies, young men, street people, and slickies sat watching . . . *nothing*. The old theater screen was blank. But they all sat there staring raptly, googles on, plugged into data ports along the backs of the seats. A bunch of them oohed, then aahed. One guy yelled "Yes, Lord! We hear you!"

"What are they watching?"

"Sermon on the Mount," said Michael. "We've got a really great syntho Jesus. Tonight he's doing the sermon. When we do the crucifixion, we need a doctor present. People faint." He seemed really proud of that fact. I took my googles out and held them up, as if to ask his permission. He nodded, and I sat down and plugged in. I found a joystick attached to the armrest, put on my glasses, and plunged into a virtie world.

I was in a broad, sunlit desert, at the foot of a small rocky rise, with other avatars floating all around me. Most of them took the form of bearded saints and other biblical-looking guys and women with shawls. But some were like ones I saw in the Mirror—colored geometric forms or animals like cats or dogs, or statues of Greek gods. I wondered what my default avatar was, since my processor with my Hemingway avatar was now in some evidence locker at Manhattan Center station.

Against a brilliant, cloudless blue sky stood a tall figure in a flowing white robe, with hair blowing, like in a faint breeze. He raised his hand and blessed the avatars. I plugged in my earphones.

". . . So, if you apply your algorithm to somebody else, that same algorithm will be applied to you. And if you detect some little bug in his moral coding, you'll miss the major bug in your own . . ." I listened some more, but it didn't sound much like what was in Mom's Bible. I unplugged.

"Modern service, eh, Michael?"

"Yes, this is the cyberspeak service, for people more comfortable with computer jargon. We do other versions in political, academic, business—"

"Sounds righteous," I said. But it was really just a little too virtie for me. I liked my Jesus more traditional, a plaster guy on a wooden cross.

"You'd be surprised who we bring to the Word this way."

"Like who?"

"The fellow who invented the cat."

I tried to remember the little guy's name, the one I'd seen on the screen at Animata. "Rozoff?"

"Yes. He came here a long time ago for our blessing-of-the-animals service. He came back several more weeks for the cyberspeak services. Then he didn't come back. We only later realized it was him."

I'd have to chew on that one a while. Imagine it; the guy who started the whole genetic animal industry showing up smack in the middle of the opposition!

"And he didn't speak to anybody?"

"I tried to get him to share his feelings, but he just wanted to keep to himself. So, we respected that."

Michael realized he was keeping us on his tour too long and apologized. He offered a meal, and I accepted quickly. He took Lulu and me up to the theater's balcony, which they'd walled off into a kitchen and some sleeping rooms. He fed us some hot vegetarian loaf with bread and water. It was pretty basic, but I ate like crazy, not having had anything since the soft eggs at Mushie's.

Soon, though I'd be master of my nutritional fate again. Back to tacos, fried rice, knishes, and slabs of steak at the steak house where they gave you onion rings the size of bicycle tires. But for now I ate their holier-than-grease food dutifully, and afterward Michael showed us to a little room with a cot and a lamp.

I hopefully asked Lulu, "You want to stay and talk a while?"

"I've got to go find *Mother*." She said it a little too emphatically. Maybe she knew I had my own definition of "talk," and she was determined to get out of there before she got tempted. At least I hope that's what her tone meant.

"Yeah, okay. Nighty-night."

"I'll be back in the morning. We'll find out whether that guy, Salvo, will help you find the cat." Then she hugged me too quickly for my liking and left.

I thought about stripping off the secondskin, but it really felt like part of me, so I left it on. Good thing, because I fell asleep so fast, I probably wouldn't have made it through the de-skinning, and ended up half me, and half that other anonymous-looking guy. The last thing I remember was wondering how we'd steal the cat back from Genipet.

CHAPTER 23

"The cat's not at Genipet," Lamb said in his gurgly-resonant voice, his statement ringing with certainty. Lulu, Callie and I sat in Salvo's living room the next morning, with Lamb staring into cyberspace. He sat in the same big chair in the same position. I wondered whether they just hauled him away at night, chair and all. Salvo wasn't as interested in me today, though. I was the same old Tim, I'd made sure of that. I'd taken off the secondskin to avoid becoming another hash mark on Max's hand when he didn't recognize me.

Ignoring me, Salvo appreciatively scanned Lulu, who still wore a little bitty sparkly party dress—apparently work clothes from the night before. And Callie looked at Salvo like he was some kind of bug. She was mad partly because her bag was lighter, since Max had taken the two pistols out. Yani was notably absent; this was business, and Max stood as usual in the corner like a huge metal-topped floor lamp watching all of us. Today, he'd dressed formally, his steel skull cap sporting a chrome eagle's head mounted on the front like a hood ornament.

"You searched the whole company?" I asked Lamb. I tried to get myself into his line of sight, as if that made any difference. "You sure you could have seen it if it was at Genipet?"

For the first time, Lamb showed an emotion. He was insulted. "If it was there, I would have found it. I can tap into the company's security cameras. I did find it."

"You did? Well, why didn't you say so? Where?"

Lamb paused, actually being dramatic. Two emotions in one day was probably a strain for him..

"Animata."

"*What!*" Lulu, Callie, and I said in unison, looking at each other, startled. I thought I'd heard wrong.

"You got 'em mixed up. You mean Genipet," I said.

"I mean Animata." Lamb's voice sounded like somebody flushing a toilet.

I stood and paced. "Animata! Why would they get the cat back and not tell anybody?"

Salvo laughed. The first time I'd ever heard him do that. It was not a pretty sound. "You are one dumb son-of-a-bitch gringo. They probably got some insurance scam going."

"Or maybe . . ." Callie paused to get our attention. "They stole it themselves in the first place."

"Okay, so why would they do that, *Mother?*" Lulu uncrossed her long legs, attracting Salvo's cool gaze once more.

"Don't know, dear. But it's a possibility."

"In any case, we got to tell the cops." I pictured Lieutenant Rocky taking the big Animata building with a SWAT team, guns ready, cameras on. "They can go in. They can sort it out."

Salvo laughed again. We were providing him considerable amusement today. "Shit, man, cops go in, they find nothing. Animata gets rid of the cat, and you're still in deep shit. You got to get the cat."

"Me? Me?" I remembered the big guns the Animata guards wore, the explosive security bracelets, and all the other stuff they had to keep people like me out.

"Yeah. It's your problem. You go in," said Salvo. "We get you in easy, but we get half of any insurance reward."

"I'll go in," said Callie. "It's me who got this whole operation going."

I guess my young macho hormones kicked in then, because Callie's volunteering evaporated just about all my reluctance. "Callie, you saved my butt already. I owe you. This is what I owe you." I could see she was ready to object, but I gave her my determined look. The Gopher was a determined guy when he wanted to be.

She looked at me hard for a long time before speaking. "Okay, then, but these guys have to prove the cat's there."

We all looked at Lamb expectantly. Salvo nodded to the 'liner, and he pointed to his processor. "Plug in. I'll show you."

I moved down the couch so I was close enough to Lamb, put on my googles, and plugged into a port on his processor.

Suddenly I was floating in the cavernous virtual lobby of Mirror Animata. But this time, instead of my angel, a black sphere hung in front of us, an ominous-looking object that didn't seem to reflect any light at all. It was like a hole in cyberspace. "Is that the daemon?" I asked Lamb.

"Yes," said Lamb, ever talkative. Just as we'd seen before in the virtual lobby, the friendly young guy-avatars floated around, greeting other visiting avatars as they came through the big front doors. One floated toward us, but passed without saying anything. I realized we were invisible to it! Something else dawned on me.

"Lamb, did you follow me to Mirror-Animata the first time?"

"Yes."

"Did you delete that knight?"

Salvo's voice intruded on the scene. "I told him to keep track of you. You gave the knight some files. We wanted to find out what they were."

I realized with a shock that I'd witnessed a cyber-murder. "So you deleted him."

Salvo: "He would have gone, anyway. He was sick."

I was sure Salvo would "delete" real people just as readily as Mirror avatars. I almost bailed out of the whole deal then, but decided to stow my doubts. Finding the cat was more important.

In the Mirror, Lamb's virtual hand touched his little control box, and we eased forward, the daemon floating in front. We passed all the same exhibits I'd seen before in the Mirror Animata. But now *all* the virtual doors were visible—doors that I'd only seen at real Animata.

The daemon could let you see things that the security system normally hides from regular avatars! No security system could keep it out! I shivered at the power the daemon gave people like Salvo.

Lamb's virtie hand touched another button and the doors and walls faded to a filmy partial transparency. Through them, I could see virtual machines, avatars, and white cubes that signified data storage

"Take us to security," Lamb instructed the black-sphere daemon, which responded by changing its shape from sphere to cube and back. We floated, ghostlike, up through transparent virtual ceilings, from floor to floor, then sideways through a couple of data-storage rooms, and into a virtual security center. One of its walls was covered with viddie security monitor screens and glowing buttons. Another wall showed a map of the Animata complex, with moving colored icons marking people. A couple of avatars, basically cubes with guys' faces on them, hovered before the screens, scanning corridors, rooms, laboratories. One of the faces was Miravelle's, and I flinched before I realized he couldn't see me. He was probably using the Mirror from a remote location to check on the security status of Animata headquarters.

We floated unseen in the corner, until Miravelle and the other avatar abruptly vanished, done with their business, leaving us alone in the virtual security center. Through the transparent wall, I saw another avatar float past in the virtual hallway. Now I knew why Lamb was so strange. He spent his days as an invisible cyberspook haunting the Mirror, watching everything.

"Now I will show you." Lamb reached out his virtie disembodied hand, and touched controls on one of the screens. The image of a room appeared on the screen, bare, except for a carrying case and food and water bowls.

And the Cerulean! The cat paced back and forth, his rich blue fur glistening in the light.

"Damn!" I whispered as if somebody might hear me. The cat was as mesmerizing as before.

"What?" asked Callie's voice.

"It's him. It is him. He *is* at Animata." The cat stopped and stretched his large body, the little gold chain reflecting the light. He yawned, showing sharp white teeth, and continued to pace. Lamb touched a control, and the screen grew to cover the entire wall. He scanned the camera, and we saw a bolted door with a small window in it. I took off my googles, and I was back in Salvo's living room. I took a second to readjust. "I just can't figure it."

"So, you going to get him? The cat?" asked Salvo.

"Well, yeah, but I don't know how."

"Easy. We do this all the time. Lamb, he takes over the security system when nobody's looking. He opens the doors for you. Makes you invisible to the cameras, the body temperature scanners. He's a 'liner; he can do about anything, eh?" He inclined his head at Lamb, who stared blankly back at him.

I thought about the guards with the big guns and the ever-watchful computer. "And if something goes wrong, I'm in there alone."

"Like I say, we do it all the time. You just got to have the guts." Salvo looked sideways at Max, the big solid floor lamp, who registered a slight flicker of satisfaction on his big face, maybe at the memory of a successful job.

"So, when?"

"Tonight. Maybe two, three in the morning when nobody's around. Meantime, we put you in a crib somewhere safe. Not here. Cops pegged you at the scene where those guys were killed. They're after you heavy. We'll pick you up from the crib tonight, take you to the company. We wait in the car and you go in. You get the cat, we haul ass. We drop you someplace with the cat. Give you a disk with the security camera viddie proving you got the cat there. You take the cat and the disk to the cops, and you're clear. And we get half the reward."

"Yeah, okay." I nodded and got up.

Salvo uncoiled and stood, his body taut, like he was anticipating a real charge out of this operation. "But only you." He looked at Lulu and Callie. "We keep the numbers to a minimum. We don't need anybody to be in the way."

"Look, I want to be there to watch his back," objected Callie.

"Then it's off," said Salvo, turning to go into the bedroom with one last appreciative glance at Lulu. "No skin off me, eh?"

I patted Callie's shoulder to reassure her. "Okay, Miguel. Your way. Thanks for everything."

"*De Nada,*" he waved his hand. "You help Mama. You . . ." he didn't finish the sentence before he left. But I sort of knew what he wanted to say. He thought helping me might get him back in her good graces.

Max escorted us out, and Callie demanded her guns back and got them. We stopped outside where we'd part company, with Callie and Lulu going back to Lulu's. They stood and looked somberly at me for a long time with those matching blue-gray eyes. I could tell they were both deciding whether to put up a fuss about leaving me.

"You're a good kid," said Callie, hugging me. "You be damned careful."

Lulu patted me on my good shoulder. She didn't say anything, but her chin was very stiff, like she was trying to keep it from trembling. Lulu the toughie.

Salvo's limo took me to a little hotel in mid-town, whose pudgy, nervous desk clerk didn't ask questions. I got into my little room and ordered out sandwiches from a deli down the street. I got a roast beef and a big pastrami, one of those kind where the pastrami is juicy and as tender as butter. I got extra half-sour pickles. I saved the roast beef for a late snack.

I watched the Cop Network on the room's viddie. The news update confirmed that the cops were looking for me now. In the viddie, they made cop-noises about me being suspicious and wanted, even though they couldn't charge me with anything. They said the DNA lab reports showed my blood at the murder scene. A commentator speculated that I might have given false evidence to throw the cops off the real trail.

Talbot appeared on the screen, looking all smooth and confident. He had his sad face on. He said they were worried that something had happened to the Cerulean. Of course, the human deaths were of utmost concern, he said. But unfortunately, the outlook for the Cerulean was not good, he said.

I still couldn't figure all this out. Talbot has this great moneymaking cat dumped in his lap. Then it's kidnapped. Then he talks about it being dead.

Maybe Lyman and Squatty did do the kidnapping alone. Maybe they were bad guys and wanted to ransom it back. Or maybe sell it to Genipet, so Genipet could develop its own animal.

Or, maybe, for some screwy reason, Talbot and Miravelle hired them, which would've been really strange.

But whatever the case, the two guys got ripped apart, and the cat ended up back at Animata. But Talbot didn't admit it. Maybe because he used a Big Nasty to kill the guys. But why do that?

I let all this churn round and round in my brain. As my head hit the pillow, I thought about messaging Mom and Dad. But I figured I'd better not involve anybody else in this until it was over. And it would be over soon.

CHAPTER 24

"This is *real!*" I panted to myself, on the knife-edge of a panic meltdown. "This is *really* real!" I stood on the deserted road leading to the service entrance to the big Animata laboratory. Salvo and Max had let me out of the electric limo and sped away whisper-quiet into the darkness. We chose this entrance, because it was the only one that didn't go through the headquarters building.

I took a deep breath, psyching myself. Pumping up the brain cells. Persuading the muscles, the pounding heart, the swimming head, to go in.

Max had fitted his metal skull cap to be particularly hazardous this time, with a row of razor-sharp serrated blades screwed in down the center. He was ready, but was I?

I adjusted the earphone Lamb had given me, so I could hear his instructions and his warnings. He sat back at Salvo's place, no doubt in that same chair with his big feet on the floor, plugged in, ready to ask his daemon to break in invisibly to Animata's security computer. It was dead-quiet at 2:30 in the morning. A guy in a white t-shirt walked by on the sidewalk, but kept his head down. He didn't want to make face-to-face with whoever was out this late at this strange place, either.

I walked up the narrow service road, staying in the shadows, and reached the gray-painted steel access door beside the big overhead freight door. I grabbed the steel handle and pulled. It didn't budge. I backed up and fiddled nervously with the fake Animata security bracelet Lamb had given me so I'd arouse less suspicion. Yeah, right, I thought. Like this buzz-freaked kid wandering the halls at night wouldn't arouse suspicion.

"It's not opening," I whispered to Lamb.

"I'm still working," he gurgled in my earphone. "Hold."

"Hold?! *Hold?!* I'm out here with God and everybody watching and you want me to hold? Christ, can't you—"

The door clicked and Lamb said "Try it."

I yanked and the big metal door swung open with a faint creak that in the quiet night sounded like a fifty-pound screech owl. I walked into a big shipping room, crowded with boxes, barrels and empty cages on rollers.

"Go through the door on the right," I heard in my ear. I walked up to the door, and just as I reached it, the lock clicked, unbolting. So far, so good. I stepped into a long hall, bare except for an emergency shower jutting from the ceiling.

I decided the way to get through this was to act like I owned the place. Be the Gopher. Cocky Gopher. Look cocky, feel cocky, be cocky. I strolled cockily down the hall, legs wobbling.

"Take the elevator to the fifth floor," Lamb told me, as he tracked me on the Animata security viddie screens.

"You sure I'm not showing up as an intruder?" I found the elevator and it sensed I was there, as the display over the door showed it starting down the floors.

"No. The computer thinks you're a night technician."

I froze. "And what does this guard think who's heading toward me?" A large security guard had rounded the corner ahead. He had a bad hangover problem: his belly hung over his belt, his jowls hung over his collar, his eye bags hung over his face. He had one of those really big pistols strapped to his hip. He looked me over and eyed my security bracelet. I nodded. He stopped to get on the elevator with me.

"Working late?" he asked.

I tried to remember I was the cocky Gopher. "Yeah. Got this thing Mr. Talbot wanted out. New . . . uh . . . snake."

The big man scowled. Did I screw up? Was this the end? I tensed.

"Hate them damned snakes. They try to make 'em fancy, but they're still snakes."

"Yeah, slimy and all." The elevator door opened, and I got on. The guard followed me and punched four. I punched five, and we waited together as the silence grew awkward. I tried to look cocky. After what seemed like about thirty years, the door opened on four and he got out. He turned back.

"Y'know, I haven't seen you before." He stood there holding the elevator door.

I thought furiously about what to answer. "I was at the other place."

"Which one?"

I wanted to slap his hand off the door and take my chances that he couldn't get his pistol out before the door closed. "Uh . . . up north."

"North?" He looked puzzled. I tensed again. "Oh, you mean out west up north."

I breathed a silent sigh of relief. I hoped he thought the sigh was just a comment on the place. "Yeah. West north."

"How'd you like it? I got a chance to go work up there. Turned it down."

"Good for you. Cold. North, y'know."

"Yeah, I bet. Utah's pretty, but I couldn't take the isolation. Well, see ya." He let the door close and I backed up against the wall for support.

I emerged onto the fifth floor into another long empty hall, lined with dark metal doors. Lamb told me to go right, four doors down. I did and stopped before a blank steel door with a brushed metal silver handle.

Lamb in my ear: "Try the handle."

I pushed it down, and it swung open into an empty, dark laboratory. I'd settled myself down. I found lights, switched them on, and shut the door behind me. The big, fluorescent-lit room had lab benches against the walls and what looked like two animal treatment tables in the middle. There was a third stainless steel table that had a kind of trough on top and a cart of surgical instruments beside it. That must be a dissection table. The room was lined with doors that probably led to cage rooms.

"One of these rooms?" I asked Lamb.

Before he could reply, something stirred in the corner, awakened by the lights and my voice. A familiar growling arose from a carrying box on the floor, and a Little Nasty emerged, its dead black-marble eyes blinking at the light, his lips showing the early beginnings of a snarl. He was just like the one I'd seen in my apartment, with one unfortunate exception. I didn't have a gun to shoot this one!

He loped out into the room on powerful bow legs carrying a sleek, low-slung muscular body, and glared at me, head low, still growling.

"Lamb, you missed one of the security systems."

"What's going on?" Lamb asked, but I didn't have time to reply. I was working hard at being friendly.

"Hi," I said, realizing how stupid that was to say. "Nice . . . Nasty." That was even stupider. He didn't believe for a second I belonged here. He went into a full snarl, curling his little black lips to show razor-sharp canines that would plunge deep into my throat very nicely, if he reached it. He slinked back and forth looking for an opening, muscles tensed for a spring.

I jumped for the cart, grabbed a tray full of instruments and flung it at him. The clanging and clattering of metal instruments confused him for a second, and he backed up. He snarled again, Nasty-drool glistening on his fangs, and extended claws that would do a good job tearing out my innards.

I grabbed a shiny metal saw and waved it back and forth, making what I hoped were intimidating anti-Nasty grunts. Unimpressed, he loped forward into an attack leap.

Behind me came a poof, like a balloon popping under a towel. A bloody hole blossomed in the Nasty's side and he yelped, twisted and snapped at air, trying to bite whatever had attacked him. He staggered sideways and started to drag himself toward me, fangs bared, eyes dull with shock and pain. Another poof, and the top of his head flew off in a pink spray, and he collapsed dead.

I turned to see Max standing just inside the door holding his pistol fitted with a silencer. He'd come in to rescue me!

"Man, am I glad to see you!"

But Max just looked around the room, checking for more Nasties. That was fine. We didn't have to be best pals, as long as he took care of Nasties.

"What happened?" I heard in my ear. I informed Lamb about his error, adding a muttered insult about him having wires crossed. He replied, "I guess that wouldn't have shown up on the cameras."

"Well, we learn something every day, don't we?"

He directed me to the middle of three doors. I pulled it open and found the Cerulean, sitting there, blue and incredible, his tail curled around him, watching me calmly.

"Hi, pal. Been a while since we saw each other."

He started to talk cat-speak to me, meowing and making sounds in his throat. The throat sounds abruptly became a growl.

"I'll take him," said Max behind me, putting away his pistol and moving forward. But the cat laid his ears back and bared his teeth, sending more growling sounds from deep in his throat. His claws unsheathed. They were unnaturally long.

"I don't think he likes you, Max. He doesn't know you like I do."

I stepped forward cautiously and picked up the cat. He allowed me, but continued to growl at Max. It was like picking up one big solid sinewy muscle. He twisted around to grip my shoulder with his front paws, and I could feel his power. One of my fingers got tangled in his gold collar with its round tag. His fur was incredibly thick and soft and a lustrous blue. Holding him was almost addictive, and I'm not a guy who goes strange over cats.

I made myself slip him gently into his carrying box and latch it. Inside, he turned and I could see his face looking out the little wire mesh window on the door. He didn't take his golden eyes off Max.

"More guards coming. Get out," gurgled Lamb in my ear. We did, moving quickly down the hall to the elevator. I could tell the door was being held open by something, but I couldn't figure out what, until I got close. It was the guard's body! I whirled to face Max.

"My God, what have you . . ." But I stopped. He had his pistol out, leveled at me. From inside the case, the cat growled and spit so loud it sounded like a steam train chuffing.

"He was trying to stop me. I had to get to you." Max had this hoarse whiskey voice. I realized I'd never heard it before.

I stared at the gun, rage building. Something was deeply foul here, but I decided to keep quiet until I could figure it out. Max dragged the guard's body into the elevator and hefted it against the back wall. It had been nothing but a door-stop to him, I thought disgustedly. I stepped in with the cat, who growled steadily at Max. I couldn't blame him.

Except for the cat growl, we rode down in silence, as I stared at the face of the dead guard and the red stain on his blue uniform. I thought about him sadly. He hated snakes. Probably close to retirement. Maybe a little house in Florida. I barely held the rage in check, but I had to keep clear, to think. We'd just reached the ground floor when I realized what was so weird about all this. Max hadn't had enough time to get to me, if he started out when Lamb first heard the Nasty over his earphones. Max had followed me from the very beginning. Maybe if he hadn't needed me to handle the cat, I'd be dead, too!

Chapter 25

When Max and I piled into the car, Salvo confirmed that my being alive wasn't part of his plan.

"What the hell's he doing here?" he barked, as we sped away into the darkness, jouncing along Philly's rutted streets.

"Cat wouldn't let me touch him," said Max, holstering his pistol, which settled the cat down some. I'd set the carrying case directly across from Max, so the cat could keep glaring at him, which he did. I could see the cat through a side vent, sitting, eyes fixed on Max, with his nose right up against the window in the carrying case door.

Salvo lounged across from me in his expensive gray suit with the black silk shirt. He stared at me, thinking. He didn't like unfinished business, which I was. I stared back, letting him know I wouldn't be finished easily.

"So, you and Max had plans I didn't know about?" I asked.

"Yeah, plans. Old plans. Now we just make new plans." Salvo pushed a button to lower the partition to the driver's compartment and told the driver to head for "the place." The car accelerated with an electric snap onto the freeway, weaving past trucks and other cars. I wished the windows hadn't been tinted. The people craning their necks at the limo would have gotten a real eyeful.

"So, after Max killed the guard, he was going to kill me next? Leave me there?" My rage bloomed, wiping away any fear, fueling cold calculation. So, we were going to "the place" to finish me off. That meant I had time to play with Salvo's head, maybe get an advantage. I'd had good practice on my brother, rat-boy Kyle, but this was playing for my life. "Dumb plan, Miguel. That would've been really syntho-brained."

Now Miguel's eyes briefly flashed in anger. None of his toadies ever questioned his intelligence like that.

In a flash, he whipped a knife from his pocket and pressed its point against my throat. I gulped. "Dumb? *Cabrone,* we got you. We got the cat. Pretty good plan, I'd say." He pressed the knifepoint enough to draw a drop of blood. He enjoyed having me under his control. Then, his honor preserved, he stowed the knife and leaned back. He didn't handle such messy chores. He would have just as soon let Max earn another hash mark right there, but my blood and guts would mess up the upholstery.

He smiled and leaned back his head, sprawling extravagantly in the leather cushions. He waved his hand at Max, who poured him a tequila shot. He downed it with a flick of his wrist and looked at me with this satisfied expression like he was looking forward to the amusement I would provide.

I tried using guilt. "What about your mama? She said for you to help me."

Salvo shrugged. "You going to just disappear. I didn't have nothing to do with it." He smiled. "You're a murderer, and murderers disappear. And Mama wouldn't like you no more, anyway."

"Murderer? What do you mean? The security cameras would show Max killing the guard and me taking the cat, and—"

"What cat? There wasn't no cat! There wasn't no Max!" Now Salvo really laughed, opening his eyes wide. Even Max showed small twitches around his ugly lips that could have been the hint of a smile.

I looked puzzled, and Salvo liked that. He reached over and touched a button on a little viddie screen on the limo's bar. It glowed to life, showing the hallway of the Animata lab building.

"My 'liner, he's a real master. He downloaded this to me. He changed the security viddie. This was the viddie he left at the company." On the screen, I came walking down the hall just like I had before. But I held a gun in my hand now. I stopped at the elevator and pressed the button. The guard's voice on the viddie said "Working late?" I shoved the gun into the back of my jeans just before he stepped into the picture.

"Yeah," I said like before. "Got this thing Mr. Talbot wanted out. New . . . uh . . . snake."

"Hate them damned snakes. They try to make 'em fancy, but they're still snakes."

"Yeah, slimy and all." The elevator door opened like before, and we got in.

The scene changed to another camera. Fourth floor. The elevator door opened and the guard got out, stopping and holding the door like I'd remembered.

"Y'know, I haven't seen you before."

This time I pulled out the gun and fired, and the guard staggered and slumped to the floor, blood oozing from his chest. I poked my head out of the elevator and looked up and down the hall, then dragged the guard into the elevator as the door closed.

Salvo flicked off the viddie. I must have looked pale, because he said "Not so smart-ass now, are you, little shit?"

"But that didn't really happen," I said weakly.

He laughed again. "It did according to them cameras. And they also show you just poking around some on their computers and leaving. No cat. No Max. Story'll be you got it in your head you could steal secrets and sell them. This is just business, you understand? We sell the cat to whatever company bids highest. *Si,* it's a fine piece of business. Animata'll pay big and keep their mouths shut. Good deal for them. They don't have to say nothing about them having the cat, because viddie don't show no cat. And that other company, Geni . . . whatever . . . if they bid higher, they keep it quiet, too."

"And me?"

"You? Viddie proves you just a little dumb shit that got all screwed up in his head and broke in and killed a guard. We had a good plan before. Before, viddie'd show you and the guard killing each other. Nice and neat, and we don't worry about no extra body. But now we got a new plan . . . now viddie shows you killing the guard. Then, the cops find you all keeled over in a vacant lot with the gun in your hand, fulla fairy dust, you'll be just another overdose. That'll work, too."

That couldn't happen, I thought. I wasn't scared for myself at all. What would my folks have to go through? And Callie and Lulu? They'd know the truth, but they couldn't say anything. As Salvo sat there smugly enjoying himself, I realized with a shock that he would probably kill them, too, just to tie up loose ends.

But I kept my mouth shut, furiously thinking, as we got on the Jersey Turnpike, heading into Newark. I figured "the place" where I was to die was in Newark. Salvo's twisted sense of order dictated that I had to die at this particular place, his killing field. I didn't have much time, so I had to start something pretty soon. At someplace that was busy. We came to the end of the turnpike and drove down into a slummy area of Newark, twisting and turning through the dark streets. Salvo turned around and said something to the driver. The driver fumbled in the front seat and held up a plastic bag. I could see a syringe and a bottle of white liquid in it. The means of my death. The time was now.

"YOU CANKY LITTLE SPIT-BRAINED PIECE OF DOG TURD!" I bellowed. "YOU'RE NOT GOING TO DO THIS TO ME!" With my right hand, I punched at Salvo, who easily dodged, but it had the desired effect. Max drew his pistol and poked it in my face. The cat reacted to the pistol, yowling in rage, spitting and clawing at the case door. I kept grabbing at Salvo with my right hand to keep his attention, but with my left I unlatched the case.

The cat exploded out of it like a big blue bullet, ricocheting around the inside of the car, yowling his lungs out. Max waved the pistol around, trying to get a shot at it.

Salvo twisted around as the cat leaped into the front seat. "*CABRÓN! IDIOTA!* DON'T SHOOT IT! CATCH IT!" Max hauled his mass out of his seat and turned around. As he leaned over into the front seat trying to grab the cat, his skull-cap blades embedded themselves into the limo's headliner, holding him fast. Just what I'd hoped. Still trying to pull his head free, he swiped at the cat, who hissed and leaped square into the driver's face. The driver swerved the limo wildly back and forth, ramming it into a parked truck with a bone-rattling crash that slammed us all forward. I hit the button on the side window, praying that it would lower fast enough.

The cat scrambled wildly all over the front seat, and I could see Max fumbling for him, managing to grab a handful of fur. Max roared in pain as the cat sank its needle-sharp teeth into his hand.

Just then, Salvo realized I'd lowered the window and twisted back toward me, reaching for his knife. For an instant, he left himself open. With immense satisfaction, I hauled back my leg and plunged my foot deep into his crotch. The black little eyes bugged out of their sockets and he uttered a heartfelt "oooooffffff." I flipped around and, using Salvo's crotch as the launch pad, shot my skinny body out the car window.

"Now I know why your mother hates you!" I hollered back at him, rolling once, leaping up and sprinting down the street, leaving the commotion behind. I passed a couple of guys leaning against a building drinking beer, and reached an alley. From behind me, the sound of balloons popping, and the guys with the beers slammed against the ground, hollering curses, as bullets ricocheted around them. I swerved into the alley, still running at top speed. I thought I could run pretty damned fast, but I was nothing compared to this furry blue streak that zipped past me and down the alley into the darkness ahead. The cat had made it, too! Cool!

The alley ended in a board fence, which the cat and I both scrambled over just as car lights lit up the alley. A string of balloon pops, and a Swiss-cheese of splintery holes erupted in the fence behind us.

But we were long gone.

CHAPTER 26

So, this anonymous-looking guy who was a little older than me, with a fatter face, broader nose, pointier jawline and bigger ears walked down the street where Lulu's loft was. He limped a little, walking differently than me so the gait-recognition scanners wouldn't detect my walk. He wore a Manhattan Delivery Co. baseball cap that he'd swiped out of a truck. He carried a cardboard box, like he was delivering it.

I thought the secondskin made a pretty good disguise, especially because nobody in New York ever really looked at each other. So, none of the people I passed would notice if my face peeled away a little. Or that the heavy box I carried kept bumping around, making me almost drop it a couple of times. The Cerulean was being patient, but he wanted out, and I half expected him to burst through the top. Even New Yorkers would notice an electric blue Cat-in-the-Box.

I didn't see any cops or Salvo's black electric limo, now with a smashed front end, or any slickie security types from Animata. Sure, everything was okay now, but I knew it was only a matter of time before I got caught. The cat shifted inside the box again, and it almost tipped. I needed a plan. I needed to get out of town, and Lulu and Callie could help.

I scanned the street again, and not seeing any cameras or people watching me, took the big old freight elevator to the set of lofts that included Lulu's. I stepped out onto her floor. The cat shifted again, but stayed quiet. I was glad he wasn't a meower. I reached Lulu's door and knocked.

"Delivery," I said in my best deep New York voice. I waited and knocked a couple of times. I tried the door and it was open, which was especially weird in New York. Inside I found the usual mess. Shank sprawled on the back of the couch, looking up and baby-crying loudly. He leaped down, walking toward me, tail up in greeting. Priss spied me from the kitchen and rubbed a chair leg as practice for rubbing mine. I heard a thump, and Albert poked his head in from the bedroom door. The blob sculpture woke up, swayed back and forth and sagged downward, turning blue. It looked sad.

"Nobody home, guys?"

Shank answered with another complaint. Priss rubbed up against me, and Albert plunked down and began grooming his fur, as if to say "It's okay that you showed up, but I'm not especially excited to see you."

I set down the box. "I brought you guys a really incredible playmate." I opened the top and the Cerulean's large blue head emerged.

The effect was as if I'd zapped each cat with a cattle prod. Shank screamed and leaped over the couch, eyes wide. Priss arched her back and danced away sideways, growling. Albert simply vanished like a fat ghost. Then, so did the other two, so fast I couldn't see where they went.

I'd never seen any reaction like it. I couldn't believe the Cerulean's reaction, either. Nothing. He leaped out of the box as if the other cats hadn't even existed. He paced around the loft, sniffing the shifting blob sculpture, staring at the art on the walls, finally walking into the kitchen. With a hiss and a white streak, Priss flashed out of the kitchen and into the bedroom.

"Senile felines," I muttered to myself, dredging up one of Mom's palindromes. I went into the kitchen to find the Cerulean peacefully drinking water from the big plastic bowl Callie had left for the vanished trio.

But there was no Callie and no Lulu to be seen. A big, fat worry-lump began growing in my chest. Something had happened to them, or they would've waited for me here. I had to figure out what to do and get out quick. We were all in deep trouble. Ironically, the absolute best thing that could happen would be that the cops would catch me, I'd be framed for murder, and I'd spend the rest of my life trying to convince big convicts named Hulk that I didn't want to be their boyfriend.

I sat down at the kitchen table, noticing immediately its uncharacteristic lack of junk. Everything had been swept onto the floor, including the sweet potato in the glass of water, which lay drying under the window.

Except for a cell phone, sitting in the middle of the table. Just a plain old-time voice cell phone, not even a genius-phone. A note stuck on it said. "For Boatright." I picked it up and turned it over in my hand, thinking what to do. I almost flicked it on; then I got smart. Somebody wanted me to call them, so this phone was probably a scrambled direct line to whoever it was. But they also wanted to find me, so the second I turned it on, no doubt a GPS would activate, and they'd get an instant fix on me.

All this time the cat watched me like he expected me to say something, so I did.

"Look, pal, we've got to get out of here. I think this phone means something, but I've got to use it where we've got a chance to escape. Okay?" The cat jumped into my lap, thoroughly filling it, and nuzzled the cell phone. I scratched his ears, trying to figure out what to do. He started to purr, but he was so big it sounded like a diesel generator. I fiddled with the round little gold tag on his gold collar. It had some writing on it that said "Home is where the Heart is." That made no sense. Animata sure didn't put that on him, so maybe Rozoff did. Something about that gold collar tickled at my memory, but I'd think about that later.

The cat jumped down, walked over to the box, and with a graceful leap jumped back in. I just stared at the box trying to figure out what I'd just seen. Did this cat understand what was going on, what I'd just said?

I slipped the phone into my pocket and started to pick up the box, then remembered Callie's cats. On a piece of paper, I scribbled "I had an emergency. Could you please take care of my cats? Thanks. Lulu." I picked up the box, and on my way to the elevator, slipped the note under the door of the apartment next door. Knowing Lulu, she probably had friends all over the building, and somebody would take care of Shank, Priss, and Albert. That is, if the cats ever showed their faces again.

Out on the street, my mind still churned away at terahertz speed. Lulu and Callie were in huge danger, and so was I. But before I could help them, I had to get myself someplace safe, where I could check out the phone and plan how to protect them. A plan began to form. I needed a car. I found a public linkbooth and called the cab dispatcher at my company. He said he didn't want me anywhere near the place, but I talked him into patching me through to Mushie. I told Mushie what I needed: a solid, old, untraceable gas car, no GPS, and a full tank.

As always, Mushie was ready to jump in. "I will come and get you. You cannot be out there all alone. Let me help. The guys will help."

"Mushie, you do that, I'll never show up. You've helped enough. Just get the car. I'll send you cash."

"Okay. I know a man who has such cars."

I got his bank account code and told him to leave the car by the subway stop near the cab barn, with the keys under the front mat. After I hung up, I found a bank terminal and took out all my money, eight thousand dollars. I filled Callie's untraceable cashcard with five thousand and transmitted the other three to Mushie's account. Five thousand wasn't much, but it would hold me for a while. Then I carefully descended the steps into the subway, still looking like a delivery guy with a big package. Both the cat and I were tired of lugging him around in a box, but soon I'd have a car.

I swiped the cashcard through the reader to get onto the subway platform. A burly transit cop strolled down the platform, stopping and eyeing the box for a long time. Luckily, the printing on the box said it had originally held a small viddie screen, so as far as the cop was concerned, I'd bought a new one for my apartment. I tried to stand there and hold the box nonchalant-like, hoping the cat wouldn't move around. He shifted, the box tipped a little, and I bobbled it and grinned like an idiot at the cop.

"You'd think they'd figure out how to make these light."

He didn't say anything, just moving on to check out the other end of the station.

184

When the train came, I got on. Rush hour was over, and I found a seat in the corner for me and my boxed cat. An old guy, the kind who always talks to people on subways, took a seat across from me, looking like he was going to get friendly. So, I coughed and hacked like I was dying of some contagious disease, and he decided to move on. I waited until the train was out of the station and flipped on the cell phone.

"Voice check," said a computer voice. "Please talk into the phone." I counted to ten and jabbered some nonsense, and the phone said "Your identity is confirmed, Timothy Boatright." Whoever it was had a sample of my voice to check against.

"Hello, Tim." I recognized Julio Miravelle's voice.

"What's this about? Where are Lulu and Callie?"

"You have the cat, don't you?"

"Where are Lulu and Callie? If they're hurt, you're dead." I surprised myself. I really meant it.

"They're fine. They're staying with us for a while, until you return our property."

"Once we do that, we're all going to be fried and digested, right?"

"No, no, no, Timothy. We have kept the whole matter to ourselves. We have a viddie of you doing something very bad. As of now, the guard is merely missing, but his body could appear, along with the video, if you decide to mention the cat to the police. Simple, no?"

I didn't have much time. By now, they had me pinpointed on the locator. So, I had to get off quick, but still let him think he had me. I also had to string him along, so Callie and Lulu stayed safe.

"Look, I'll think about it. Let me call you right back." I slipped the cell phone under the seat and stood up with the box. At the next station, I got off, made my way around to the other side of the platform and boarded a train going the other way. Thanks to the New York subway system, they'd have a hell of a time catching that phone. Now I just had to figure out what to do with the time I'd bought.

I rode to the station near the cab garage and lugged the cat up the stairs. He was incredibly patient, like he knew what I was going through. Just outside the station, a couple of cars waited at the curb. Which one was it? The first one, a brown Chevy, was locked. A guy in a suit waiting for a cab outside a deli and eating a bagel looked at me funny when I tried the car's door. I gave him my nonchalant look, but I didn't really know how expressions translated through secondskin. He looked even more suspicious when I went over to the other car, a rusty blue Ford, and tried its door. It opened, so I felt around under the mat.

The guy walked inside the deli, and I saw him talking to the girl behind the counter. She picked up the phone. I kept fumbling, found the key, loaded the box into the back, got in and eased away from the curb.

I don't think I took a breath until I was about seven blocks away. I headed out of Manhattan across the George Washington Bridge, moving slow in mid-morning traffic.

I was really thinking long-term strategy now, like the next ten minutes. I couldn't go east, because that's where the Atlantic Ocean was, so I guessed I'd go west. Once I was on an open freeway, I reached in the back and flipped open the box. The cat climbed out and into the front seat, rubbing his face against my hand as I petted him, then sitting there almost incandescent, his blue fur reflecting the sunshine. I had to figure out a way to make him less conspicuous.

In Paterson, I took an exit that took me to a mall with a Safeway store. I put the cat back in the box and asked him to stay there. Talking to him like that seemed a natural thing to do. He looked at me with those understanding eyes and curled up at the bottom of the box.

I went into the mall and spent about five hundred dollars on food, beer, blankets, cat food, cat bowls—just about everything I thought we'd need for the trip, wherever the hell we were going. I felt lost wandering the endless aisles of the big brightly lit stores, with all their shelves of everything anybody could possibly want. Lost in a lot of ways. For the first time, I had no plan at all. Lulu and Callie were God-knows-where, and everybody in creation was after me.

As I piled all the food and stuff in the car trunk, I felt a big knot grow in my throat. For the first time since I was a kid, I just felt like sitting down and crying. I pitched the blanket in the front seat and crawled in the back seat with the box, lifted the cat out and petted him. It was good therapy, and I knew I could do it without being seen, because I was way off in a corner of the Safeway lot, parked so I could see anybody coming.

I remembered the palindrome Mom had recited when I told her I wanted to come here. She'd said "Not New York, Roy went on," with a sort of sad resignation. She'd been right, and so had old "Roy," whoever he was.

"Well cat, what do we do now? What do we do now? Do I go home? My folks would be in big trouble if Animata or Salvo or the cops showed up." He rubbed his face gently against mine and began to purr to console me. I buried my face in his thick, warm fur and tried to think of something. He shifted his great head, and I felt his collar tag against my face. I wondered idly whether there was anything written on the back. I looked at it again, and found that if I held it just right, I could see an inscription that said "If lost, return to Vasily Rozoff, Qualton, Wash."

Well, I sure was lost, I thought. I turned the tag back over. The inscription said "Home is where the Hear is." Wait a second. I looked again, realizing I'd read wrong the first time. There was no "t" on Heart. It said "Hear." I looked the cat in those big shining eyes.

Something about that collar had tickled my memory before. Now the tickle was turning into a poke, a prod. Mom always taught me to revere words, to respect their power. The word "Hear" was like a big crowbar, prying up memories.

Rozoff, gold, collar . . . bracelet!

The collar was like the bracelet Rozoff had worn in the viddie! It *was* the bracelet! At the time, I'd thought the bracelet seemed out of place on Rozoff, being gold and fancy. I shut my eyes, scrunched my face, and tried to remember the bracelet. The cat sat patiently on my lap, purring, waiting for something to happen.

Yes! I was sure they were the same. Rozoff had put his bracelet on the cat and added a tag with this inscription. I stared intently at the cat.

"Did your master just give you this thing just as a present?"

I answered myself. "Not likely. He was a scientist, and they aren't usually very sentimental. He did it for a reason."

"And did he make a mistake on the word "Heart"?"

I answered myself again. "Again, not likely. This guy made sure every detail of you was perfect, cat. He sure wasn't going to screw up even a word on a little tag he gave you."

The cat meowed and looked me square in the face, like he wanted to get in on the conversation. I remembered one of our barn cats who got loaded into a delivery truck by mistake and ended up halfway across the county. He'd found his way home. Cats go home. Cats always want to go home. This cat wanted to go home.

"So that means he made that inscription on purpose? Home is where the *Hear* is?"

"Meow."

"And he knew that you would trust whoever you let get this close to you without slicing them up?"

"Meow."

"And that means he wanted the person to read the tag? To go to this place in Washington where he invented you? Your home?"

"Meow."

I lowered the cat into the front seat, crawled in beside him and started up the old gas engine. I'd sure stitched together a long chain of assumptions. But as flimsy as the chain was, it was the only one that led to some kind of action. And I needed some kind of action.

"Well, okay, cat. If you and Rozoff say Washington, that's where we're going!"

Chapter 27

So, that was how I got here, sitting huddled on this windy, wet porch in Seattle, staring out through the dark, drizzly Seattle night, having lost the cat. I bring myself back to the present, and my imagination takes over. I'm sure I see out there in the gloom the predatory gleam of Big Nasty eyes, or hear the metallic clink of gun bolts being drawn.

On our trip across the country, I drove until I was exhausted and flopped down wherever I could, to sleep. To gas up the old car, I'd slap on the secondskin and the baseball cap and hide the cat in his box. I'd fill the tank at an automated station, zip the untraceable cashcard through a reader at the pump, and be off in a flash. Police cruisers lurking for speeders fed my paranoia, so I stayed schizzed most of the time. Thank God for the cat. He calmed me down with that placid cat-confidence of his.

We sped across a thousand miles of dry, dead Midwestern farmland desolate from global warming. We would stop mostly in dusty, abandoned farmhouses or barns way up dirt roads where we wouldn't be seen. I would flop down on an old mattress, falling into a dead-man sleep. But night time was the cat's prowling time. He slept all day on the seat beside me, but he became edgy and cat-alert in the total blackness of the moonless nights. I'd see the evidence of his patrolling littered about the area the next morning—bunches of dead mice and rats. Even all the genetic tinkering Rozoff had done to create him hadn't engineered out his hunting instinct.

I think he was actually guarding me. One night I woke up to pee and saw him silhouetted in the gloom, sitting stock-still in a window, his back to me, seeming to scan the landscape outside the old farmhouse we'd camped in. I found it easier to fall back asleep, knowing that he was on the lookout.

He might have been doing more than scouting. One morning, I found a huge, dead coywolf out by the car—one of those coyote-wolf hybrids that prowled the abandoned farms. I couldn't figure out how it had died. It wasn't squished, like it had been run over, or mangled like it had gotten into a fight. It just laid there, stiff and glassy-eyed, with only a few scratches on its muzzle and dried foam on its mouth.

We soon left the farmland behind, crossing the alien, moonlike landscape of South Dakota's badlands, and the rolling brushy plains of Wyoming. I decided to move as fast as possible through there, since there were no more farmhouses to hide in.

There was only one stop I really *had* to make. Ketchum, Idaho. In the middle of the night, so nobody would see us, I drove cautiously through the former ski resort—now all but a ghost town since its winter snows had disappeared—to the Ketchum Cemetery and through the simple gate. I found the flat granite slab in a grove of massive cedars, with the inscription "Ernest Miller Hemingway," and the dates of his birth in 1899 and death by suicide in 1961. The gravestone was covered with coins left as tributes, as well as beer cans, liquor bottles, a cigarette, a cigar, and three fresh yellow roses. It was strange to see the coins, since nobody used them anymore.

A cold drizzle was beginning to fall, but I ignored it. This was important. I sat down on the bare ground beside the gravestone, leaning against a tree. The cat circled around to the other side and sat, too, curling his tail around his feet like cats will do. He looked at me as if he expected me to say something profound. So, I did, sort of.

"He was a great writer . . . like I hope I can be," I told the cat. "But he suffered. He was in plane crashes, had depression, took drugs, alcohol. And in the end he gave up. But I won't give up. *Ever.* I'll get us out of this. I promise."

I guess the cat liked what I said, because he padded over and sat beside me in the darkness, while I thought about what I'd have to do.

In the still night, sitting there beside the grave, I found new resolve, got a second wind. So, we got back into the car, and headed for Seattle.

Looking back on the trip, I realize that something important happened. The cat and I became fast friends. Like in the graveyard, I began to talk to him like a person, which I'd never really done with an animal before. During the rest of the drive to Seattle, I told him my short life story, told him what I'd do if I got out of this mess. I'd even sung a couple of old songs I knew to him. And since it was night, he was fully awake, sitting on the front seat in that luminous fur, watching me with those shining eyes, as if he knew what I was saying.

His cat-calm helped a lot after we got into the apartment house, when I'd turned on the Cop Network in my room to see the viddie of me shooting the Animata guard. Now I was wanted for murder. They interviewed Mom and Dad, who stood in front of our house with sad, stubborn looks on their old faces saying "He didn't do it. He's not that kind of boy."

They also interviewed Uncle Ned, who made a crack about the cops that got bleeped out.

Of course, Talbot and Miravelle knew the viddie had been faked, because it didn't show the cat. But giving fake evidence to the cops didn't bother them if it discredited me.

In one viddie report, Talbot stood there in his perfect haircut and fine suit and said "We can confirm that the guard who Mr. Boatright killed was, indeed, among those assigned to the Cerulean when it was taken. We are cooperating with the police to establish a link between them."

That really freaked me! All the breaks were going to the bad guys.

Looking smooth and somber, Talbot went on to say "The possibility, of course, is that Mr. Boatright probably stole the poor animal in the first place, and returned to Animata to silence his partner, and perhaps to obtain more genetic data. Greed knows no bounds, y'know."

I would've kicked in the viddie set, but it would've scared the cat and drawn the landlady's attention. Talbot, Miravelle, and the cops had fitted all the pieces into a picture of me with "guilty" stamped on my face. And when they caught me, I'd have the cat, proving my guilt even more. Well, not exactly. Since I'd managed to lose the cat, they sure couldn't use that piece of evidence against me.

Sitting on the porch listening to the splatter of water sluicing out the downspout, I must have nodded off again. Something brought me awake, a presence. Not a sound, just a presence, like when you know somebody's in a dark room with you.

When I looked up, sitting in front of me, like he'd been there an hour, was the charcoal-gray cat with the golden eyes. I jumped out of the chair and scooped him up, and he tolerated me.

"Wow! I thought you'd taken off or gotten killed or something! Are you okay?" I held him out and examined him. He was only damp, and the gray dye hadn't run. I swear he looked back at me with disdain.

"C'mon, I didn't mean to hurt you or anything. Don't you understand I had to change that fur color?"

He wriggled to be let down, walked over to the food with that confident tiger-walk of his, crouched down on all fours and began eating fastidiously, showing an "I'm-not-sure-I-forgive-you-yet" attitude.

The landlady trundled out onto the porch in a taped-up plastic raincoat and grimaced at the cat.

"Didn't see that cat before," she said. "Damn big cat." Her parchment-wrinkled face squinched in displeasure, no doubt angling a way to gouge me for more money.

"You didn't say no pets," I reminded her.

"He craps all over, and you pay extra." She flipped open a faded yellow umbrella and stepped off the porch into the rain. "Well, I'm going for a little drink or three," she said over her shoulder. "If I get back and find any cat crap on the porch, it'll cost you extra."

"Have a nice time," I said to her umbrella bobbing away into the darkness.

The cat finished his food, walked to the door and turned around. With an expression of tolerant annoyance—if cats have expressions—he meowed to be let in. I guessed he'd decided to forgive me.

We both slept well the rest of the night and woke to a soggy gray Seattle morning. After sharing some scrambled eggs, we started out for

Qualton. My only plan was to find Rozoff's place and maybe get inside, to see what was there. I didn't know what I was looking for, but maybe I'd know when I found it.

I didn't have my processor and my angel, so I had to get an old-fashioned GPS gadget at the gas station. Its mechanical voice guided me out of the Seattle suburbs and onto a narrow, winding country road through thick green forests that seemed to crowd in on both sides, resenting the road's intrusion. Qualton was an hour outside Seattle, a little town consisting only of a country store, a shop that sold handmade wood furniture, a couple of gas stations and a cafe. It nestled in the woods, smack up against the Olympic National Forest, so I couldn't figure out where Rozoff could have had a house.

Back home, if you wanted to know anything, you asked at the store, so I left the cat in the car, made sure my secondskin was intact, and headed in. The front window was plastered with sheets of colored paper advertising fishing guides, pancake suppers and puppies for sale. Inside, an older man with an incredibly rotund beer belly and industrial strength suspenders holding up his pants stood behind the counter sorting through a box of screws, nuts, and bolts. His jowls sat comfortably on his chest as he bent his head poking at the pile.

I picked up some cold cuts, a loaf of bread, a couple of plastic-sealed pickles, and three cans of Croke. I remembered the cat and piled on a can of tuna, carrying the armload to the cash register. I knew I'd get better information if I bought something, and if I tried to be helpful.

"Fixing something?" I asked, laying my stuff on the counter.

The owner grunted and nodded. "Damn back door came off. I got this little fart of a grandson, he likes to swing on it. Fat little kid. I got to figure out how to bolt it on so he can't tear it up." He stopped to scratch sparse graying black hair before he came up with one long lag screw, eyeing it with satisfaction.

"Yeah, kids," I agreed. "I've done doors so they'd hold. It's not easy. Got to cross-brace 'em." I leaned against the counter like I had all the time in the world and peered into the box of hardware. A grizzled old man with a polished cane hobbled in and fished a stick of beef jerky out of a jar and chewed on it while we both watched the big guy paw through the hardware. We both gave sage advice about hinges and bolts and door frames. And children.

"Maybe just backhand the kid," said the old man. "That worked with mine."

"Wife doesn't hold with that . . ." said the storekeeper ". . . unfortunately."

I helped go through the box, and we came up with a couple of good-sized screws. The storekeeper said his name was Johnny, the old guy said he was Carl, and I said my name was Nick Adams.

I started easing my way toward the information I wanted. "Who could put together a good door for you around here? Know any good carpenters?"

"Carpenter up in Clinston. Guy named Izzy Bolton." Johnny had found all the hardware he needed, and he asked Carl to watch the front while he looked for some wood to reinforce the frame. He told Carl to stay out of the jerky unless he was going to pay. I offered to keep help- ing, saying I had some time. Johnny accepted gratefully. I knew he'd have trouble bending his big, round belly to get to the bottom hinges.

"The reason I ask about the carpenter is I know this guy who lives here who needed a carpenter. Guy named Rozoff." I followed him back as he lumbered toward the rear of the store, past the beer cooler, gripping the precious hardware in his fat hand. He looked at me suspiciously. "Rozoff? Ain't seen him in a long time. Sheriff said he's missing. You see him?"

"Missing? Gee, I talked to him a long time ago. More than a year. He said to come see him if I came through town."

"Well, you won't see him. He's missing."

"Wow, and he's got that nice house, I heard. Up that road. What's the name?"

Johnny got his tool kit from the store room and dug through it to find a screwdriver and drill.

"Cedar Canyon Road. I been up there. I brought groceries up to him a couple of times. He didn't want my stuff, usually. Most of the time, he had a truck up from Seattle delivering frozen. Biggest log house I ever saw. All fancy computers inside. Way the hell up that road. Twenty miles maybe. About the only private land up there surrounded by the national forest."

I helped him heft the door back into place, and we figured how to reinforce it and bolt it on. All that time, I circled round and round what I needed to know about Rozoff, gathering more and more bits of information.

"Yeah, that was a nice house," said Johnny. "He was always having fancy people come up there. Limos, they drove. Vans. Kinda dangerous-looking people, if you ask me."

By the time we got the door done, I had a pretty good idea of what I had to do. I couldn't drive straight up the road. The house might be under surveillance, so I had to go through the woods.

"That ought to hold the little porker," said Johnny. "Now all I got to do is figure out how to keep him from grabbing stuff off the shelves and eating it."

He thanked me and rang up my food, throwing in the drinks for free.

Carl took the jerky stick out of his mouth and waved it to get our attention. "If he's going in the woods, you ought to warn him, Johnny."

"Oh, right. You planning to go hiking?"

"I thought I might. It's nice weather."

"Well, keep an eye out. Last week, a guy lost a couple of hunting dogs in there. And one of the rangers found a deer all tore up. The dogs were kind of wild anyway, so they're probably taking down the deer. They scare away easy, but guard your food, just the same."

"Sasquatch," grunted the old man. "People said they saw Sasquatch. This is his country, y'know."

"Ain't no Sasquatch," said Johnny. "Last time there was a sighting, it was some bum from Seattle with a long beard. But just be careful."

"Thanks, I will." I went back outside and stood looking into the thick, dark woods. Getting to Rozoff's wouldn't be easy. Back in the car, I told the cat everything, and he listened, paying particular attention when I opened the tuna.

I drove back to Seattle, and over the next two days went around the city buying what I'd need. I got different stuff at different stores, so I wouldn't stand out. A backpack, flashlight, hunting knife, poncho, hiking boots, forest hiking map, packaged food. The cat thoroughly investigated each purchase to determine whether it would be useful to him.

That night, I watched the old television in my room, learning that there were lots of sightings of me and the cat—none mentioned in Seattle, though—and that the police were confident of an arrest soon. Lieutenant Rocky was his usual tough-jawed self, and Talbot smooth as ever.

Finally, I was ready for what would be a real Nick Adams trek through the woods, but this was not fiction. If I failed, real people would die.

CHAPTER 28

The cat woke up before me, pacing the dark room, waiting for me to haul my sleepy self out of bed. I fed him and made myself a big ostrich and cheese sandwich, which I ate as we drove through the quiet Seattle streets and out the deserted road to Qualton.

We made it just as the darkness turned to a slate-gray light. The weather was still overcast, the woods still gloomy. I decided I couldn't risk running into people, so I drove the car about fifty yards up a fire road and ran it deep into a grove of thick bushes. As the cat explored the area, I pulled on my pack and strapped on the hunting knife.

A gas car rattled past out on the main road, and I froze, even though I knew the driver couldn't possibly have seen me. I was especially jumpy because I'd left my secondskin off and I looked like Timothy Boatright, who everybody wanted to find. The secondskin was deteriorating, anyway, and I figured I didn't want to screw up the last set I had by getting it ripped off on some bush. Besides, I knew I could hide well enough in the woods so that nobody would get a look at me except for some squirrels. Feeling more like my woods-tramping self, I figured out my location from the map and the GPS locator. I plotted a heading to the cabin, called the cat, and plunged directly into the thick forest.

But these weren't the North Carolina woods I'd explored as a kid, full of scruffy tangled underbrush with gnarled oaks, tall skinny pines and a summer organic smell. No, this was a thick, damp primeval rain-forest, columned with massive trees tall as buildings that filtered the light to an eerie dimness. Dead tree limbs were hung with tattered gray moss like gnarled fingers. They hovered over an unrelieved jumble of fallen, rotting logs, shrouded in thick green lichens and overgrown with luminous-green ferns. Trees also sprouted from the dead logs, some so large their thick spider-leg roots had clutched the log in a stranglehold. In some places, the logs had rotted away, leaving the trees standing on stilted roots, offering dark hidey-holes for God-knows-what creatures.

No path offered itself across this alien green obstacle course, so I jumped, crawled and clambered over the spongy logs and slogged through the icy slow-moving streams, making sure with the locator that I stayed on course. The cat easily kept up, leaping lithely from log to log and climbing trees occasionally. After a bit, he started to lead the way. He knew where he was going better than I did. His certainty increased my certainty that I'd chosen the right thing to do.

I felt the terrain rising, checked the map and read my position on the GPS. The cat had led us unerringly up the mountain that Rozoff had built his house on. After three hours, I sat panting with fatigue on a rock, my clothes soaked, pulled a bag of trail mix out of my pack and began munching on it. I dug out a tin of cat food and opened it, but the cat wasn't interested. He kept slipping off into the thick undergrowth, only to come back and stare at me impatiently, as if demanding that I get up and get going.

I finally got my wind back and obliged him. As I hiked on, my locator showed we were getting closer and closer to the coordinates of Rozoff's house. Finally, in the sun-dappled mid-afternoon, I rounded a lichen-covered boulder and glimpsed a light brown log wall through the trees. It could only be Rozoff's. But when I looked down, the cat was gone! Jesus, I thought, if he just blunders in there and somebody's waiting, we're all dead!

I dropped my pack and slithered on my belly up to the edge of the clearing, staying well down in the thick ferns. I parted them and peeked through. Old Johnny in the store was right that Rozoff had built one really big log house. It had a two-story main building and sprawling side wings, all surrounded by a broad porch. The front had big picture windows, and I could see through to more big windows in the back. There was no movement in the house, no lights on. I waited and watched, hoping the cat hadn't just gone right up to it. A flash of gray caught my eye on the porch. The cat walked slowly across it, ears swiveling this way and that, eyes searching. He stopped. Had he seen something? I widened the hole in the bushes to get a better look at the whole house. Still nothing. The cat moved across the porch and disappeared. I waited a long time, and was preparing to scooch back into the woods to figure out what to do next.

"Meow."

I jumped like I'd been snakebit! The cat sat right beside me. "Jesus, you scared me! Where did you go?" I felt stupid, not only for letting the cat sneak up on me, but for talking to him like I expected an answer. I was glad none of our barn cats back in North Carolina had heard me.

The cat moved a couple of steps into the clearing, then looked back. I had this weird feeling he wanted me to follow him. My woods sense told me there was nothing moving in the area, so I decided to go along with him. I got myself up into a crouch and moved forward. The cat loped around to the back, and I followed, still crouching. After a short distance, I decided being a foot or so shorter wouldn't help my chances if somebody had a rifle trained on me, so I stood up. I didn't get shot. So far, so good.

"So you're basically saying there's nobody home," I whispered to the cat. He kept going around the house, past a big woodpile, past a pump house, coming to a rear door. I tried the knob, finding the door locked, but the cat slipped through the flap of a cat door. I shrugged, went back and fetched my pack from the woods, laid down on my belly and wriggled through myself, pulling my pack after me. The door had obviously been sized for a big cat like him, so since I was a skinny human, I had no problem.

I found myself in a big kitchen with a fancy refrigerator, microwave, and stove. It had a granite-topped center island with all kinds of copper pots hanging above it. The cabinets were light pine, just like the logs of the house, and a control panel and viddie screen were inset in a wall over a desk beside the refrigerator. The cat rubbed against the counters, getting reacquainted with his home. He moved around the center island, and I followed, entering a two-story living room with brown overstuffed sofas, a big recliner with remote controls set into the arm and a massive stone fireplace you could almost stand up in. The shelves on either side of the fireplace held books, animal skulls and big chunks of fossils on little plastic stands. Rozoff must have used them for inspiration in designing his creatures. I moved over to examine the skulls.

The cat had other ideas. He went over to a corner of the room beside the viddie screen and sat there meowing. He stood on his hind legs and put his paws up on the side of the viddie screen, looking back at me and meowing again. I'd learned that it was a good idea to listen to the cat, so I went over to him. His paws were kneading a spot on the viddie screen frame, like he was trying to point, except he didn't have fingers.

I looked where he was pawing, to see a small unobtrusive slot in the frame, about the size of one of the old quarters my dad collected.

"So? What's this about?" I asked the cat. He sat on his haunches, looked up at me and meowed again.

We looked at each other for a minute. Something must go in that slot, I thought. What would fit in that slot? He looked at me like I was becoming a disappointment. I thought harder.

His disk-shaped tag, of course!

I bent down and unfastened the bracelet from his neck and pushed the little disk into the slot.

"Hello," said a voice.

I jumped back, startled, ready to run or fight.

"Welcome to my *dacha*," said the accented voice. "No doubt, with the help of my Familiar, you have figured out code key and inserted it."

I backed out into the room to see on the viddie screen, looking straight at me, the face of Vasily Rozoff.

CHAPTER 29

Rozoff's face looked haggard, thinner than when I'd seen him in the Mirror-Animata viddie. The dark beard and hair messed up like he hadn't thought about them in a year. His eyes looked desperate. This guy had seen some terrible things and couldn't shake them.

"I am Vasily Rozoff," he continued in the thick Russian accent, "but you already know that or you would not be here. However, I am not here." He gave a wry, sad smile. "I am taken away or I am . . . dead. I have left this secure recording for whoever my Familiar brings back to my dacha. The house sensors confirm that my Familiar is with you."

"Yeah, he is," I answered, before remembering that this was a recording.

"*Privet,* Druzhok," said Rozoff. "*Ya schastliv, chto ti verrulsya.*"

The cat meowed back at Rozoff as if he understood Russian, settling himself onto the couch and staring at the screen. I thought I'd decided on my own to come here, but after seeing that cat in action, I could be wrong. He had his own cat-plan.

"I have just greeted my Familiar," explained Rozoff in English. "I am sure he trusts you. He must think you are good person, or he would not have shown you how to use code key. A camera has scanned your eyes, and my house has determined that you are not Kenneth Talbot, Julio Miravelle or any of other people who have done such great wrong. So now you listen to my message."

As Rozoff began to speak, I wandered around the room, checking things out. I found it hard to look at the three-foot-tall face of this desperate man. I examined the fossils on the shelves and fiddled with a big baseball-sized fossil egg sitting on the coffee table. I think it was a dinosaur egg, if I remember correctly from my paleo class.

"My Familiar has many secrets. But just in case Mr. Talbot is smarter than I think, I will not tell you all of them." He kept using that word. "Familiar." I'd heard it somewhere before, but I couldn't remember where. "But if he trusts you, you will learn them. You will learn why I made him. Everybody will learn."

The cat still watched the viddie screen intently. I asked "You trust me cat?" I'd never seen a cat watch a screen like that before, except when there were birds on. I poked my head through doors leading to the other wings of the house. One wing was a large bedroom with bath, strewn with e-papers, and with a rumpled bed. The other opened into a virtie-room, where Rozoff must have designed the Cerulean. I'd investigate that later.

Rozoff continued. "One thing you should understand. One important thing. Do not think of my Familiar as just cat. He is much, much more. I have only used cat as convenient genetic platform."

Suddenly I felt sorry for the Cerulean. He didn't understand he was nothing but a "genetic platform." He thought he was a living, breathing animal. But he was all alone, a freak of, well, *un*-nature. As if he sensed my pity and resented it, he stood up, looked right at me and jumped off the couch, ambling into the kitchen for a drink of water from a custom-made bowl kept continually filled by a valve.

As I watched him lap water with cat-like precision from the bowl, I remembered another of Mom's palindromes. "Was it a car or a cat I saw?" The people at Animata, at Genipet, the collectors, the exhibitors—they all saw these animals as machines. Nothing but meat machines, with no more feelings than a car. I wondered whether this was Rozoff's intention, to make us understand that—like Lulu had said—we'd become low-rent Frankensteins.

"If the cat trusts you, he will now lead you to something that will be of great help to you." That got my attention, so I sat down and watched Rozoff again. "I have made e-paper containing everything I know about Talbot, Miravelle, Animata, and all my work . . ." He paused and smiled slightly, a strange sad smile, mixing pride and shame. ". . . except, of course, about my Familiar. He will never be duplicated." His voice rose, as if he knew the cat had moved into another room. *"Ko mne, Druzhok."* The cat walked back into the room and sat in front of the viddie screen, watching Rozoff's face.

"Druzhok, pokashi svoemu drugyu safe. Safe, Druzhok," instructed Rozoff. The cat looked over at me, then moved toward the wing that held the VROOM. He stopped at the door, and I let him in. I followed him into the large room with a large control-studded easy chair in the middle. A pair of googles rested on one arm of the chair, and I put them on. The floor was strewn with food wrappers, books, and e-papers. The cat went to one side of the room and stopped, pawing the dark blue carpeting. Rozoff appeared standing before me, slouching like a very tired man. He was smaller than I had imagined. I bent down where the cat was pawing and found a place where the carpet could be lifted up. The cat sat beside me, intently watching the spot. I lifted it up and discovered . . . nothing. Just a smooth floor.

Rozoff must have figured the floor would puzzle whoever encountered it, because he said "When you see floor, hit it with hand. Hard."

I smacked the floor and the faintest outlines of a square crack appeared. I hit it again, and the crack widened. It was a safe hidden beneath a thin layer of plaster. At the same time, a chunk in the middle popped out to reveal a ring I could lift with my finger. Apparently, the code key had unlocked this safe, because when I pulled on the ring, it opened, sending small bits of plaster down into it.

Inside the small safe sat a single e-paper page. Rozoff must have rigged his house computer to detect when the safe was opened, because he began to speak again.

"Take this information and use it as your conscience dictates. My Familiar trusts you. So do I. *Do svidanya I udachi.* Goodbye and good luck." The virtual Rozoff disappeared. I sat on the floor in the darkness, the only light spilling from the open door to the main room, and wondered what to do next. The cat laid down, nestling his large, warm body against my leg. I petted him, and he rested his big handsome head on my knee, almost sadly.

"Well, pal, let's find out what's on this e-paper. But first, I'm hungry."

"What would you like to eat?" The woman's voice made me leap from the floor and whirl around, looking for its source. "Hello? Who are you?"

"I am the house."

It dawned on me. That's what Rozoff meant when he said "my house" earlier. This was a sentient house. Naturally, Rozoff would have rigged his house with all the modern high-tech conveniences, like voice-activated systems that recognized statements like "I'm hungry." Since I'd inserted the code key, the house would now respond to me.

"What do you have?"

"If you mean what is there to eat, my records show a wide range of entrees, soups, casseroles . . ." The voice droned dutifully on, listing what was in the freezer and cabinets. I stopped the listing by asking for meat loaf and mashed potatoes, two helpings of each. I got up and went into the kitchen, where I heard the faint whining sounds that must have meant a meal was being transferred from a freezer behind the wall into the microwave. I found the glasses and filled one with water. I also found a cabinet full of expensive cat food and spooned some into a bowl for the cat. He made an appreciative purring sound and went to work on it.

The microwave said my meal was ready, and I took out two covered plates full of what looked like real meat loaf with brown gravy and a mound of fluffy white potatoes, also with gravy and a steaming helping of corn. Thank God Rozoff liked real food!

I set the plates on the kitchen island, found some silverware and pulled up a stool, putting the e-paper page beside the plates. I touched the page, and it lit up and displayed a table of contents. As I worked my way through the savory steaming meat loaf and buttery thick mashed potatoes, I also worked my way through the information on the e-paper. It held tons of data, including bios on all the people, plans of all the facilities and videos and detailed descriptions of all the animals of Animata, except, of course, for the Cerulean.

I called up Talbot's bio, and it wasn't flattering. Boy, it sure wasn't! His history showed him to be the black sheep of an upper-crust British family, which was ironic considering the animal-making business he'd gotten into. He'd squandered most of his inheritance on drugs, gambling, and expensive yachts. Then he tried to get it back by drug-dealing. Not just nickies, but the really bad stuff. The old standbys, heroin and cocaine, and the new synthetic spirit-boosters that let you live with the gods for six months and left you a head-empty husk for the rest of your life. And the hypersex drugs that gave you a three-day orgasm, which led people to commit suicide to escape the unrelenting pleasure.

Scanning the data, I also discovered the truth about Talbot's handicap. The medical reports and Rozoff's notes said he had not fallen from a sailboat mast. He'd been shot in the back running away from a drug dealer he'd cheated.

What I read next astounded me so much, I actually stopped eating! Besides tearing apart his spine so badly it couldn't be regenerated, the bullets had bounced around inside Talbot, messing up his internal organs. So surgeons had installed a pig heart in him. Actually, pigs are pretty noble animals; I really pitied the poor pig who got sacrificed for the likes of Talbot. I chewed a little meatloaf and thought a bit; maybe that was how Talbot got so interested in Animata; him having a pig heart genetically engineered not to be rejected, and all.

The pig heart was obviously an improvement, because the records showed that Talbot didn't have much of a human one. When Miravelle and Talbot had abandoned a girl at the scene of the shooting, she was later found floating in the Thames River. Rozoff must have really done some digging to come up with all this dirt.

In any case, Talbot made enough money from his drug-dealing to weasel his way into Animata . . . an appropriate metaphor. He figured he could make as much money from the animals as from drugs, so he bribed, blackmailed, and threatened enough board members to get himself made chairman and CEO.

Julio Miravelle had been his second-in-command and link to the bad guys, so he came on board as security chief.

Talbot also brought in his buddies—freaks, shifties, hustlers, and winklers—to make up the rest of the Animata board, taking it away from Rozoff, making him nothing more than hired help. The e-paper also held data on Rozoff's family back in Russia, telling how Talbot threatened them if Rozoff didn't work for him.

I hit a few buttons, did a search of the e-paper and found the Animata animal descriptions, zeroing in on information about the GenESents like the Big and Little Nasties. I found a whole history of the "product line." Talbot had lied about them. They weren't really meant as sentries but highly efficient remote-controlled assassins. Talbot had forced Rozoff to invent them, and even after he'd licensed them to Genipet, he still made Rozoff develop improved models in secret. And Talbot didn't just want to sell them to the military. He wanted to make clones to sell to hoods and terrorists. The descriptions on the e-paper said that the Nasties were only the beginning. Talbot wanted to develop a whole line of vicious assassin animals with the honed hunting instincts of predators. They could even be equipped with weapons like shoulder-mounted remote-controlled machine guns, so a human controller could give them firepower. With that strength and cunning, and the added hardware, they could outmaneuver and kill any human cop or soldier.

I called up a picture of the first prototype. It's the one I'd named a Big Nasty. God, was it a mean-looking critter! A witch's brew of genes from a grizzly, baboon, hyena and a bat, pumped up to three hundred pounds with three-inch fangs, razor claws, night vision, natural sonar, and a built-in homicidal tendency. The description said the designers implanted electrodes in the pleasure centers of the creatures' brains. So, when one made an assigned kill, the handler just flipped a switch to give the beast a jolt of electric bliss. So the monster was addicted to killing!

That's what had sniffed around on the other side of the closet door, fortunately not yet programmed to my scent.

I clicked off the reader and concentrated on what remained of the two plates of food, thinking about what I'd just learned. Clearly, when Rozoff had been forced into developing these animals from hell, he needed some strategy to get himself free, in fact, to wreck the whole Animata enterprise. He was practically a prisoner, so it had to be a very clever strategy to get past Talbot and Miravelle.

The Cerulean cat was his solution, and I'd have to be just as clever to figure out what the cat was all about. I mulled over all this new information as I watched the cat finish his food and begin to fastidi-ously wash his face. I had to find out where Miravelle was holding Callie and Lulu; it had to be an Animata facility for the privacy. So, I switched the reader back on and called up the listings of Animata facilities around the country. Talbot wouldn't risk keeping Callie and Lulu at headquarters in Philly. He'd have taken them somewhere remote, somewhere he could control, so I began going through the list of Animata ranches.

Suddenly, the cat interrupted my search by leaping onto the coun-ter, arching its back, laying back its ears, and baring its teeth, looking toward the front of the lodge. Its throat rumbled with a low growl as the house-lady-voice announced, "You have a visitor." I clicked off the reader and slid to the floor, crawling low to the front picture window. The cat stayed on the counter, preferring the high ground, erupting a loud, hissing spit.

Luckily, I hadn't turned on any lights yet, even though the daylight was beginning to fade. Boards on the porch creaked, like something heavy walked across them. The cat growled and spat again. I raised up to peek out the window.

And faced a Big Nasty! It glared back at me with hateful black slit-eyes, a grotesque gnarled face and bat-ears. It snarled, curling back its dark lips to reveal a fang-filled hyena-like maw that could bite my head off in one crunch. It opened its mouth in a window-rattling roar, showing a wet, pink tongue the size of my hand that offered a welcome mat to its dark gullet.

It stood its seven-foot hulking body on its hind legs and slammed a massive claw against the window, so intent on killing me that it had forgotten about the glass. But the thick plate glass held, and the animal roared again, the sound piercing the house as if the walls didn't exist.

A blast of adrenaline surged through my brain, and I scrambled back against the sofa and toward the kitchen. The animal turned, show-ing a bearlike body with brown fur, and made for the front door. The cat stood his ground, back arched, spitting, but I grabbed him and the e-paper and leaped in the opposite direction. Behind me, the front door exploded into flying glass and splintered wood, leaving the doorway filled with a snarling Big Nasty.

I slammed to the kitchen floor, shoved the cat through the cat door and launched myself through. Behind me another gut-shaking roar and the crash of furniture slamming against the wall. Outside the door, the cat still acted like he planned to fight the Nasty, but I scooped him up and sprinted for the forest, slashing my way into the damp brush, scrambling over the rotting logs. Tearing through the undergrowth, I made it about a hundred yards before another crash behind me told me the Nasty had burst through the back door. A rain shower began to patter the forest floor, and I could hear heavier rain approaching from the distance.

I kept running flat out, dodging limbs, scrambling over logs, leaping streams, not letting up for an instant. I clutched the cat firmly, until there erupted at the forest edge a roar from a cavernous throat and the crack of tearing brush. The Nasty had plunged into the thicket after me. His killing program ended only with my death.

"You got a better chance on your own!" I whispered to the cat. "Take off!" I hefted him onto the forest floor, but he stayed with me. As I plunged on, I made scatting noises, but he just ran ahead, turning occasionally to make sure I was staying up. "Dumb cat!" I panted. The rain grew into a deluge, and I became soaked to the skin.

Closer behind, another enraged roar and the ripping of brush told me that the Nasty had gained on me, so I kept up a blistering pace, pushing myself, ignoring my jackhammering heart. I knew I had an advantage. If the Nasty lost, he only missed a kill; I ran for my life.

I veered sharply off to the left, so he couldn't track me in a straight line. I leaped onto a large log and paused long enough to see if I could spot him. A few hundred yards away, a small tree slashed to earth like a twig, and a dark shape burst through the tangle of its limbs. I'd gotten into deep, deep trouble. I realized the rain would be my best friend, washing away my scent enough so that maybe I could lose the monster.

CHAPTER 30

I leaped off the log and ran like I'd never run before, plunging past the giant trees, tearing my own trail through thick ferns and bushes. I promised myself I wouldn't stop until I just couldn't run any more. Then, if it was still with me, I'd fight. I'd fight what would likely be the last fight of my life. But now, running hard might give me an edge. Most predators are only sprinters. The big cats, the wolves, can go for a short distance, then it's not worth it to keep up the chase. But I would be a long-distance-running prey. I would not stop. Through the hiss of the rain, I heard a roar close behind me, making me realize with stomach-churning certainty that this predator was different. He wanted to kill me down to the very depths of his genes. He had been programmed to follow the scent of prey to kill it, no matter how long it took, and I was at least five hours from the highway and my car. But I kept running.

The cat stayed stubbornly with me, darting ahead, then looking around and back at me. Every so often I panted a "Scat!" at him, but still he stayed with me.

As it grew dark, a moss-covered rock embedded in the ground made my decision to stop for me. I clipped it hard with the toe of my shoe and slammed to the sodden ground, knocking the breath out of me. When

I stood up, I realized my running was over, legs weak, body bruised, all the energy drained from me. As I tried to breathe, the cat bounded up and rubbed my leg, as if to say "Keep going."

"I can't," I told him. "This is it. You really gotta go, cat." But still he didn't. I panted hard a few times, then held my breath to hear any sound of the animal pursuing me. I listened hard. I thought I heard a thump of footsteps over to my left. Maybe the swish of a limb shifting to my right. But I heard no growling, no obviously animal sounds. I wouldn't. This hunter would know to approach me stealthily in the dark. He'd know to use his night vision and sonar to get right up next to me before attacking, taking a murderous swipe with those vicious claws and ripping my throat out before dismembering me.

The cold rain continued, still good news. Maybe it would have washed away enough scent that I could hide long enough to recover.

I needed a secure place to take a stand. In the waning light, I could make out a big rotting log that had fallen over a couple of boulders, leaving a little hollow underneath. I picked up the cat and crawled into the hollow as far as I could, scrunching myself up deep in its soggy interior, setting aside the e-paper and pulling out my knife. I smiled at myself in spite of my predicament. The Gopher was in his element. The hollow smelled richly organic, of fungus and rotting wood. Maybe it would mask my smell even more. The cold rain chilled me all the way to my soul, and I drew the cat closer to warm us both. I held out the knife, ready to slash at the animal should it emerge out of the rainy darkness.

I figured if I got a good stab at him, maybe I'd slice open an artery, maybe stab him in his ugly face. Maybe before he killed me, he'd be mortally wounded himself. But I knew it was a lousy plan. I had one knife. He had about fifty teeth and ten claws and a hatred beyond reasoning.

I petted the cat's soft fur and scratched his head. His gray had been all but washed away, except in patches, and his blue fur began to glimmer its old glimmer. I could tell by feeling his perked up ears and the taut muscles in his neck that he was watching the woods beyond, looking for the same thing I was—glowing eyes, a glint of teeth, the shifting of a bush. He hadn't hissed or spat, or arched his back, so he must not have seen anything.

I crouched for hours, trying to stay vigilant, petting the cat. But the rain kept up a steady, lulling patter and I started to doze. Fuzziness seemed to soak into my brain and I shook myself awake, even poking my hand with the point of the knife. But I started retreating gradually into sleep. First I slumped down a little more, pulling into a fetal position around the warm cat. Then I nodded my head, resting it on the side of the cold, wet log. Then I let the knife rest on my leg. Then I was gone.

A roar jerked me awake. It had sounded like maybe a quarter mile away. I was teeth-chattering cold, and I couldn't figure out why. Then I realized the cat had gone! Another roar, but now an added sound that I knew well: the scream of the cat, rising to a vicious crescendo then tapering off with an echoing end. The Nasty had caught the cat! I cursed myself as I scrambled out of the hollow and stood up, peering all around, trying to figure the direction of the scream. It must have been near dawn, because the darkness had given way to a gray morning mist rolling through the forest. Another roar. Another cat scream, this one ending abruptly. I started forward in the sounds' direction, then stopped myself, cursing. I knew what had happened, and there was nothing I could do. My throat lumped up and tears started to roll down my face.

The cat was dead. There was nothing I could do. I had to save myself. Willing myself with all my might, I forced my stiff leg muscles to obey me, to turn and run. My clothes were soggy heavy weights, but I pushed ahead, my muscles limbering up, clenched-jaw determined. I slogged away from the deadly sounds for about a mile, then stopped to check the GPS now that there was enough light. Its small screen showed only a spider web of cracks. It had been smashed, maybe against a tree, or maybe when I scrambled through the cat door. I had to dead-reckon. Ironic phrase, dead-reckon.

I willed myself to feel my surroundings, to let my old backwoods instinct take over. I hoped I still had it after a year in New York. I sensed that the way back was a little to the right. It was downhill, too, which made me even more sure. So I took off running again, the e-paper in one hand, the knife in the other. My heart pumped vigorously with the run, but somehow at the same time it felt like a big chunk of lead sitting in my chest, matching the lump in my throat. The Cerulean was dead, and I'd gotten him killed.

CHAPTER 31

I finally staggered out of the woods onto a stretch of featureless road that didn't give me a clue about where I'd ended up. Just solid forest in either direction. I was sure I'd reached the road into Qualton, but I didn't know which side of town I was on. I slumped against a tree and tried to figure out which way to go. I knew that if I sat down I wouldn't be able to drag myself back up. I stared desperately at the shattered GPS like it would suddenly fix itself once I got to the road.

The rain had drizzled to a stop and the gray had brightened. The woods lay dead still, except for the occasional spatter of raindrops, but I had this dread that any instant a claw could reach around the tree and tear my throat out. That fear forced me into action. I pushed myself away from the tree, turned to the right and started down the road as fast as my rubbery legs would carry me. I still clutched the knife in one hand and the e-paper in the other, holding both like my life depended on them. And it did, and so did Callie's and Lulu's. A truck engine revved from down the road, and I ducked back into the woods to hide, luckily remembering that I looked like Timothy Boatright, not like my secondskin older self.

The day brightened even more, and a little sun dappled the road. It was a good sign and a bad sign. I could see farther into the woods, but if the Nasty lurked in there, he could see me better on the road. I crossed over to the other side from where I'd come. At least the Nasty would have to cross the road to get me, and I'd have a little more time to react. It's funny how random thoughts pop into your head at the most stressful times. Now I knew why a Nasty crosses the road. To kill me.

I rounded a bend to come up to a road sign that looked familiar—a squiggly arrow warning of curves ahead. I thought I'd seen it a mile or so before the town, which meant . . . . Yes! There it was! The fire road where I'd parked the car. I felt more energy now, but more fear. For some weird reason, the fact that I was near safety made the danger from the Nasty seem more immediate. Like after you've just washed the car you're more worried about rain, only this was a zillion times more intense.

I turned up the dirt road and saw a glint of glass behind the bushes, marking the car. I jogged up to the turnoff point, and something moved on the car. I stopped, frozen at the movement of an animal on the trunk. I held out the knife.

The animal meowed!

I ran through the bushes to see the cat uncurl himself, stretch, yawn and look at me like "Where have you been, for God's sake?"

I hollered a "Yesss!", hefted him up, hugged him and danced around like a complete idiot!

"Kittycat, kittycat, kittycat! You big old good lookin', meowing, blue thing! I thought you were . . ." I didn't even want to say it. I just hugged him again until he meowed a complaint, as if to remind me that there was a 300-pound Nasty still out there. Actually, if he wasn't a cat, I'd have sworn he was embarrassed, but cats don't seem to get embarrassed.

I unlocked the car, laid him in, slid behind the wheel, started it up, slammed it in reverse, lurched backward onto the road, popped it into drive, and spewed dirt getting out of there.

Once I'd turned onto the main road, I drove for about fifteen miles, until I was sure I was out of the range of even the most fleet-footed Nasty. I pulled into a state park, which wasn't occupied because of the cruddy weather, found a bathroom and got my first look at myself in a mirror. I was so raggedy and messed up I would have scared little kids. I scrubbed my face, combed back my hair and took my last set of secondskin out of its plastic bag. I was as careful putting it on as my tired trembling fingers could manage. I finished and made a few faces to make sure it had stuck on and was looking natural. I looked okay, except that my jeans and jacket were so canky I'd have to burn them.

I drove back toward Seattle, stopping just before the freeway at a drive-through window at McDonald's to pick up three bacon-and-egg breakfast biscuits. And a big coffee. I handed over my cashcard and realized I only had a couple of thousand dollars left. I'd better watch my expenses. As we reached the freeway, I gave some bacon to the cat and chewed on a biscuit of my own. I exited off the freeway and wound through the streets to the one where the old boarding house was. The houses, bars, and shops looked even more shabby in the morning sun.

I neared the house and realized something didn't seem right. A couple of the cars parked on the crummy block looked out of place, too shiny to belong in the neighborhood. I pulled over a ways up the block from the house and thought. Maybe the old woman had figured out a way to make more money off me by turning me in to somebody—maybe cops, maybe Animata, maybe Salvo.

I petted the cat and laid the blanket over him. He lay still. I eased past the house. My room was downstairs, front right. My shade was up, but I knew I'd left it down. I kept driving, turned right and with my hands gripping the wheel and my eye glued to the rear-view mirror headed back for the freeway.

I was pretty sure I had made it okay. The Cop Network had taught me a lot about avoiding the cops. I'd always parked my car a block away, so the old lady never got a good look at it. And I'd thrown away all the dye boxes and tried to clean the dye and my fingerprints off everything in the room. Sure, if they were brought in, the forensics people would find the cat hairs, but they probably wouldn't be. All the old lady would tell the cops was a half-baked story about a guy who didn't look like me with a cat that didn't look like the Cerulean. That is, if those were cop cars parked on the block. The old lady could have mentioned me to some punk in the bar who called Animata for a reward. And Animata might have even sent Salvo, if they decided to hire him for the dirty work. Or, maybe I was just being paranoid. Maybe some people on the block just had nice cars.

In any case, I'd made myself homeless.

I drove all the way across town on Interstate 5, finding an exit near the airport that led to a row of mini-malls and cheap hotels. I found a motel that had off-street parking and checked in, smuggling the cat in under the blanket. I left the cat in the room and went out to the mini-malls and bought some new jeans and t-shirts, a jacket, people food, cat food, and some bowls for the cat. There was a Really Cool Stuff Outlet Store, and I looked around in there, buying one of those big floppy green hats that smoothie-baldies wore. And in a party store nearby, I found a fake moustache.

I bought them because during the drive, I'd come up with a new plan, one that was so great it gave me a nice jolt of optimism. I also had new confidence, because, after all, we'd learned all kinds of new information from the e-paper, and escaped a Big Nasty, so now I firmly believed the cat and me could take care of a little daring rescue with no problem.

Back in the motel room, I ate a self-heating fake Salisbury steak dinner and put on the hat and the moustache. In the mirror, I was another guy entirely, a really weird-looking guy. A guy who was going to find out where Callie and Lulu were.

I turned on the e-paper and took up where I'd left off before I'd been interrupted by the Nasty. I called up the data base of Animata facilities. Rozoff had been a thorough data-compiler, including names of personnel, phone numbers, maps—everything I'd need. The cat had stretched out on the bed watching me, his eyes opening and closing, opening and closing, finally closing. He'd had a busy couple of days.

I let him rest, slipping out the door with the e-paper and my disguise in a paper bag. I drove the car to one of the mini-malls that had a virtie shop with a row of viddiebooths and linkbooths in it. I settled into a viddiebooth, shut the door, put on the floppy hat and pasted on the moustache under my secondskin nose. I set up the reader, inserted my cashcard in the slot and searched for the viddie number of the first Animata facility on the list, a ranch in Texas. I entered the number of the main house, and the call went through in a few seconds. A little round Mexican lady answered, probably a house manager.

"Is Julio there?"

"Julio who?" asked the lady.

"Miravelle."

"No, he not been here long time. Year maybe."

I thanked her and hung up. I tried a research lab in Florida and an island in the Bahamas, where the company raised genetically engineered fish. No Miravelle in either place. I tried the ranch in Utah.

A rough-looking character with deep lines in his face, a scar creasing the forehead and scraggly brown hair answered the call.

"Yeah . . . Animata ranch."

"Is Julio there?"

"Miravelle? Why you calling here?" He looked annoyed. Another dead end. I was about to apologize and hang up, when he said. "Why don't you use his cell phone?" Something in the way he said it made me decide to hang on a little longer.

"I'm supposed to show him something. I needed to get him on viddie."

"He's not here."

"Where is he?"

"The cabin. Out in the cabin. Don't you know?" His eyes narrowed. He was testing me to see if I knew where the cabin was. Out of his line of sight, I punched search buttons on the reader to bring up a map of the Utah ranch. The ranch included a main research complex, with labs and barns, but also a cabin way off in the mountains, isolated, that would be a perfect place to hide two kidnapped women.

"Yeah, I know the cabin. Up Reese Canyon. I got the number." And I did. The guy punched off. I took a deep breath and tried to settle myself. I was going to face Miravelle, try to fool him. I had to really be convincing, so he wouldn't even suspect it was me.

I punched in the number, and after a minute, the screen showed another bigger guy who also had a mountain-road-map face, but a huge mop of gray and black hair, and one thick black eyebrow running all the way across his forehead.

"Yeah."

"Is Julio there?"

"Who are you?"

"Nick."

"What do you want?"

"It's about the women."

His single brow dipped into a frown, like a hairy garage door going down. "What the hell you calling on a public line for?"

"Just let me talk to him."

One-eyebrow-guy moved off-screen and after a second Miravelle appeared, the same slickie I remembered. He peered at me suspiciously.

"Who are you?"

"It's Nick. You're not Julio. Who're you?" I made my voice lower and tried to lose the southern accent.

"What the hell—"

"I wanted Julio . . ." I hadn't thought to think up a last name. I looked around the virtie shop desperately for inspiration. I got it. ". . . Xerox."

"What the—!"

"Julio Xerox. You're not Julio Xerox. I got a wrong number. I was calling about a date Julio and me got with these two women." I punched off and he disappeared from the screen. Christ, what a dummy I was! I hoped he hadn't recognized me.

I took off the hat and moustache and stuffed them into the bag. I extracted my cashcard from the slot, flicked off the e-paper and sat very still in the linkbooth, fighting a bad case of the shivers.

Now I knew where the cat and I had to go next, and what we had to do.

CHAPTER 32

I stood on top of the Utah mesa, as the dry cool wind whipped around me. The high sun and clear day gave me a view all the way across the broad valley to low rolling mountains. Animata ranch covered the entire valley; its research complex a large collection of buildings, barns, and corrals visible even from this mesa. That's where they field-tested all the exotic big animals that they sold to circuses and zoos and rich people with big estates who wanted living conversation pieces.

But if Rozoff's map was right, fifteen miles farther down the valley hidden from view sat the big, isolated cabin that served as a guest house for buyers who wanted to preview their animals in a natural setting, away from the research complex. But now the cabin served as a prison for Callie and Lulu. The ache and fear I felt for them gave me more courage than I thought I ever had. I would go down there and do whatever necessary to save them. Whatever necessary. It surprised me. I'd always been this kid just trying to get along in life, but now I'd turned into a guy with a sense of steely purpose.

The cat jumped up on the hood of the car and rubbed against me, holding his head high and sniffing the wind.

"That's it, pal. That's where I'm going." I tried to shake off the dead-tired fatigue from the trip. I wouldn't rest, but would immediately start on the long hike in, because that would put me at the cabin in late afternoon. Then, I could hide in the brush and get a good look at the place before maybe moving in at night.

I sat in the car for a while, using the e-paper to go over the security information on the ranch. I zoomed in on the map of the research complex itself—covered with cameras, sensors and all kinds of heavy-duty security computers—because that's where they kept all the secret stuff. Then I scanned around the map covering the rest of the thousand-acre ranch, including the cabin. No cameras or electronic monitors showed up there, except at the gates. The animals running free on the ranch had electronic tracking tags attached, so they couldn't be stolen. And they'd already been offered to buyers, so they weren't secret. I also suspected the cabin was kept free of cameras so that rich buyers could have their privacy, to do whatever rich people like to do in privacy.

So, if I was careful, I could slip through what looked like a simple fence on the map, onto the ranch property and make it to the cabin unnoticed.

The cat and I climbed into the car and drove the last twenty miles down to the valley floor. Halfway to the main entrance to the ranch, a rutted dirt road led away to the left across the rocky terrain. I checked the e-paper, trying to memorize as much as possible. This dirt road took me along the valley to a place where I could go through the fence and along a small canyon that would take me right up to the cabin. I swerved off the paved road, keeping an eye out for other cars, jouncing along across a small stream and through brushy woods. I checked the new locator I'd bought. It said I was about a mile from where the map showed the canyon began.

Just before I reached the canyon's mouth, I found a dry stream bed and drove the car up it and around a little bend, parking on a sandy area. The car wasn't visible from the dirt road. I clipped my canteen to my belt, along with my knife. The knife was all I carried for protection. I guess I should have tried to get a gun earlier, but I doubted if any gun shop would have given a gun permit to Timothy Boatright, wanted murderer.

I got out of the car and turned to the cat, who sat on the seat looking at me expectantly.

"Okay, now you've got to stay—"

In a blue streak, he was out the door and twenty feet back down the stream bed toward the dirt road. I thought about trying to catch him, but was smart enough to know better.

"So, I guess you're going, then." By now, it wouldn't have surprised me if he'd nodded back.

I followed him to the dirt road, crossed it, and picked my way over rocks and brush, going deeper into the woods to the beginning of the canyon. As usual, the cat ranged around, scouting ahead, but always keeping tabs on me. I wondered who was taking care of whom.

After about a mile, I came to a high barbed wire fence, checking it for sensors or cameras, then flattening myself and sliding under it. Now I'd entered Animata property. I stopped and listened for sounds of engines or voices or anything that might have been a patrol. An occasional bird twittered, and the cool breeze gently whispered through the brush, but I heard nothing more, so I continued on.

I figured I'd hiked to within five miles of the cabin when the canyon began to deepen. I liked that. It gave me better cover. Walking the canyon proved easy, because it had a flat grassy bottom, littered with only an occasional boulder, and sheer thirty foot walls on either side that hid us well.

The cat had been ranging ahead of me, but he abruptly doubled back to move close by my side, his ears cocked forward, his tail twitching nervously. He meowed softly, maybe his version of a warning whisper. Ahead, I glimpsed what may have been a horse and rider through the brush, but couldn't be sure. When we reached the spot, nobody was there.

After about ten minutes, as I hiked along, a faint rumble hinted at distant thunder, but the clear sky meant I didn't have to worry too much about rain or a flash flood through the canyon. I kept hiking, and the rumble increased in volume, seeming to echo from up the canyon, beginning to shake the ground.

I'd just realized that thunder didn't shake the ground, when the cat suddenly scurried straight up a steep cliff, pulling himself onto a narrow ledge. I turned to tell him to get down, when rounding the bend ahead, heading right for me in a rolling cloud of dust, burst a massive wall of stampeding animals.

I stood paralyzed, watching a hundred tons of chests, hooves, tusks, and big wild eyes bearing down on me.

It's funny how time slows in a crisis. In only the instant I stood there, I could pick out the individual animals, all these weird genetically engineered creatures. A giant birdlike thing loped along on two muscular legs like an ostrich but had a horned-toad head. Two longhorn cattle with corkscrew horns galloped along, shoulder-to-shoulder with a huge gray ox whose horned head looked like a pig. Was it a pox? Following them ran a cow with long silky hair as white as new snow; a horizontal-striped zebra, and a creature that looked like a cross between camel and buffalo—call it a camalo? Towering over them all came a massive gray beast that thumped along like an elephant, but had a greenish scaly hide and big toothy alligator mouth. Must have been an alliphant.

Just as the thundering wall of weird meat bore down upon me, I un-paralyzed and dove for the meager shelter of a small boulder sticking up from the ground on one side of the canyon. I landed with a thud, huddling in its shelter. The herd roared by, shaking the ground like an earthquake, giving me a scarifying close-up at the massive bellies of the animals and hooves that would have ground me into unrecogniz-able road kill. The huge gray pox tried to leap the rock but stumbled, its hoof scraping across my back something fierce. The pox recovered its balance and pounded away, disappearing into the thick, roiling dust cloud. I hunkered down even more.

The rumbling faded as the animals disappeared down the canyon, and a voice emerged from the noise. I stayed down, hearing a whistle and a shout. Somebody had stampeded that herd of animals from genetic hell on purpose

A white horse galloped past the rock, and the rider reined it in, holding a long-barreled revolver high and ready.

"There y'are. Figured we'd catch ya. Guess your buddy's somewhere around here mashed underfoot." I raised up enough to see the rider peering up at the cat from beneath a sweat-stained cowboy hat. The cat glared down at him, showing teeth and hissing. I saw my chance.

I leaped up and sprinted for a low rock about four feet to the right of the horse and rider. I leaped onto the rock, shoving off as hard as I could, sailing into the rider, smashing into his shoulder, ripping him off the horse. We slammed to the ground in a dusty flailing heap, with me on top.

Now I figured we'd have a big movie fight. I'd slug him, making this loud whacking sound. Then he'd hit me with another bone-crunching whack. Then he'd break a tree limb over my back and I'd be all bloody and down. Then I'd come back like this big hero and whale the living daylights out of him.

At least that's how I figured it would be. I stood up, fists clenched, ready to go, but he just laid there on the ground curled up in a ball. His hat came off his head and rolled brim up onto the dirt.

"Shit," he wheezed. "You . . . landed . . . right on me. Can't . . . breathe." He rolled over on his back and tried to suck in air.

"Well, you tried to kill me."

"Didn't . . ." He tried again and drew a rasping breath. "Didn't give you no call . . . landing on me like that."

He eased himself onto his stomach and tried to stand up. I found the revolver and held it on him. I realized a straggler was watching us—the long-haired white cow standing there with a dumb cow look. I guess she'd gotten tired of stampeding.

"So, you saw me coming?"

The cowboy struggled to his feet, but stayed bent over, his hands on his knees. His stringy blond hair had been flattened against his skull by his cowboy hat, except for those dumb-looking little wings of hair that stick out above the ears.

He breathed in, wheezed out and spat. "I was out here checking on the herd. Saw you up the canyon with the cat and called in. They said it might be you . . . Boatright. They said not to risk getting close; just to stampede the animals down, let them do the work." He squinted sideways at me. His sunburned face was covered with sparse young-kid stubble. "They said you could be a sneaky little shit."

Obviously, I needed a new plan. The cowboy almost certainly hadn't called in since the stampede. And he was about my size.

"Take off your clothes," I commanded.

"You some kind of sissy?"

"Nope. Just need your clothes." I waggled the gun at him for emphasis.

Within ten minutes, I had on his clothes and he was tied up with my boot laces sitting over in a shady part of the canyon. The cat had climbed down and monitored the process with apparent approval. As the cat, the cowboy, and the cow watched, I pulled the hat down low on my brow, and checked the gun. I tried to psych myself up for the masquerade I was going to attempt.

"Reviled did I live, said I, as evil I did deliver!"

"What's that?" asked the cowboy, trying to scooch himself up into a comfortable position against a rock.

"A palindrome," I said. "Seemed appropriate."

I followed after the horse, which had wandered off down the canyon a bit, cropping some grass. I hadn't paid too much attention to the horse, being occupied with the rider. It was a huge, muscular white horse from the rear. Then it turned its head around to look at me with sapphire-blue eyes. A three-foot spiral pearl-white horn jutted straight out from its forehead. A unicorn! The cowboy must have been saddle-training the animal for a buyer.

I climbed aboard the incredible mythical beast, and called to the cat, who with a great leap bounded onto the saddle, settling its muscular body in front of me. I reined the unicorn to the right and gave it a kick. The fine, broad-backed animal launched into a solid trot up the canyon, his horn waving up and down as if he was directing an orchestra with it. Riding this great animal, with the amazing cat as my ally, I began to feel like maybe I could be a hero after all.

CHAPTER 33

Deep twilight had fallen when the people outside the cabin saw their guy in his cowboy hat ride out of the gloom on the unicorn. They waved. I waved back and held up the cat in triumph. I'd spent an hour watching the cabin from behind a screen of bushes. I'd seen only two of Miravelle's men standing guard outside, with another two people in the house, almost certainly along with Callie and Lulu.

"So it was him!" shouted one of the men out front. "The stampede got him? And that's the cat?"

I waved a fist in triumph, keeping my hat pulled low.

"You should've called," said the other, holding a rifle across his chest. I waggled the cowboy's cell phone like I was disgusted with it. "Yeah, shit," said the guy. "Bouncing around knocks 'em out on me, too."

I was close enough for my trick, if the cat would cooperate. I leaned down to him. "Okay, now run for it!" I gave him a nudge, and he cooperated perfectly, leaping off the saddle and streaking away around the side of the house.

"Damn!" I hollered, trying to sound like the guy I was impersonating. The two guys took the bait—that is, the cat—and hustled after him, with shouts of "Get 'em!" and "Miravelle will be pissed!" leaving me free to hit the house.

I slid down off the unicorn, tied it to the porch post, and slipped into the cabin, leaving the door open for a quick escape. The cabin had a mud room with big, rough-hewn wood benches on either side for taking off boots and rows of pegs to hang skis and guns. Through a door on the left was a big darkened dining room with long wood tables and benches and a stone fireplace. On the right, a closed door showed a slice of light through the crack at the floor. I pulled the gun, took a deep breath and kicked open the door.

Miravelle started from his chair in front of the fireplace, still holding his glass of wine. Standing in front of the fireplace was the one-eyebrow-guy I'd talked to on the viddie, with his mountain-road-map face and mop of hair. He started to reach for a gun in his belt holster, but saw my revolver leveled at him and thought better of it, slowly raising his hands.

Callie and Lulu sat on a big leather couch across from the fireplace, their wrists handcuffed in front of them.

"Who the hell are you?" asked Miravelle, peering at my secondskin-covered face.

"Just looking for Julio. Don't you recognize the voice?"

The scowl on his face told me my phone trick had dawned on him.

"Timmy!" exclaimed Callie, leaning toward me. "My God, what are you doing here!" Her cheek showed a big purple bruise. Miravelle would pay for that.

I stepped to one side of the door, so if anybody came in I'd get the drop on them. "You okay? Came to get you." I cocked the gun and told Miravelle and One-eyebrow to put their guns on the floor. One-eyebrow dropped his, and Miravelle slowly opened his coat and turned around, revealing that he wasn't carrying one.

Lulu stood up, her face pale with fear and just said "Oh no, Timmy. There's—"

But Miravelle backhanded her with a wallop that sent her sprawling backward over the couch and onto the floor.

Callie leaped for the gun, but Miravelle kicked it away beneath a large bookcase across the room and grabbed her, wrenching her in front of him as a shield. She took up Lulu's warning "Tim, there's a—"

Miravelle leaped to the right and my gun followed him.

"ATTACK!" he shouted.

He'd distracted me from the door to my left, which burst open. With a deep-throated growl, a huge blur hurtled out of the darkness and slammed into my body, knocking the gun away. I collapsed to the floor, the suffocating mass on top of me and wrenched my body around to look into the snarling face of a Big Nasty. In desperation, I slammed my fist into its jaw, tearing my knuckle on a fang, but having no effect on its utter determination to rip me apart. I tried to grab for my hunting knife, but the Nasty pinned my arms beneath its legs, crouching on my chest, leaving me unable to breathe.

Lulu rolled from her position on the floor and kicked hard at the Nasty, slugging it solidly in the side. But the Nasty lashed back with a huge claw knocking her away like a rag doll and slashing her jeans.

Callie, still in Miravelle's grip, shouted "For God's sake, stop it!"

The Nasty wrapped a taloned claw over my face, tearing my secondskin. It wrenched back my head to expose my throat and opened its massive jaws. The stink of its flesh, its hot animal breath enveloped me, and I prepared to die.

But I didn't. Instead, the Nasty suddenly roared and sat straight upright, throwing back its ugly head, taking its claw from my face. It stood up on its hind legs, towering over me, groping frantically to reach something behind it. From the floor, my vision blurred from the impact, I could only tell that its brown back appeared to have grown a furry, blue hump. The Nasty spun around, grasping behind it, and I realized the hump was the cat! It had vice-clamped its jaws down on the Nasty's neck, its back legs braced, its front claws raking bloody welts in the Nasty's furry shoulders.

The Nasty lurched around the room roaring with rage and pain, smashing lamps, slamming into the couch, trying to dislodge the cat, who hung on and continued its attack. I rolled over, trying to see where the gun had gone. One-eyebrow fled, and Miravelle held Callie tight, flattening himself against the wall, waiting for the cat's death and mine. Lulu leaped to the corner, avoiding the Nasty's powerful flailing, also looking for the gun.

I knew the cat didn't have a chance. Once the Nasty reached him, he was dead. Then it was our turn to die. I drew the knife and looked for an opening to stab the Nasty without hurting the cat. But all I could see was a spinning blur of locked animals and flailing claws careening around the room.

Then the cat vaulted himself free of the Nasty, who recovered and turned toward us, its face contorted in the most vicious, snarling rage I have ever seen. The cat landed against the wall near me and turned to face the Nasty, who advanced with its fangs bared, its front claws reaching, anticipating the pleasure of tearing us into bloody chunks.

Strangely, the cat just sat there and watched impassively. I crouched, holding the knife in front of me, knowing what a futile gesture it was. For a second time, I faced certain death. But I'd do as much damage as I could before it took me. Maybe I could hurt it enough to save Lulu and Callie. The Nasty growled once more, but then stopped only feet away, panting strangely.

I stood up from my crouch and looked into its grotesque face. The snarl had faded into a dazed expression. The obsidian-black eyes grew glassy. A gelatinous foam began to dribble from its lips. It stumbled and reached out a claw toward me, a faint guttural sound coming from its throat. I held the knife ready, but somehow knew I wouldn't need it.

Then it collapsed onto its belly with a thud that shook the room. The cat still sat and watched with that peculiar calm. Miravelle froze, a look of stunned disbelief on his face, giving Callie the opening she needed to elbow him in the gut, wrench free, grab a poker from the fireplace and hold it at his chest.

"Move and you've got a new part in your nice hair," she said.

Lulu shouted a cry of discovery and hurdled the couch, bent down and rose up holding my revolver in both handcuffed hands. A clunking of boots came from the front porch and three men, including One-eyebrow, filled the doorway, holding guns. Cool as she could be, Lulu stepped behind Miravelle and jammed the muzzle against the base of his skull.

"Let's just think things over, okay, guys? The guns?" she said calmly. Miravelle nodded at the men to pitch their guns into the room.

The Nasty's breaths now had a rattling finality to them. I stepped over to it, my knife ready, and nudged it with the toe of my boot. It shuddered and jerked its arms as if trying to rise and attack. But then with a final wheeze, its breathing stopped, and the stink of its bowel emptying rose from it.

"What did you do?" I asked the cat, who walked calmly over to the Nasty, sniffing it delicately and circling its inert hulk. Satisfied that the animal was dead, he turned and nuzzled my leg.

"You got 'em under control?" I asked Lulu, who answered by pushing the gun even more firmly against Miravelle's skull. He raised his hands, showing his gold wristwatch.

"We're fine, sport," she said. Callie retrieved the handcuff keys from One-eyebrow and proceeded to uncuff herself and Lulu.

I bent down to check the cat for injuries. I still couldn't figure out why the Nasty had died. I ran my fingers across the cat's head, neck and back to check for wounds from the Nasty and found none. I lifted a front paw, finding it wet, but not with blood. I gently pressed the pad, making the claws extend. They were formidable-looking weapons, but not enough to kill. Then, from the tip of each claw exuded a glistening droplet.

I stood up, stunned.

"God!" I breathed the word. "My God!"

"What?" asked Callie.

"Poison. This cat has poison."

"It's been poisoned?" asked Lulu.

"No, it's poisonous. Like a snake. It's got venom in its claws."

Miravelle's mouth dropped open, the first time I'd ever seen him so rattled.

"Didn't know that, eh, Julio?" I asked him. "A little surprise from the guy who made the cat. Rozoff really was a genius."

But as the realization sunk in, I got a thermonuclear case of the shudders myself. One scratch from that cat would have killed me, too. I remembered the dye job, holding him yowling and fighting in the bathtub. He could have killed me then, but he knew his own power. And he knew I was his friend. I steadied myself and picked the cat up very, *very* carefully and went to stand behind Lulu.

"We're moving out now," I commanded. Miravelle nodded, and they did so. Callie and I both picked up guns that the men had dropped and we started outside onto the lighted porch.

I asked Lulu to find rope, and she ran for a nearby barn. I had everybody stand in pairs, back to back, against the porch pillars. Lulu brought rope back, twirling one end with obvious satisfaction at the prospect of tying up her former captors.

"Wait a second," I said, handing my gun to Lulu. I peered at Callie's face to gauge where her bruise was. Then I reared back and slugged the holy shit out of Miravelle in the same place. He grunted and went down hard in the dirt, thoroughly soiling his nice suit.

"That's for Callie and Lulu," I told Miravelle as he struggled back up, glaring at me.

"Nice shot," said Callie, as Lulu nodded in agreement.

My hand hurt, but it was worth it. I shoved the stunned Miravelle over to a porch support and took the gun back while Callie and Lulu lashed the men to the posts. They frisked all of them, finding Miravelle's expensive googles and processor. Callie and Lulu gathered all the processors and cell phones we could find and stuffed them into the unicorn's saddle bag. I yanked the central processors out of the four-wheel-drive trucks and added them to the bag. We would pitch the whole bunch out into the brush somewhere.

Finally, I picked up the cat and dipped his paws in a water trough, very gently washing away the dried venom. He wasn't especially pleased, but I didn't need an accidental scratch killing me after all I'd been through.

Miravelle had recovered, as he sat against the post with his hands tied to the guy behind him.

He looked groggily up at me. "You know, this is not the end. I always get revenge. But if you just give us the cat, I will forget. We will clear you with the police. And we will let the whole thing drop. Otherwise—"

"Otherwise what?"

"You will all die." He said it offhandedly, with that smooth accented voice that would have scared me any other time. But I'd just proved to myself that Julio Miravelle could be brought down like anybody else.

"Well, Julio, right now it looks like I've got the upper hand. And after all, you tried to kill me."

"Matter of business." He shrugged, which was as close to an apology as he could probably come.

"By trampling? Ripped apart by a Nasty? That's pretty rotten business. Look, Julio, once we get some distance between us, we'll call. Maybe we'll negotiate then." I knew I'd never give up the cat, but I wanted to leave them guessing while Callie, Lulu and I figured this whole thing out.

I mounted the unicorn, tapped the saddle horn and the cat leaped up in front, settling against my stomach. I helped Lulu up, and she pulled up Callie behind her. Lulu put her arms around my waist and it felt really good. We had a fully loaded unicorn, but it was one big animal, so it took our four light bodies without complaint.

I gave the massive animal a nudge in the ribs with my heels and we cantered away into the darkness, its waving, pearlescent horn directing some silent symphony.

CHAPTER 34

The flat, sun-blasted desert slid by outside the car window, mile after sandy mile. "So, you're sure this guy is okay?" I asked, sitting in the front seat, with the cat curled up beside me. Callie drove my car, peering out the windshield from behind big wraparound sunglasses. The bruise showed dark and ugly on her face. Lulu sat in the back seat, leaning forward between us.

"*Mother,* going there is dumb," she said. "Tim, this is the guy they call Mad Matt . . . Matt the Bat. He's a loony, burned-out old spook. *Mother,* you're nuts."

"I can handle Matthew," she said, her set jaw showing her annoyance at Lulu. "Besides, his place is impregnable. And it's got all the equipment we need."

As usual, Callie had come through at a critical time. We'd needed a place to hide out, to regroup, and she insisted that her old spy friend Matthew Winn would put us up, even if we arrived unannounced. So we'd driven all night from Utah to put distance between us and Miravelle.

We had no choice but to hide out. We'd already agreed we couldn't go to the cops, because that viddie showing me killing the guard might prejudice them against me . . . just a little bit. And even if I did agree to surrender, the news would be in the Mirror, Salvo's 'liner would find out, and I'd be dead before I got there. I felt like thirteen thunderclouds hung over me. My family and friends thought I'd killed somebody; maybe even Callie and Lulu thought so, too, a little bit. And Miravelle and Talbot wouldn't give up until they'd gotten the Cerulean back and killed me like they'd done poor Rozoff.

Talbot was the key. The only way out was to catch Talbot in his lies, to prove he was behind it all, so nobody had any doubt. But I had no idea how. Callie insisted Matthew could help us, if Matthew hadn't gone completely off the beam since she'd last seen him.

As Lulu leaned between us, awake and argumentative, I still held the sweet memory of her curled up in the back seat napping, her face so perfect, so pretty, in sleep. I'd tried not to make it obvious when I turned around and stared at her. I remembered the soft line of her jaw, the elegance of her eyes when they were closed.

Besides just enjoying the view of her, I'd kept looking because I was still puzzling over how she'd behaved after we got away from Miravelle. Callie had hugged me and given me a big loud smack on the cheek and said I was a very brave boy. But Lulu had just stood there in the darkness beside the car, looking at me strangely with that straight-on gaze of hers.

Once or twice, Callie had caught me stealing glances at Lulu sleeping.

Finally, she said real soft "Timmy, are you in love with my daughter? Or in lust?"

I'd smiled back at her, I guess with this dopey look on my face. "Well . . . uh . . . love."

She blew a sigh and shook her head. "Then you'll have trouble, son."

"What do you mean?"

"You'll find out."

And that's all she would say on that subject.

I could tell Callie was tiring, so we pulled over and did a switch, with Callie climbing in back to sleep and Lulu sitting up front. Still, the cat stayed right beside me on the seat.

Lulu glanced down at the cat, curled up sleeping as peacefully as cats sleep. She stroked its stunning blue fur, which glimmered in the light with each stroke.

"It's hard to believe that's a deadly animal. The poison claws."

He probably knew we were talking about him, but he didn't move, except for the gentle rise and fall of his chest. "Yeah, but I should have suspected something. I found a dead coywolf one morning when we were traveling. It only had scratches on it. That's all. And when he just showed up after that other Big Nasty chased us in the woods, I should have figured out he did more than just get away. A Nasty wouldn't have given up or lost our track."

"There's more to him, though." She placed her hand gently on the cat's head. His ear twitched and he flicked his tail, but he remained asleep.

"I know. There is something else. I don't know what it is, but there's something else. There's got to be a reason for this whole business. The catnapping. Talbot having those guys killed to get the cat back. Then keeping it a secret that they had it. I just can't figure."

After a while, Callie stirred in the back, sat up and stretched. Then I remembered what I wanted to ask her. "Callie, what's a Familiar?"

"A familiar what?"

"Not a familiar anything. Rozoff called the cat his Familiar."

Callie leaned forward from the back seat, smiling. "That's appropriate. A Familiar is a friendly spirit that inhabits an animal. Like a witch's Familiar is a black cat."

Out in the desert, a tan wispy dust devil whirled across the flatness, sucking up soil and bits of brush.

I stroked the cat, my fingers accidentally touching Lulu's. Well, not really accidentally. "You a friendly spirit?" I asked the cat. He didn't stir. "Hmm, well, cool. I guess that makes me a witch. But I think wizard's more like it." Callie chuckled and said something about me being a little full of myself. The cat continued to snooze, oblivious to my new profession.

We drove hours more, taking turns, stopping only to fill up with gas, use the bathroom, and grab whatever snacks and drinks we could eat in the car. Despite the danger, Callie insisted on making a phone call to Lulu's neighbor to make sure Shank, Priss, and Albert were all right. We had to practically tear her away from the phone, because she insisted on giving ultra-detailed instructions on how the neighbor should take care of each cat and explain her absence to it.

The only other long stop was at a station in the middle of an isolated desert town, when Callie decided that her blouse was too torn and dirty to wear. So, in the little gift shop she bought a big floppy t-shirt with a fierce-looking mountain lion on it. Lulu made some adjustments to her wardrobe, too. Since the dry desert heat had risen with the sun, she borrowed my hunting knife, went into the ladies' room and cut off her jeans to make shorts.

I visited the bathroom, too, to check my secondskin in the mirror. It was the last set, and after being mashed by the Nasty and being exposed to the desert sun, it looked kind of crinkly and dried out. I looked old and wrinkled, maybe about forty, but still convincing. At most stops, we just allowed ourselves the brief luxury of standing for a minute and stretching in the eyeball-searing desert wind that sucked moisture from our bodies. The cat would leap from the car, gazing at the horizon, then at us. He knew we were going somewhere, and seemed worried that we weren't there yet. So, we'd all climb back in the car and drive some more.

When Lulu took a turn driving, I sat there enjoying the lines of her slim body in the little t-shirt, her smooth brown legs sticking out of the cutoff jeans, ending in those cute clunky hiking boots. Then I drove again, just as the straight-arrow highway entered ranges of brown-gray mountains whose peaks traced jagged lines against a cloudless sky. The great jumbles of boulders were bare, except for the tall, massive saguaro cacti that seemed to stand a polite distance apart, stretching their long thick arms to the sky. The old ones had drooping arms with holes eaten in them by birds. The young ones were vertical gray-green prickly pillars, some with the first knobby hints of sprouting arms.

Finally, Callie directed me to slow the car, as she peered intently at the passing roadside. "Turn!" she barked abruptly, as we reached nothing more than a dusty path through a break in the fence. It stretched straight south across the desert floor, like a white scar in the desert scrub, to a notch in a distant mountain range. I shrugged and turned off the highway, bouncing onto the path and speeding across the desert. I squinted in the rear-view mirror, trying to see through the dust cloud whether we were being followed.

The car left the broad desert basin and entered a winding, sun-baked arroyo between the mountains. I swerved back and forth, skirting boulders and easing over deep potholes.

"You sure anybody lives out here?"

"*Mother,* this can't be the right road." Lulu sat in the back again, leaning forward with her elbows on the back of the front seat.

"It's the right road." Callie said from the shotgun seat, scanning the desert terrain.

"How far do we go?" I held tight onto the wheel as we kachunked into a pothole and bounced out.

"Until we're stopped."

"What's going to stop us?"

Callie just chuckled. I drove on for another few minutes, trying to figure out why she'd chuckled.

Then I found out. A bone-jarring whoomph, and an explosion tore a new pothole right in front of us, erupting a major chunk of desert into the air, raining sand and rock clattering down onto the car. I grabbed the cat and bailed out of the car, sprinting through the cloud of dust and out into the flat arroyo, glancing back to make sure Lulu and Callie had done the same, but Callie still stood beside the car.

"STOP!" boomed a disembodied voice from somewhere down the arroyo. I stopped, figuring a voice that loud had lots more explosives. I started toward a nearby boulder to hide behind. "YOU'RE IN A MINE FIELD," the voice boomed again. "STOP WHERE YOU ARE."

I was persuaded. I stopped, turned and looked back. Lulu had stopped, too, standing like she was in a snake pit, looking around her warily. But Callie calmly-as-she-pleased squinted up the arroyo shading her eyes with her hand.

"Matthew? Don't set off any more charges. It's me. Callie Lawrence."

A pause. We remained frozen in place.

"NO, ITS NOT," came over the loudspeaker.

Callie gave an exasperated wave of her hands. "Matthew, I should know who the hell I am, right?"

"YOU LOOK OLDER THAN CALLIE."

"You idiot! That's because it's been ten years since you've seen me!"

"WELL, MAYBE. PROVE YOU'RE CALLIE."

"Matthew, get the kids and the cat out of the minefield."

Another pause. The cat wriggled to be let down, but I held him tight. I didn't think even he was smart enough to detect mines.

"THE MINES ARE OFF FOR ONE MINUTE. WALK AHEAD UP THE TRAIL."

We all hustled back to the car and hiked up the arroyo, pocked here and there with other potholes, probably created for the benefit of other visitors.

We reached a small cinderblock building with a loudspeaker on top that was the source of the voice.

"ONE BY ONE, STEP INSIDE AND SHUT THE DOOR. STAY THERE UNTIL THE GREEN LIGHT COMES ON."

Even though I'd been taught ladies first, I figured the rule didn't really apply here. So I handed Lulu the cat and stepped in. I stood in the dark, stifling building, as a faint electronic hum rose, along with the whine of a small fan.

"What's this all about?" I asked anybody who could answer.

"You're being sniffed, scanned," said Callie through the door. "Gas chromatograph. Magnetometer. X-rays. Microwaves. Computer's checking you for explosives, weapons."

A green light flashed on and I stepped outside into the desert glare. I held the cat, as Lulu and Callie took their turns. Just as Callie came out, a man appeared up the pathway.

I always liked the word "gaunt" when I took creative writing in college. It had a great, soulful sound. Gaunt. I'd tried to use it as much as possible, but my teacher got tired of it. Especially one time when I wrote "It was a gaunt day."

Well, this guy defined gaunt. He wore baggy old jeans that would have been tight on anybody else. And his ratty t-shirt hung on a frame that made a skeleton look porky. A stained straw cowboy hat shadowed sunken cheeks with leathery, wrinkled skin, and a scraggly excuse for a beard. He had a haunted look. Gaunt and haunted. Sounded good together.

He held up a machine pistol, not quite pointing it at us, but not quite pointing it away.

"Prove you're Callie."

Callie put her hands on her hips. "Matthew, I see you're the same."

"Have to be. He's still after me."

"*He's* dead. Been dead for six years."

"Clever son-of-a-bitch wants me to think that. Prove you're Callie."

She marched toward him, her mountain lion blouse billowing in the desert breeze. He brought up the pistol, but she didn't stop. She got right up to him and said something real low in his face. He stepped back, startled, and lowered the pistol. Callie turned and motioned to us.

"This is Matthew Winn. An old friend." She put her arm around Matthew who stiffened as if he hadn't had human contact for a long time. She introduced Lulu and me. The gun came up again.

"That's not Timothy Boatright," he growled. "I watch the viddies." He gripped the gun, bracing himself for the recoil when he shot.

"MATTHEW, DON'T!" Callie moved to get between us, but I stepped away so she wouldn't get hit. I stared at the dark gunhole where the bullets would come out, trying to figure out what was going on. Then it dawned on me. I reached up and tore off the secondskin. As my real cheeks, nose, forehead and chin showed, Matthew still peered suspiciously at me from beneath the old hat. But he brought the gun down a bit.

"Okay, yeah. I recognize the face from the viddies." He lowered the gun all the way. "That the Cerulean?" He gestured with the gun barrel at the cat.

"Yes, that's the famous cat," said Callie.

Matthew cocked his head and looked suspiciously at the Cerulean. "That ain't no cat."

I looked down at the cat, who also watched Matthew steadily. "Funny, that's what the guy who made him said."

"I watch the viddies real close," mumbled Matthew. "I watch all the viddies. Watch 'em close." He turned and climbed up the trail.

We followed and Callie walked alongside him, explaining that we needed some place to hide. And we needed his help because of his "capabilities." I didn't know exactly what his capabilities were, but the explosive part might be helpful.

Matthew didn't like the idea at all. "Can't do it. I got security problems enough. I'll give you food and water. Then you leave."

"Matthew, you remember Columbia?"

Matthew trudged silently up the trail a few steps.

"You can stay a day. Then you leave."

"Caracas?"

Another pause. Another few steps in silence. "A few days. Week maybe. Then you leave."

"La Paz? You'd be rotting in a shallow grave there, except for me."

Pause. "Damn. Okay. Long as you need."

The trail passed a couple of burned-out cars and a beat-up but functional Jeep and wound up out of the arroyo. After quizzing Matthew to make sure the area wasn't mined, I let the cat roam ahead of us. We climbed the narrow trail that cut across the south face of the mountain, higher and higher, until we came onto one end of a broad rock ledge that looked out over the desert floor to the shimmering horizon. The desert heat baked us, and the wind sucked away our sweat, so that by the time we'd reached the ledge, we were parched.

Matthew led us through a square mineshaft entrance in the mountainside and into a dark, cool tunnel that led into the mountain's depths. He opened a big steel door set in the side of the tunnel and we stepped into a chamber that stretched for forty feet beyond. But the chamber was well lit, and as we stepped in, I realized why. One wall of the chamber consisted of thick, clear, floor-to-ceiling glass, likely bulletproof, with a broad view of the desert to the south. A door led outside to the ledge beyond, which ended with a low rock wall punctuated with gun ports.

Inside the big rock chamber, a telescope and tripod-mounted binoculars pointed out into the desert. The far wall held solid banks of electronic equipment—junky old stuff, but with all its lights blinking.

The side across from the window held another door into the mountain, a battered old picnic table, a saggy bed, a night stand and piles of books all around. Matthew hung his machine pistol on a large rack beside the door that also held a multitude of clean, well-oiled weapons of every sort, from a little snub-nosed revolver up to a large-bore cannon that could punch holes in a tank. I also recognized three long-range shoulder-mounted missiles and a laser-illuminator to guide them.

The cat began exploring, first circling the room, then tentatively nosing each piece of furniture and equipment.

Matthew stood, uncertain what to do next. He didn't have to decide. Callie decided for him.

"Get these kids and me some water. You got any food?"

"Beans, tortillas."

Lulu laughed. "Beans? It must get pretty smelly up here in Fort Apoo-calypse."

Callie gave her a scolding look, but she made a funny face back. Then, to Matthew, "How about you heat up the food? You got any beer?"

"Dulls the senses," said Matthew as he stepped through the doorway cut in the rock and into what must have been a kitchen and storage area.

Callie could tell I was very disappointed about the beer. "Yeah, we wouldn't want dull senses," she said, with a wry smile.

We roamed around looking at all Matthew's military stuff until he appeared with a pot of beans and a pile of tortillas on a paper sack. He set them on the picnic table, and came back with a plastic jug of water, plastic glasses and big army-issue spoons. As we sat down, he moved a sack of oranges and a magnifier off the table.

I poured water into one of the glasses and held it down for the cat to lap up with his big pink tongue. I pulled out a tin of cat food I'd brought up from the car and opened it, spooning some onto a piece of sack paper. He finished drinking and started to eat.

Then I poured myself a big glass of water and gulped some down. It tasted like distilled, with no minerals, no chlorine. I looked at the oranges. "Mind if we have an orange?"

Matthew held up one in each hand. "You can have these two. I'm still checking the rest out."

I completed my guzzle. "For what?"

"Needle marks."

"Like hypodermic?"

"I check all the produce."

Lulu smiled that mischievous smile of hers and began to peel an orange. "You check grapes? That must be tedious."

Matthew furrowed his brow. "Yeah, it is. Don't eat many grapes."

"You analyze all your food?" Lulu chewed an orange slice thoughtfully. I needed more substance, so I started on the beans, packing steaming gobs of them in a tortilla and chomping away. Matthew had obviously perfected his beans recipe over a long period, because they were spicy and good.

"He's afraid he'll be poisoned, right, Matthew?" Callie spooned beans onto her plate and began eating.

Matthew's face clouded up as he examined his plate of beans carefully before taking the first mouthful. "You never know where he'll strike. I run everything through a lab I got in the back. Chemical, biological. Check everything. You'd be surprised what I find. Parts of *Periplaneta americana. Blatta orientalis.* Hairs of *Rattus rattus.*

"Whattus whattus?" asked Lulu.

"Roach parts. Rat hairs. I got a collection I can show you . . ."

Lulu made a blechhing sound, but Matthew didn't notice.

". . . I do species analysis. Look for South American variants. It tells me whether the food might have come from South America, where he could've poisoned it."

"Who?" I asked. Callie arched an eyebrow as if to tell us to prepare ourselves for Matthew's delusion.

"Rojas." Matthew's already haunted-looking face got even more so, with a blank stare like he was seeing ghosts.

"Romulo Liberio Rojas," said Callie. "Meanest drug lord in South America. Anywhere, really. Matthew thinks Rojas has been after him for the last twenty years."

"He is," said Matthew.

"Was. Maybe. But he's dead."

"Then his family."

"Matthew, you killed his family."

CHAPTER 35

Matthew seemed to deflate a little at the memory, his old eyes growing sadder than usual.

Callie tried to comfort him. "Look, Matthew, you couldn't help it. You didn't know." Then, to us: "Matthew was in charge of a mission to stop this drug shipment. Big one. He used a shoulder-mounted missile to bring down the plane he thought was carrying it. Turned out, Rojas had rescheduled the shipment and decided to send his whole family on a Christmas shopping trip to Miami. They all died. Rojas vowed to get Matthew, and that's how he ended up here."

Matthew mumbled something about doing his daily scan and went off to the bank of computers and viddie screens. He stood there lost in fiddling with controls, bringing up telescopic images of the desert.

Lulu decided to change the subject. "Listen, I've got to take a shower. Get some of this road gunk off." Matthew told her his bathroom was back in the depths of the mountain, and she went off in search of it.

A kathumping sound emanated from speakers attached to the bank of computers.

"Matthew, what's that?" asked Callie.

"Rabbit. He lives in the area." Matthew touched a few buttons and the viddie screen lit up with a close-up of a skinny, big-eared jackrabbit crouched in the shade of a desert bush. The rabbit hopped. The speaker sounded kathump.

"He's usually in sector R546 in the afternoon. Guess he prefers R565 this afternoon. I track him."

"You've got quite a monitoring system," I said, trying to figure out all the buttons, dials, viddie screens and optical storage consoles.

"Yeah, visual, infrared, radio. I see it all."

"The Indians still call you Strange Hawk?" Callie sat down in a creaky old chair by the control panel and crossed her legs at the ankles.

"Yeah," said Matthew, with only a trace of pride.

"The Indians love Matthew. He's found a couple of their kids lost in the desert over the years. And the DEA loves him, too. Basically, the drug runners know he's got this whole section of the desert locked down tight. They never go through here. DEA has him on their payroll, right, Matthew?" A bunch of kathumps sounded through the speakers.

"Rabbit's moved to S456," announced Matthew, peering intently at the screen.

I realized Matthew could probably do all kinds of interesting things with his equipment. "I need to call my folks," I said. "Can you help? Can you make it untraceable?"

Matthew smiled a crooked half-smile, still fiddling with the controls to sweep the expanse of desert to the south. "Yeah, sure. Soon's I do my afternoon scans. I have to do my afternoon scans. Maybe in a couple of hours, I'll set it up."

Lulu showed up after a while looking fresh and scrubbed, with her wet hair slicked back, and I decided I needed a shower, too. The cat still roamed the room, restless. I figured he needed some freedom, so I asked Lulu if she'd like to go up the trail I'd seen to the mountain summit after I took my shower. She said sure, why not.

The shower consisted basically of a big chamber cut into rock with a little waterfall you could turn on by pulling a rope. I figured Matthew had somehow rigged a cistern that caught the summer rains and stored them. I stood there happily letting the cool water sluice over me and thinking of the cat and my folks and Lulu.

When I came out, the sun had lowered to near the horizon, bathing the desert in a golden-tan light. Matthew still occupied himself with his scans, and Callie had taken off for town. She decided that we needed more than a diet of beans and tortillas, and certainly needed beer, so she'd headed for the nearest store. However, before she left, she'd gotten Matthew to admit that he kept one six-pack for celebrating, although I couldn't imagine what he'd celebrate in his cave. Callie agreed to buy him new beer, so she split the six pack with Lulu and me, two each. I stuffed one can in my pocket and opened the other and took a big swig. The taste was a little stale, but delicious, and I was thankful for the buzz. Lulu decided to save both hers for the mountaintop. I hefted the cat, and we started for the door.

I remembered something really important, if we were to come back in one piece. "Matthew, could you turn off the mines? I want to let the cat run."

"Yeah, but keep your head down." He turned away from the computers to stare at us with a slightly mad stare that made his face look like a crumpled leather shoe. "Snipers."

I held back a smile. "We'll watch it."

We stepped outside to find that the desert wind had died to a soft, cool, dry breeze. I took a deep breath, smelling the tang of desert brush, and Lulu said "Move it, nature-boy. Let's take a hike."

We found the trail we'd come up on, and it continued upward, so we climbed it. I put the cat down, and he bounded ahead making a "meeyowp" that I took to mean he was happy to be outside. The trail wound around boulders and over ledges, and after about fifteen minutes, we reached the mountaintop—a flat, rocky area with nice sitting boulders around the edge. It also held a forest of Matthew's antenna dishes and transmission towers, aiming every which way.

The cat leaped over a rock and disappeared, probably to hunt and do stuff that cats do, while I'd enjoy the view. And Lulu.

She climbed onto a rock looking out over the desert, sat down and stretched out her long, tanned legs, and opened a beer. I climbed up beside her. The sun had just set, leaving a rich orange, red and pink glow across the sky. The low-angle light made every bush and cactus across the desert floor below seem to have a personality of its own. The saguaros looked like soldiers getting ready to stand guard for the night. The other bushes . . . I think they were creosote or sagebrush or something . . . seemed to huddle in shadow as if they were keeping some secret.

"This is sure a different kind of place than I grew up in," I said, making conversation. "It's all browns and tans. No green."

Lulu took another swig of beer and leaned forward, hugging her knees. "Pretty, though. Stark beauty. I know a guy who came out here for a year. Artist. When he came back, he'd made some incredible paintings."

"And you sold them for him? You're like an agent?"

"Yeah . . . an agent."

"But I know there's more to it than that. C'mon, what do you really do?"

"I'm an agent."

"You can tell me."

"You'll tell *Mother*." Always there was that wry snap of her voice when she said "Mother."

"I won't tell if you don't want. And what's the problem, anyway?"

She looked at me. It was the closest our faces had been. I enjoyed the play of the soft desert light on her oval face, her little straight nose with the delicate nostrils. "The problem is . . ." She rolled her eyes in frustration. ". . . look, my mother and I just have this relationship thing. This problem. I don't want to be like her. But I am. And I don't want her to know that."

"And you also want to make her suffer a little, not knowing what you do? Maybe keep her in the dark like she did to you, about her life?"

She took another drink and shrugged. "You're pretty smart for a kid."

"So what do you do?"

She took another slow drink of beer. She seemed to be buying time to think, making some decisions. I opened my second beer and we both drank together in silence.

"Well, okay, I'm not exactly an agent. I'm kind of a hustler. Okay, I'm an art hustler."

"And what does an art hustler do?"

"Well, I get to know artists. Ones I think are really promising. Or, sometimes ones that are already really hot. And I hustle paintings out of them. Or sculptures, or holos, or virties . . . whatever they do."

"You get them free? Like that big blob sculpture in your apartment?"

"Yeah. That'll fetch a couple of million in a year or so." She took a big drink, lay back and stretched out on the rock, and stared up at the darkening blue-gray sky, now just a little darker than her eyes.

I didn't know if I was going to like the answer to the next question. "And how do you persuade them to give you their things free?"

She smiled at the night sky. "Not the way you think, filth-brain. I tell them where the money will go when I sell them."

"Where."

She took a deep breath, and her breasts rose and fell beneath the thin t-shirt. "Damn. Well . . . orphans."

"Like, you mean kids?"

"That's usually what orphans are. Yeah." She talked like it was a tiresome thing to admit. "I give it all to these places that take in kids who don't have parents . . . they died or left. Foster families. Institutions. The artists keep it quiet. They don't want collectors to know they give their stuff away, even to orphans."

"Wow . . . orphans . . . that's really nice, Lulu."

"I'm just like Callie. Saving the damned world."

"How do you live?"

"Grandma left me all her money. I don't need much."

I laid down on my side beside her and put my hand on her cheek. It was the first time we'd been horizontal together. We were getting somewhere.

"And so you're helping kids who you think are like you were? Abandoned by their parents."

She took a deep breath, and I thought I could see her eyes glistening. She was silent a long time before she said to the sky "I wasn't abandoned. I never had parents."

"You've got your mother. Callie."

She turned her head toward me, tears filling her eyes, watching my face intently, but I didn't know for what. "Callie's not my mother."

"Who then?"

"Nobody. I'm a clone. I'm Callie's clone."

I must have flinched without meaning to, because she sat bolt upright, breathing hard, almost sobbing. "I knew you'd react like that. Like I'm a freak. I just knew!"

"But how—"

"When she was a spy, she disappeared in South America. The CIA thought she was dead. Back then they had a clause in their contracts that said they'd clone whatever agent was lost, as a kind of compensation to the family. The technology was new then, and of course they'd been messing around with it in secret."

"So, they made you."

"My grandma was so crushed at losing her daughter that she agreed to it, maybe without really thinking it through. So, nine months later I got delivered to her doorstep by some scientist, and she raised me. Callie did show up a couple of years later. She'd been held prisoner and was finally traded. Then when I was ten, I found some papers that made me realize Callie couldn't be my mother because she'd been in South America. I realized I wasn't *me,* I was *her.* I was a policy decision."

"She loves you."

"Yeah, right. She loves herself."

"No, you . . . Lulu. I can tell. Because—"

"Because you're such a smart kid?"

"Because I understand it. Because I love you."

Now *she* flinched. She stood abruptly, silhouetted against the darkening sky, trembling with emotion. Fear? Anger? Hurt? Probably all. "But there's no me to love. There's only Callie."

"Wanna bet?" I stood and wrapped my arms around her slim body and kissed her. Now, I really do have a great kissing technique, but this was more than technique. This was world-class, from-the-heart persuasion that I loved this woman, and that she was special.

I put my soul into this one, starting with a soft kiss on her lips, feeling their lovely shape. She sob-hiccupped, but didn't pull away. With one hand, I stroked her cheek, wiping away tears. With the other, I reassuringly caressed the smooth curve of her back. I kissed deeper, and she kissed back. I stroked her soft hair. She made a little squeak and melded her body to mine, arms around me, hugging tight.

I paused. "See," I whispered into her small, delicate ear. "I love you, Lulu."

But she abruptly stiffened again and pushed me back, her jaw clenched, tear-stained face visible in the dying desert light. "No. I'm just not . . . I don't . . . Look, you're Callie's friend. You just can't be my . . ." She jumped off the boulder and stomped away down the trail. She kicked this big rock as she went, sending it clattering away down the mountain.

I stood for a while dumfounded before it began to dawn on me. Lulu wouldn't be ranting around like that unless she really loved me, too. I slowly began to grin like an idiot at what I'd just realized. I knew she'd come around once she thought about it. I'd be her rock, the source of her confidence that she was truly Lulu, not a copy of Callie. I'd be her love, and someday her lover.

I drained my beer as a celebration and wandered around the mountaintop, letting the realization sink in. The cat showed up with a dead rat in its mouth and laid it on a rock. He'd had a good evening, too. The cat watched me attentively with those big golden eyes, its head up, ears forward.

"Y'know, she loves me," I said to him. "She right surely does." I noticed she'd left her second beer, another sign of her love, so I also popped it open and started to drink. As I drained it, I felt better and better about the day's events, I examined Matthew's radio dishes and big antenna towers.

I pitched rocks at the cans sitting on the boulder. Missed every time. It wasn't just the beer; I'm a lousy pitcher. I'd had only one pitch in my Little League career, which whacked the coach's wife, who was standing by her car getting a glass of lemonade. After that, I played outfield.

But I was good at some things. I jumped up on the next boulder over from the cat, and defying the snipers let a terrific roaring belch out into the vast desert night. Like I was a foghorn warning ships away. The unimpressed cat toyed with its dead rat and licked its fur carefully. I felt really Hemingway-like now, standing alone and looking out over the wild desert, knowing this great girl loved me. Nick Adams would've approved.

A dust cloud off in the distance caught my eye. I could barely make it out in the fading light, but it looked like the cloud behind a car. My car. Callie was speeding down the dirt road, coming back from the store. I stomped the rock-dodging beer cans into pancakes and gathered them up. I requested the cat to come but please leave the rat, and we picked our way down the darkening trail to the entrance to Matthew's cave fort. I let myself in the big steel door and held it open for the cat to slither in after.

And I turned to find myself looking into the black barrel-hole of a big damned machine gun. Lulu stood beside the door, stock still, staring silently at the same barrel.

"God damn you!" snarled Matthew. He stood across the room, his hands clenched around the gun, his knuckles white, his face scrunched up with rage, "You're all dead!"

CHAPTER 36

It was a truly big gun and it would shoot a truly big bullet that would leave a big hole.

"What's going on? Why do you want to—"

"Let me see it!" Matthew jerked the gun at me, his eyes wild, crazy.

"See what?"

"The transmitter. You got a transmitter."

"I couldn't have."

"I did my scan, I got a strong transmission. Right next to the antenna. And you were up there." He jerked the gun at Lulu. "She comes down, and the transmission's still going on. It's you."

Then a steam line broke. At least that's what it sounded like, until the cat let out another steam-sounding hissy spit, leaping up on the table to Matthew's right, arching its back and laying back its ears. Then it loosed a low growly rumble.

Matthew glanced over at it. "Shut up, cat."

"Uh, Matthew, you've got a problem."

"No, I've got the gun, and you're going to die."

The door behind me opened and Callie pushed in, loaded down with grocery bags.

"Could you help me with—" Then she saw Matthew. "What is this? Matthew, put that gun down."

That cat crouched for a spring, tensing its back legs. Ironically I had to save Matthew's life, and he held the gun.

"Matthew, unless you put that gun down, the cat'll attack."

But Matthew only made it worse, holding up the gun, his finger tightening on the trigger. "Don't care about no cat scratches." The cat coiled, preparing to leap.

"Matthew, that cat's poisonous! He's got poison in his claws. Unless you quit threatening me, he'll kill you!"

"He's right Matthew," said Callie, still holding the groceries. "I've seen it."

"I have, too," said Lulu. "It killed a big animal just by scratching it."

Matthew's eyes flicked to the cat and back. A few muscles on his face twitched, sending a message of doubt.

Callie took a step forward. "Look, Matthew, we'll figure this out. You know me. I'll help you figure this out."

Matthew twitched some more. Then he slowly lowered the gun, and I leaped over to the cat, scooping him up, petting him. He still glared at Matthew with an animal's instinctive hatred, but I felt his muscles relax.

"I don't have a transmitter on me. I'm sure I don't."

"Well, it sure as hell can't be the cat," said Matthew.

Callie set the groceries down and took Matthew by both shoulders. "You can check, can't you? You could scan him."

Before I knew it, I was standing in the middle of the room, with Matthew running a loop of antenna wire over me and staring at an oscilloscope screen. The glowing line on the green screen stayed as flat as the desert horizon outside. He clicked some knobs and kept scanning. Still flat. He scratched his scraggly-haired head.

"I know there was a signal. I know it." He set the loop down on the picnic table and started to examine the metal studs on my jeans. This made me a little nervous. A man doesn't like another man examining his studs. Matthew stood up, still mystified. "Maybe it switched off. It could be in one of these rivets and just turn itself . . ." He glanced at the oscilloscope. Skittering across the screen were glowing, squared humps.

"That's it! That's the signal!" He peered intently at the screen, then we all looked over to see the cat nosing the wire loop curiously. "Damn if it ain't coming from the cat!"

Matthew edged toward his gun, but I put myself in his way. "If you shoot the cat, you'll never figure it out. You'll never know where this signal was going. And besides, there's a really good chance the cat would kill you first." I moved over to the cat and picked it up. I figured Matthew's paranoia would demand that he know what the signal was all about. I was right. He took a deep breath and looked to Callie, who nodded encouragingly.

"Yeah, okay. I'll do it." He moved over to his bank of computers and began to fiddle with a storage console. "We'll record some of the signal and do a fast Fourier transform, and . . ." his voice trailed off in the mumbling-to-self that people do when they live alone.

I handed the armload of cat over to Lulu. The cat seemed as happy to be in Lulu's arms as I'd been earlier.

"Look, can you link me up with my parents first? I really need to let them know I'm okay."

Matthew nodded and motioned for Lulu to hold the wire loop beside the cat. He set up the recording of the cat's transmission, then started the process of calling my folks.

"I don't have a land line, so it'll be low-def, no three-D."

"Yeah, whatever you can do." I sat down on a stool in front of the viddie screen beside Matthew's bank of equipment. The red light on the camera at the bottom of the viddie screen blinked on. The "Call Attempting to Connect" flashed on the screen for a long time. I thought I might get their voice message when Uncle Ned appeared on the screen. He had the same dark tousled hair, carefully trimmed beard, and tired eyes that had seen lots of crazy stuff. The resolution was low and two-D, since it was over-the-air transmission. But even that resolution showed him surprised.

"Timmy! My God, boy, are you all right?"

"Fine. I just called to tell my folks I'm fine. Where are they?"

His expression revealed his worry. "They're gone, Timmy."

"What do you mean gone? Where?"

"We don't know. Your dad didn't show up at a meeting at the factory, so his people called home and got no answer. And Kyle didn't go to school. By the time I got here, Sheriff Rainey was checking the house. They've gone. Your mother, too. Dinner dishes still on the table. We're afraid they were kidnapped."

I felt my throat knot up tight as a boiling rage built. "Talbot! Miravelle!" Lulu moved up beside me, holding the cat. I felt Callie's hand on my shoulder, and she stared at the screen, her face grim.

CHAPTER 37

When Matthew brought Talbot up on the viddie screen, and he saw it was me calling, he didn't seem surprised. And he didn't flinch when I bellowed at him "YOU SLIMY SON-OF-A-BITCH! IF YOU HURT THEM IN ANY WAY, I'LL FIND YOU, AND I'LL KILL YOU!" I wished I could reach right through the screen and choke the life out of him.

He just stood there in front of a big shelf of leather-bound books, looking calmly at me. Likely, he was enjoying having the upper hand. After a moment, he glanced questioningly to the side, as if he was looking at somebody off-camera.

He finally said "All we want is the cat. Will you give us the cat? Then we'll make everything right."

"You prove they're safe!"

"They're . . . not available. But they're safe. You have my word."

"Right. Your word."

"Yes, my word. It would be foolish of me to go back on my word. So here's what we demand—"

"Look, I'll bring the cat to you in two weeks. At Rozoff's house. Just you and Miravelle. Nobody else. As you've probably figured, I have access to the systems in Rozoff's house and all the sensors around there.

So, I'll know if you try to gang up on us." It was a good plan, meeting at Rozoff's far out in the woods. I'd have more control over the situation there. I gave Talbot a date and time, gave him another warning, and disconnected.

"Are you really going to give him the cat?" asked Lulu, stroking the brilliant blue fur.

I petted the beautiful animal that was also my friend, who'd saved my life. "I need to go think." The thunderclouds hung heavy over me, now. I grabbed a flashlight and opened the big door. The cat jumped from Lulu's arms and slipped out into the darkness ahead of me.

Lulu started after him, but Matthew said "It's okay. I got enough signal recorded to figure out what's going on." She stopped, unwilling to go up the mountain with me again. Callie huddled with Matthew, talking over the analysis they would do.

I strode through the tunnel and emerged into a cool desert night and the vast desert silence that I needed right now. I picked my way up the dark, winding trail holding the flashlight, with the cat stalking ahead, fully comfortable in his nocturnal element. At the top, I flicked off the flashlight and sat watching the dark desert and the explosion of stars glittering across a coal-black sky. Across the blackness, a meteor trail traced a glowing scratch that quickly faded. Back home on nights like these I'd lie out with my buddies and we'd look for the big space stations sailing across the starfield. We'd drink beer and talk about what life was like on the stations. We'd try to spot satellites. We'd talk a lot about girls. But tonight I just had to figure things out.

I plunged hard into thought, not seeing anything. There had to be some way to get all of us out of this mess. I was the only one who could do it, because I was the deepest into this thing.

I came up for mental air and realized the cat was gone. Not again! My eyes had become dark-adapted, but I couldn't see any faint movements that would reveal his presence in the shadows. I checked around boulders, peered over cliffs. I heard his meow and he strode into sight. I picked him up and decided I wouldn't let him go again. Sitting down on a flat boulder, hanging my feet over the edge, looking out across the desert, I held the cat in my lap and petted him, and he started that diesel-generator purr. I looked him deep in those glow-in-the-dark eyes.

I'd never really looked into them like that. They had a depth of intelligence I'd never seen before in a cat.

"Y'know, I had a cat like you, used to disappear all the time. He'd go for a few days, then show up all scratched. Big tomcat. Name was . . ." I stopped. A little tiny, bright light of realization suddenly flickered on in a deep part of my brain. And it started growing, and other realization-lights came on in other parts of my brain, and they started coming together in one big searchlight like a train roaring down the tracks toward me.

I jumped up and held the cat up in front of me. He just stared at me, calmly, like he always did, being a rational, logical cat.

"DAMN! DAMN! JESUS! WOW! I KNOW!" And I did know! I knew why this whole thing had started. I knew why Rozoff had invented this cat! And I knew why Talbot had done everything he had done!

I sat the cat down on a rock and petted him a couple of times. Then I hooted and whooped and stomped and danced around that mountaintop like a madman. Because I knew! I really knew!

Hauling butt down the trail with an armload of barely tolerant cat and without a flashlight, I almost ran off a cliff twice. When I slammed open that big steel door with a loud clang, Matthew instinctively reached for his gun.

I jabbered and jabbered and told them. I told them the whole thing from the very beginning, up to the cat running away, and my hyperultimate-very-cool genius in figuring it all out.

After I'd finished, Callie sat down on the table and just stared at me. Lulu picked up the cat and called him "You remarkable animal. You rascal."

"Well, now, we've got something else to tell *you*," she said, shaking her head. "This is just as incredible."

She and Matthew told me about the signals. How they were coming from the cat, and what they meant. Now it was my turn to sit down and stare at them dumfounded. But I was doing more than just being dumfounded; I was hatching one hell of a plan to save my folks and Kyle, to get us all out of this mess, and to stop Talbot and Miravelle for good.

"Won't cat lovers revolt? Act now!" I exclaimed triumphantly to myself. A very appropriate palindrome.

CHAPTER 38

I stood on the broad front porch of Rozoff's lodge after two weeks of waiting. My anger hadn't faded, my fists clenched as I watched the black electric limousine ease silently around the bend in the road, heading toward me. Its silence in the calm, overcast, rain forest morning allowed me to listen for any telltale sounds from the thick woods that might betray any of Talbot's human or animal henchmen. But the forest remained dead quiet, confirming what the sensor system surrounding the property indicated. No other people within miles. Talbot and Miravelle had heeded my warning.

I managed to unclench the fists. They seemed to have a life of their own, and they wanted like crazy to pound Kenneth Talbot and Julio Miravelle into bloody, unrecognizable pulps. But my head, not my fists, had to control what would happen here today. The complicated plan had to work precisely right or we'd all die like Rozoff certainly had. Phase one, phase two, phase three—they all had to come off like clockwork.

The car rolled to a stop, and Miravelle eased out of the driver's seat, showing the satisfyingly large greenish-yellow healing bruise I'd produced on his right cheek, and holding a black attaché case in his hand.

He stood looking coldly at me like a snake regards something it's about to eat. He scanned the cabin and the surrounding woods, then opened the limo's back door and spoke to someone inside.

Talbot emerged from the car, rising ponderously on his electrically operated paralyzed legs and stood, assessing me, still no doubt trying to figure if I was up to more than he knew. My fists reminded me again what they wanted to do, but the head kept control. Talbot smiled! The son-of-a-bitch smiled! His right hand held the little control box, and he manipulated it with his thumb and fingers to launch himself plodding robot-like toward me. Miravelle followed, and they stopped at the bottom of the porch steps.

"Hello, Timothy," said Talbot. "I know we've had our problems. But let us settle this unfortunate situation amicably. Quietly. With profit for all."

"Where's my family?"

"Safe. They're just fine. Shall we go in?"

I stepped through the front door that was still smashed from the Nasty's attack, gaining great confidence from the knowledge that two Big Nasties now lay dead thanks to the Cerulean. The cat and I could make this plan work.

In the big, high-ceilinged main room of the lodge, I faced them. Miravelle set his case down on a table and opened its lid to reveal an electronic control panel. He flicked a switch, jiggered a few knobs, then took out his googles and plugged them into the case. His eyes hidden behind the dark glasses, he scanned the room, taking in every corner and carrying the case about the room to see behind furniture and into closets and adjacent rooms. After a silent minute, he took off the glasses.

"No active cameras, no transmitters in the room," he reported. "No guns. No explosives."

"Good fellow, Timothy," said Talbot cheerfully. "Our own scans also showed no inconvenient intruders. So, you kept that part of the bargain. Now, let us see whether you kept it all. The cat?" He gestured expectantly with one hand, the other holding his control box, and raised his eyebrows expectantly.

"Prove you'll let my family go."

"Timothy, it would be foolish of me to continue to hold them, given the resources you've shown. Callie's contacts, y'know. They'll be released the minute I have the animal. The very instant, Timothy."

True, Callie had proved to be one formidable woman, given that she knew people like Mad Matt. Convinced, I turned toward the kitchen. "Okay!" I shouted. After a moment, the back door opened and Lulu stepped through the kitchen into the room, lugging a case shrouded by a dark cloth. She set it down on the big coffee table in front of the sofa beside the large petrified dinosaur egg, slid off the cloth and stepped back, glaring at Talbot. A blue face showed at the wire case door, golden eyes also riveted on Talbot.

"Now let my folks go."

Talbot smiled tolerantly. "Timothy, Timothy, Timothy. We need to make sure that is, indeed, our cat. Could you please let it out?" I unlatched the cage door, reached in and gently lifted out the cat, who still gazed steadily at Talbot, flicking his eyes occasionally over to Miravelle. I held the cat, petting his glistening blue fur. But he ignored me and continued to stare at Talbot with a purpose Talbot hadn't yet guessed.

He nodded with satisfaction. "That is just fine, Timothy." He smiled again, a signal for Miravelle to make a subtle movement toward his coat, one which I expected. "Now, we'll just conclude our business."

The cat was in place; now for phase two. "Well, not quite," I said. "I've got something else you'd be interested in."

"Oh?" Talbot's question signaled Miravelle to relax his arm.

Lulu left for the kitchen, and called into the woods.

"After we left your ranch, I figured out something important," I said. "I came up with quite a theory. And I asked Callie and Lulu to do some poking around in Seattle to prove my theory."

Callie walked in carrying a big yellow tabby in one arm and a cat carrier in the other. The tabby and the Cerulean immediately locked gazes, recognizing one another.

"So, you have another cat," said Talbot. "I only want the Cerulean, thank you." He stepped away from Miravelle, as if to be out of the line of fire. "But, Tim, there's this problem of the box Callie's carrying. We wouldn't want any cameras or weapons being brought in, now would we?" Miravelle moved over to Callie and held out his hand for the carrier, which Callie handed him with an ironic crooked grin, also setting the yellow tabby on the sofa. He opened the carrier and peered in.

Julio Miravelle's cheek flinched, a telling crack in his cool expression. "What?" asked Talbot. "What is it?"

"They know," croaked Miravelle, like he was going to be sick. He set the carrier on the sofa beside the tabby. A tiny fluff of blue fur emerged, with a round little blue head and little blue ears. It mewed. The tabby padded over to it, nuzzling it maternally.

"Unh," Talbot grunted out hard—the only sound he could manage, so deep was his shock. Lulu's and Callie's smug expressions probably matched mine.

Another blue kitten scampered from the carrier, and another, then a yellow, then a last blue. Now four little brilliant blue kittens and one yellow wandered around on the sofa, climbing the back and mewing. Their mother nuzzled one, then another, checking her babies. And, I swear to God, the Cerulean looked proud! I let him down onto the sofa to inspect his offspring, but after gently nuzzling each one, he turned his attention quickly back to Talbot. Perfect, I thought, since I wanted the cat's gaze riveted on Talbot.

Phase two complete, I thought. Now to get Talbot talking.

Talbot, who still had his mouth open, had some difficulty answering when I asked "Nice litter of kitties, eh, Talbot? Callie and Lulu had to do quite a bit of searching in Seattle to find the Cerulean's mate, but Callie used to be a spy, so they managed. Y'see, the Cerulean disappeared one night in Seattle. I thought he was mad at me, but he was really courting a female in heat. He is a male cat, you know."

Talbot took a deep breath and sighed, recovering himself. "All too well. And I gather you now understand what this has all been about. Who else knows about this?"

I sat on the sofa petting the cat. Talbot would let us live until he had the cat and the answer to that question. So I could keep him talking. "Rozoff outsmarted you. He found out you planned to make Nasties and sell them on the black market, so he invented this incredible cat, and turned it over to you. But it was, well . . . a Trojan cat with a big surprise inside. And like he planned, your greed made you announce the cat publicly before you really knew what Rozoff had done—made a *fertile* genetically engineered animal. And a venomous one at that."

"Vasily was a very clever person," said Talbot, just a little too smoothly, hiding his tension.

I continued. "A fertile animal would have made the feds shut down the whole industry, right? They would've stopped you cold. No more animal pets. No more money. You'd be ruined."

"Well, it was certainly an unfortunate situation that had to be remedied. Why don't you just give us—"

"But wait, there's *more!*" I declared, sounding like those too-good-to-be-true offers on the shopping viddies. "The way we figure, these kittens were born only weeks after the Cerulean met his lady friend. *Weeks*, not a couple of months like regular cats. Rozoff engineered the Cerulean to trigger faster gestation times in mates. So, he showed that mutant cats . . . and any other such animals . . . could breed like, well, rabbits."

Now Talbot was speechless. His face hardened into a barely contained rage. I continued to goad him. "When you realized the cat was fertile, you had it kidnapped, right? That way you didn't have to make up excuses for the cat disappearing. If you told everybody it up and died, your reputation would've gone pffft. And neutering might have killed it, and would've been obvious to any vet, tipping everybody off. But a kidnapping gave you sympathy, publicity." Talbot started to speak, but I stopped him. "Then there's your greed. You figured you could study the cat in secret—even dissecting it—and develop a sterile version to auction off for big, big money."

Talbot took a deep breath and steadied the tremor in his voice. "Yes, of course. But we can still work an agreement here. Give me all the cats Tim, and we'll—"

"But Lyman and his guy double-crossed you, right? They wanted to sell the cat to Genipet. So you had them killed by the Big Nasty and took the cat. But you didn't know I was in that closet."

Talbot fiddled nervously with the control box for his legs. He faced too many uncertainties to start shooting just yet—the Cerulean in the line of fire, the kittens scampering about. And he was still not certain that news of the kittens had been contained. And, his huge, arrogant ego didn't brook any lectures from an insolent kid like me. I'd counted on that. I glanced at the cat to make sure he was taking all this in.

Talbot retreated to his fallback position, cold arrogance. "You naive little fool," he spat. "We did what we had to do. Sometimes it's unfortunate, but, one must sometimes do unpleasant things."

I sensed that he was deciding to let Miravelle kill us. "And you also had Rozoff killed. Where is he?"

"Around here," said Talbot smiling smuggly. Miravelle showed the cold-blooded smile of a satisfied predator.

"Around here?"

"Sometimes our creatures get a little carried away." He waved at the woods around the cabin.

I shivered. A Big Nasty had torn Rozoff apart, just like the one that slaughtered the kidnappers. "And you gave the police Salvo's faked tape of me killing the guard to frame me."

Color rose on Talbot's face. He didn't like me getting the better of him. "Of course, you stupid little prick. It cost me to keep that greasy little gangster quiet, but it was a worthwhile investment." His caution was evaporating in the heat of his anger, and he nodded to Miravelle.

Miravelle pulled out a pistol and aimed it at Callie and Lulu, who joined hands, glaring defiantly at him. The Cerulean didn't see the gun, because he was still paying rapt attention to Talbot.

"Now for the last time, Timothy, who else knows about these animals? Then we'll take the cats and go." Yeah, right, I thought. No doubt, after killing us. Talbot was a cool liar. But I was cool, too.

Now for phase three of my plan. "There's one other thing I think you should see."

Talbot waved his hand to stop Miravelle. "These surprises are becoming tiresome."

I glanced at the cat to make sure his gaze remained fixed on Talbot. "House, please turn on the viddie screen. To the Cop Network."

"Very well," said the female voice of the house.

The viddie screen brightened and an image formed. The lower right corner of the screen showed the Cop Network logo, with the words "Live transmission" across the bottom.

And the image on the screen showed billionaire Kenneth Talbot standing in a log house, a stunned realization dawning on his face. The Talbot image looked off-camera and said "Goddamnit, Julio, I thought you checked for cameras!"

Miravelle shrugged in puzzlement. Talbot looked back and forth at the screen and the room, confused. Then he realized that the low angle of the image meant it was coming from . . .

"THE CAT! THE GODDAMNED CAT!"

Talbot lost all his cool. He punched his leg controls and twisted around from the screen, clumping toward the cat and me. The cat's gaze followed him, and so did the image on the screen.

I moved to protect the cat. "Yes, it's the cat. We found out right before we arranged our little meeting. Rozoff was more clever than you ever imagined." Now it was my turn to be smug.

"A *chip*," growled Talbot. "A bloody camera chip in the cat's eye!" Anger began to contort his face.

"Yeah, a biochip camera. New stuff. Microphone, too. All the size of a little bit of dust. Implanted with nanosurgery. And the cat was trained to fix its gaze on interesting things. Like you."

"When—?"

"From the beginning, since Rozoff first brought him to Animata, the camera has transmitted everything this cat has seen and heard. Rozoff planned to release the viddies to the cops and tell the world about the cat, until you murdered him."

Talbot's jaw jutted out, his breath coming in furious gasps, his blood pressure no doubt skyrocketing. "Where—?"

"The cops traced the transmissions to a company in Philly. DataDump, Inc. A viddie storage unit there has automatically recorded everything. Cops had a big problem, though. You hadn't implicated yourself on that viddie. You were smart enough to stay away from situations that spoiled your deniability. Until now. Rozoff got you. I got you. We patched the viddie nationwide. Now all you can do is give up."

My phase three plan had ended with the calculating bastard seeing the wisdom of just giving up. But Talbot had his own phase three—unreasoning, animal rage.

His face transformed totally, as if a mask had dropped away to reveal a monster beneath. His expression contorted in fury, his eyes gleaming with madness. He bellowed curses that sounded like an animal's scream, a spray of spittle erupting from his mouth. He jammed his hand into his coat pocket, tore out a silver pistol, and aimed it at me.

CHAPTER 39

At the sight of the pistol, the Cerulean sprang at Talbot, ears flat against his skull, front legs extended, poison-glistening claws unsheathed. But Talbot instantly transferred his aim to the cat and fired a deafening shot that exploded from the barrel, catching the Cerulean in midair, spinning him around in a bloody blur of red and blue. The image on the viddie screen spun wildly, ending with a canted picture of the fireplace. The cat lay still.

Miravelle swung his pistol to take care of Callie and Lulu, but they leaped behind the kitchen counter just as he fired, blowing a chunk of granite off the counter top, the blast pounding the big room.

As blue kittens scattered and the tabby yowled in fright, Talbot paused for an instant, dismayed by the realization that he'd just put a bullet into a billion-dollar business deal. That instant gave me the time to act before he put a bullet into me. Spying the big round fossil egg on the coffee table, I grabbed it and heaved it at Talbot as hard as I could.

Naturally, my pitch missed Talbot's gun hand, instead slamming into the hand grasping his control box. I cursed my pitching arm, as the black box sailed from his hand and skittered away to come to rest near the smashed doorway. I realized that doorway was my only refuge, and in the second before Talbot recovered, I dived toward it, sliding across the wooden floor and scrambling over the wreckage of the door.

Another shot exploded behind me, and a vicious pain ripped through the back of my thigh, right below where it became my butt. I kept scrambling until I was out the door, and another shot came from inside, sounding like Miravelle shooting at Callie and Lulu.

Blood soaked the back of my leg, and the searing pain ate into my consciousness. I dragged myself over to the big front window and peeked up at the window's corner. Miravelle took Lulu and Callie as his targets of choice. He moved toward the kitchen, ready to finish them off. The metallic rattle of silverware sounded from behind the kitchen island. Callie's hand thrust upward holding a kitchen knife, which she expertly zinged at Miravelle, burying it solidly in his shoulder. He screamed and staggered backward as Lulu popped up and whipped another knife at him slicing past his ribs. Callie had taught her clone well. Miravelle yanked out the knife and, leaning against the wall, grimacing in pain, fired another shot, keeping a respectful distance from the kitchen.

A glimpse of yellow appeared out the front door, as the tabby mother emerged, carrying a bright blue kitten in her mouth. She skirted a puddle of my blood and disappeared into the woods.

Talbot fired at me, blowing a jagged bullet hole in the front window, and I ducked, then poked my head back up for another look. His control box gone, legs not working, he faced into the room twisting to shoot at me almost over his shoulder. To get a better shot, he jerked his body around by throwing himself off balance and letting the brace's automatic balancing system keep him upright. In the righting process he twisted toward me. Soon, he'd be lined up for a good shot.

I needed a weapon! A gun, or rocks, or a stick. Anything! Another shot exploded from inside, as Miravelle advanced on the kitchen. Another shot from Talbot and another hole erupted in the window.

I remembered the control box. If I could get it, I did have a weapon . . . Talbot's legs! I hauled myself along the porch, leaving a smear of blood, until I reached the doorway. Maybe I could get in, get the controller and get out before either of them could get a shot off. Talbot would expect me to still be by the window, and Miravelle wouldn't bother with me until he'd killed Callie and Lulu.

I pushed off with both legs, scrambling through the doorway, grabbing the box and rolling back out, just as a shot from Talbot blew a hole in the floor. The tabby emerged from the woods and bounded into the house to retrieve another kitten. I examined the box. The leg controls consisted of some buttons and a joystick. Kyle was better than me at figuring out video games, but maybe I could do this. This time, the tabby appeared with the yellow kitten.

I poked my head up to look into the window and hit a few buttons. Talbot raised one leg, then the other. A look of utter surprise dawned on his face, and he stared down at his legs, realizing I hadn't just swiped the control box to keep him immobile. He fired another wild shot through the window. Before he could warn Miravelle, I jammed the joystick forward, marching him to the attack. Talbot's look of surprise turned to sputtering, impotent rage. He twisted and jerked his upper body, trying his best to get another shot off at me, but I still don't think he realized exactly how I planned to use his legs.

Miravelle hadn't noticed Talbot's gyrations. He was too busy bleeding, firing, and dodging kitchen knives. So when I walked Talbot toward him, he missed the significance.

"JULIO!" shouted Talbot. Miravelle glanced around, his gun still trained on the kitchen. A knife zipped toward him and clanged off the rock fireplace. "JULIO! HE'S GOT THE—"

But by this time I had Talbot in position, punched buttons, and lashed out with his right leg. His shoe smashed into the side of Miravelle's knee, producing a crunching sound and a bellow from Miravelle, who collapsed to the floor, dropping the gun.

"DID THAT HURT, JULIO?" I shouted. "I HOPE SO!" I poked buttons to draw Talbot's leg back and slash it forward, catching Miravelle with a vicious, muscle-tearing kick to the stomach. He oofed and doubled up.

Boy, Talbot had powerful muscles. If I'd had muscles like that when I had kicked Salvo in the crotch, his grandkids would've felt it. The tabby appeared at the doorway with another blue kitten, destined for the safety of the woods. Even gunfire didn't deter a mother cat.

"GOD DAMN YOU!" Talbot bellowed, but he couldn't do a thing about it. Miravelle rolled over and crawled for the gun. I waited, for just the right moment, hit a button, and knocked him cold with another Talbot-kick to the back of the head.

"GIVE IT UP TALBOT! IF I GOT THE BOX, I GOT YOU!" I hollered back.

But Talbot had gone beyond reasoning. He spewed a stream of curses and managed to get another shot off at me. By now I'd figured out how to finish with him. I yanked the joystick, marching him forward a ways, lining him up just right. Lulu and Callie stood up from behind the counter, each holding knives at the ready.

I jerked the joystick and Talbot lurched backward, legs pumping, gathering speed and slamming hard into the fireplace. But he cleverly protected the back of his head with his hands and bent forward so his head didn't hit, so all I did was knock a little wind out of him.

But I knew how to top his strategy. Fiddling with the controls, I started him spinning in place.

"Round and round you go, and where you stop, nobody knows!" I taunted. He fired the gun, but in his merry-go-round mode he came nowhere close to hitting anything.

I stopped him and his top half swayed back and forth, showing that his dizziness had totally disoriented him, left him vulnerable.

Now I marched him away from the fireplace and slammed him backward into its stone face, his cranium impacting with a dull thunk.

His eyes glazed and his top half swayed back and forth even more, but he still held the gun, trying to raise it. The tabby appeared with still another blue kitten destined for the woods. I wanted to tell her it would all be over very soon.

Again, I moved Talbot forward and rammed him backward against the fireplace. His body sagged, his head lolled, and he finally dropped the gun. I hauled myself to my feet and limped through the doorway, leaning on it for support.

"Where is my family?"

"Kiss my—," he mumbled, dizzy and half-conscious.

I collided him with the stone fireplace again, and the breath whooshed out of him.

"Where?"

Blood trickled from his nose. "Screw—" I introduced him to the stone fireplace again. Now blood streamed from a gash on his scalp, staining his expensive suit.

"Where?"

"I di'n' have them."

Callie ran to the bloody Cerulean and knelt over it. Lulu hurried over to me with a big towel, bent down and pressed it against my leg. I stumbled.

"You what? Tell the truth!" I marched him forward a good ways this time, centering him on the big oak mantle, knowing that it would shatter his skull when he hit. He glanced groggily over his shoulder, his eyes barely focusing. He knew it, too.

"I lied! Stop . . . don't . . . please!" He wiped the blood from his face and tried to straighten himself up. "You called and I didn't . . . know. . . what you were talking about at first. I found out Salvo took them, your goddamned drug guy. He said if I paid him, he'd agree to let you think it was me. It's the truth. Please, for God's sake!" He stood there under my control, his body slumping in pain and defeat.

The whuffing of helicopters in the distance announced that Lieutenant Rocky and the Seattle police would arrive soon with plenty of cops and medical help. He'd gone along with my plan, and now he had his evidence and his criminals and really great viddie. The tabby gathered the last kitten gently in her mouth and trotted out the door. Her job was done, too. But mine wasn't.

Bleeding badly, my head all woozy, I pitched the control box onto the couch and let Lulu help me over to the Cerulean. I lowered myself onto the floor beside him and stroked his bloody fur. His eyes were closed. A lump rose in my throat and tears streamed down my face. I began to cry, as Lulu and Callie put their arms around me.

CHAPTER 40

The desperate yowling echoed all the way down the vet hospital corridor. I hobbled as fast as I could, considering that the thick plastic bandage over my butt-wound kept yanking tight, reminding me to take it easy. Lulu ran alongside me, steadying me when I'd stumble. We did a little "'Scuse-me" dance with a big nurse who got in our way, circling her and making it to the door.

Standing outside the room were three vets with matching white coats and worried looks—a big tall lady vet, a short roundish male vet, and a little bald male vet.

"Thank God you're here!" exclaimed the little bald vet who wore a badge that said Calvin Strittman, DVM. "I'm deeply sorry. We're just not experienced with dosages on this animal. We had him out of the cage to check his cast and he woke up enough to be aggressive. We had to evacuate . . . the poison you know. You know the most about him."

"Yeah, I know. I'll go in."

"Tim, he's going to be crazy," said Lulu. "He may not know you."

"He'll know me." I pushed open the door and slipped in. More yowling rose from the corner on the floor, a pitiable mix of pain and fear. I moved around the big examining table and peered into the dark space between a big cage and the wall. The Cerulean had dragged himself there, his golden eyes flashing wild, struggling to move his immobile hind end, which was encased in a big white cast.

"Hey, pal, it's me. It's me." I crouched down, my butt-bandage pulling to remind me I was wounded, too. He spit and laid back his ears and pulled back his lips to reveal his needle-sharp teeth. He raised one paw, each razor-tip talon dripping with a clear droplet of venom. "Calm down. I'm here." The ears came back up. The lips lowered back over the teeth. The claws retracted. I reached gently into the space and petted his magnificent head, smoothing the ruffled blue fur. He seemed to relax.

"Okay, now let me just come down and see you." I stood back up again and gently rolled the big metal cage away from the wall far enough so I could lower myself to lay down beside him on my good butt-cheek. I stroked his back, gently touching the cast to make sure it was still intact. I thought it was, but I needed a better look. He slumped down exhausted and looked at me with half-closed eyes showing a glazed relief.

"Y'know, you took a big hit, there. Lots of damage to your pelvis. You were in surgery seven hours. Lots of restorative work, but you had the world's best vet surgeons. You'll be fine, pal." I rubbed his face and took a paw, still damp with venom. He withdrew it and used both his front legs to drag himself over to nestle against me. As I stroked him, I heard the beginning of his diesel-generator purr. The door opened behind me.

"You okay?" Worry colored Lulu's voice. "What're you doing on the floor?"

"We're just talking. Just give us some time, here. I've got a lot to tell him."

"You're two of a kind," she snorted, and the door shut again.

"Lulu finally admitted she's in love with me," I told the cat. "She finally decided I loved her as Lulu, not as Callie's clone. And I'll tell you a secret . . ." The purring grew louder, and the Cerulean lowered his great head onto my chest and closed his eyes. But I knew he was still listening. ". . . We made love. Not sex . . . *love*. It was incredible, cat. After I got out of the hospital, and we made sure you were okay, we got this big hotel room and we made monkey-love all over it—bathroom, kitchen, closet, entry hall. Yeah, and the bedroom, of course. Except I couldn't be on the bottom, unless I sort of hung my butt half off the bed.

It reminded me of the palindrome my Uncle Ned used to recite about his girlfriends: 'Now, Ned, I am a maiden nun; Ned, I am a maiden won.'"

I paused, and the cat opened his eyes and looked up at me like he wanted to hear more, but I needed to get him off the floor. I pulled myself up and reached under him, scooping him up in my arms. He meowed, and his eyes took on a little of that wild look. But when I laid him on the padded table, he relaxed again.

"There's lots more to tell you. My folks are safe! Turned out Talbot wasn't lying, for once in his canky life." I leaned over to examine the cast. It was scuffed and had a small crack by his left haunch, but looked solid. The cat reached out a paw and laid it on my hand. He wanted to hear more.

"Miguel Salvo had Max kidnap my folks and Kyle. Well, Uncle Ned took care of that. See, cat, Uncle Ned had friends we didn't know about. I knew Uncle Ned had done jail time back in the 2030s for selling nickie tobacco. So, he had big-time gang contacts up in New York; people he'd protected when he served time. They found out that Max and his buddies were holding my folks and Kyle on a farm in Richmond. So, Uncle Ned raided the farm with a bunch of those big monster guys who move sofas at my dad's company." The cat twitched his tail. My story had him hooked.

"Kyle told me that my crazy Uncle Ned kicked in the door hollering 'Bombard a drab mob!' another one of Mom's palindromes. Uncle Ned used an oak table leg on Max's skull cap. That steel cap wasn't as hard as it looked. Max ended up with a skull fracture in the Richmond county jail infirmary, and the cops picked up Salvo and his 'liner in New York. Uncle Ned got the skull cap and bolted it on the hood of his truck as an ornament."

My story had relaxed the Cerulean almost to sleep, his bright blue chest rising and falling in gentle steady rhythm. But when I would stop talking or petting him, he'd open his eyes to make sure I was there. I had to keep talking.

"Of course, Talbot and Miravelle will rot in jail for a long time, even with all their fancy lawyers. Lieutenant Rocky and the district attorney's office piled up a zillion charges on them. And every time the prosecutors go over another part of the camera recording from your eye, they come up with more. Live not on evil! That's a great palindromic lesson for them, eh, cat?"

"Oh, yeah, and Callie took your kittens to Washington to appear before a Congressional committee. Your kitties played around on the witness table with their mom while some scientific experts told this committee all about you being fertile. The USDA shut down the whole genetic pet industry. They ruled that every last animal . . . even every bug . . . whatever . . . has to be recalled for examination and sterilization if necessary. So are the other countries. They all agreed that you proved that there was a danger of a God-knows-what kind of mutant breeding going on, if somebody accidentally or on purpose created other fertile mutant animals." I paused, feeling a little sorry for calling the Cerulean a mutant, but he didn't seem to mind. Calvin Strittman, DVM, poked his head in, but I waved him off, whispering, "Not quite yet."

"Oh, yeah, I got a call from my old girlfriend, Elizabeth. I told her I was in love with Lulu, and I was taking Lulu to meet my folks as soon as we knew you were okay. She said fine. She said she really wanted to offer me a book contract. *Seventy million dollars!* She wanted me to do a syntho, but I said I wanted to do a printed book. Like Hemingway. So, we agreed I'd do both kinds. Cool, huh?"

He really had gone back to sleep now. I eased over to the door and opened it, signaling with a finger against my lips for the vets to be quiet. Dr. Strittman sneaked in and began to examine him. I stayed close, just in case he woke. I stroked him gently, while Strittman gave him a shot of cat tranquilizer and antibiotic. Satisfied that the cat was under control, he invited the other vets in, and they crowded around, fascinated.

As I watched them, I felt the deep sadness that had haunted me since I'd come to love the cat. What would happen to this poor cat? Would he be poked, prodded and experimented on, forced to live his life in a cage with only strangers to take care of him?

The big, tall lady vet turned back to me. "There's a lawyer out there to see you. He asked to be called the next time you came in."

Worried that I'd gotten into some other trouble, I stepped out into the hall and hobbled down to the waiting room, to find Lulu sitting on a couch talking to a very trim-looking blond guy in an expensive vested pin-stripe suit. He had his expensive leather briefcase open on the coffee table, sitting on a pile of old issues of *Cat Quarterly* and *Dog's Life*. Lulu smiled up at me with a peculiar puzzled/happy expression.

"You'd better sit down, Tim."

"I can't," I reminded her, patting my bad cheek.

"Then you need to lean against something. Really, Tim."

I obediently leaned against a shelf of animal toys, and the lawyer reached out a hand with a wrist that had a very expensive platinum watch around it. I shook his hand and straightened up to relieve the pull of my butt-bandage.

"I'm Gus Joiner. I was Vasily Rozoff's lawyer, and I'm executor of his estate."

"God, I'm so sorry for what happened to him. Did they find him?"

"Unfortunately they did. Out in the woods. Enough to identify with DNA analysis, anyway."

"So why do you need me?"

"Well, to discuss the matter of the cat."

"I want to do whatever I can to make sure he's safe, happy. After all, I owe him my life. We all do. But Animata owns him, right? So, I guess there's nothing I can do."

Lulu smiled mysteriously. "You're going to be surprised at what you can do."

The lawyer smiled, too. "You see, Mr. Boatright, Kenneth Talbot is a lawless man. And lawless men don't pay too much attention to the legalities of situations. Actually, the cat belongs . . . belonged . . . to Vasily Rozoff."

"How can that be? He worked for Animata."

"Yes, but Talbot's lawyers weren't very good, mainly crooks themselves. They didn't bother to include an ironclad exclusivity clause in Vasily's contract. They thought they could rely on threats and violence. So, Vasily asked me to get around his contract, and he created the cat under the auspices of another company, Blue Sky, Inc., which Kenneth Talbot didn't know about at first. Unfortunately, he did find out, which was one of the reasons he had Vasily killed."

"So what happens to the cat? Is he going to be a prisoner in a zoo or something?"

"This gets even stranger," said Joiner, pulling a fat, blue-covered legal document out of his briefcase and laying it on the table. "Vasily knew there was a likelihood he . . . well . . . he wouldn't survive. And he knew his cat possessed incredible intelligence."

"Yeah, I should know."

"Well, then you'll appreciate what Vasily decided. He stipulated in his will that the cat itself would decide who it would be with . . . who should own it."

Lulu squinched up her pretty face in a happy "isn't-that-wild?" expression.

"So, who did the cat decide on?"

Joiner shrugged. "I've done a lot of interviews over the past few days. It's pretty obvious from what I heard. And I was watching what happened in that room just now. The cat has decided on you, Mr. Boatright."

Lulu was right about me needing to lean against something. I staggered a bit against the shelves and knocked a few cat toys off. "Me? I . . . I don't know how to handle all the—"

"Mr. Boatright, it's pretty obvious you're closer to that cat than anybody. So, as executor I'm going to turn full ownership of the Cerulean over to you."

"Really? You can do that?" I asked. "Just like that?"

"Well, we may have some court hearings to go through. But as I said, Mr. Boatright, I'm the executor. I have full legal power to do whatever I believe satisfies the terms of Mr. Rozoff's will. And I've decided." Then he rattled on, explaining about signing papers and stuff, but I didn't hear him. My mind was still trying to wrap itself around the idea of owning the world's most incredible cat. Then he stood up, shook my hand, and left me, still leaning against the shelves like an idiot.

Lulu's hug brought me to my senses. "You love that cat, Tim. You're the only one who could take care of it right."

"And what about the kittens? What happens to them?"

Lulu hugged me again, even harder. "The mama was apparently a stray. So, when we collected her and her kitties, they became ours. So, we'll keep them safe, too."

I enjoyed the hug . . . a lot. But I had doubts. "Yeah, this is all great and all. But I don't particularly want to be famous and all. You saw how we've been mobbed by reporters and viddie vampires and stuff."

"Well, imagine what will happen to the cat and kittens without you. And, Tim, I know you can cope with the fact that they're going to bring in billions of dollars. Everybody's going to want you to show them. And there's commercial endorsements, and movies, and God-knows-what else." She looked me in the eyes and smiled that great smile. I hoped our kids had that smile.

That's when I decided about the cats. "How about this? We all take care of the cats. Callie will help us decide what's best for them. How to manage them. And maybe we do make a billion dollars. And we give the money away to your orphans."

She really liked that idea, and her smile broadened beautifully, with major cheek-dimpling. That's the smile I was after. She gave me a great sloppy kiss and patted my good butt-cheek. Then she put her arm around my waist and helped me hobble down the hall to wake the cat and tell him the good news.

Read on for an exciting preview of
Dennis Meredith's new novel

The Happy Chip

For more information, go to
www.TheHappyChip.com

CHAPTER 1

James Preston pushed open the apartment building's heavy oak door and stepped out into an icy wind that whipped the driving rain down the darkened Boston street. His thin raincoat gave little protection from either the cold or the downpour. He huddled against the weather, thoroughly chilled . . . grinning like a fool.

He'd just finished about the most incredible first date ever! It started with a delightful first meeting, followed by a cozy dinner in which he and the incandescently beautiful Toni discovered they had tons of stuff in common. They'd totally clicked. During intimate after-dinner drinks at her place, they even agreed to sync their Happy Chip data—unheard of on a first date. Even a date arranged by the very expensive dating service Total Resonance. And they'd discovered, to their delight, that each registered a stunningly high physiological reaction to the other.

It was awesome to feel so great after weeks of going through his crazy up-and-down moods. He'd felt the blackest funk one minute and a top-of-the-world elation the next. He'd guessed it was just all the crap at work, some run-ins with so-called friends and worries over the date.

But now he almost skipped down the rain-slick steps, not even caring what the guy standing at the curb with the umbrella thought. In fact, Preston decided maybe he'd ask the guy if he could borrow his

1

umbrella and do the goofy, fun, *Singin'-in-the-Rain* dance. He checked his watch. It was midnight, and the trains were still running. He decided he'd better just head for the entrance to the subway's Green Line down the block. Maybe he would just do a little jig along the way.

He'd walked only a few hundred yards along the deserted block in the swirling deluge when the street was lit by headlights from a car approaching behind him. Maybe it was a taxi. Yeah, he should take a taxi. He was feeling too terrific to let the mood fade, getting soaked, waiting for a train and coping with the drunks and rowdies and bums on subways at night.

A smile still on his face, he turned toward the headlights, and realized it was not a cab, but a van. The side door slid open, and he found himself staring at a guy crouched in the van and dressed in black.

Before he could say anything, a sound behind him—the whoosh of an umbrella closing—made him start to turn. But powerful hands gripped his head from behind and a vicious, expert twist snapped his neck, killing him instantly. His mouth gaped open, his dead-glassy eyes wide with a remnant horror of his death, as the rain washed down his face in a final, tragic baptism.

Before his body could crumple to the ground, the killer grabbed him beneath his arms, and together with the man in black, they shoved him into the van.

The killer picked up the umbrella, quickly scanned the street, saw no witnesses who would also have to be dispatched, and climbed in.

"Go," he said simply to the driver, and the van sped away, winding through back streets for a dozen miles into an industrial area and to a warehouse where an overhead door slid up to admit it.

The driver, a muscular, sandy-haired man with carefully groomed face stubble, slid out of the van and opened the back door. A slim man dressed in blood-stained surgical gloves and blue medical scrubs appeared with a gurney.

"Any problems?" he asked.

"Clean kill, clean extraction," replied the driver, as the two men in the back hefted Preston's body onto the gurney and helped wheel him into a large, clear, brightly lit plastic tent. They halted the gurney beside a stainless steel autopsy table, transferring the corpse. Nearby sat other, smaller tables laden with scalpels, saws, and other surgical instruments, all clotted with dried blood.

The three men from the van sat down outside the tent on folding chairs, one lighting a cigarette.

"You need to do this fast," the driver told the surgeon. "By the time we get this one to the chopper, it will be three a.m. We have to finish the mission before dawn."

"It'll take whatever time it takes!" snapped the surgeon, quickly cutting away the corpse's clothes, leaving Preston's pale body lying naked and still under the light. "Besides, the mission's not finished until you get them all. That's only nine. One left." The surgeon picked up a small box with a glowing screen and carefully began to scan Preston's body, scrutinizing the display.

"Not our fuckin' problem!" spat the driver. "That's Recon's job, and you know goddamned well she's disappeared. I just talked to Recon. She hasn't been to work in a week, hasn't used credit cards, hasn't seen any family, friends . . . fuckin' gone. Somehow, she must have known some of the other subjects, and found out about the loony behaviors, the suicides."

"She's probably dead, anyway," said the surgeon, stopping his scan at Preston's chest. "Shit," he said to himself. "It attached in the heart. Why couldn't it be in a damned extremity!"

"What do you mean she's dead? You mean suicide? What's all this with the suicides, anyway?"

"Above your pay grade," said the surgeon, still scanning the chest.

"So, what's inside me? What's in them?" he said pointing at the other two men.

"Not to worry, soldier. It's not the same chip." He stood up and looked at the driver. "I'll need help. Put on scrubs. I've got to crack him open."

"Oh, hell, no!" said the driver, looking over at the other two expectantly.

They both shrugged, and the man who had murdered Preston said, "Dude, you're team leader. We did the kill, the extraction. We moved the body."

Their argument was interrupted by the whine of a surgical saw, which lowered in pitch as the surgeon applied the saw to slice into Preston's chest.

"Okay, you want to be out of here in time, you got to get a little messy," he said.

The driver muttered a curse, quickly donned a surgical suit, boots, cap and gloves, and pushed his way into the plastic tent. He smelled the cloying, metallic-fleshy odor of blood, but he was used to that smell.

He took up a rib spreader and jammed it into the gaping incision in the corpse's chest, ratcheting it open. With the dull snap of cracking ribs, the opening into the chest cavity widened to reveal Preston's inert, pale yellow heart. The surgeon scanned the small box over the heart and nodded his head. "Chip's there."

Taking up a scalpel, he quickly sliced through the arteries feeding the heart and lifted the organ out of the corpse's blood-filled chest, dropping it into a tray beside the table. Again, he used the scanner on the excised heart, now merely a lump of dead muscle.

"Yup, it's there." He sealed the heart in a plastic bag, marked it with Preston's name and pitched it into a cooler onto a pile of similar flesh-filled bags."

"Let's get him wrapped," said the surgeon, and he and the driver quickly slid a body bag under the corpse, enveloped it and zipped it up.

The other two men had rolled the gurney into place and they quickly loaded the body into the van.

• • •

The Black Hawk helicopter was already spinning up its rotors, creating a gale of icy rain, when the van rolled up to its open passenger bay door. The two men hefted Preston's body out of the van and dumped it onto a pile of other body bags in the helicopter. They climbed in, followed by the driver, who'd parked the van near the helicopter's hangar.

Its door slid shut, the helicopter roared into the coal-black sky, its landing lights flashing, and swooped out over the storm-roiled waters of the Atlantic Ocean. The three men donned headsets and settled in, crowded against the pile of body bags.

"How far?" asked one. "This ain't exactly the most comfortable ride."

"I want to get well into the offshore currents."

"Hell, that'll take an hour!" shouted the other man."

"Yeah, well, the currents will keep the bodies from washing up, and we got hungry friends out there. Great Whites."

The other two settled into a bored sulk until the leader slipped into a harness, clipped its safety line to a ring in the ceiling, and directed the other to do the same. They heaved open the hovering helicopter's metal door, and rolled the nearest body to the edge. The leader raised a hand to stop their progress and hauled out a shotgun, waving the other two away. He leveled the gun at the body bag. A thunderous shotgun blast rang in their ears, even over the noise of the storm and the helicopter.

"Helps them sink. Attracts the sharks," shouted the leader, motioning for the others to roll the shredded, bloody bag out the door, watching it flutter down the beam of the helicopter's searchlight into the black waters. Eight more times shotgun-blasted bags rolled out the door, until, despite the whipping wind, the helicopter bay was filled with the acrid stench of burned gunpowder.

Finally, they hauled up buckets of seawater to sluice down the floor and rinse away remnants of blood and tissue, and slammed the door shut.

"Bleach the shit out of this copter when we get back," instructed the leader, giving another command to the pilot through the headset. The helicopter banked forward into a swooping turn back toward the mainland.

CHAPTER 2

Andy Davis nearly collided with a matronly woman as he walked through the glass-domed atrium lobby of NeoHappy, Inc. He'd been staring up at the massive, transparent globe suspended high in the three-story space, light shining through it from the skylights.

The glimmering, transparent sphere was studded with long, winding filaments and pierced with apertures that connected to a maze of glass pipes and chambers. Electronic circuitry crowded the globe's interior, surrounding the chambers. A profusion of twinkling lights traced what were probably the pathways of electrons through the circuitry. The effect was of a massive, high-tech Christmas tree ornament.

So that's what a Happy Chip looks like enormously magnified, he thought. Millions and millions of people had the actual chips, each the size of a cell, injected into them. He'd studied photomicrographs of the chip when he'd explored the NeoHappy.me web site, but this sculpture really revealed what an amazing technical achievement the nanochip was.

And just *maybe* he'd get a chance to write a book about the scientific virtuoso who invented it! He took off his glasses and rubbed his eyes, tired from a day reading up on the company, cramming for the interview. Unfortunately, he couldn't wear contacts, so it was glasses, which made him look like more of a geek than he really was, even given his sallow complexion, skinny frame, and somewhat out-of-control mop of reddish hair.

He announced himself to the stocky, rather intimidating receptionist sitting beneath the giant sculpture. She actually looked like a female wrestler, he thought. He wondered whether even this tough-looking woman ever got nervous, with the massive structure looming overhead. Seemingly at ease, though, she checked the schedule and said with some mild reproof, "I have you down for half an hour from now. Is that correct?"

"Uh . . . well . . . I am a little early. I'll just sit and wait." His premature arrival made him look overeager, but he *was* eager. He noticed that the woman glanced with some unspoken signal at a hulking blue-blazered guard, who regarded him with a stern, perhaps even suspicious, stare. The atrium contained a number of such guards, who patrolled along the long gallery. This company used some serious security, unlike the many other high-tech firms Andy had visited for his articles. He wondered why.

After about twenty-five minutes, the guard approached him. "Sir, you can go up now. You can sign in at the desk." The security man escorted him to the elevator, using a key card to access the top-floor executive offices. As he rode up with Andy, the man stood feet-apart, hands clasped in front of him, staring impassively straight ahead. A bulge in his jacket told Andy the guard wore a shoulder holster.

The doors opened into a thickly carpeted foyer, where a trim, middle-aged woman sat behind a chrome-and-glass desk. Her desk sign read Irene Crawford, and lettered on the cherry paneling above her was the company slogan, "Knowledge for the Best Life You Can Live." The guard disappeared back into the elevator, and the woman said cheerily "Mr. Davis, if you don't mind, Marty is running a little behind. Can you wait a moment? Can I get you something to drink? Coffee? Soft drink?"

Andy declined, fearing he would manage to spill something, he was so jittery about the meeting. He settled into one of the foyer's leather armchairs and tried to calm himself by taking the time to check his bank account on his smartphone. But that act wasn't calming. The damned payment still hadn't been deposited for the corporate speech he'd ghosted. He needed the money. Lisa wouldn't get her paycheck until next week, and there were overdue bills.

"Hi, I'm Marty," said a voice startling him. He jammed the phone into his coat pocket, looking up to see that famous, smiling, boyish face that had become nearly ubiquitous on TV and the web. He struggled to his feet and shook the hand that was offered.

"Andy Davis," he answered back, realizing that his coat and tie made him embarrassingly overdressed compared to the khakis, polo shirt and sneakers that Fallon wore.

"C'mon in. I'm sure Jenny offered you something to drink. You sure you don't want anything? I'm having a vitamin water."

Again Andy declined, following the slightly built, multi-billionaire techno-genius into a huge office strewn with papers, computer stations and electronic parts. One wall held massive display screens and another was covered by a shelf full of models of the company's products. He recognized some, particularly the implantable clinical blood analyzer that had launched the company.

But what surprised Andy, and slightly intimidated him, was that the office also held three other people, all with tablet computers in front of them, sitting around a large conference table. This interview would be something of a grilling, he thought with trepidation. The three stood and introduced themselves: Mindy Carroll, a perky, animated young woman who headed corporate communications; John McClellan, the towering, balding company lawyer; and Clair Roberson, a bright-eyed twenty-something with long hair who was Mindy's assistant. He only knew Carroll through the emails they had exchanged when she'd contacted him.

"I've read your books, your articles," said Fallon, gesturing for Andy to sit at the head of the table and settling into one of the chairs, leaning back and propping his feet on the chair beside him. He took up a tablet computer, sliding his finger across the screen, flipping through what Andy recognized as a collection of his magazine and web pieces. *Really* liked them. I like your biography of the Harvard biologist. And the pieces for *Scientific American* and the *New York Times Magazine.* And I see from your resume you've done corporate writing."

"Speeches and so forth. Freelancers need to mix it up quite a bit to stay solvent."

"And I see you're born and bred in Boston."

"My mom calls me a Green Line baby," said Andy, referring to the Boston trolley lines that extend westward from downtown. "Born at Brigham and Women's Hospital. Grew up in Brookline. My folks lived there until they moved to California. Went to college and learned science writing at BU. Heck, I first met my future wife at a performance of the Newton Community Theater. She was in the cast and I met her at the cast party. And our two daughters were born at Brigham. Now we live in Newton." He stopped, realizing that he had been babbling nervously.

"Yeah, one of my kids was born at Brigham," said Fallon, taking his feet off the chair and leaning forward. "So, what do you think about the project?" He gave Andy a disarmingly intense look.

Andy had read about Fallon's signature style—seemingly offhanded, but then zeroing in on a target to try to rattle them. He knew the tactic because he used a version of it in hostile interviews, to poke the interviewee to see what new facts would emerge.

Recovering from his babble-fest, he managed a reasonably poised answer "Well, from what Mindy has told me, it sounds really exciting," he said.

Fallon leaned forward even more. "So, why should *you* write my biography?"

"Because I'm good." Now they were on a topic Andy was comfortable with. He *was* a good writer.

Thankfully Fallon laughed at Andy's show of confidence, apparently not thinking it arrogant. "Okay, well, what if I said it's too early for me to write my memoir?"

Andy clicked into his sell-the-assignment mode, another comfortable place for a freelancer. "I'd say it should be the first of several memoirs—not *the* memoir." Andy leaned forward, grinning. In addition to persuading this famous billionaire that the book should be written, he wanted to show him that this writer had done his research. "Y'know, the whole world wants to know your story. How you started grad work at MIT in nanofluidics, nanoelectronics, and molecular engineering. How you founded your company to build nanomachines at twenty-five. Then built your first nanofluidic analyzer. And how you then bet *everything you had* on the Happy Chip. And how you went round and round with the FDA about approval. I read the transcripts of the review hearings. And finally, how the chip just went viral. Y'know, by the time the book comes out, most everybody will have one."

Mindy chimed in. "Marty does have his doubts about the project . . ." she said to Andy." . . . but I hope I've convinced him it's critical to the company. And to getting his position out there, given the critics of the chip and the controversy it caused before it was finally accepted."

"Are you chipped?" Asked Fallon abruptly. Andy took it as a sign that he'd passed whatever initial test Fallon had been giving him.

"Well . . . no . . . haven't had the money or time to—"

"If you decide to take on the project, we'll chip you as part of the deal. And we'll pay for the app, of course. We're all chipped here. Then you'll be able to see for yourself how . . . well . . . *happy* everybody is with their chips."

One phrase riveted Andy's attention: *"If you decide to take on the project . . ."* It triggered his internal assignment detector! Every poverty-stricken freelancer had one, and it pretty reliably detected whether an editor was about to hand out a paying assignment. Until Fallon had uttered that phrase, Andy thought he was just one of many being interviewed for the gig!

"Well, sure, that would be terrific," he managed to say coolly. Now Fallon had managed to rattle him even beyond his initial jitters.

"Okay, then," said Fallon. "Let's just spend a little time making sure we're compatible. Then if we are, Mindy and John can work out contractual details."

Andy tried to tamp down his excitement. He took a deep breath. He needed to ask a key question, without seeming too money-grubbing.

"Well, I do need to ask about one detail that's kind of important. The writing fee." Andy determined not to let the lure of the project and Fallon's charisma divert him from his prime objective of thickening the thin financial ice he and his wife Lisa were skating on.

For too long, Lisa had been the chief breadwinner, with her nurse's salary and benefits. She had been more than tolerant of his love of the journalistic juggling act of freelancing—pitching editors, investigating and writing fascinating science stories; and unfortunately of waiting and waiting for payment. She understood his excitement at watching geneticists pin down a lethal cancer gene, or tracking jaguars with conservationists in Central America. But it was a financially precarious profession and brought no benefits.

"Ah, yes, the financial consideration," said Fallon, leaning back in his chair.

"Writing a book will take at least a year, probably more," declared Andy. "It's a time I almost certainly won't be doing any other projects."

Mindy tapped on her tablet screen, consulted the result and gave an answer. "I did research on the standard fees for a book like this . . ."

Andy steeled himself for the news that he would have to spend at least a year with little income.

Mindy continued. ". . . They run a max of two dollars a word. But we want to make it *really* worth your while. And we want your complete involvement. So, we'll give four dollars a word. Plus expenses, of course."

Awesome! thought Andy. He struggled to keep himself from leaping up and dancing around the room. "And what length do you think?" He switched on his mental freelance income calculator.

"Oh, we're thinking a hundred thousand words . . ."

Andy's mental calculator melted! He tried to focus on the rest of what she was saying, but *Four hundred thousand dollars!* His shock meant that at first he didn't grasp the import of Carroll's recitation of the payment schedule.

". . . a hundred thousand on signing, another two hundred when you deliver a satisfactory manuscript, and the last hundred when it's published . . ."

A hundred thousand dollars up front! Andy wondered whether hugging the woman would be out of line.

". . . and the fee's a guarantee against half the royalties."

The last word ramped up his excitement even more. *Royalties!* This wouldn't be just a work-for-hire project! He'd also be a co-author on the book contract, and the book would likely be a bestseller! And a movie!

"So, you okay with that?" asked Fallon.

"Uh . . . well . . . sure . . . that would be fine," Andy choked out.

McClellan the lawyer chimed in. I'll have a contract drawn up. You'll want your agent or lawyer to check it over, of course. And there will be a standard non-disclosure agreement. You'll also be party to the contract with the publisher, when the bidding is over. I should mention that Marty's giving his share of the advance and his royalties to charity.

Andy refrained from declaring that his favorite charity would be the Davis Family Trust for Solvency-at-Last!

"So, let's take a walk, show you the place, have some lunch," said Fallon, standing and heading toward the door. Andy barely had time to shoo the dollar signs from his mind and follow.